THE
COLD COLD
GROUND

A DETECTIVE SEAN DUFFY NOVEL

THE
COLD COLD
GROUND

BOOK ONE
THE TROUBLES TRILOGY

ADRIAN McKINTY

DISCARD

SEVENTH
STREET
BOOKS™

59 John Glenn Drive
Amherst, New York 14228–2119

Published 2012 by Seventh Street Books™, an imprint of Prometheus Books

Top cover image © Shutterstock
Bottom cover image © AP Photo/PA
Cover design by Grace M. Conti-Zilsberger

Inquiries should be addressed to
Seventh Street Books
59 John Glenn Drive
Amherst, New York 14228–2119
VOICE: 716–691–0133
FAX: 716–691–0137
WWW.PROMETHEUSBOOKS.COM

16 15 14 13 12   5 4 3 2 1

Library of Congress Cataloging-in-Publication Data

McKinty, Adrian.
    The cold cold ground : a Detective Sean Duffy novel / by Adrian McKinty.
        p. cm. — (The Troubles trilogy ; bk. 1)
    "First published: London: Serpent's Tail, an imprint of Profile Books Ltd., 2012"—T.p. verso.
    ISBN 978–1–61614–716–7 (pbk. : alk. paper)
    ISBN 978–1–61614–717–4 (ebook)
    1. Police—Northern Ireland—Fiction. 2. Gay men—Crimes against—Fiction. 3. Catholics—Fiction. 4. Serial murderers—Fiction. 5. Northern Ireland—History—1969–1994—Fiction. I. Title.

PS3563.C38322C95 2012
813'.54—dc23

                                                    2012023528

Printed in the United States of America

It is rumoured that after concluding his song about the war in Ilium, Homer sang next of the war between the frogs and rats.

—Jorge Luis Borges, "The Immortal," 1949

CONTENTS

1: THE THIN BLUE LINE

The riot had taken on a beauty of its own now. Arcs of gasoline fire under the crescent moon. Crimson tracer in mystical parabolas. Phosphorescence from the barrels of plastic bullet guns. A distant yelling like that of men below decks in a torpedoed prison ship. The scarlet whoosh of Molotovs intersecting with exacting surfaces. Helicopters everywhere: their spotlights finding one another like lovers in the Afterlife.

And all this through a lens of oleaginous Belfast rain.

I watched with the others by the Land Rover on Knockagh Mountain. No one spoke. Words were inadequate. You needed a Picasso for this scene, not a poet.

The police and the rioters were arranged in two ragged fronts that ran across a dozen streets, the opposing sides illuminated by the flash of newsmen's cameras and the burning, petrol-filled milk bottles sent tumbling across the no man's land like votive offerings to the god of curves.

Sometimes one side charged and the two lines touched for a time before decoupling and returning to their original positions.

The smell was the stench of civilization: gunpowder, cordite, slow match, kerosene.

It was perfect.

It was *Giselle*.

It was *Swan Lake*.

And yet . . .

And yet we had the feeling that we had seen better.

In fact we had seen better only last week when, in the hospital wing of The Maze Prison, IRA commander Bobby Sands had finally popped his clogs.

Bobby was a local lad from Newtownabbey and a poster boy for the movement, having never killed anyone and coming from a mixed Protestant-Catholic background. And bearded, he was a good Jesus, which didn't hurt either.

Bobby Sands was the *maitreya*, the world teacher, the martyr who would redeem mankind through his suffering.

When Bobby finally died on the sixty-sixth day of his hunger strike the Catholic portions of the city had erupted with spontaneous anger and frustration.

But that was a week ago and Frankie Hughes, the second hunger striker to die, had none of Bobby's advantages. No one thought Frankie was Jesus. Frankie enjoyed killing and was very good at it. Frankie shed no tears over dead children. Not even for the cameras.

And the riots for his death felt somewhat . . . *orchestrated*.

Perhaps on the ground it seemed like the same chaos and maybe that's what they would print tomorrow in newspapers from Boston to Beijing . . . But up here on the Knockagh it was obvious that the peelers had the upper hand. The rioters had been cornered into a small western portion of the city between the hills and the Protestant estates. They faced a thousand full-time peelers, plus two or three hundred police reserve, another two hundred UDR and a battalion-strength unit of British Army regulars in close support. The Brits on this occasion were the Black Watch who, notoriously, were full of Glaswegian roughnecks looking for any chance of a rumble. There were hundreds of rioters— not the thousands that had been predicted: this hardly represented a general uprising of even the Catholic population and as for the promised "revolution" . . . well, not tonight.

"It looks bad," young Constable Price offered as a conversational opener.

"Ach, it's half-hearted at best for this lad," Detective Constable McCrabban replied in his harsh, sibilant, Ballymena-farmer accent.

"It's no fun being the second hunger striker to croak it. Everybody remembers the first one, number two is no good at all. They won't be writing folk songs for him," Sergeant McCallister agreed.

"What do you think, Duffy?" Constable Price asked me.

I shrugged. "Crabbie's right. It's never gonna be as big for number two. And the rain didn't help him."

"The rain?" McCallister said skeptically. "Forget the rain! It's the Pope. It was bad luck for Frankie to kick the bucket just a few hours before somebody tried to kill the Pope."

I'd done an analysis of Belfast riots from 1870–1970 which showed an inverse proportion between rain and rioting. The heavier the downpour the less likely there was to be trouble, but I kept my trap shut about that—nobody else up here had gone to University and there was no gain to be had from rubbing in my book-learning. And big Sergeant McCallister did have a point about John Paul II. It wasn't every news cycle that someone shot the Holy Father.

"He was a scumbag was Frankie Hughes. A rare 'un. It was his ASU that killed Will Gordon and his wee girl," Sergeant McCallister added.

"I thought it was the wee boy who was killed," McCrabban said.

"Nah. The wee boy lived. The bomb was in the car. The wee lad was severely injured. Will and his young daughter were blown to bits," McCallister explained.

There was a silence after that punctuated by a far-off discharge of baton rounds.

"Fenian bastards," Price said.

Sergeant McCallister cleared his throat. Price wondered what that meant for a beat or two and then he remembered me.

"Oh, no offense, Duffy," he muttered, his thin lips and pinched face even thinner and pinchier.

"No offense, *Detective Sergeant* Duffy," Sergeant McCallister said to put the new constable in his place.

"No offense, Sergeant Duffy," Price repeated petulantly.

"None taken, son. I'd love to see things from your point of view but I can't get my head that far up my arse."

Everybody laughed and I used this as my exit line and went inside the Land Rover to read the *Belfast Telegraph*.

It was all about the Pope. His potential assassin was a man called

Mehmed Ali Agca, a Turk, who had shot him in St. Peter's Square. The *Telegraph* didn't have much more information at this stage but they padded out the story with the shocked opinions of local people and politicians and a few right-wing Protestant nuts, like Councilor George Seawright who felt that this was an "important blow against the Anti-Christ."

Sergeant McCallister poked his big puffy face and classic alky nose round the back of the Land Rover.

"You're not taking the huff at Price, are you, Sean?" he asked in a kindly manner.

"Jesus no. I was just getting out of the rain," I replied.

Sergeant McCallister grinned with relief. One of those infectious grins that I had not been blessed with myself. "That's good. Well, look, I was thinking, do you want to call it a day? No one is going to be needing us. They're more than covered down there in the riot. They've got redundancy in spades. Shall we bog off?"

"You're the senior sergeant. It's your call."

"I'll log us in to midnight, but we'll skip, what say you?"

"Alan, I think that's the most sensible thing I've heard since we bloody came up here."

On the way back down the mountain McCallister put a cassette in the player and we listened to his personal mix tape of Crystal Gayle, Tammy Wynette and Dolly Parton. They dropped me first on Coronation Road, Carrickfergus. "Is this your new manor?" McCrabban asked, looking at the fresh paint job on number 113.

"Aye, I just moved in couple of weeks ago, no time yet for a house-warming party or anything," I said quickly.

"You own it?" Sergeant McCallister asked.

I nodded. Most people still rented in Victoria Estate, but a few people were buying their council houses from the Northern Ireland Housing Executive under Mrs. Thatcher's privatization plans. I had bought the place vacant for only £10,000. (The family that had lived here had owed two year's rent and one night just upped and vanished. To America, some said, but nobody really knew.)

"You painted it pink?" Price asked with a grin.

"That's lavender, you color-blind eejit," I said.

McCallister saw that Price clearly hadn't got the message yet. "Hey lads, you know why Price nearly failed the police entrance exam? He thought a polygon was a dead parrot."

The lads chuckled dutifully and somebody punched Price on the shoulder.

McCallister winked at me. "We have to head, mate," he announced and with that they closed the back doors of the Rover.

"See you!" I shouted after them as they drove off, but it was unlikely they heard me through the bulletproofing and armor plate.

I stood there looking ridiculous with my full riot gear, helmet and Sterling sub-machine gun.

A wee lad was gawping at me. "Is that a real gun, mister?" he asked.

"I certainly hope so," I said, opened my gate and walked down the garden path. It wasn't a bad house: a neat job in the middle of the terrace, built in the 1950s, like the rest of Victoria Estate, Carrickfergus for the Protestant working poor. Of course these days hardly anybody was working. The ICI textile plant had closed last year, in the autumn of 1980, and they had employed one in every four men in Carrick. Now the town had an unemployment rate of twenty per cent and it would have been worse but for emigration to England and Australia and the brand new DeLorean factory that had just opened in Dunmurray. If people bought DeLoreans in anything like the numbers predicted then Carrickfergus and Northern Ireland had a chance. Otherwise . . .

"Busy night?" Mrs. Campbell asked from next door.

Mrs. Campbell . . . I smiled and said nothing. Best not to. She was trouble. Thirty-two. Red hair. Looker. Husband away on the North Sea oil rigs. Two weans under ten. There was no way.

"You know, what with the riots and everything?" she insisted while I hunted for my keys.

"Aye," I said.

"I suppose you heard about the Pope?"

"Yes."

"You could find about a dozen suspects on this street," she said with a cackle.

"I'm sure you could," I agreed.

"Personally, mind, I find it shocking, really shocking," she said.

I blinked a couple of times and looked straight ahead. This statement worried me. It meant that she was trying to show empathy, which led me to the inescapable conclusion that she probably fancied me and that she (and everybody else on the street) knew that I was a Catholic.

I hadn't been here three weeks, barely spoken to anyone. What had I done in this time to give myself away? Was it the way I pronounced the letter "H" or was it just that I was marginally less sour than Coronation Road's dour Protestant population?

I put the key in the lock, shook my head and went inside. I hung up my coat, took off my bulletproof vest and unbuckled the handgun. In case we'd been needed for riot duty I'd also been issued with a CS gas canister, a billy club and that scary World War Two machine gun—presumably to deal with an IRA ambush en route. I carefully put all these weapons on the hall table.

I hung my helmet on the hook and went upstairs.

There were three bedrooms. I used two for storage and had taken the front one for myself as it was the biggest and came with a fireplace and a nice view across Coronation Road to the Antrim Hills beyond.

Victoria Estate lay at the edge of Carrickfergus and hence at the edge of the Greater Belfast Urban Area. Carrick was gradually being swallowed up by Belfast but for the moment it still possessed some individual character: a medieval town of 13,000 people with a small working harbor and a couple of now empty textile factories.

North of Coronation Road you were in the Irish countryside, south and east you were in the city. I liked that. I had a foot in both camps too. I'd been born in 1950 in Cushendun when that part of rural Northern Ireland was like another planet. No phones, no electricity, people still using horses to get around, peat for cooking and heating, and on Sundays some of the crazier Protestants rowing or sailing across the North Channel in little doreys to attend the kirk in Scotland.

Aye, I'd been whelped a country boy but in 1969, right as the Troubles were kicking off, I'd gone to Queen's University Belfast on a full scholarship to study psychology. I'd loved the city: its bars, its alleys, its character and, at least for a while, the university area was immune to the worst of the violence.

It was the era of Seamus Heaney, Paul Muldoon, Ciaran Carson, and QUB was a little candle of light held up against the gathering dark.

And I'd done well there if I say so myself. Nobody was doing psychology in those days and I'd shone. Not much competition, I suppose, but still. I'd gained a first-class degree, fell in and out of love a couple of times, published a little paper on the unreliability of eyewitness testimony in the *Irish Journal of Criminology* and perhaps I would have stayed an academic or gotten a job across the water but for the incident.

The incident.

Why I was here now. Why I'd joined the peelers in the first place.

I stripped off the last of my police uniform and hung it in the cupboard. Under all that webbing I had sweated like a Proddy at a High Mass, so I had a quick shower to rinse out the peeler stink. I dried myself and looked at my naked body in the mirror.

5' 10". 11 stone. Rangy, not muscled. Thirty years old but I looked thirty unlike my colleagues on sixty cigs a day. Dark complexion, dark curly hair, dark blue eyes. My nose was an un-Celtic aquiline and when I worked up a tan a few people initially took me as some kind of French or Spanish tourist (not that there were many of those rare birds in these times). As far as I could tell there wasn't a drop of French or Spanish blood in my background but there were always those dubious sounding local stories in Cushendun about survivors from the wreck of the Spanish Armada . . .

I counted the grey hairs.

Fourteen now.

I thought about the Serpico moustache. Again dismissed it.

I raised an eyebrow at myself. "Mrs. Campbell, it must be awful lonely with your husband away on the North Sea . . ." I said, for some reason doing a Julio Iglesias impersonation.

"Oh, it's very lonely and my house is so cold . . ." Mrs. Campbell replied.

I laughed and perhaps as a tribute to this mythical Iberian inheritance I sought out my Che Guevara T-shirt, which Jim Fitzpatrick had personally screenprinted for me. I found an old pair of jeans and my Adidas trainers. I lit the upstairs paraffin heater and went back downstairs.

I turned on the lights, went into the kitchen, took a pint glass from the freezer and filled it half full with lime juice. I added a few ice cubes and carried it to the front room: the good room, the living room, the lounge. For some arcane Proddy reason no one in Coronation Road used this room. It was where they kept the piano and the family Bible and the stiff chairs only to be brought out for important visitors like cops and ministers.

I had no toleration for any of that nonsense. I'd set up the TV and stereo in here and although I still had some decorating to do, I was pleased with what I'd achieved. I'd painted the walls a very un-Coronation Road Mediterranean blue and put up some original—mostly abstract—art that I'd got from the Polytech Design School. There was a bookcase filled with novels and art books and a chic looking lamp from Sweden. I had a whole scheme in mind. Not my scheme admittedly, but a scheme none the less. Two years back I'd stayed with Gresha, a friend from Cushendun, who had fled war-torn Ulster in the early '70s for New York City. She'd apparently become quite the professional little blagger and hanger-on, name-dropping Warhol, Ginsberg, Sontag. None of that had turned my head but I'd done a bit of experimenting and I'd gone apeshit for her pad on St. Mark's Place; I imagine I had consciously tried to capture some of its aesthetic here. There were limits to what one could do in a terraced house in a Jaffa sink estate in far-flung Northern Ireland, however, but if you closed the curtains and turned up the music . . .

I topped off the pint glass with 80 proof Smirnoff vodka, stirred the drink and grabbed a book at random from the bookcase.

It was Jim Jones's *The Thin Red Line* which I'd read on my World

War Two jag along with *Catch 22, The Naked and the Dead, Gravity's Rainbow* and so on. Every cop usually had a book going on for the waiting between trouble. I didn't have one at the moment and that was making me nervous. I skimmed through the dog-eared best bits until I found the section where First Sergeant Welsh of C for Charlie Company just decides to stare at all the men on the troop ship for two full minutes, ignoring their questions and not caring if they thought he was crazy because he was the goddamned First Sergeant and he could do anything he bloody well wanted. Nice. Very nice.

That scene read, I turned on the box, checked that the Pope was still alive and switched to BBC2, which was showing some minor snooker tournament I hadn't previously heard of. I was just getting a little booze buzz going and quite enjoying the loose match between Alex Higgins and Cliff Thorburn (both them boys on their fifth pint of beer) when the phone rang.

I counted the rings. Seven, eight, nine. When it reached ten I went into the hall and waited for a couple more.

When it reached fifteen, I finally picked up the receiver.

"Aye?" I said suspiciously.

"There's good news and bad news," Chief Inspector Brennan said.

"What's the good news, sir?" I asked.

"It's nearby. You can walk from there."

"What's the bad news?"

"It's nasty."   •

I sighed. "Jesus. Not kids?"

"Not that kind of nasty."

"What kind of nasty, then?"

"They chopped one of his hands off."

"Lovely. Whereabouts?"

"The Barn Field near Taylor's Avenue. You know it?"

"Aye. Are you over there now?"

"I'm calling from a wee lady's house on Fairymount."

"A wee fairy lady?"

"Just get over here, ya eejit."

"I'll see you there in ten minutes, sir."

I hung up the phone. This is where the Serpico moustache would have come in handy. You could look at yourself in the hall mirror, stroke the Serpico moustache and have a ponder.

Instead I rubbed my stubbly chin while I extemporized. Pretty nice timing for a murder, what with the riot in Belfast and the death of a hunger striker and the poor old Pope halfway between Heaven and Earth. It showed . . . What? Intelligence? Luck?

I grabbed my raincoat and opened the front door. Mrs. Campbell was still standing there, nattering away to Mrs. Bridewell, the neighbor on the other side.

"Are you away out again?" she asked. "Ach, there's no rest for the wicked, is there, eh?"

"Aye," I said with gravity.

She looked at me with her green eyes and flicked away the fag ash in her left hand. Something stirred down below.

"There's, uh, been a suspected murder on Taylor's Avenue, I'm away to take a gander," I said.

Both women looked suitably shocked which told me that for once in my police career I was actually ahead of the word on the street.

I left the women and walked down Coronation Road. The rain had become a drizzle and the night was calm—the acoustics so perfect that you could hear the plastic bullet guns all the way from the center of Belfast.

I walked south past a bunch of sleekit wee muckers playing football with a patched volleyball. I felt sorry for them with all their fathers out of work. I said, hey, and kept going past the identical rows of terraces and the odd house which had been sold to its tenants and subsequently blossomed into window treatments, extensions and conservatories.

I turned right on Barn Road and cut through Victoria Primary School.

The new graffiti on the bike shed walls was jubilant about the Pope: "Turkey 1, Vatican City 0" and "Who Shot JP?"—a none too subtle *Dallas* reference.

I slipped over the rear fence and across the Barn Field.

The black tongue of Belfast Lough was ahead of me now and I could see three army choppers skimming the water, ferrying troops from Bangor to the Ardoyne.

I crossed a stretch of waste ground and a field with one demented looking sheep. I heard the generator powering the spotlights and then I saw Brennan with a couple of constables I didn't yet know and Matty McBride, the forensics officer. Matty was dressed in jeans and jumper rather than the new white boiler suits that all FOs had been issued and instructed to wear. I'd have to give the lazy bastard a dressing down for that, but not in front of Brennan or the constables.

I waved to the lads and they waved back.

Chief Inspector Tom Brennan was my boss, the man in charge of the entire police station in Carrickfergus. The bigger stations were run by a Superintendent but Carrick was not even a divisional HQ. I, a buck sergeant with two months' seniority, was in fact the fourth most senior officer in the place. But it was a safe posting and in my fortnight here I'd been impressed by the collegiate atmosphere, if not always with the professionalism of my colleagues.

I walked across the muddy field and shook Brennan's hand.

He was a big man with an oval face, light brown, almost blondish hair and intelligent slate-blue eyes. He didn't look Irish, nor English, there was probably Viking blood somewhere in that gene pool.

He was one of those characters who felt that a weak handshake could somehow damage his authority, which meant that every handshake had to bloody hurt.

I disengaged with a wince and looked about me for a beat or two. Brennan and the constables had done a hell of a job contaminating the crime scene with their big boots and ungloved hands. I gave a little inward sigh.

"Good to see you, Sean," Brennan said.

"Bit surprised to see you, sir. We must be a wee bit short-staffed if you're the responding officer."

"You said it, mate. Everybody's away manning checkpoints. You know who's minding the store?"

"Who?"

"Carol."

"Carol? Jesus Christ. This would be a fine time for that IRA missile attack we've all been promised," I muttered.

Brennan raised an eyebrow. "You can joke, pal, but I've seen the intel. The IRA got crates of them from Libya."

"If you say so, sir."

"Do you know Quinn and Davey?" Brennan asked.

I shook the hands of the two reserve constables who, in the nature of things, I might not see again for another month.

"Where's your gun?" Brennan asked in his scary, flat East Antrim monotone.

I picked up on the quasi-official timbre to his voice.

"I'm sorry, sir, I left my revolver at home," I replied.

"And what if my call to you had been made under duress and this had been an ambush?" Brennan asked.

"I suppose I'd be dead," I said stupidly.

"Aye. You would be, wouldn't ya? Consider this a reprimand."

"An official reprimand?"

"Of course not. But I don't take it lightly: they would just love to top you, wouldn't they, my lad? They'd love it."

"I suppose they would, sir," I admitted. Everybody knew the IRA had a bounty on Catholic coppers.

Brennan reached out with his big, gloved, meat-axe fingers and grabbed my cheek. "And we're not going to let that happen, are we, sunshine?"

"No, sir."

Brennan give me a squeeze that really hurt and then he let go.

"All right, good, now what do you make of all this?" Brennan said.

Matty was taking photographs of a body propped up in the front seat of a burnt-out car. The car was surrounded by rubbish and in the lee of the massive wall of the old Ambler's Mill. The vehicle was a Ford Cortina that been had jacked and destroyed years, possibly decades, before. Now it was a rusted sculpture, lacking a windscreen, doors, wheels.

A shock of mid-length yellow hair was visible from here.

I walked closer.

The cliché of every cops and robbers show—the dead blonde in the garbage tip. Course the blonde was always a bird, not what we had before us: some chubby guy with yellow tips in a denim AC/DC jacket.

He was sitting in the driver's seat, his head tilted to one side, the back of his skull gone, his face partially caved in. He was youngish, perhaps thirty, wearing jeans, that jacket, a black T-shirt and Doc Marten boots. His blond locks were caked with filth and matted blood. There was a bruise just to the right of his nose. His eyes were closed and his cheeks were paler than typing paper.

The car was on a rise above the high grass and wild blackberry bushes and only a few yards from a popular short cut across the Barn Field itself which I myself had used on occasion.

I pinched the skin on the corpse's neck.

The flesh was cold and the skin stiff.

Rigor was on the gallop. This boy was killed some time ago. Most likely the wee hours of the morning or even late last night.

They had either marched him here and shot him or shot him and dragged him here from their vehicle on Taylor's Avenue. Good place for it. There would be no one here late to witness a killing or a body dumping, yet someone would find the corpse soon enough in the daylight hours. Ten more minutes up the road would have brought you into the countryside but you couldn't be too careful with the Army throwing checkpoints up all over the place.

I looked again for footprints. Dozens. Matty, Tom and the two reserve constables had come over for a look-see at the body. They didn't know any better, God love them, but I made a mental note to hold a little seminar on "contaminating the crime scene" perhaps in a week or two when everyone knew who I was.

I circled away from the car and walked up to the high mill wall, which, with the broad limbs of an oak tree, formed a little protected area. It was obviously some kind of former druggie or teenage hangout. There was a mattress on the ground. A sofa. An old reclining chair.

Garbage. Freezer bags by the score. Hypodermics. Condoms. I picked up one of the freezer bags, opened it with difficulty and sniffed. Glue. Nothing was fresh. Everything looked a couple of months old. The teenagers had obviously found an abandoned house in which to get high and create a new generation.

I checked the sight lines.

You could see the car from the road and from the Barley Field short cut.

They—whoever *they* were—wanted the body to be found.

I walked back to the vehicle and took a second look at the corpse.

Those pale cheeks, a pierced ear, no earring.

The victim's left hand was by his side, but his right was detached from the body and lying at his feet on the accelerator pedal. He'd been shot in the chest first and then in the back of the head. There wasn't much blood around the hand which probably meant that it had been cut off after the victim's heart had stopped pumping. Severing a limb while he still lived implied at least two men. One to hold him down, one wielding the bone saw. But shooting him and then cutting off his hand was easy enough to do on your own.

I looked for the customary plastic bag containing thirty sixpences or fifty-pence pieces but I didn't find it. They didn't always leave thirty pieces of silver when they shot informers but often they did.

Here's the hand that took the dirty money and here's the Judas's bargain.

The right hand looked small and pathetic lying there on the accelerator. The left had scars over the knuckles from many a bout of fisticuffs.

There was something about the other hand that I didn't like, but I couldn't see what it was just at the moment.

I took a breath, nodded to myself, and stood up.

"Well?" Brennan asked.

"It's my belief, sir, that this was no ordinary car accident," I said.

Brennan laughed and shook his head. "Why is it that every eejit in the CID thinks they're a bloody comedian?"

"Probably to cover up some deep insecurity, sir."

"All right what have you got, Sean? First impressions."

"I'd say our victim was a low-ranking paramilitary informer. They found out he was snitching for us or the Brits and they killed him. In typical melodramatic fashion they cut off his right hand after they topped him and then they left the body in a place where he could easily be found so the message would go out quickly. I'd say the time of death was sometime around midnight last night."

"Why low-ranking?"

"Well, neither you nor Matty nor I recognized him so he'll just be some crappy low-level hood from the Estates; also this place, bit out of the way, so the killer will be somebody local too. Somebody Carrick at least. I'll bet Sergeant McCallister can ID our stiff, and I'll bet you we find out who ordered the killing through the usual channels. Who called it in?"

"Anonymous tip."

"The killer?"

"Nah, some old lady out walking her dog. Unless you think the terrorists are using old lady hit men?"

"What time was the call?"

"Six fifteen this evening."

I nodded. "That's a bit later than our killers wanted but he was seen in the end. I'm sure we'll have the prints by tomorrow. I'd be very surprised indeed if this boy doesn't have a record."

Brennan slapped me hard on the back. "So, you're happy enough to take this as lead?"

"What about the Ulster Bank fraud?"

"White-collar crime is going to have to wait until we're back from the edge of the abyss."

"Nice way of putting it."

"It's going to get worse before it gets better, don't you think?"

I nodded. "Aye, I do."

"Have you handled a murder before, Sean?"

"Three."

"A triple murder or three separate murder investigations?"

"Three separate."

"What, may I ask, were the results of those murder inquiries?"

I winced. "Well, I found out who did it on all three of them."

"Prosecutions?"

"Zero. We had good eyewitness testimony on two but no one would testify."

Brennan took a step backwards and regarded me for a second. He opened my raincoat. "Is that bloody Che Guevara?"

"It is, sir."

"You're a big pochle, aren't ya? You turn up at a crime scene with no gun, wearing trainers and a Che Guevara T-shirt? I mean, what's the world coming to?"

"A sticky end more than likely, sir."

He grinned and then shook his head. "I don't get you, Duffy. Why did a smart aleck like you join the peelers?"

"The snazzy uniforms? The thrilling prospect of being murdered on the way to work every morning?"

Brennan sighed. "Well, I suppose I should leave you to it." He tapped his watch. "I might be able to get a wee Scotch and soda at the golf club."

"Before you go, sir, I've one question. Who will I get to work this one with me?"

"You can have the entire resources of the CID."

"What, all three of us?" I asked with a trace of sarcasm.

"All three of you," he said stiffly, not liking my tone at all.

"Can I put in a secondment request for a couple of constables f—"

"No, you cannot! We're tighter than a choir boy's arse around here. You've got your team and that's your lot. In case you hadn't noticed, mate, civil war is a bloody heartbeat away, *après nous* the friggin flood, we are the little Dutch boys with our fingers in the dyke, we are the . . . the, uh . . ."

"Thin blue line, sir?"

"The thin blue line! Exactly!"

He poked me in the middle of Che's face. "And until the hunger strikes are over, matey-boy, you'll get no help from Belfast either. But you can handle it, can't you, Detective Sergeant Duffy?"

"Yes sir, I can handle it."

"Aye, you better or I'll bloody get somebody who can."

He yawned, tired out by his own bluster. "Well, I'll leave this in your capable hands, then. I have a feeling this one is not going to cover us in glory, but we have to file them all."

"That we do, sir."

"All right then."

Brennan waved and walked back to his Ford Granada parked behind the police Land Rover. When the Granada had gone, I called Matty over.

"What do you make of it?" I asked him.

Matty McBride was a twenty-three-year-old second-gen cop from East Belfast. He was a funny-looking character with his curly brown hair, pencil thin body, flappy ears. He was little was Matty, maybe five five. Wee and cute. He was wearing latex gloves and his nose was red, giving him a slight evil-clown quality. He'd joined the peelers right out of high school and was obviously smart enough to have gotten himself into CID but still, I had grave doubts about his focus and attention to detail. He had a dreamy side. He wasn't fussy or obsessed, which was a severe handicap in an FO. And when I had politely suggested that he look into the part-time degrees in Forensic Science at the Open University, Matty had scoffed at the very notion. He was young, though, perhaps he could be molded yet.

"Informer? Loyalist feud? Something like that?" Matty suggested.

"Aye, my take too. Do you think they shot him here?"

"Looks like it."

"March him out here and then chop his paw off with him screaming for all and sundry?"

Matty shrugged. "Ok, so they killed him somewhere else."

"But if they did that, why do you think they carried the body all the way over here from the road?"

"I don't know," Matty said wearily.

"It was to display him, Matty. They wanted him found quickly."

Matty grunted, unwilling to buy into the pedagogical nature of our relationship.

"Have you done the hair samples, prints?" I asked.

"Nah, I'll do all that once I'm done with the photos."

"Who's our patho?"

"Dr. Cathcart."

"Is he good?"

"She. Cathcart's a she."

I raised my eyebrows. I hadn't heard of a female patho before.

"She's not bad," Matty added.

We stood there looking into the burnt-out car listening to the rain pitter-patter on the rusted roof.

"I suppose I better get back to it," Matty said.

"Aye," I agreed.

"Is the cavalry coming down from Belfast at all?" Matty asked as he took more pictures.

I shook my head. "Nah, just you and me, mate. Cosier that way."

"Jesus, I have to do this all by myself?" Matty protested.

"Get plod and sod over there to help you," I said.

Matty seemed skeptical. "Them boys aren't too brilliant at the best of times. Question for ya: skipper says to go easy on the old snaps. Do you need close-ups? If not I'll skip them."

"Go easy on the snaps? Why?"

"The expense, like, you know? Two pound for every roll we process. And it's just a topped informer, isn't it?"

I was annoyed by this. It was typical of the RUC to waste millions on pointless new equipment that would rot in warehouses but pinch pennies in a homicide investigation.

"Take as many rolls of film as you like. I'll bloody pay for it. A man has been murdered here!" I said.

"All right, all right! No need to shout," Matty protested.

"And get that evidence lifted before the rain washes it all away. Get those empty suits to help you."

I buttoned my coat and turned up the collar. The rain was heavier now and it was getting cold.

"You could stay and help if you want, I'll give you some latex gloves," Matty said.

I tapped the side of my head. "I'd love to help, mate, but I'm an ideas man, I'd be no use to you."

Matty bit his tongue and said nothing.

"You're in charge of the scene now, Constable McBride," I said in a loud, official voice.

"Ok."

"No shortcuts," I added in a lower tone and turned and walked back to Taylor's Avenue where the police Land Rover was parked with its back doors open. There was a driver inside: another reserve constable that I didn't know, sitting on his fat arse reading a newspaper. I rapped the glass and the startled constable looked up. "Oi, you, Night of the Living Dead! Close them rear doors, and look alive, pal, you're a sitting duck here for an ambush."

"Yes, sergeant," the unknown constable said.

An idea occurred to me. "Shine your headlights onto the field, will ya?"

He put the headlights on full beam giving Matty even more light. I looked for a blood trail from the road to the corpse and sure enough I found a few drops.

"There's a blood trail!" I yelled to Matty and he nodded with a lot less excitement than I would have liked. I shrugged, did up my last coat button and went back along Coronation Road. It was well after midnight now and everyone was abed. The rain had turned to sleet and the smell of peat smoke was heady. No people, no cars, not even a stray cat. Dozens of identical, beige Proddy curtains neatly shut.

So all these Jaffa bastards know I'm a Catholic? I thought unhappily. That was the kind of quality information the IRA would pay good money for, if anybody around here was imaginative enough to sell it to them.

I walked up the garden path, went inside, pulled my vermillion curtains, turned on the electric fire, stripped off my clothes in the living room and found an old bath robe. I made myself another pint of vodka and lime. The TV was finished now and it was test cards on all three channels. I put *Double Fantasy* on the record player. I flipped the lever for repeat, lay down on the leather sofa and closed my eyes.

Darkest Ulster in the Year of our Lord 1981: rain on the gable, helicopters flying along the lough, a riot reduced to the occasional rumble . . .

The problem with *Double Fantasy* was the arrangement whereby they alternated John Lennon tracks with Yoko Ono tracks. You couldn't escape Yoko for more than four minutes at a time. I lowered the volume to two, snuggled under the red sofa comforter and, taking the occasional sip from my vodka gimlet, fell into the kind of deep sleep only experienced by men whose lives, like those of C for Charlie company, are lived on the edge of the line.

2: YOUR TINY HAND IS FROZEN

The occasional rumble of riot, gunfire and explosion. Nothing that Carrickfergus's seasoned sleepers couldn't handle. But then the comparative quiet was shattered by the apocalyptic turbines of a CH-47 Chinook. Everything began to rattle. A coffee cup fell off my mantelpiece. A picture came down.

The helicopter passed overhead at a height of 200 meters, well below the recommended ceiling. The Magnavox flip clock said 4 a.m. The British army had woken me and half the town in a hubristic display of raw power. Yes, you control the skies. And this, guys, is how you lose the hearts and minds.

I thought about that as I lay there in the big, empty double bed on Coronation Road. And when my anger subsided I thought about the vacuum on Adele's side of the mattress.

Of course I had asked her if she wanted to come to Carrick with me, but there was no way she was going to "that stinking Proddy hell hole," was her response. I hadn't been heartbroken but I had been disappointed. She was a schoolteacher and it wouldn't have been difficult for her to switch education boards as all the good teachers were going to England and America. The house was paid for, she would have been bringing in the dough, we would have been living high on the hog.

But she didn't love me and the truth was I didn't love her either.

I lay there in the darkness wondering if sleep was an option.

My mind drifted back to the murder victim on Taylor's Avenue.

The crime scene had been nagging at my unconscious.

I had missed something.

In my haste to get out of the rain I had overlooked a detail.

What was it?

It was something about the body, wasn't it? Something hadn't been quite right.

Wind tugged at the gutters. Rain pounded off the window. I shivered. This was evidently going to be another "year without a summer" for Ulster.

For obscure reasons the previous tenants had blocked up the chimney so that you couldn't light a fire in the upstairs or downstairs grates. I'd reckoned I wouldn't have to worry about this until November but now I was obviously going to have to get someone in to see about it.

I lay there thinking and the Chief's question came back to me.

Why *had* I joined the police?

And for the second time in twenty-four hours I thought about *the incident*.

Don't look for it in my shrink reports. And don't ask any of my old girlfriends.

Never talked about it with anyone.

Not me ma. Not me da. Not even a priest. Unusual for a blabber like yours truly.

It was May 2, 1974. I was two years into my PhD program. A nice spring day. I was walking past the Rose and Crown Bar on the Ormeau Road just twenty yards from my college digs.

It was the worst year of the Troubles but I hadn't personally been affected. Not yet. I was still neutral. Trying to keep aloof. Trying to do my own thing. The closest I'd come to assuming a position was after Bloody Sunday when me and Dad had attended the funerals in Derry and I'd thought for twenty-four hours about joining the IRA.

Funny how things turn out, isn't it?

May 2, 1974.

The Rose and Crown was a student joint. I'd been in there for a bevy maybe three hundred times in my years at Queens. It was my local. I knew all the regulars. Normally I would have been at that bar at that time but as it happened I'd been meeting a girl at the Students' Union and I'd had enough to drink already.

It was a no-warning bomb. The UVF (the Ulster Volunteer Force, an illegal Protestant paramilitary group) claimed responsibility. Later the UDA (the Ulster Defence Association, another Protestant paramilitary group) said they did it. Still later the UVF said it had been an IRA bomb that had exploded prematurely.

I didn't care about any of that.

The alphabet soup didn't interest me.

I wasn't badly hurt. A burst eardrum, abrasions, cuts from fragmenting glass.

Nah, I was ok, but inside the bar was carnage.

A slaughterhouse.

I was the first person through the wreck of the front door.

And that was the moment—

That was the moment when I knew that I wanted to be some small part of ending this madness. It was either get out or do something. I chose the latter.

The police were keen to have me. A university graduate, a psychologist, and that most precious thing of all . . . a Catholic.

And now seven years later, after a border posting, the CID course, a child kidnapping, a high-profile heroin bust, and several murder investigations, I was a newly promoted Detective Sergeant at the relatively safe RUC station in Carrickfergus. I knew why they'd sent me here. I was here to stay out of harm's way and I was here to learn . . .

I sat up in bed and turned on the radio and got the news about the Pope.

Still alive, the tough old bugger. I genuflected and muttered a brief, embarrassed prayer of thanks.

"Why is it so bloody cold!" I said and bundled up the duvet and pillow and carried them to the landing.

I knelt down in front of the paraffin heater.

From the Arctic to the tropics.

I assumed the fetal position on the pine floor. I immediately fell asleep.

Rain.

Such rain. Lugh draws the sun and sea and turns them into rain.

I stirred from a dream of water.

Light.

Heat.

My body floating on the paraffin fumes above the river and the sea.

Next door children's laughter and then something heavy smashing against the wall. They were always going at it, the Bridewell boys.

I opened my eyes. My throat was dry. The landing was blue because of the indigo flame of the paraffin heater. The heater had been a gift from my parents when I first moved to Belfast and I had lugged it to Armagh, Tyrone and lastly to Carrickfergus. Even now the gorgeous, heady kerosene aroma time-travelled me across the decades to my childhood in Cushendun.

For five minutes I lay there listening to the rain pouring off the roof and then, reluctantly, I went downstairs.

I made tea and toast with butter and marmalade. I showered, dressed in a sober black polo-neck sweater, black jeans, black shoes. I put on a dark sports jacket and my raincoat. I put the revolver in my coat pocket and left the ridiculous machine gun on the hall table.

I went outside.

Grey sky that began fifty feet above my head. Drizzle. There was a cow munching at the roses in Mrs. Bridewell's garden. Another was taking a shit in Mrs. Campbell's yard.

When I looked to the left and right I could see other cows further along the street wandering stupidly to and fro. I'd been here three weeks and this was the second time the cows had escaped from the field next to Coronation Road. It would never have happened in Cushendun. These Carrick eejits were not good cattle farmers. I walked down the garden path ignoring Mrs. Campbell's cow and buttoning my coat. There was a frost in the high hills and my breath followed me like a reluctant *taibhse*.

I checked under the BMW for car bombs, didn't find any, looked a second time just to be sure, turned the key in the lock, flinched in expectation of a booby trap, opened the door and got inside.

I did not fasten my seat belt. Four police officers had died in car accidents this year, nine police officers had been shot while trapped in their vehicles by their seat belts. The statistical department of the RUC felt that, on balance, it was better not to wear a seat belt and a memo had been sent around for comments. This memo had obviously been seen by someone in the Chief Constable's office and quick as a flash it had become a standing order.

I stuck on Downtown Radio and got the local news.

Riots in Belfast, Derry, Cookstown, Lurgan and Strabane. An incendiary attack on a paint factory in Newry. A bomb on the Belfast to Dublin railway line. A strike by the Antrim Ulsterbus drivers in protest at a series of hijackings.

"Because of the Ulsterbus strike schools in Belfast, Newtown-abbey, Carrickfergus, Ballymena, Ballyclare, Coleraine and Larne will be closed today. Now a little George Jones to soothe your morning," Candy Devine said.

I flipped to Radio 1 and drove up Coronation Road listening to Blondie.

"It's like bloody India," the milkman said to me coming down the street in his electric float. "Aye and without the cuisine," I muttered and drove slowly to avoid killing a cow and thus incurring an unfavorable incarnation in the next life.

I turned right on Victoria Road and saw a bunch of teenagers in school uniform waiting for a bus that was never going to come. I wound the window down.

"School's off, I just heard it on the radio!" I yelled across to them.

"Piss off, ya pervert!" a seventeen-year-old slapper yelled back, flipping me the bird as she did so.

"I'm the bloody peelers, ya wee shite!" I thought about replying but when you're in an insult contest with a bunch of weans at 7:58 in the morning your day really is heading for the crapper.

I wound the window back up and drove on to the sound of jeers.

Two hundred yards further on I went past a Twelfth of July bonfire which was already two storeys high and stacked with pallets, boxes and tires. On the top someone had a stuck an effigy of the Pope wearing a blood-stained bed sheet.

Nice.

I pulled into McDowell's newsagents.

Oscar was serving two hacks from the Associated Press. You could tell they were hacks from the Associated Press because they were wearing jackets that said "Associated Press" in big yellow letters on the back and because they were trying to buy a couple of Mars bars with a fifty-pound note.

I bought the *Guardian* and the *Daily Mirror*. The headlines were about the Pope and the Yorkshire Ripper trial. Nothing about Northern Ireland on the front page of either. The AP men were probably selling their stories to the papers in Boston.

At the bottom of Victoria Road there was an army checkpoint. Three green armor-plated Land Rovers and a bunch of Scottish soldiers smoking Woodbines.

I showed them my warrant card and they lifted their rifles and waved me through.

"Nice Beemer," a big Jock squaddie said as I drove on. Was he implying that because I was driving a BMW, I was a corrupt cop on the take to the paramilitaries while he was a hard-working son of Caledonia trying to keep the murderous Paddies from killing one another? Maybe, or maybe he just dug the wheels.

I drove south west along the sea front.

Ahead of me Carrickfergus Castle, the town and harbor.

To my right a dismal line of houses and shops, to my left the—always—gun-metal grey waters of Belfast Lough.

The police station was about half a mile along the front.

A small two-storey brick affair, surrounded by a blast wall and a high fence for deterring hand grenades and Molotov cocktails.

I nodded to Ray behind the bulletproof glass. Ray raised the gate barrier and I drove into the police station compound. There was hardly anyone in because everyone had been up the night before on riot duty. I easily found a parking space next to the entrance.

I got out gingerly. The yard was full of potholes and puddles and since all the police Land Rovers leaked oil, you could really take a nasty spill if you didn't watch your step. I said "Good morning, Miss Moneypenny," to Carol and went upstairs. The second floor was open plan with an interview room, an incident room and offices for the senior sergeants and Chief Inspector Brennan.

CID had all the window desks overlooking Belfast Lough. The view was pleasant and on a clear day you could see Scotland, which was nice if you ever wanted to see Scotland on a clear day. Detective Constable "Crabbie" McCrabban had built an elaborate and paranoid conspiracy theory around these prized window desks. It was his feeling that CID were given this prime position so that we would get it first in the event of an IRA missile or RPG attack, but I chose to believe that Brennan had assigned us these desks as reward for our hard graft day in and day out.

I sat down in my swivel chair and flicked through the report that Matty had inexpertly typed up:

Carrickfergus RUC, CID Div. Case #13715/A. Homacide. Barn Field, Taylor's Avenue, Carrickfergus, 5/13/1981. Srce: anon tip Wed evening. Victim: victim unknown. Victim's personal effects: none. Other evidence: blood sample, victim's hair sample, victim's right hand, CS photographs. Remarks: victim found in abadoned car, one hand severed, prints taken. Victim not yet IDed. Patho Rept: awaiting patho rept. #13715/A CS: Inq. to Det. Sgt. Duffy. 5/14/1981: body devilered to Carrick Hospital c.o. pathologist Dr. Cathcart.

Matty had written nothing about getting prints off the victim's clothes. I wondered if he'd done it and found nothing or just not done it. It was a toss up.

I went to the coffee machine and pushed the buttons for white coffee and chocolate simultaneously. Armed with this dubious concoction I went back to my desk. Matty had not left me the photographs but I found them in the darkroom hanging on the drying line. 7×10 glossies of the body, the hand, the car, the pool of blood, the AC/DC jacket, the victim's face, other aspects of the crime scene and a few of the moon, clouds and grass.

I gathered the pics and took them to my desk.

Other officers started to arrive, doing whatever the hell it was that they did around here. I said good morning to Sergeant McCallister and showed him the pics of our boy. It didn't ring a bell.

McCrabban appeared twenty minutes later sporting a black eye.

"Jesus, mate! Where'd you get that shiner?" I asked.

"Don't ask," he replied.

"Not the missus?"

"I don't want to talk about it, if that's all right with you," he said taciturnly. These Proddies. They never wanted to talk about anything.

McCrabban was a big, lanky man with a carefully engineered old-school peeler tache, straight ginger hair and pale, bluish skin. With a tan he'd look somewhat like a Duracell battery, but he wasn't the type to get a tan. He was from farmer stock and he had a down-to-earth conservative millenarian quality that I liked a lot. His Ballymena accent conjured (in my mind at least) Weber's stolid Protestant work ethic.

"A big Jock was giving me a hard time about my Beemer. It's a '77 E21. That's not flashy, is it? You need a reliable car as a cop, don't you?" I said.

"Don't ask me. I have a tractor and an old Land Rover Defender."

"Forget it," I said and showed him the case notes and Matty's photographs of the victim.

"Recognize our poor unfortunate?" I asked.

Crabbie shook his head. "You're thinking informer, I suppose," he said.

"Why, what are you thinking?"

"Oh, I'm with you, with his right hand cut off? Standard operating procedure."

"Do me a favor, take some of the headshots down to Jimmy Prentice and see if he recognizes our boy. I already asked the Chief so I'm a bit skeptical that Jimmy will have an ID but you never know."

"He mustn't be local. If Brennan doesn't know him he isn't worth knowing," Crabbie said.

"If Jimmy draws a blank, fax them up to the Lisburn Road and ask them to cross-reference with all the informers on their books, especially ones that haven't called in in the last day or two."

Crabbie shook his head. "They'll never tell us about the MI5 boys."

"I appreciate that, Crabbie, but they'll have the army list too, so let's at least try and narrow the field down a wee bit," I said with a slight edge in my voice.

Crabbie grabbed a couple of the face pics and took them downstairs to Jim Prentice who ran all the informers in Carrick. Because of the sensitive nature of his work he was stationed in a locked little office by himself next to the armory. Prentice was the paymaster for all the touts, informers and grasses in our district so if the victim had ever taken a government shilling for information Jimmy would know it. If not, the fax to Belfast would set the ball rolling on their lists. Crabbie was right about MI5 though. MI5 had its own network of informers, some in deep cover, and because MI5 fundamentally didn't trust anyone in Northern Ireland the names of their agents were never shared with us even when the eejits got themselves shot.

Matty appeared shortly before lunch and over coffee and sandwiches the three of us had our first case conference. Matty told us he had done the victim's clothes but there were no lift-able prints. He had fingerprinted the victim's right hand and faxed the printout to Belfast, but so far nothing had showed up in the RUC database. Crabbie told us that no one had called in a missing person's report in the last twenty-four hours and Jimmy Prentice had told him that our victim was not one of his lads.

"Did you find any bullets in your search of the scene?" I asked Matty.

Matty shook his head.

"Footprints, hair samples, anything unusual about the victim's clothing?"

Matty shook his head. "The T-shirt was a black Marks and Spencer XL, the jeans were Wrangler, the shoes Adidas trainers."

"Any claims of responsibility yet?" I asked Crabbie.

Crabbie shook his head. "No one's said anything."

"So we've got no prints, no physical evidence, no recovered slug, no claim of responsibility, no missing person's filings, absolutely nowt," I said.

The other two nodded their heads.

"Right fool I'll look going to Brennan with this."

"We could put his picture on TV," Matty said. "Get an artist to fix up a sketch of his face pre-gunshot."

"Brennan won't like it, asking the public for help. Hates that," Crabbie said.

"Does he now?" I muttered. He seemed like a man with a yen for the bright lights of a BBC studio, but that was maybe just me projecting, and again it made me think that *Prods were different and Prods from East Antrim were even differenter.*

"Aye, he does. He doesn't want a lot of focus from the powers that be on our wee set-up down here," Crabbie explained.

The three of us sat there for a minute looking at a filthy coal boat chugging down the lough. Matty lit a Rothmans. Crabbie began assembling his pipe. I played with a paper clip. I sighed and got to my feet. "Maybe the doc will help, who wants to come?"

"Will they be cutting him open?" Matty asked.

"I expect they will."

Matty coughed. "You know what? I'll stay here and chase up on our boy's prints," he said.

"I'll pass too," Crabbie muttered.

"You're both a couple of yella bellies," I said and put my coat on.

Crabbie cleared his throat. "If I could make an observation before you head off, Sean," he said.

"Go on."

"Very unusual this for these parts. No prints on anything? Believe me, I know these local hoods and no one in the Carrick UVF or the Carrick UDA is this careful. It gives ya pause for thought," McCrabban said.

"Aye, it does," Matty agreed.

"And no 'thirty pieces of silver' either," I said. "They usually love that shit."

Brennan saw me on the way out and dragged me to the Royal Oak public house next door.

He ordered two Guinnesses and two Bushmills.

"That's some lunch. I'll have the same," I told him. He smiled and we took the drinks to the snug.

My pager was going like the clappers and under Brennan's withering look I turned it off.

"What news, kemosabe?" he asked when we'd drunk our chasers.

"Drawing a blank so far, skipper, but I still have the patho to see and the victim's prints are up in Belfast getting run through the database as we speak."

"Thought I told you last night to handle this ourselves," Brennan muttered with a scowl.

"Not the leg work too, surely? Besides, them boys in records have nothing better to do. If I sent Matty up there to do it manually it would take him two hours just to drive through the police road blocks."

Brennan nodded. He fixed me with his Viking peepers. "And I heard you authorized 'additional photography'?"

"Yes sir, but I'll pay for that," I replied.

"See that you do. I have to account for every penny."

"There was some thought among the lads that we could go on the BBC and put our mystery man's face on the telly, but Crabbie has crushed my show-business dreams by saying that's not your policy? Sir?"

Brennan pointed heavenwards. "No. Let's keep this nice and discreet. Once *they* start breathing down your neck . . ."

"Ok to authorize flyers and a poster of our poor unfortunate on the board outside the station?"

"One poster and don't make it grim, let's not upset the natives."

Sergeants Burke and McCallister spotted us and joined us at the table, but I had things to do and couldn't afford a lunch-time session with them boys. After I finished my Guinness, I went back in the cop shop and got my car. Carrick Hospital was a small Victorian building on the Barn Road, only about three hundred yards from the police station as the crow flew, but the crow could juke over a railway line, a stream and Carrick Rangers FC so it took me ten minutes to get there in the Beemer.

The waiting room was full of people with runny noses, colds and other complaints. A child was vomiting into a bag. A teenage hood stinking of petrol was holding a singed hand. A man with a face caked with dried blood was wearing a T-shirt that said "No Pope Here." Considering his present condition, the Pope could consider himself lucky. There were, however, no young men lying on gurneys with their kneecaps shot off, which you always saw in the bigger Belfast hospitals.

I walked to the reception desk.

The nurse behind the counter was channeling Hattie Jacques from the *Carry On* films. She was fidgety, scary and enormous.

"What's the matter with you?" she asked in one of those old-timey upper-crust English accents.

"I'd like to see Dr. Cathcart," I said with what I hoped was a winning smile.

"This is not one of her days."

"It's not? Oh? Where is she?"

"She's doing an autopsy, if you must know."

"That's what I wanted to see her about," I said pulling out my warrant card.

"You're Sergeant Duffy? She's been trying to reach you for the last hour."

"I was busy."

"We're all busy."

She showed me the way to the morgue along a dim black and white tiled corridor that seemed unchanged since the 1930s.

A leak was dripping from the ceiling into a large red bucket with the words "Air Raid Precautions" stamped on the side.

I stopped outside a door marked: "Autopsy. Strictly No Admittance Without Permission of Staff Nurse."

I knocked on the door.

"Who is it?" a voice asked from within.

"Sergeant Duffy from Carrick police."

"About time!"

I pushed the door and went inside.

An antiseptic, freezing little room. More black and white tiles on the floor, frosted windows, a buzzing strip light, charts from a long time ago on "hospital sanitation" and "the proper disposal of body parts."

Dr. Cathcart was wearing a mask and a white cotton surgical cap. A little Celtic cross was dangling from her neck and hanging over her surgical gown.

The star of the show was John Doe from last night who Dr. Cathcart had opened up and spread about like a frog on a railway line. There were bits of him in various stainless steel bowls, on scales and even preserved in jars. The rest of him was lying naked on the table uncovered and unconcerned by these multiple violations.

"Hello," I said.

"Put on gloves and a mask, please."

"I don't think he's going to catch anything from us."

"Perhaps we'll catch something from him."

"Ok."

I put on latex gloves and a surgical mask.

Cathcart held up the severed right hand. "Were you responsible for fingerprinting this hand?" she asked. Her eyes were blue and I could see the hint of black hair under the cap.

"One of my officers did it, but I take full responsibility for him. Why, did we do something wrong?"

"Yes, you did. Your officer cleaned the fingers in white spirit before taking fingerprints from this hand. We therefore lost any evidence that may have been under the victim's nails."

"Oh dear, sorry about that."

"Sorry doesn't fix things, does it?" she said sternly in what I realized now was some kind of posh South Belfast accent.

I really didn't like her tone at all. "Love, in a murder investigation getting the fingerprints is a priority so that we can establish who the victim was and hopefully trace their final movements and question witnesses when things are fresh in their minds."

She pulled down her mask. Her cheeks were pink and her lips a dark red camellia. Her eyes were a vivid azure and her gaze icy and disturbing. She was imperious, attractive and she probably knew it.

"I prefer 'Dr. Cathcart' rather than 'love' if you don't mind, sergeant."

Now I felt even more like an eejit.

"Sorry, Dr. Cathcart . . . look, we seem to have got off on the wrong foot, I mean, uhm, just because we're police officers, it doesn't mean that we're total idiots."

"That remains to be seen. This hand, for example," she said, picking up the severed right hand.

"What about it?"

"It seems that none of you noticed that this hand does not belong to the victim. It's from a completely different person."

Shit.

That was what my subconscious had been trying to tell me all night.

"Nope, we missed that," I admitted.

"Hmmm."

"What else have you found out?" I asked.

She put the hand back on the autopsy table and gave me a plastic bag containing a bullet slug.

"You'll want this," she said. "Recovered from his chest."

"Thank you."

She read her notes. "The victim is a white male around twenty-eight years old. His hair has been dyed blond but it was originally brown. The lack of compression of the blood vessels in the arm or ligature marks on the wrists leads me to the conclusion that the victim's right hand was cut off postmortem. After he was murdered."

"We prefer the term 'unlawful killing' at this stage, Dr. Cathcart. It's the mens rea of the killer that determines if he or she is guilty of murder as opposed to some other kind of unlawful homicide," I said to get a bit of my own back and annoy her—which I could see was mission accomplished.

Dr. Cathcart sniffed. "Shall I continue?"

"Please."

"Another man's hand was placed at the scene. This man was considerably older than the victim. Perhaps sixty. For what it's worth this hand shows evidence of callusing on the fingers in a pattern which suggests that he played the guitar. Perhaps professionally."

"How long ago was this hand removed? Days ago? Weeks ago?"

"It is difficult to say. However there is no evidence of freezing and thawing in the blood or skin cells so I would assume that it was removed around the same time as the victim was killed."

"When was the victim killed?"

She picked up her notes and read: "Between 8 and 11 pm on 5/12/81."

"The cause of death was the gunshot wound?"

"The chest wound probably killed the victim but he was then shot in the head, execution style."

"Anything else?"

"The victim had had sexual intercourse with a male before or after he was killed."

"How can you tell that?"

"The victim's exterior sphincter was stressed and I found semen in his rectum."

"Was this consensual intercourse?"

"If the sexual encounter was also postmortem then I would hazard a non-consensual encounter."

This was beginning to look a little less like your ordinary run-of-the-mill execution of an informer.

"Leaving aside the sexual episode, the chronology of the murder seems to have been this: the victim was shot in the chest, shot in the head, there was an interval of some time and then the assailant removed the right hand with a hack saw," she continued. She stifled a yawned.

"Tired or already jaded by death?"

"Sorry. Helicopters woke me up last night. Couldn't get back to sleep. We couldn't possibly do the rest of this outside, could we?"

"Certainly. Over a cup of tea or something?" I asked.

"That would be nice," she said and smiled.

"I'll just need to fingerprint this character. Is that ok? We've got the prints from the other hand working their way through the system."

"Yes, that's fine. But I should show you this first."

She went to one of the stainless steel bowls and I winced involuntarily as she reached inside and gave me something large and slippery. I opened my eyes and was relieved to see that it was merely a plastic bag with a curled-up piece of paper inside.

"What's this?"

"I also recovered this from the victim's anus and perhaps this was where the subcutaneous stressing came from."

"Jesus Christ! That was up his arse?"

"Yes."

"The bag and all?"

"Just the paper."

"I see."

"Why don't you meet me in the hospital cafeteria in ten minutes while I wash up?" she said.

"Ok," I replied. I took out my kit and fingerprinted John Doe's left hand. I went back outside and along the gloomy corridor until I found Hattie Jacques again. "I need to make a phone call," I said.

Her eyes bulged as if I had asked for her firstborn but then she directed me to an inner office. I called McCrabban and told him to get over here right away not sparing the horses. I went to the cafeteria, got a pot of tea and waited for both of them at the window seat next to the garden. I examined the bullet: 9mm slug shot at point-blank range. I looked at the bag Dr. Cathcart had given me.

Keeping it within the plastic I unrolled the piece of paper she had recovered.

"What the fuck?" I said to myself.

The paper was soiled and faded but it was clearly the first twelve bars of a musical score:

I examined it for a minute. Some things were obvious. It was for solo tenor and piano but clearly transcribed from an opera score. I hummed it to myself. It was vaguely familiar, but I couldn't quite place it. The words had been removed from the transcription, which wasn't that uncommon. I hummed it again. It was something quite famous. Italian. Verdi or Puccini.

But which opera and what were the words? I needed an expert. While I was thinking Crabbie showed up.

"Jesus, how did you get here so fast?" I asked him.

"Out the back doors, over the railway lines. Is one of them teas for me?"

"No. Here," I said handing him the bag. "Dr. Cathcart found this shoved up the victim's arse. Get Matty to open it with full forensic caution. When he's done that, please get him to make me a photocopy of it and get one of those reserve constables to send the photocopy back over here ASAP. Make sure Matty does his best work on this. The killer might not have expected us to find it and he may have been a bit more careless."

"This was in the victim's, uh, behind?"

"Yeah. Here, take it."

"Ok, boss," Crabbie said taking the plastic bag with distaste.

"And take this," I said handing him the fingerprints.

"What's this?" Crabbie asked.

"That hand next to the body last night? It was from somebody else."

"Seriously?"

"Me and Matty missed it. Right eejit I looked in front of the patho."

"A different bloke's hand next to the body? What kind of a case is this?"

"There's more."

"I'm listening."

"He had semen in his arse too. It's a possibility that he was raped postmortem. Raped, a piece of music shoved up his arse, his hand cut off. We're into weird territory with this one, Crabbie."

His eyes were wide. "If the press get a whiff of this . . ."

"But they won't, Crabbie, will they? Not until we're ready."

"No way, Sean. No way."

"Good. Now here's the slug. Get that up to the ballistics lab. And have that photocopy back here as quick as you can."

Crabbie went off looking thoroughly unhappy.

When he was gone I took out my notebook and wrote: "Shot in the chest. Rape? Musical score. Nineteenth-century opera. Hand removed and kept for trophy? Second victim? Tortured? Informer? Something else made to look like murder of informer?"

I looked through the cafeteria window at the darkening sky.

The wind had picked up and it begun to rain. A harsh sea rain from the north east. The flowers in the well-kept hospital garden were getting a battering. I flipped a page of my notebook and sketched them: syringa wolfii, syringa persica—here under the great shadow of the railway embankment May was the month that bred lilacs out of the dead land.

Dr. Cathcart sat down. She'd showered and changed into civvies. A tight, mustard-colored jumper, black slacks and high heels. Her hair was a long cascading stream of black that fell ever so precisely over her right shoulder. She was the spit of the evil Samantha on Bewitched.

"Shall I be mother?" she asked, pouring the tea.

"If I can be the pervy uncle."

She made the tea like a surgeon. Milk, then tea, then more milk and your bog-standard two sugars. In the long caesura an army helicopter flew low overhead.

"Do you have any more questions, Sergeant Duffy?"

"The semen in the victim's rectum, is there any way we can use that to help identify the killer?" I wondered.

"It's an interesting question. I have read a few papers about this. At the present moment, no, but perhaps in a few years they will be able to do DNA sequencing or something like that. I've frozen a sample just in case."

I nodded. She was good.

We sipped our tea.

"Where's the music?" she asked. "I thought we could figure it out together."

"I gave it to McCrabban. It's a nineteenth-century opera. Italian. Other than that I have no idea. He's getting it photocopied, either that or he's run off screaming to the Witchfinder General. Good lad, McCrabban, but he's from Ballymena. Different world up there."

"And you're not from up there, are you?"

"Geographically a little. Spiritually, no."

We looked at one another.

"So what's a nice girl like you doing in a place like this?"

"How do you know I'm a nice girl?"

"The Malone Road accent, the fact that you're a doctor . . ."

"What's your accent?"

"Cushendun."

"Cushendun? Oh, that's way up there, isn't it? What primary school did you go to?"

"Our Lady, Star of the Sea."

And just like that she had established that I was a Catholic. Of course I'd known she was a Catholic from the get-go because of the cross around her neck.

She took another sip of her tea and added a decadent third cube of sugar.

"No, seriously, you could be earning a fortune over the water," I said.

"Does it always have to be about money?"

"What should it be about?"

She nodded and tied back her hair. "My parents are here and my dad's not very well."

"I'm sorry to hear that."

"It's his heart. It's not fatal. Not immediately fatal. And both my little sisters are still here. What about you? Brothers, sisters?"

"Only child. Parents still up in Cushendun."

"Only child?" she asked incredulously. She obviously thought that all country Catholics had twelve children each. The only possible explanation was that something terrible had happened to my mother. She gave me a pitying look that I found adorable.

"So where did you go to uni, Queen's?" I asked.

"No, I was at the University of Edinburgh."

"And you still came back?"

"Yup."

She didn't ask me where I had gone to uni because in general coppers did not bother with college. She was more relaxed now and that lovely smile came back again.

I was starting to like her.

"So what do you make of everything that I told you?" she asked.

I shook my head. "This was a pretty complex killing possibly disguised to look like the simple execution of an informer."

"Badly disguised."

"Maybe he thought we would never find the paper in the victim's rectum."

"No, it was sticking out. It was quite obvious. And that's what made me check for signs of rape."

"So he's signposting everything. His working assumption is that we're lazy and incompetent and he needs to underline everything. He put the body where he knew it would be found fairly soon. He's bold and a bit too sure of himself and he has contempt for us. I imagine he's had a few dealings with the cops over the years if that's his attitude."

"Is the RUC not noted for its competence?" she asked with a slight sarcastic edge to her voice.

"Oh, there are worse police forces but it's not exactly Scotland Yard, is it?"

"You're the expert."

"When was the last time you've seen a male rape in the course of your duty?" I asked.

"Never."

"It's not in the paramilitaries' MO, is it?"

"Not it in my limited experience."

"Both sides are extremely conservative. And the normal way they deal with informers is virtually identical."

"Is that so?" she asked, her eyebrows arching with interest.

"There's really no difference at all between your average IRA man and your average UVF man. The markers are always the same: working class, poor, usually an alcoholic or absent father. You see it time and again. Identical psycho-social profiles except for the fact that one identifies himself as a Protestant and one as a Catholic. A lot of them actually come from mixed religious backgrounds like Bobby Sands. They're usually the hardcore ones, trying to prove themselves to their co-religionists."

"Sorry, you lost me there. Do you want a slice of cake or something? I'm starving. I haven't eaten since breakfast."

"I'm all right, but you go ahead," I said. "Seeing John Doe all disemboweled like that has somewhat smothered my appetite."

"Speaking of appetites, his last meal was fish and chips."

"I hope he enjoyed it."

"The fish was cod."

"You're just showing off now, aren't you?"

She grinned, got up and came back with two slices of Madeira cake. Despite my protestations she gave me one of them.

"How come you ended up in the police?" she asked.

Her real question had been "So what's a nice, bright, Catholic boy like you doing in the peelers?"

I thought about what I'd said to Brennan last night. "I just wanted to be part of that thin blue line holding back the chaos."

"Thin green line," she said.

She was right about that too, bless her: in the nineteenth century British peelers had been given a blue uniform to distinguish them from the Red Coats, but the Royal Irish Constabulary had worn dark (very dark) green uniforms from the start. The successor to the RIC after partition was the Royal Ulster Constabulary, based in Belfast, and the uniform hadn't changed even though green was a color associated with Irish nationalism.

"Thin green line doesn't really work as a metaphor though, does it?" I said.

"No," she agreed. She ate her slice of cake and looked at her watch. "Do you have any more questions or are we about done here?"

I shook my head. "I can't think of anything. You'd better give me your number though, in case something comes up."

"You can reach me here," she said.

She hadn't liked that. It was too sly. Maybe the direct approach: "What are you doing later? Do you want to go out for a drink or anything?" I asked.

"You're fast," she said.

"Is that a no?"

She didn't say anything, just tapped her fingers on the Formica table.

"Look, I'll be at the Dobbins from nine o'clock onwards, if you fancy a quick drink, drop in," I said casually.

She stood up. Got her bag. Gave me the once over. "Maybe," she said.

In an odd, formal gesture, she offered me her hand. I shook it.

"It was nice meeting you," she said.

"Nice meeting you too," I said and gave her a conspiratorial wink. Here we were: two wee fenian agents in Proddy Carrickfergus.

I watched her walk into the car park and saw her get into a green Volvo 240.

I finished my tea and was thinking about the remaining cake when Sergeant McCallister showed up with the photocopy of the musical score from poor John Doe's arse.

"What are you doing here, Alan? I asked Crabbie to send this over via some useless ganch."

Alan took off his hat and fixed his thin thatch of greyish brown hair.

"No, Sean, no reserve constables this time. You're going to have to be more careful about the protocols, mate. Looks like you've got yourself a freaky one."

"Aye, you're right," I thought, slightly chastened. The reserve constables were all chatty bastards.

"There's been two phone calls already this morning asking for the head of Carrick CID."

"Shit."

"Carol said that Sergeant Duffy was not available and could she take a message."

"And?"

"They hung up."

"The press?"

"My advice: don't give them anything."

"Did you hear about the rape?"

"I got Crabbie to tell me everything. Different hands? Pieces of music? Queer sex? This thing's far too complicated already," McCallister muttered darkly.

McCallister was close to fifty, a twenty-five-year man with a lot of experience both before and after the Troubles.

"Have you ever seen anything like this before?" I asked.

"No, I haven't and I don't like it."

"Me neither."

"Are you eating that cake?"

Alan walked me back to my car and I drove to the center of Carrickfergus.

A bunch of kids were walking around aimlessly. There was nothing for them to do with school cancelled except that there was always potential for a rumble since the Proddy kids were easily identifiable by their red, white and blue school uniforms and the Catholics by their uniforms of green, white and gold.

There were few actual shoppers. Since ICI had shut down the center of Carrick had withered. The bookshop had closed, the shoe shop had closed, the baby clothes shop had closed . . .

I easily found a parking place on West Street and dandered past a boarded-up grocers before I came to Sammy McGuinn, my chain-smoking, short-arsed, Marxist barber.

He'd given me two good haircuts since I'd come here which was a high batting average for Ulster and probably why he was still in business.

I went in and sat down in the waiting area.

He was finishing work on a man in a brown suit with a ridiculous comb-over. Sammy was only five five and he had lowered his customer practically to floor level.

"Nationalism is a plot by international capitalism to keep the working classes from uniting. Irish independence separated the working classes of Dublin, Liverpool and Glasgow which destroyed the union movement forever in these islands just when capitalism was entering its crisis stage . . ." he was saying.

I tuned him out and read the cinema reviews in Socialist Worker.

Raiders of the Lost Ark sounded promising despite "its patronizing caricatures of third-world manual laborers."

When Sammy was finished with his customer I showed him the musical score.

As well as being Carrick's only remaining barber Sammy was a violinist with the Ulster Orchestra and had two thousand classical records in his flat above the shop. A collection he had shown me when he'd found out from Paul at CarrickTrax that I bought the occasional classical record and that I'd done ten years of piano. Ten years of piano under protest.

"What do you make of that?" I asked him, showing him the photocopy of the music.

"What about it?"

"What is it?"

"Surprised at you, Sean. I thought you knew your onions," he said, with an irritating sneer.

Like a lot of barbers, Sammy was completely bald and that chrome dome really invited a Benny Hill slap right about now.

His lips were tightly shut. He wanted the words:

"No, I really don't know," I said.

"Puccini, La Bohème!" he announced with a laugh.

"Aye, I thought it was Puccini," I said.

"You say that now. Anybody could say it now."

"The words are missing, aren't they? It's not the overture, is it?"

"No."

"You don't happen to know what the missing words are, by any chance?"

"Of course," he said with an eye roll.

"Go on then!"

"Che gelida manina, se la lasci riscaldar. Cercar che giova? Al buio non si trova. Ma per fortuna é una notte di luna, e qui la luna, lCabbiamo vicina," he sang in a surprisingly attractive baritone.

"Very nice."

"Do you need a translation?"

"Uhm, something about hands, fortune, the moon?"

"Your little hand is freezing. Let me warm it for you. What's the use of looking? We won't find it in the dark. But luckily it's a moonlit night, and the moon is close to us."

I got out a pencil and made him say it again and wrote it down in my notebook.

"What's this all about?" he asked.

"Nothing important," I said and drove back to the police station.

I knocked on Chief Inspector Brennan's door.

"Enter!" he said.

He looked up from the Daily Mail crossword. "You seem worried, what's going on, Sean?" he asked.

"We may be in trouble," I said.

"How so?"

"I think we have a sexual murderer on our hands, perhaps even a nascent serial killer."

"Have a seat."

I closed the door. His cheeks were ruddy and he was a little the worse for drink.

"What makes you think that?" he asked in a cold burr, leaning back in his pricey Finn Juhl armchair. I filled him in on all the details but he was skeptical of my thesis. "Northern Ireland's never had a serial killer," he said.

"No. Anyone with that mindset has always been able to join one side or the other. Torture and kill with abandon while still being part of the 'cause.' But this seems different, doesn't it? The sexual nature of the crime, the note. This is not something we've encountered before."

"I already put the paperwork through that this was a hit on an informer," Brennan said with a trace of annoyance.

"I'm not ruling anything out, sir, but at this stage I'm thinking it's not that."

"Let me see that piece of music."

I passed across the photocopy under which I had written: "Your tiny hand is frozen. Let me warm it for you. What's the use of looking? We won't find it in the dark. But luckily it's a moonlit night and the moon is close to us."

He examined it and shook his head.

"He's mocking the victim, sir. And us. He's taking the piss. He's telling us that he's cut the victim's hand off and he's taken it somewhere else. He's making game of us, sir."

Brennan shook his head and leaned forward. He took his reading glasses off and set them on the table. "Look, Sean, you're new around here. I know you want to make a name for yourself. You're ambitious, I like that. But you can't go bandying words like 'serial killer' around for all and sundry. The shit's hitting the fan everywhere. You cannae throw a brick out there without clobbering a journalist. They're all looking for an angle, aren't they? And believe me, I know Carrick, so I do. Serial killers. Come off it. We don't do that in these parts. Ok?"

"If you say so, sir."

He smiled in a conciliatory manner. "And besides, for a serial killer you need more than one victim, don't you?"

"Our guy in the Barn Field and then the hand from the other bloke. That's two."

Brennan passed the musical score back across the table. He took a sip of cold coffee from a mug on his desk. "Who else have you told about this theory of yours?"

"McCrabban and Sergeant McCallister. I'll have to tell Matty too."

"Good. Nobody else. What's the status of your investigation?"

"We might get a break soon, sir. Now we have two sets of fingerprints working their way through the channels."

He nodded and put his glasses back on. I could see that I was being dismissed. I got to my feet. "Do your job, do it well and do it quietly," Brennan muttered, examining the *Daily Mail* again.

"Yes, sir."

"Sean, one more thing."

"Yes, sir?"

"'Idle fellow but he gives us a buzz.' Thirteen across. Five letters."

I thought for a second. "Drone, sir?"

"Drone? Drone, oh yes. Ok, you may go."

I exited. It was late and the place was emptying out.

I borrowed a couple of ciggies from someone's table and headed out onto the fire escape to think.

There was trouble up in Belfast again. Potassium nitrate flares falling through the darkening sky. A Gazelle helicopter flying low over the lough water. Little kids walking past the police station showing each other the best technique for lobbing Molotov cocktails over the fence. Jesus, what a nightmare.

This was a city crucified under its own blitz.

This was a city poisoning its own wells, salting its own fields, digging its own grave . . .

3: A DIFFERENT MUSIC

I smoked the fags and when the rain came I climbed back inside, locked the evidence in the CID room and drove home.

The cows were gone. The cow shit had been scraped up and bagged by entrepreneurs. Mrs. Campbell told me all about the great bovine escape and how Arthur's prized roses had been ruined and how he would be furious when he got back from the North Sea, which wouldn't, she added, be for two more long, lonely weeks.

I went into the kitchen and made myself a pint-glass vodka gimlet. I threw frozen chips in the deep fat fryer and dumped a can of beans in a pot. I fried two eggs and ate them with the chips and beans.

At seven o'clock I shaved and changed into a shirt, my black jeans, leather jacket and DM shoes. I put on a black leather waistcoat. It looked good but there was a slight Han Solo vibe so I hung it back in the cupboard.

I went out. A stray dog began walking beside me. Black lab. Cheerful looking character. Victoria Estate had dozens of stray dogs and cats, fed, and sometimes adopted, by the local children.

I was halfway along Barn Road when a guy ran out of his house wearing a white singlet and waving a ten-pound sledgehammer.

"Now you're going to get it!" he screamed at me. "You're really going to get it!"

"For what?"

"Your dog just took a dump against my gate. I finally caught you, you dirty bastard! You and your dirty dog. You are going to pay, mate! Oh yes!"

"That's not my dog," I said.

His consternation and disappointment knew no bounds. I could sympathize: there is nothing, nothing in this world more deflating than the realization that the lumping villain who has been tormenting you is not going to get an arse-kicking after all.

He asked me if I was sure it was not my dog but I just kept walking.

I went by a DeLorean broken down on the Scotch Quarter, gull wings askew, steam coming from its rear engine, which did not bode well.

The Dobbins was deserted and I got a seat next to the massive sixteenth-century fireplace. I ordered a Guinness, took out my note-book and looked over my bullet points from the day. Twelve pages of notes. Lots of questions marks and exclamation points. This was a case already spiralling out of control.

I nursed my pint until 9:30.

She didn't show.

"The hell with it!" I said, got up and began walking home along West Street.

"Sergeant Duffy!" she called out.

I turned. She was wearing old jeans and a red blouse, ratty sneakers. She hadn't dressed up and her hair was wet. Spur of the moment decision?

We went back in. I got her a gin and tonic. Another pint for me.

"Look, it's a wee bit late in the game to ask this but . . ." I began.

"Yes?"

"What's your name?"

She laughed. "I must have told you."

"Nope."

"Laura."

"Mine's Sean."

"I know. Although I bet they all call you the fenian or the left footer or something, don't they?"

"Who? The other cops?"

"Yeah."

"It's not like that. At least not to my face. The constables call me 'Duffy' or 'Sergeant Duffy.' I'm Sean to everybody else except Carol who calls me Mr. Sean cos she's from Fermanagh. I'm only mildly exotic. Catholic hiring has gone up since Mrs. Thatcher seized the reins. Even the dyed-in-the-wool bigots are going to have to get used to us soon enough."

She seemed unconvinced.

"I'm CID," I further explained. "Believe me, that's more of an issue. Some divisions are more important than others and detective versus beat cop is the historic peeler schism."

"If you say so."

"Did you have any trouble being an RC in medical school?"

"You knew I was a Catholic? My name's Laura, I'm a doctor, how could you—"

I pointed to her crucifix. "Proddies don't wear those unless they've got a morbid fear of vampires."

"You don't see many Catholic policemen. Your father was a peeler?"

"God, no. A clerk, then a country solicitor. Yours?"

"Country doctor."

She had taken precisely one sip of her gin and tonic when her pager went.

She found a telephone.

She came back ashen.

"What is it?" I asked.

"The Peacock Room Restaurant, South Belfast," she said, her voice trembling.

"A bomb?"

"Incendiary."

"How many?"

"Six burned alive. A dozen more in the Royal Victoria Hospital. The coroner asked me if I would help ID the victims in the morning."

"What did you say?"

"What can you say?"

She downed her gin and tonic. I took her hand to stop it shaking. It was cold.

"Let's get out of here," she said.

Back on West Street it was drizzling and we could hear the sound of rioting in Belfast again, distant and ominous.

"Walk me home," she said.

I walked her to one of the new flats on Governor's Place opposite the castle. We put on the TV news. All three channels were carrying it. It was a blast bomb that had been placed next to an oil drum filled with petrol and sugar—IRA napalm. The victims hadn't had a chance.

After five minutes she turned off the tube.

"I've been to that restaurant," she said.

She began to cry.

I held her.

"Will you stay?" she asked.

I stayed.

Later. Her bedroom overlooking the harbor. Laura, asleep in the moonlight. The harbor lights dead on the black water. A Soviet coal boat tied up along the wharf. Six people. Six people trying to seize a piece of normality in an abnormal world. Burned alive by incendiaries.

Tiocfadh ar la. Up the revolution. Our day will come.

I wondered why that particular target. Maybe they hadn't been paying their protection money? Maybe they had but it had been full of Belfast's high society and it was just too tempting to pass up. And then there was the whole business of the oil drum, maneuvering that into place implied careful planning and possibly someone on the inside . . .

I sighed—all these were questions for a different team of detectives. I had my own problems. The sheet had fallen off Laura's back. I looked at her long legs tucked up beneath her breasts. I fixed the sheet, slipped out of the bed, pulled on my jeans and sweater. I dressed, grabbed her keys from the dresser and went outside to have a cigarette.

Water. Reflections. Pencil lines of light.

The silence of 3 a.m. Sporadic gunfire. Choppers.

I could see it even if no one else wanted to. This was the Götter-dämmerung. This was a time of opportunity for people who wished to walk on the grass, to embrace the irrational, to hug the dark.

I walked down to the harbor's edge.

Somewhere deep down I heard music. Not Puccini. Schubert's piano trio in e-flat. His opus 100. The fourth movement where the piano takes the melody . . .

I looked at Laura's apartment from the outside. I looked at the sleeping town.

The phosphorescence of bulb and beam.

You're out here too, aren't you, friend? You're awake and wondering about me. Have the peelers got your message? Do they know what's in store?

We know.

I know.

I walked back to the apartment. I put the key in the lock.

Quiet.

The hall.

Quiet.

The bedroom.

Quiet.

"Where have you be—"

"Sssshhh. Sleep."

"Sleep?"

"Yes. Sleep."

And I got in beside her and we moved from one dream to another . . .

4: BONEYBEFORE

I could smell coffee. She cleared her throat. I opened my eyes and looked at her. She was wearing my shirt, no kacks and she was holding a mug of Nescafé.

She smiled but she didn't look happy.

I didn't envy her her task today up at that awful morgue in Belfast.

"Thanks," I said and took the cup.

"I didn't know how you liked it so I just made it with milk and two sugars."

"That's fine."

"You want some breakfast?"

"If you're having something."

"It's already made, come and join me in the living room."

"Ok," I said.

She took off my shirt and laid it on the bed.

"And get a move on," she said.

I admired her small breasts, trim, sexy body and pert arse as she walked away. She was like one of the girls you'd meet out in the country somewhere, you on a bike covered in mud spattle and she trotting past on some massive chestnut hunter. I liked that image. And I liked her. But it was evident that I was being given the bum's rush.

She wanted me to dress, eat and go.

I pulled on me kit and shoes and followed her into the lounge.

The place looked good in daylight. Very chic: blurry black and white photographs, pastel shades, German furniture and a kitsch kitty cat lamp (at least I hoped it was kitsch). The view through the big windows was of the harbor and the twelfth-century castle.

She'd made porridge and an Ulster fry.

My porridge came in a packet, hers had been slow cooked for twenty minutes with full cream milk, salt and brown sugar and was so thick that you could stand a spoon vertical in it.

It was damn good.

The fry was fine too, sizzling: sausage, egg, bacon, soda bread and potato bread. After this I'd last until dinner or my coronary—whichever came first.

A doctor, a looker and a cook.

She was a catch.

"So what's your home number?" I asked as I started on the last egg.

"Uh, you won't need it. We won't be doing this again."

I looked for the kid, but there was no kid. She was serious.

"What? Why?"

"It was a momentary . . . weakness. I am not the kind of girl who bangs on the first date."

She was looking at me, her eyes wide and her face frowning. It was, no doubt, an expression she had practised in the mirror for telling patients bad news.

"Neither am I," I said.

She gave me a thin smile. "I'm no slag. And it's not just that."

"Something about me?" I wondered aloud.

"No. Not you. Timing. I just got out of a long-term relationship. It wouldn't be fair on you."

"I'd be the rebound guy?"

"Exactly."

"I'll take my chances."

She shook her head. "No. No. It's all too soon. You understand, right? And we'll be friends. I'm sure I'll see you around, on a, uh, professional basis."

She put out her hand again for that odd formal handshake.

I was having none of it.

I pulled her close and she was having none of that.

"No," she said and shoved.

She got up from the table, went to the radio and turned it on. Juice

Newton was singing "Queen of Hearts." It was a song I had grown to hate over the previous week.

I regarded her with amazement and she returned my gaze with a fixed, impatient look of her own.

"I suppose you think you're better than me," I very nearly said but didn't.

I finished my tea in a gulp.

"All right. I imagine I'll see you around then, Dr. Cathcart," I said, pushing the chair back.

"Yes," she said, not looking at me now.

I got my coat, opened the front door and was down the steps and half way to the cop shop before I regretted the abruptness of my departure.

It was petulant. It lacked finesse. Cary Grant would have made a joke or something.

Annoyance changed into self-pity. The first woman I'd liked since Adele and somehow I had ballsed it all up. "Eejit," I muttered to myself.

I walked along the Scotch Quarter past a bunch of confused looking school kids with no school to go to and nothing else to do but make trouble or sniff glue.

I went into Sandy McGowan's newsagent next to the Royal Oak. I looked at the headlines but didn't buy a paper: the local news was terrible, the British news irritating.

"How's the Pope doing?" I asked Sandy.

Sandy was yet another fenian fifth columnist in Proddy Carrickfergus. Decent bloke. A bald wee fella from County Donegal. Rap sheet for smuggling cigarettes across the border but who hasn't got one of those?

"Bless him, he's on the mend, he'll live to see a hundred," Sandy said.

"I'll put a tenner on that. Cheers, Sandy," I said and headed for the door.

"Are you not buying a paper?"

"Improve the news, mate, and then I'll get one."

I walked past the Oak and stopped to look at a big convoy of army trucks and APCs going south along the Marine Highway. They were fresh painted and obviously coming straight from the ferry in Larne.

The soldiers were nervous and seemed about seventeen.

I gave them the black power salute just to get in their heads. Several of them looked suitably terrified and I had a bit of a laugh to myself.

The RUC barracks.

First one in again. Keep this up and I'd get a reputation.

I went to the coffee machine and got a coffee choc and then I checked the faxes but there was no news from Belfast. I followed up with a phone call.

Yes, they had both sets of fingerprints.

No, they had no results as yet. Yes, they knew it was a murder investigation. Did I appreciate that they were very very busy?

At nine o'clock Brennan came in with sergeants Burke and McCallister and asked if me and my CID lads wanted to earn some riot pay. It was Frankie Hughes's funeral this morning, all RUC leave had been cancelled and trouble was expected.

"No thanks, chief, some of us have an actual job to do around here," I said.

Brennan didn't like that but he didn't bust my chops.

"You'll mind the store?" he asked.

"Aye," I said.

The station emptied. Just Carol, a couple of part-time reservists, Matty, Crabbie and me.

I told the boys about the Puccini and both of them saw the same angle that I did.

"He's taking the piss," Matty said.

"He's drawing attention to himself. That's his method. Like Bathsheba combing her hair. There's a reason for it," Crabbie said.

I liked Crabbie. The sixth of nine boys. The rest of his brothers were farmers and farm laborers except for one who was a Free Presbyterian missionary in Malawi. He was the family brainbox. He had bucked the trend by not leaving school at sixteen and immediately getting married.

Instead he had done his A levels, got an HND certificate at Newtown-abbey Tech and joined the peelers.

He was married now, though, to a twenty-two-year-old from the same Free Presbyterian sect and she was already pregnant with twins. Doubtless they were planning to sire an entire clan.

"He? You're thinking solo? One guy?" I asked him.

He nodded. "If they're topping an informer it's going to be a team of hit men from the UVF or UDA, but if it's some pervert I reckon he's a loner."

He was dead right about that.

Double acts were rare in this kind of case.

The three of us talked evidence, ran theories and got nowhere.

We waited for the fingerprint data or ballistics or any good ideas. Nothing.

"Do either of you know anything about women?" I asked them as I made a fresh pot of tea.

"I'm the expert," Matty claimed.

Without mentioning Laura's name I told him how I'd been turfed out this morning.

"You underperformed, mate. Simple as that. They say it's all about having a good sense of humour and a nice smile and all that bollocks but when push comes to shove it's all about what you do upstairs. Some of us have it, Sean, some of us don't. You clearly don't," Matty said.

Crabbie rolled his eyes. "Don't listen to him, Sean, he hasn't had a girlfriend since he took Veronica Bingly to The Muppet Movie."

The rioting at Frankie Hughes's funeral began exactly at twelve and we could see black smoke from hijacked buses five miles across the lough in the center of Belfast.

"My treat for lunch," I said and took the lads to the Golden Fortune on High Street. We ate your typical low spice Irish-Chinese chips, noodles and spare ribs. We were the only customers.

I got us a trio of brandies and we milked the lunch hour well past two o'clock.

On the way back to the barracks I sent the boys on and I stopped off at Carrick Library.

There was a preacher outside who tried to give me something as I went in. It was a pamphlet about the imminent "Second Coming." He was young and had the insolent air of the recently converted. I refused the pamphlet and went straight to see Mrs. McCawley. She was wearing a yellow polka-dot dress that I hadn't seen before. You don't expect old folks to go swanning around in polka-dot dresses, yellow or otherwise, but somehow Mrs. McCawley pulled it off. She'd been a beauty in her day and had run away to America after the war with some GI, only returning after his heart attack in the '70s.

I told her she looked nice and then my problem.

"Dewey 780-782," she said right off the top of her head.

I got the score of La Bohème from 782 but The Grove Dictionary of Music was missing from the reference shelf. I was about to go back to Mrs. McCawley and complain but who should I spot reading it in the Quiet Area? None other than Dr. Laura Cathcart.

I sat next to her. "Good afternoon," I said.

She gasped, surprised, and then she smiled. She slid the dictionary entry across to me.

She was looking at the entry on La Bohème. "How did you figure that out?" I asked.

"How did you?"

"I had to ask someone," I said.

"I had a pretty good idea. At St. Brigid's we did a musical and an opera every year."

"You were in La Bohème?"

"No, I auditioned for Mimi and didn't get it. Still, I recognized it."

"You should have said something yesterday."

"I didn't want to until I was completely sure."

She bit her lip. She seemed pale and she looked like she'd been crying. I remembered her appointment at the coroner's office. "Did you go up to Belfast?"

"Nah. They called it off until tomorrow. Nobody could get into town because of the funeral."

"Makes sense."

She put her hand on mine. "I'm sorry," she said.

"About what?"

"You know. Us." She made a dramatic face and put her hand on her forehead like a silent-movie actress: "What might have been!"

"What still could be."

She shook her head firmly. "No, definitely not. I just can't. I went out with Paul for two and a half years. It's a long time."

"Of course."

"He went to London. He wanted me to go with him. I said no."

"You don't have to explain," I said.

She cleared her throat and slipped her hand from mine.

"You can get on with your wee thing if you want," she said.

"Wee thing! It's police work, darling, serious police work."

I read the libretto for La Bohème but there were no more obvious clues. I passed it over to her.

I watched her face while she read.

Her lips were moving. She read the Italian and the English silently to herself. She enjoyed the sound the Italian words made in her mind. I was digging on that when my pager started beeping.

"Excuse me," I said.

I asked Mrs. McCawley if I could use her phone.

I dialed the station.

It was McCrabban.

"Another one," he said.

"Jesus! Another body?"

"Aye. Sounds like it's our boy from the mystery hand."

"You're joking. Where?"

"Boneybefore."

"Where's that?"

"Out near Eden Village."

"Assemble the gear, sign out a Land Rover."

"And there's been another press call for you. This time from the Carrick Advertiser, they were asking about the body in the Barn Field."

"Bollocks. What did you tell them?" I said.

"Nothing. But they'll keep calling until you give them something," Crabbie muttered.

"Tell him something like: an anonymous tip led Carrickfergus RUC to a body in an abandoned car on Taylor's Avenue. A homicide is suspected and leads are being pursued by Carrickfergus CID. The victim was a white male in his early thirties, as yet unidentified. Police officers kindly request the public to phone in tips or information about this incident to the Confidential Telephone or Carrickfergus CID. Sound ok?"

"Aye."

I hung up the phone and went back to the Reading Area.

She saw my face. No poker player me.

"What is it?" she asked.

"I have to go. The other shoe dropped."

Her eyes widened. "The second victim?" she asked.

I nodded.

She got to her feet. "Walk you out?" she asked.

"I've no objection to that."

Outside the library the preacher was gone and over Belfast there was a pall of heavy black smoke that looked like an evil genie emerging from a lamp.

"Listen, I'm at a bit of a loose end today. I'll walk you out the Quarter too, if you don't mind."

"Sure."

We walked past a funeral home, half a dozen houses for sale and a boarded-up ice cream shop. I thought she was going to talk but she had nothing to say.

I offered some remarks about the weather and such but she wasn't biting on those either.

"Hey, you said you were at a loose end. You wanna come? We could do with your expertise," I suggested and that was the hook she was looking for.

"To the murder scene?" she asked. "Am I allowed?"

"Of course you're allowed. I'm the big Gorgonzola in these parts. Although fair warning, it might be on the grim side."

"You don't know grim, pal, trust me . . . Still, I'm not really dressed for it," she said.

She was wearing a wool coat, slacks, heels, and a white blouse.

"Go home, get changed."

"All right," she said, perking up. "It'll take my mind off things. Meet me at the flat in fifteen minutes?"

"Ok."

She turned and walked briskly in the other direction.

It's all on/off off/on with that lass, I thought.

I went inside the barracks. Matty had the Land Rover out of its parking spot and Crabbie was standing next to it raring to go.

"Jump in, Sean," Crabbie said.

"Hold your horses lads. With Chief Inspector Brennan gone to Belfast and with Burke and McCallister away too I'm senior officer here. I can't just tear out of Dodge. We've got to go organize things."

On the way inside Carol stopped me.

Wonderful woman Carol. Ageless. Thin, stooped, piercing blue eyes, hard as an iron bar. Had worked in Carrick station since 1941. On her second week on the job the barracks had been bombed by the Luftwaffe. A big Heinkel 111 who saw a target of opportunity near the railway station. The Luftwaffe! You gotta love it.

"Mr. Sean?" she said.

"Yes?"

"I was wondering if I could go home early today, I wanted to watch that program about Lady Diana on BBC2."

"That's fine, Carol," I told her. I couldn't really spare her but I knew better than to come between the great British public and Lady Di. The world could be going to hell in a handbasket but the Royal Wedding was in two months and that's all that mattered.

I went upstairs and asked which of the reservists had the most seniority.

A trainee dentist called Jameson, who looked about eleven, put his hand up. He'd been in the force since '79 which would have to do. I told him to call Inspector Mitchell who was technically Brennan's deputy but in fact was almost never here because he more or less single-handedly ran the RUC sub-station in Whitehead.

"Tell Mitchell that I've had to leave, maybe for the day and he probably should close Whitehead station and get up here. It's his call, of course."

"And if he doesn't come?" Jameson asked nervously.

"Then you're it, mate. The skipper's gone and the sergeants are gone and now Carol's gone."

He opened his mouth to speak, didn't know what to say and closed his gob again. He looked petrified.

"Out with it, man!" I ordered him.

"Well, uh, I was just wondering what I should do if the IRA attack us while you're away?"

"Break out the machine guns and return fire. And don't kill any tax-paying customers. Ok?"

He nodded.

"You know where the armory key is?"

"No."

"On the hook next to the fire extinguisher. Got that?"

"Yes."

"Jesus," I muttered as I went back downstairs. If I was an IRA mole in the RUC, this would be my moment to shine . . .

I got in the Land Rover and kicked Matty out of the driver's seat.

I drove out of the station and over the series of speed bumps that were supposed to be a deterrent for a drive-by attack. I got into second gear and finally third and took the heavy vehicle along the Marine Highway.

"We're going to pick up Dr. Cathcart on the way, lads," I said.

Neither Matty nor McCrabban seemed fazed by this.

We stopped outside her place and she was already changed into Wellington boots and a white forensic boiler suit. "What does she look like!" Crabbie muttered.

"Clockwork Orange," Matty concurred.

"We all should be wearing them things to avoid contamination," I said. "Do you boys ever go to the training seminars?"

"What training seminars?" Matty asked.

"You wouldn't catch me dead in one of them," Crabbie said, although his orange shirt, paisley tie and beige jacket weren't exactly Savile Row.

"You lads get in the back. Our guest can ride up front with me."

There was an ancient police superstition that if you changed seats in an armored Land Rover you were sure to cop it during the next rocket-propelled grenade attack while the person you switched with would escape completely unscathed. Why the jinx would only apply to you, and not him, was a secret known only to the elect.

"Come on lads, move it!" I had to say again and they got in back, grumbling. I opened the passenger door and Laura climbed up and in.

"Morning, Dr. Cathcart," I said stiffly.

"Oh, good morning, Sergeant Duffy," she replied. "Where are we going?"

"Boneybefore."

"Stick on the radio for us, will ya?" Crabbie said from the back.

I turned on Downtown Radio but they were in some kind of conspiracy to make Juice Newton a millionaire. I switched to Radio 1 and we listened to Spandau Ballet as I drove us along the Marine Highway and the Larne Road.

"Do you like Spandau Ballet, Dr. Cathcart?" Matty asked from the back.

"I don't really know them," she replied.

"They're the latest thing. What about you, Sean, you like 'em?"

I tried to come up with a witty answer and after some deliberation I said: "Spandau Ballet are to pop music what the Cretaceous-Tertiary Event was to dinosaur music."

Stony silence. Nobody laughed.

"Am I the only one around here that reads New Scientist?" I asked.

Evidently I was. I kept my bake shut after that.

Boneybefore. A village eaten up by the Carrick expansion sometime in the '50s. A white thatched cottage almost on the lough shore. Another unknown young reserve officer standing by the door.

I parked the Land Rover and we got out.

"What are the facts, constable?" I asked the reservist.

"Postman noticed the door was slightly ajar on the second post today. He pushed it open and found the victim. He called us."

"Anybody touch anything?"

"Nope. But I had a wee look in."

"What did you see?"

"I noticed that the victim had been shot and that his hand had been cut off, so I called Crabbie."

I put on latex gloves and went inside the cottage.

The victim had been shot once in the head, probably as he had opened his front door, because he was still lying in the hall. He was a thin, dapper, grey-haired man in shirtsleeves, black tweed trousers and slippers. His hand had been cut off and the hand of—presumably— John Doe had been tossed, almost idly, on his chest.

I found a wallet on the sideboard and quickly ascertained that the victim was one Andrew Young, a sixty-year-old music teacher at Carrickfergus Grammar School.

The place was untouched. The killer had come inside only to kill Young and cut his right hand off.

We did a thorough inspection but Matty agreed with me that the killer had not even entered the rest of the house.

"Time of death?" I asked Laura.

"He's been dead about forty hours," she said, examining the corpse.

"Which one did he kill first?" I asked.

"If you put me on the spot I'd say he killed the man in the car first. But only by a few hours," Laura said.

Matty began taking photographs and dusting for prints.

Laura examined the body.

McCrabban grabbed my sleeve. "Word with you outside, Sean?" he said.

We stepped out into a salt wind coming off the lough.

"What is it, Crabbie?"

"I know this character, Sean. He runs the Carrick festival. He's headteacher at the school. He met Princess Anne. Upstanding citizen and all that. But . . ."

"But what?

"Like I say, decent bloke and everything, but he's a known poofter."

"Are you sure?"

"As sure as eggs is eggs."

I saw the implications immediately. "So what do you think we have here, Crabbie? Someone going around killing homosexuals?"

Crabbie shrugged. "I don't know, but it's beginning to look like it, isn't it?"

"And there's the bloody music connection again, isn't there?"

Crabbie nodded and began filling his pipe.

Of course homosexuality was illegal in Northern Ireland but that didn't mean that there were no homosexuals.

Everybody knew somebody . . .

"Don't mention anything for the moment, let's get the old routine working," I said.

We went back inside.

Photographs.

Prints.

Interviews with the neighbors.

A recovered 9mm stub from the wall.

I reminded Laura to look for another concealed score when she did her autopsy.

The day lengthened.

Waned.

We drove Laura home and thanked her for her help.

We had another case conference at the station.

Of course now that we knew who he was, the first set of finger print data came through from Belfast: Andrew Young DOB 3/12/21. 4 Lough View Way, Boneybefore, Carrickfergus. No known next of kin. No criminal record.

The second set was still being processed.

We bagged the evidence.

I sent the lads on.

It was midnight when I got home. After I'd gone back out to Boneybefore to supervise the removal of the body to Carrick hospital by a private firm of undertakers because the police were overstretched. After I had changed into a shirt and tie and went to make the notification to Young's employer Jack Cook, the headmaster of Carrickfergus Grammar.

"Andrew? I can't believe it! Andrew was one of our best teachers. He was a terrific man. How? When? No, he had no enemies. Are you joking? Everybody loved Andrew."

Midnight and I poured myself a vodka gimlet and listened to the bad news on the radio and put on *La Bohème*.

A 78. Toscanini's own hurried, strange 1946 version.

When I got to Mimi's famous first aria I picked up the lyric sheet and read along: "My name is Lucia. But everyone calls me Mimi. I don't know why. *Ma quando vien lo sgelo. Il primo sole è mio.* When the thaw comes, the sun's first kiss is mine."

I read and listened until I fell asleep but no great revelation was at hand.

No, that wouldn't come until the first post in the morning.

5: MERCURY TILT

The tinker rag-and-bone man woke me up calling out "Tuppence for rags! Tuppence for rags!" I listened to the clip-clop of his ancient horse and then I heard those other heralds of a society attempting to keep order: the milkman, the postman, the bread man.

I'd fallen asleep in the living room under a thin duvet and I was freezing.

La Bohème had been playing on repeat all night and I'd probably ruined the grooves on what was a very rare recording.

I lifted the stylus and examined the 78. It seemed ok. I blew off dust and put it carefully back into its sleeve.

I padded into the kitchen and turned the kettle on. I flipped on Radio Ulster for the news: "Our headlines at a quarter past the hour. Fresh rioting rocked sections of Belfast last night as hunger striker Frankie Hughes was laid to rest. A police reservist was shot dead outside his house in Bangor in the early hours of the morning. A police station in County Tyrone was attacked by rockets and mortars . . ."

I turned off the radio and walked into the hall.

That absurd Sterling sub-machine gun was still sitting there on the hall table.

"If someone breaks in and steals that thing Brennan will have my guts for garters," I said to myself.

I wondered if I could sign the gun back in on a weekend when the armory officer was off duty.

I grabbed the post from the hall floor and opened the front door to take in the milk before the starlings got at it. Mrs. Campbell was bringing in *her* milk. She was holding her dressing gown closed with one hand, picking up the bottles with the other. I could see the curve of both breasts.

"Morning, Mr. Duffy," she said.

"Morning, Mrs. Campbell," I replied.

"Did the filthy tinkers wake you too?" she asked.

"No, Mrs. Campbell, I was already up," I lied to pre-empt a racist rant about "tinkers," "gypsies," and the like. She smoothed a loose strand of red hair back onto her scalp, smiled and went inside.

Up in the fields beyond the cow pasture I could hear the crack crack crack of repeated clapping. Perhaps a local virtuoso was practising a modernist piece by Steve Reich, I thought sardonically . . . Sardonically because, of course, it was in fact someone shooting at targets with a .22 pistol.

A couple of annoyed starlings flew onto the porch looking for milk bottles to vandalize and rob but I had out-generalled them this morning.

I closed the front door and carried the milk and the post to the kitchen.

I lifted up a brown electricity bill and underneath saw a postcard. I picked it up. It was a picture of the Andrew Jackson presidential homestead in Boneybefore.

A little white-washed cottage not unlike that of . . .

I flipped it over.

A first-class stamp. Posted yesterday.

I read it.

A note.

For me.

From the killer.

In lower-case letters: "I found out your name, Duffy. You are young, careful. Your circumspection mirrors my own. Perhaps we are opposites who share the path through the λαβύρινθος. Perhaps we are not true opponents, but key and lock, eternal duellists forced into the fray by rules of which we have no understanding. As a brother of the mirror I have one request of you: do not let them say that I hate queers. I do not hate them.

I pity them. My task is merely to free them from this world and let them have true judgement before the Lord. He, not I, will decide their fate."

I set the postcard on the counter, put on a rubber glove, turned on the fluorescent lamp and read the whole thing again.

λαβύρινθος.

Of course the Jesuits had beat Latin, Greek and Irish—the languages of culture—into us but still I couldn't quite remember the word until I had sounded it out.

Lah, Buh, Ree, N, Thos . . . λαβύρινθος was "labyrinth."

We share the path through the labyrinth together. You and I. Theseus and the Minotaur. Man and monster. I put down the postcard and went to the phone book lying in the hall. It was the newest edition. I looked up "S Duffy" and sure enough I was the only one in Carrickfergus: "S Duffy, 113 Coronation Road, Carrickfergus Tel: 67093." He gets my name from the switchboard, he looks me up in the book. He's no mastermind.

I called McCrabban at home. "Hello?"

"Crabbie, it's me."

"Sean? What's the matter, is there—"

"It's all happening, mate. The killer sent me a postcard. Case conference at nine thirty. I'm inviting the big white chief and Sergeants Burke and McCallister. It's all hands on deck. If Matty's late he's getting my boot up his arse."

"I'll tell him."

I hung up and looked at the postcard a third time. Aye, who do you think you are? Sending this? Name-dropping your dead languages. You're nothing special. Big fish. Little pond. My fucking pond. You'll see pal. "You'll see."

I went out to the car and started her up.

I was at the site of the bonfire on Victoria Road when I remembered that I had forgotten to check underneath for bombs. I slammed on the brakes in front of dozens of wee muckers building a Twelfth of July pyre out of tires, pallets and furniture. Not that it was in need of further construction—the thing was already massive enough to endanger the entire estate.

The kids all turned to look at me. Sleekit wee shites with skinheads, hardman T-shirts and DM boots. "Hey, check out yon Beemer!" one of them called out and they all began walking over to the car. One wee lad was carrying a tin of red paint for painting the curbstones around the bonfire red, white and blue, his dripping brush making a trail on the cement behind him.

There was no way I was getting out and doing a full inspection on the vehicle in front of them.

I put my foot on the accelerator and drove on.

It was stupid, very stupid.

The way a mercury tilt switch works is by establishing an electrical current through the mercury which then sets off a charge in a detonator. The detonator explodes into a pancake-sized wedge of Czech Semtex or Libyan C4 which then reacts and expands in a violent decay of heat and gas that would be powerful enough to eviscerate me and disintegrate the car. I'd seen pics of IRA car bombs that had thrown the vehicle two hundred feet and transformed the occupants inside into offal.

I kept on going.

Dolly Parton came on the radio, singing an old bluegrass song.

My knuckles were white. The downslope was coming up.

The reason the IRA used mercury tilt switches is that they only work when the mercury establishes contact on an incline or decline. While the mercury remains level the bomb is safe, thus it could sit under a car for days or even weeks. As soon as it was driven, however, eventually you'd encounter a hill . . .

I looked out the window.

This is what death would look like.

Victoria Council Estate, a grim appendage of consumptive Carrickfergus, itself a distension of the dying city of Belfast. Grey, wet, unloved. A ghetto supermarket, a bookies, a derelict house and on the gable terrace a massive mural of crossed AK-47s above the Red Hand of Ulster.

The downslope grew steeper. I held my breath as Dolly made her point:

When I was young and in my prime,
I left my home in Caroline,
Now all I do is sit and pine,
For all the folks I left behind . . .

I clenched my fists.
Counted. One. Two. Three.
The road flattened out.
The bomb had not gone off.
There was no bomb. The danger had passed.
I pulled into the car park in front of the newsagents.
Reborn.
My whole life ahead of me . . .
Until the next fuck up.

6: THE LONG BAD SATURDAY

I turned off the engine and sat in my little existential prison before going outside into the bigger existential prison of Northern Ireland.

The car park was empty and I checked under the car just to be on the safe side. Nothing, of course.

I said hi to Oscar McDowell and perused the front pages.

"Liz Taylor Collapses" was the headline in the Sun and the Daily Mirror. "Ripper Trial Final Days" was the offering from the Daily Mail. "Royal Wedding Mix Up" was the lead in the Daily Express. A couple of the Irish papers covered the Frankie Hughes riot and were speculating about which of the hunger strikers would die next, while the others led with the ex-Mrs. Burton.

"What happened to Liz Taylor?" I asked Oscar.

"Buy the paper and find out," he said.

I bought a packet of Marlboro Lights, a Mars bar and a Coke instead.

Oscar gave me a funny look with my change.

"What?" I said.

He examined his shoes, cleared his throat.

"You're a copper, aren't you, Sean?"

"Yeah," I said suspiciously.

"Look, is there . . . is there nothing you can do about the boys?"

"What boys?"

"I'm fed up with it. We barely scrape by here. No one has any money any more. Magazine subscriptions are off by fifty per cent since ICI closed. And you can't tell them that . . . You know what I'm talking about."

I did. He was talking about the protection money he had to pay every week to the paramilitaries. The money he gave straight out of his till to the local hoods so they wouldn't burn him out.

Oscar was in his sixties. Everything about him radiated exhaustion. He should have sold up and moved to the sun years ago.

"What's the going rate these days?" I asked.

"Bobby asks for a hundred pound a week. I can't do it. Not in this economy. It's impossible! Can you have a word with them, Sean? Make them see sense? Can you?"

I shook my head.

"There's nothing I can do, Oscar. If you were willing to testify that would be one thing, but you're not willing to testify, are you?"

He shook his head. "Not on your life!"

"Well then, like I say, nothing I can do."

"There must be some kind of back channel, Sean, you know, where you can just talk to them. Just tell them that they are charging far too much for this economy. If I go out of business, everybody loses."

"I can't meet them. Internal Affairs would say it was collusion."

"I don't mean a formal meeting or anything, I'm only saying that in the course of your duties, if you happen to come across those particular gentlemen, perhaps you can drop a wee hint or two."

I picked up my Mars bar, smokes and Coke.

"I suppose the Bobby you're referring to is Bobby Cameron on Coronation Road?" I asked.

"You heard no names from me."

"Ach, I'll see what I can do."

Oscar sighed with relief.

"Here, you forgot your papers," he said, giving me The Times and the Guardian for nothing.

I took them as a matter of course.

I put them on the passenger's seat and looked at myself in the mirror.

"Your first freebie in your new gig, Sean. This is how it starts. Baby steps," I said to myself.

Another army checkpoint on the Marine Highway. This time the bloody Paras. They looked at my warrant card and sent me through with a sarcastic thumbs up.

Ray was back in the box at the RUC station and gave me a nod as he raised the barrier to let me into the barracks car park.

I got out into a drizzle and decided to leave the smokes. I was down to two or three bummed ciggies a day. Only bought my own for emergencies.

I went upstairs to the CID evidence room.

I reread the postcard through the evidence bag.

I wrote "eternal duellists/labyrinth/queers" in my notebook.

I checked for any faxes from Belfast.

Nothing.

I put my feet on the chair and had a think.

Two victims. Two hands. Symmetry. Mirrors, opposites, duellists, opponents, key and lock. It was all two.

All except the labyrinth.

"We share the path through the λαβύρινθος."

There was only one route through the labyrinth.

One true way. The labyrinth. Built by Daedalus the flyer . . .

Maybe that meant something.

Daedalus, Icarus, Stephen Daedalus, James Joyce, Dublin . . .

Nothing.

I rubbed my chin and thought and bounced a pencil off the desk.

I called ballistics.

"Preliminary indications were that the two slugs came from the same gun," I was told.

I grabbed a typewriter and began work on the presentation. I ate the Mars bar and drank the Coke. McCrabban showed up at 8:30. I told him about the postcard.

He read it, asked me if I'd lifted anything from it.

"You think it's the real deal?" I asked him.

"We get a lot of hoaxes on every case, but this, I don't know, it seems different."

"Any ideas about our boy?"

"He hates queers. Which makes me think that John Doe must be one too. Has to be, right?"

"Aye."

Crabbie typed up a transcript of the note, made photocopies and helped me with my presentation.

At 8:45, Matty called to say he was running late because of a bomb scare on the Larne–Carrick train.

"Where are you calling from?" I asked.

"The train station," he lied.

"How come I can hear David Frost in the background?"

"Uhm."

"Get your arse in here, you lazy hallion!" I said and hung up.

"Youth," McCrabban said.

"What about them?"

"They need more sleep than us," he said.

"You know, I don't think we can do this case with just three people."

McCrabban nodded.

"I'm beginning to feel overwhelmed," I said.

Crabbie didn't like to hear that sort of thing (or anything about anyone's feelings) and he began furiously filling his pipe to cover his embarrassment.

He lit the thing, coughed and blew a blue smoke ring out of his mouth.

"Yes," he said, which was about as much consolation as I was going to get from that dour visage.

"Do me a favor and find out who sells postcards of the Andrew Jackson cottage in Carrickfergus and Belfast and ask them if they've sold any lately and if so do they remember to whom."

"So basically call up every single newsagent in Carrick and Belfast?" McCrabban asked.

"Yeah."

"Ok, boss."

Matty finally came in and I showed him the postcard and he took it away to do more tests. He did fingerprints and the black light and the UV light. All the prints were smudged except for two sets that he suspected were mine and the postman's. I told him to send a reserve constable round to Carrick post office to print the mail carrier from Coronation Road.

At 9:05 I was done typing my presentation and did a dry run in front of the lads. They felt it was ok, although McCrabban made me cut it shorter because Sergeant McCallister had a poor attention span.

At 9:15 I called up Mike Kernoghan in Special Branch, told him about my anonymous letter writer and asked him if his boy could put a tap on my phone just in case the killer decided to get more intimate.

Mike thought this was a good idea and said that he'd send a couple of boys round this afternoon "to fix my TV."

I told him that I kept the spare key under the cactus plant and he said that his boys didn't need no key, a rusty nail could get you into a Northern Ireland Housing Executive terraced house—a fact that did not fill me with confidence about my home security.

I checked again for any faxes from Belfast and I called up the forensics lab just to make sure they were working their arses off ID'ing my John Doe. They claimed that they were and that they had a promising line of inquiry.

"Really? You're not just messing with me, are you?"

"We wouldn't do that, sir."

"When do I get the good word?"

"We like to confirm these things first, Sergeant Duffy, but I'm reasonably sure that we'll have a positive hit by the end of the day."

"Positive hit?"

"Yes."

"So you know who he is?"

"We're fairly certain. We're in the confirmation process at this moment."

"Can you give me a clue? It's not Lord Lucan, is it? DB Cooper? Lady Di?"

The forensics guy hung up on me. I called around for a next of kin on Andrew Young but his work colleagues were the best we could come up with.

When Matty was done with the prints I asked him to start running down any sexual abuse allegations against Young. An enraged former pupil would be a nice go-to guy in a case like this.

At 9:30 I assembled my team in the CID room, set them up in chairs next to me and put three chairs in front of the white board.

At 9:35 Sergeants McCallister and Burke came in. Burke was another old-school peeler about fifty-five years old. No nonsense bloke. He was ex-army and military police. He had served in Palestine, Cyprus, Kenya, all over the shop. He looked like someone's scary father. He didn't talk much, did Burke, but what he did say was usually the wisdom acquired from a long and interesting life . . . either that or total bollocks.

Chief Inspector Brennan came in last. He was wearing a top hat and tails.

"Hurry up, Duffy, I don't have long," he said.

"Aye, you don't want to be late for the play Mr. Lincoln," Sergeant McCallister said and everyone roared.

"Maybe he does a magic act on the side," Sergeant Burke said.

"I'm off to my niece's wedding. Get on with it, Duffy!" Brennan snapped.

I read them the presentation. There were seven main points:

1. The as yet unidentified victim in Barn Field had been shot execution-style by a 9mm.
2. He had had a recent homosexual encounter and a piece of music had been inserted in his anus.
3. His right hand had been replaced with the hand of Andrew Young, a known homosexual who had also been murdered in his house in Boneybefore also by a 9mm.
4. The musical score was *La Bohème* and contained the lines "your tiny hand is frozen" sung by Rudolfo to Mimi.
5. Andrew Young was a music teacher at Carrick Grammar School

and ran the Carrick festival. No, he had never done *La Bohème* at either the school or the festival.

6. The killer had apparently called up Carrick Police Station, found out who the lead detective was and sent me a bizarre postcard (photocopies of which I passed around) that might contain clues or might be a complete distraction.

7. The 9mm slugs from both victims matched.

Brennan and the two sergeants listened to the whole thing without interruption.

"What is your current working hypothesis, Sergeant Duffy?" Brennan asked when I was done.

"Obviously the two murders are linked. Dr. Cathcart feels there was a two- or perhaps three-hour delay between the two deaths. She'll know more precisely when she's performed an autopsy on Mr. Young. Therefore I feel that we have a potential serial murderer on our hands. At this stage I do not see any evidence of a paramilitary link, which would make this the first non-sectarian serial killer in Northern Ireland's history," I said.

"Why would he come out of the woodwork now?" McCallister asked.

"I don't know. Jealousy, perhaps? He's been watching all the publicity the Yorkshire Ripper trial has been generating and it's been getting his goat?" I ventured.

"Maybe the chaos of the hunger strikes has given him the cover and opportunity he needs," McCrabban said.

"Sounds like this old fruit, Young, got someone riled up and that someone went mental and decided to kill some more fruits," Burke said.

"Matty's checking to see if there are any allegations against him," I said.

"And I don't like this music angle. It's bloody weird," Burke said.

"I don't like it either. There something about it that stinks to high heaven. I've read the libretto to *La Bohème* but nothing jumped out at me," I said.

"Jesus, what will we do if this Young fella has something up his arse too?" Brennan muttered.

"Keep our cheeks squeezed together?" McCallister offered and everybody laughed again.

"We're waiting on the autopsy report on that, sir," I added when the tittering had died down.

Silence descended, punctuated by a distant rumbling in Belfast that could be anything from a ship unloading in the docks to a coordinated series of bombings.

"What's your next step, Sergeant Duffy?" Brennan asked.

I told him about the various angles we were chasing down and the fact that we were supposed to finally get the prints on John Doe today.

"And if our letter writer gets in touch again?" Sergeant Burke asked.

I told them about my call to Special Branch.

I could tell Brennan wasn't too happy about that but he didn't say anything. And besides he was getting worried about the time and he had one other fish to fry.

"Have you thought about the press?" he asked.

"Uh, obviously, we'll need to brief the press at some point," I said. "But we can probably put it off for a bit. It's not exactly a slow news week."

Brennan sighed. "This is going to blow up in our faces, Sergeant Duffy. If we don't go to the papers you can be sure that our anonymous note writer, or one of Mr. Young's neighbors, or someone will. Do you have a media strategy?"

"Uh, no, not as such, not a, uh—" I stammered. I looked at Matty and McCrabban who had both discovered something fascinating about the wall-to-wall carpet.

Brennan looked at McCallister. "What about you, Alan? It's a bloody thankless task but we need someone and DS Duffy has quite a full plate by the looks of it. You could do a good defensive briefing to a couple of the local hacks. Seen you do it before."

McCallister smiled at me and shook his head. "No, no, fellas, that's not the way to handle this at all. No defensiveness. We present this as a triumph. Through clever police work we have linked two murders. We talk about modern forensic techniques and how even during these difficult times we hard-working honest peelers are able to spend due care and attention on every single case."

Brennan nodded. "I like it."

"We won't get TV because of all the other nonsense going on but we can call in some of our pals from the Belfast Telegraph, the Carrickfergus Advertiser, the Irish News and the Newsletter and let them have it. Maybe your woman Saoirse Neeson from Crime Beat on Downtown Radio."

Brennan looked at me. I shrugged. When I'd thought this was a nothing case I was keen for the telly but now it had got more complicated there was, at the very least, an element of stage fright; however, if big Alan McCallister wanted to help out. "If Alan wants to do it, that's great," I said.

"Ok, we'll defer everything to Sergeant McCallister," Brennan said.

Hold the phone. Defer everything? What did he mean by that?

Fortunately Alan saw my face and did his best Uri Geller: "Nope. I'm not CID. This is not my case, it's Duffy's. Run everything through Sergeant Duffy. I'll only be his press officer. He tells me what to say and I'll say it and that's that."

"Well said, Alan. These CID boys are flighty, sensitive creatures who don't like their toes stepped on," Brennan said. He got up and put his arm around me. "What kind of a loony are we dealing with here, son?"

"We're dealing with a type none of us have encountered before in an Ulster context. A careful, intelligent, non-sectarian, serial murderer."

"A total freak psycho," Burke said.

"Not in the way you think. Sociopaths tend to have no regard or empathy for the feelings of others but they may in fact be personally charming with considerable charisma. I expect that our boy (and I'm pretty sure he's a boy) will challenge us, but we'll get the bastard, I'm confident of that," I said and looked Brennan in the eye.

"That's good to hear," Brennan said. "But let me just say something here. Sean, I want you to tell me if you think we're in over our heads. It's not a weakness to admit the truth. You yourself were saying it the other night. You're relatively new at all this and we are understaffed . . . we can always get a real expert in from Special Branch or even someone from over the water . . ."

The thought of having this case snatched from under me sent a chill down my spine. Because Carrickfergus was a Protestant town most of the mischief was expected to come from the Loyalist paramilitaries who were not as efficient at carrying out attacks as the IRA and who, anyway, were unlikely to attack the cops. As safe postings went, there were only four or five better ones in Northern Ireland, which is why I had initially not been that excited to end up here, a relative backwater. If you wanted to make your name you had to be in Belfast or Derry, but it would be worse if they were going to take all the good cases away from me . . .

"You yourself told me that resources are stretched thin. Belfast needs every available man until the hunger strikes and the riots are over. And running to mummy in England would be embarrassing for the whole RUC. No, I think we can handle this here in Carrick, sir, we really can."

"Ok," he said, not completely convinced. "I won't ask you again. I'll trust you to come to me."

"I will, sir."

"Any other comments?" Brennan asked but nobody could think of anything.

Brennan whispered something in Matty's ear and he got up and came back with a bottle of Jura single malt. He poured us all a healthy dose in plastic cups and raised his glass.

"Unlike some stations that have been radically transformed with fairy gold from London, we're still a small barracks, a small barracks with a family atmosphere, and this is going to be a challenge, but we can handle it if we all pull together. Can't we, fellas? Can't we, Sean?"

"We'll have to, chief."

We drank our whiskeys. It was the good stuff and it tasted of salt, sea, rain, wind and the Old Testament.

"Ok, boys, get that dram down your neck and get out there. Get working! I'll have to tell Superintendent Hollis before I tell the media and it would be nice if I had one crumb to throw at his fat, dozy face. I may pop in after the wedding but now I have to go," Brennan said.

"Yes, sir," we all replied.

We skipped lunch and made phone calls. We discussed the post-card and the music but we made no headway.

Brennan came back from the wedding and demanded progress but we had none to offer him. He went into his office to change.

I had just finished a conversation with Andrew Young's boss who denied all knowledge of Andrew's homosexuality (sensible because he could have been charged as an abetter under Section 11 of the Criminal Law Amendment Act 1885, which considered homosexual acts to be "gross indecency") when a now uniformed Brennan put his big paw on my shoulder and sat down on my desk.

"Do you know Lucy Moore?" he asked.

"No."

"How long have you been here now, Sean?"

"Nearly a month, sir."

"Lucy O'Neill was her maiden name. Local Republican family, the O'Neills. Big deal in these parts. Fairly well off Catholics. Her dad's a human rights lawyer, her mum is high up in Trocaire—that big Catholic charity. Ringing a bell now?"

"I'm afraid not, sir," I said.

"They both met the Pope when he came to Ireland in '79. Come on, you know who I'm talking about."

Brennan had that unfortunate habit of assuming that all Catholics went to the same mass in the same chapel at the same time.

"Nope."

"Ok, well, anyway, Lucy's husband Seamus goes up to the Maze Prison last year for weapons possession and for one reason and another they get divorced."

"He's IRA?"

"Of course."

"They don't like it when their wives divorce them and they're in prison."

"No, not in theory. But apparently he didn't mind too much because Seamus Moore has a wee woman on the side. More than one."

"Oh, I see."

"Anyway. They're divorced. He's up for his stretch. She's living back with her ma and da and everything's normal until last Christmas Eve. And then she goes missing. The family can't find her so they put out feelers in the community and when that doesn't work they call us."

"Seamus had her killed from the inside?"

"No, no, nothing like that. Seamus doesn't have the power for that. He's a pretty minor player. She just goes missing. It's Christmas time and we're short-staffed, so I took charge of the investigation."

"You were lead?" I asked, a little surprised.

"It was a defining case. It's my job to show that we are the cops for both sides in Carrickfergus, Protestant and Catholic. So yes, I was running it and I ran Matty and McCrabban ragged and I pulled out all the stops but we couldn't bloody find her."

"What were the circumstances?"

"Christmas Eve. Barn Halt. She was waiting for the Belfast train to come and she just vanished."

"Poof! Gone! Just like that?"

"Poof. Gone. Just like that. I was pretty aggrieved that we couldn't find a trace of her. But then in January the family started getting letters and postcards from her saying she was ok and not to worry about her."

"Genuine letters?"

"Aye. We had the handwriting analysed."

"Where were they posted?"

"Over the border. The Irish Republic: Cork, Dublin, all over."

"So she just ran away. No mystery there. Happens all the time. Not a happy ending but not a tragic one either," I said.

"That's what I thought," Brennan said with a sigh. "That's what I told Mrs. O'Neill. 'Don't worry, she's run away, I've seen it a million times. She'll be all right.'"

He got up, walked to the window, leaned his forehead against the glass. His big greying, Viking head of hair mooshed against the pane. He suddenly looked very old.

"What is it?" I asked.

"She's been found."

"Dead?"

"Get your team, get a Land Rover and drive up to Woodburn Forest. You're meeting the ranger there, a man called De Sloot," he muttered.

"Yes, sir."

In ten minutes we were in the country.

Rolling hills, small farms, cows, sheep, horses—a world away from the Troubles.

Another ten minutes and we were at Woodburn Forest, a small deciduous wood surrounded by new plantations of pine and fir. The ranger was meeting us at the south-west entrance.

"There he is," I said and pulled in the Land Rover.

He was a lean, older guy with ruddy red face and close-cropped grey hair. He was wearing a Barbour jacket, hiking boots and a flat cap.

"Everybody out!" I said to Crabbie in the front and Matty in the back.

"I'm De Sloot," the ranger said with a Dutch accent. We did the handshakes and I helped Matty unpack his gear.

De Sloot was all business. "This way, if you please," he said.

We followed him through a cutting in the wood up a steep hill and into one of the older sections of the pine forest.

The trees were tall and densely packed together. So dense in fact that the forest floor was a dark, inert wasteland of pine needles and little else. As we went deeper we had to turn on our flashlights. The hill was north-facing and it was a good five or six degrees colder than the temperature outside the wood. In hollows and against rock faces there were even patches of snow that had survived the spring rains.

"Who found the body?" I asked De Sloot.

"I did. Or rather my dogs did. A fox had been reported attacking sheep and I thought they had found him or a badger, but of course I was mistaken."

"You saw the fox?"

"No, it was a report."

"Who reported it?" I asked.

"A man," De Sloot said.

"What man?" I insisted.

"I don't know. I got a phone call this morning that a fox had been attacking sheep and it had gone into Woodburn Forest."

"Describe the man's voice."

"Northern Irish? I think. Male."

"What else? How old?"

"I don't know."

"What exactly did he say?"

De Sloot thought for a moment.

"He asked me if I was the ranger for Woodburn Forest. I said that I was. He said 'A fox has been worrying sheep. I saw him go into Woodburn Forest.' That was all. Then he hung up."

"What time was this at?" Crabbie asked.

"Around ten o'clock, perhaps ten thirty."

"And what time did you find the body?"

"Some time after two. It's quite deep into the forest, as you can see."

"Yes."

"Aye, how much bloody further?" Matty asked, struggling with his lights and sample kit.

"Gimme something," I said, taking one of his bags.

"Quite a bit yet," De Sloot said cheerfully.

The trees were even more tightly packed here and it was so dark that we'd have been hard pressed to find our way without the flashlights.

The incline increased.

I wondered how high we were up now.

A thousand feet? Twelve hundred?

I was glad that I was in plain clothes today. The polyester cop uni-

forms were murder in any kind of extreme temperature. I took off my
jacket and draped it over my shoulder.

We stopped for a breather and De Sloot offered us water from his
canteen. We took a drink, thanked him, soldiered on. On, through
the dark, lifeless carpet of rotting pine needles before De Sloot finally
called a halt. "Here," he said, pointing to a snow-filled hollow in the lee
of a particularly massive tree.

"Where?" I asked.

I couldn't see anything.

"Near that grey rock," De Sloot said.

I shone my flashlight and then I saw her.

She was fully clothed, hanging under the limb of an oak tree. She
had set up the noose, put her head in it, stepped off a tree stump and
then regretted it.

Almost every person who hanged themselves did it wrong.

The noose is supposed to break your neck not choke you to death.

Lucy had tried desperately to claw through the rope, had even
managed to get a finger between the rope and her throat. It hadn't done
any good.

She was blue. Her left eye was bulging out of its socket, her right
eyeball had popped onto her cheek.

Apart from that and the lifeless way the breeze played with her
brown hair she did not look dead. The birds hadn't found her yet.

She was early twenties, five two or three, pale and once, not too
long ago, she had been beautiful.

"She left her driver's license on the tree stump over there," De Sloot said.

"Any note?" Crabbie asked.

"No."

In a situation like this what saves you is the routine. There is something about process and procedure that distances you from the reality.
We were professionals with a job to do. That's also why you're supposed
to look under your car every morning—it isn't just the possibility of
finding a bomb, it's the heightened sense of awareness that that routine
is supposed to give you for the rest of the day.

Process, procedure and professionalism.

"Everybody stay here. Matty, get your camera and start snapping. Mr. De Sloot, have you moved anything at all?"

"No," De Sloot said. "I read the driver's license and then I went back home and called the police. I kept the dogs away."

We set up the battery-powered spotlights. I spread the team out and we combed the immediate area for footprints, forensic proofs or anything unusual.

Nothing.

Matty took the pictures and I made sure that his camera strategies were formal and correct.

The body was clean and there was no sign of anyone else having been here.

I looked at Matty. "Are you happy with the protocols? Shall we close the circle?"

"Aye. We've plenty of coverage. At least three rolls of film on just the wide shots."

"Good. Keep snapping and damn the torpedoes," I said.

I let Matty finish his photography.

"Better not fingerprint her just yet, or we'll have to deal with Cathcart," I said.

"Do you know the woman?" De Sloot asked.

"Lucy Moore, nee O'Neill. Missing since last Christmas," I said.

"Until now," McCrabban muttered.

"Until now," I agreed.

We stood there in the dark understory. It began to get very cold.

"I think we're done here, boss," Matty said.

"Cut her down, have them take her to the patho," I said.

"Have who take her? You'll never get an undertaker to come out here," McCrabban said.

"We'll bloody do it then!" I said.

We cut the body down, Matty took a hair sample and we carried her back to the Land Rover.

Thank God I wasn't in the back with her.

We drove to Carrick Hospital and left the body for Laura but the nurse told us that it would take a while because Dr. Cathcart had finally been called away to Belfast to help autopsy with the burn victims from The Peacock Room.

When we returned to the barracks it was early evening and Brennan was waiting for me at my desk.

"Was it her?" he asked.

"It was," I said. "She looked like her picture on the driver's license anyway. The patho will tell us for certain when she gets a chance."

"Suicide?"

"Seems like it."

Brennan looked cosmically sad. "I think I know why she may have topped herself."

"Why?"

"Her ex-husband joined the Maze hunger strike on Monday."

"He goes on hunger strike and she's all guilty about divorcing him and she hangs herself?"

"Must be."

"It's possible," I said and rubbed my chin dubiously.

"Hunger striker's ex-wife tops herself! Oh my God, the media are gonna love this one too, aren't they?" Brennan said.

"We can do the old 'no details released because we are respecting the wishes of the family' routine."

"Aye and speaking of that, I suppose we better go and tell the family. Her poor ma," Brennan said.

I knew what he was angling at but there was no friggin way I was going with him. "Yes, I suppose you should go, sir. It was your case after all and you know how busy I am," I said.

He sighed again.

"I'd appreciate it if you looked at the case file to see if there was anything that I missed," he said as he departed.

"Not a problem, sir."

I went to the CID filing cabinet and dug out the binder on Lucy Moore's disappearance and carried it down to The Oak. My stomach was grumbling but someone had blown up their chef's bus and he couldn't get in. I ordered a Bushmills and a pint of the black and a bowl of Irish.

I opened the file. Thin. Lucy had told her mother that she was going to go to Barn Halt in Carrickfergus to catch the 11:58 a.m. train to Belfast on Christmas Eve 1980. Her mother had not been planning to go with her but after Lucy left the house she had changed her mind and got a lift to Downshire Halt (the stop before) so she could meet her daughter on the train. At 11:54 she had gotten on the train at Downshire Halt. It was a four-minute ride to Barn Halt.

A man called Cyril Peters had been driving over the Horseshoe Railway Bridge at 11:56 a.m. He had seen a woman exactly matching Lucy's description waiting for the train at Barn Halt.

Then ...

Zero.

The train came on time but Lucy had not got on.

Her mother had looked out the train window to see if she was at the halt. She not seen Lucy and then she had walked the length of the train searching for her. There were only three carriages and it didn't take long to ascertain that she was not on board. No one had seen her. The driver hadn't remembered if there were was anyone waiting on the platform and the passengers who had got off hadn't remembered seeing her either.

Between 11:56 and 11:58 she had disappeared.

Lucy had said "I might stay over with some friends in Belfast, but I'll be back on Christmas morning."

All the friends were called. Lucy wasn't there.

There had been no ransom demand, no confirmed sightings, no physical evidence at Barn Halt or anywhere else.

Absolutely nothing for ten days until the first of the postcards had arrived with a Cork postmark on it. It was in Lucy's handwriting and explained that she "wanted to go find myself." She begged her parents not to send anyone to look for her and she promised she would keep in touch with them.

She had kept in touch, sending a simple letter or plain postcard every fortnight. Brennan had kept a photocopy of several of these postcards. Some of them referred to contemporary events but none of them revealed her whereabouts, what she was doing or who she was living with. Somewhere down South from the stamps.

The postcards closed the case for the RUC because Lucy was twenty-two and therefore an adult. If she wanted to run away to parts unknown that was her business.

I read the psych. assessment, the bio and the case summary. She'd been an easy-going, fairly happy girl in her first year of an English degree at QUB when she'd met Seamus Moore. They'd got married quickly (obviously knocked up), she'd had a miscarriage and he'd almost immediately gotten arrested for weapons possession and been sent up for four years in the Kesh.

He'd joined the IRA wing as a fairly low-level prisoner.

She'd gone to see him once a week until she had bumped into Seamus's mistress, one Margaret Tanner and there had been a blazing row right there in the visitors' hall. Hair pulling, screaming—the prison officers must have loved it.

Divorce proceedings had been initiated.

After the divorce Lucy had moved back in with her parents.

There had been eight tips about the Moore case on the Confidential Telephone. None of them had come to anything. The IRA had been contacted through surrogates and, convincingly, denied any involvement. The UDA had also denied any connection.

Then the letters and postcards to her parents and a couple to her sister and brother.

Where would we be without postcards?

After the letters came and were authenticated the case was closed. And that was it. The whole file.

I walked to the station and called up Carrick Hospital to see if Laura was back there yet.

She wasn't.

I talked to McCrabban about the Andrew Jackson postcard the

killer had sent to me. Apparently you could buy them anywhere. None of the local newsagents remembered selling one recently.

At five o'clock my phone rang.

"Hello?"

"Is this Sergeant Duffy?"

"Yes, who's this?"

"This is Ned Armstrong from the Confidential Telephone."

"Hello, Ned, what can I do for you?"

"It's what I can do for you," Ned said good-naturedly.

"All right, Ned, I'm all ears."

"A guy called in about ten minutes ago, saying that he quote, had a message for Carrickfergus CID. He said that he had quote killed the two fruits and he was going to kill more if his glorious deeds stayed out of the newspapers."

"Hold on a minute, please, Mr. Armstrong... Crabbie, pick up line two!... Go on, Ned."

"Ok, I'm reading here: the guy said that he wanted the fruits to know that he was coming for them. And this was their first and last warning. He was phoning us from a call box outside the GAA club on Laganville Road, Belfast. And if the peelers went to number 44 Laganville Road they might get a wee surprise."

"Did you tape this call?"

"No, part of the confidentiality of the Confidential Telephone is that we don't tape or trace calls."

"What was the man's accent?"

"He had a broad West Belfast accent which sounded a little broader than I had ever heard before, which meant that he was hamming it up for us. People often do that or disguise their voices."

"Anything else?"

"Not at the moment."

"You've been a big help. Thank you very much, Ned."

I wrote down the address and hung up.

The excitement was palpable. There were only half a dozen of us in the station but this was a big break.

Brennan had gone to make his notification so I sought counsel from Sergeant McCallister. "What do I do, Alan?"

"You know what you have to do. You've got to get up the Laganville Road. Take your team and a couple of boys. Full riot gear, mate, that's in the bloody Ardoyne off the Crumlin Road, so, you know, if it looks dodgy at all, don't even hesitate, scramski!"

We put on riot gear, I grabbed two reserve constables and we signed out a Land Rover.

Someone had hijacked a bus and set it on fire on the Shore Road so I drove the Land Rover along the back way. We came down into Belfast from the hills through the Protestant district of Ballysillan, which was decorated with murals of masked paramilitaries holding assault rifles and zombie armies holding Union Jacks.

We drove along the Crumlin Road and turned into the Ardoyne, a staunch Catholic estate just a couple of streets away from a staunch Protestant one—in other words, a real high heat flashpoint area.

"Does anybody know where Laganville Road is?" I asked.

Crabbie unfolded a street map and gave me directions.

We got lost twice but finally made it.

It turned out to be a small dead-end terrace, with a large graffito running the length of three houses that said, "Don't Let Them Die!" referring, of course, to the hunger strikers.

It was teatime on a Saturday night and things looked quiet. The football matches were all over and no one was thinking about going out just yet. Maybe we could creep in and out without ever being noticed.

I drove past the GAA club where the tipster had made his phone call.

"Matty, you get out and dust for prints," I said.

"Why me?"

"Cos you're the bravest."

"No, I'm not."

"Just get out. You're the FO, come on."

Matty was reluctant to leave the safety of the Land Rover so I sent one of the reservists with him. He was called Brown, twenty-two, a carpenter in real life. Matty looked shit-scared. Both of them were in full riot gear and twitchily holding their Sterling sub-machine guns. It made me nervous. "Under no circumstances are you to fire those fucking guns, is that understood? We'll be right at the end of the street. If there's trouble, point the guns but do not bloody shoot them."

"What do we do?" Matty asked.

"Come running down to us if there's real bother, ok?" I told them.

Brown and Matty nodded.

We drove down to #44.

It was derelict with the windows boarded up and the front door kicked in. I parked the Land Rover and McCrabban, myself and the other reservist got out.

"I'm going in, lads. Keep an eye out for booby traps. He said we'd get a surprise and this would be perfect for a concealed explosive device."

"In that case, I'll go first, Sean," Crabbie said.

"How come you always get to be John Wayne?" I said. "You just hold here, Crabbie. Stay well behind me, the pair of you. And if I'm killed, all my albums are to go to Matty, he's the only one that will appreciate them."

"I'll take the country albums and any of the non-poncy classical," Crabbie said.

"Fair enough. Now stay back, both of you."

I was being flippant but dozens of police officers had been killed in booby traps over the years. It was a classic IRA tactic. You call in a tip about a murder, the police go to investigate and they trip a booby trap or the provos remotely detonate a landmine or pipe bomb. Sometimes they place a time-delayed device in a car in the street so they can get the rescue workers too.

I walked down the front path.

The smell of shit and piss hit me straight away.

I looked for wires, loose paving stones or any obvious trips.

Nothing.

So far.

I drew my revolver, turned on the flashlight and walked into the house.

It was completely gutted. Holes in the roof that leaked water, a few hypodermic syringes.

The stairs were wrecked and the stench of mildew was overpowering.

"Everything all right?" McCrabban shouted from out in the street.

I walked into the downstairs living room and the kitchen. More garbage, drug paraphernalia, water dripping down from the ceiling. I tracked through the entire ground floor and the back yard. I couldn't get upstairs because of the destroyed staircase but it was obvious that no one had been in here for some time.

So why had he sent us here? Just because he could? A power trip? Was he watching us from a location across the street, laughing?

"There's nothing here!" I yelled back.

"Let's get back to the Land Rover then. There's trouble!" McCrabban said.

"What kind of trouble?"

"Bunch of lads outside the GAA club."

I went back outside. Matty and Brown were running down the street towards us. They were being chased by a dozen lads with hurley sticks and bottles.

"Don't run, you pair of eejits," McCrabban was muttering to himself.

"Ok, everybody, get in the Rover! You drive, Crabbie, I'll try and reason with the lynch mob."

I walked back down the path and was about to leave #44 Laganville Road forever when I noticed that the owners from long ago had put in a US-style mailbox with a little red flag to indicate when there was mail.

The flag was up. I opened the rusted mail box and sure enough there was a brown envelope inside. I took it out and shoved it between my flak jacket and my sweater.

Matty and a terrified-looking Constable Brown reached the Land Rover.

"Did you get the prints?" I asked.

"Are you fucking joking?" Matty said furiously. "Fucking suicide mission you sent us on."

"Ok, calm down. Get in the Land Rover and close the bloody doors, Crabbie, get her started up!"

I holstered my revolver, reached into the front seat and grabbed a plastic bullet gun that I loaded and primed.

I walked towards the rioters.

They were the kind of kids who hung around the streets and attacked the police or fire brigade whenever they saw them. With tensions running high over the hunger strikes, one solitary Land Rover was an irresistible target.

Bottles and stones started smashing all around me.

Crabbie revved the engine and I waited until all the lads were inside before walking in front of the vehicle with the plastic bullet gun.

When the mob was twenty feet away they started directing all their bricks, bottles and stones at me. If they could put a man down or disable the vehicle they'd scarper and call in the heavy brigade who would show up with grenades and petrol bombs.

I pointed the plastic bullet gun at them.

"That's enough!" I yelled.

Everyone froze and I knew I had about three seconds.

"Listen people! We are not DMSU. We are not the riot squad. We are detectives investigating a murder. We are going to leave this street right now and no one is going to get hurt!"

I kept the plastic bullet gun aimed at the guy on point and moved my way backwards towards the Land Rover. Their leader was an ugly ganch with a skinhead, a Celtic FC shirt and a breeze block in his hand.

"This is our patch, you fucking peeler bastards!" he said and hurled the breeze block at me. I dodged it but didn't avoid a couple of stones that caught me in the flak jacket.

"Get in, Sean!" Crabbie yelled.

I jumped into the passenger seat of the Land Rover as an impressive hail of assorted objects came hurtling at me.

"So how did your Gandhi act go down with the locals?" McCrabban asked with dour satisfaction.

A milk carton exploded on our windscreen.

I closed the Land Rover door.

"They have much to learn about the moral authority of non-violence."

"I think we should be leaving now," Crabbie said.

He turned the window wipers on, gave the engine big revs and drove slowly through the crowd. Perhaps one of them was our killer. I tried to see their faces but it was impossible through the milk and missiles. Bottles and bricks bounced off the bullet-proof glass and the steel plating on the sides. The mob began chanting "SS RUC! SS RUC! SS RUC!" However, after twenty seconds of this we had successfully reached the end of the street without getting a puncture.

In another five minutes we were on the Crumlin Road and five minutes after that we were safe in Protestant North Belfast.

"Everybody all right back there?" I asked the lads in the rear.

"Everybody's fine," Matty said, but I could smell shit through the grill. One of the two reservists had keeked a planet in their whips.

Half an hour later, Matty opened the envelope from #44 in the CID room with myself, McCrabban, Chief Inspector Brennan and Sergeant McCallister looking on.

It was on standard A4 paper. A typed message single-spaced:

My story still has not appeared in The Belfast Telegraph!!!! You are not taking me seriously!!!!! You have until the Monday edition and then I will kill a queer every night!!!! I will liberate them from this vale of tears. The queers on TV and in the peelers and everywhere!!!! Lee McCrea. Dougal Campbell. Gordon Billingham!!!! Scott McAvenny. I know them all!!! DO NOT TEST ME!!!!! My patience is running thin!!!!

Matty carried it to the photocopier and made us half a dozen copies before setting to work on his forensic tests. It took him ten minutes to discover that the typewriter was an old manual Imperial 55.

Lee McCrea was a BBC presenter on the late-night local news. Dougal Campbell was a talkshow host on Radio Ulster. Gordon Billingham, a sports reporter on UTV. Scott McAvenny ran Scott's Place, the only decent restaurant in Belfast. Of course they were all gay men, not out as such, but well known.

"What's the verdict, gentlemen?" I asked.

"He's a nutter!" Matty said.

"A nutter who can type without making a single mistake," I said.

Brennan looked at me. "That's good, Sean, what else jumps out at you?"

"It's not a very comprehensive list, is it? Four pretty obvious homosexuals."

"Aye, plus the two he's already topped," McCallister added.

"I suppose we better have that press conference on Monday morning," Brennan said.

"And we better give those boys protection," I suggested.

"I'll call Special Branch," Brennan said wearily.

I reread the note and sat down. I had a splitting headache. I had been hit by a dozen stones and half bricks, one right off the top of my riot helmet.

I looked out the window at the lights of ships moving down the black lough into Belfast's deep water channel.

Brennan was talking to me but I didn't hear him.

I watched as the pilot boat put out from under the castle to bring a cargo vessel into Carrick's much smaller and trickier harbor.

"... go on home," Brennan finished.

"What?"

"I said you look like Elvis at his 1977 CBS special, why don't you go on home?"

"I've things to do."

"Just go. Have a drink, have a bath. Might be the last one you take for a while, I heard the power-station workers are going on strike."

"I can't. I'm still waiting for the prints on John Doe."

"I'll wait. You go on. That's an order, Sean."

"Yes, sir."

I decided to walk home. A mistake. A downpour caught me on Victoria Road. Heavy, cold rain from a long looping depression over Iceland.

Coronation Road.

The quintessential Irish smell of peat smoke rising up to meet the rain.

Light and fear and existential depression leaking through the net curtains.

#113.

I turned the key and went inside. I had forgotten about the phone tap and was surprised to see a black box next to my telephone. Kernoghan's boys hadn't left any trace apart from that. I stripped off my clothes, went into the kitchen and opened the empty fridge. Half a can of Heinz beans. Some yellow cheese. I ate beans and toast and lit the upstairs paraffin heater and went to bed.

I found myself dreaming of the girl hanging in the forest.

It was dusk and the stars were coming out over western Scotland and eastern Ireland and the sunken realm between the two. I've never liked the woods. My grandmother told me that the forest was an opening to someplace else. Where things lurked, things we could only half see. Older beings. *Shees*. Shades of creatures that once walked the natural world, redundant now, awaiting tasks, awaiting their work in dreams.

"*Le do thoil*," I said to them in Irish, but they wouldn't listen, calling my name from behind oaks and fairy trees, mocking me, teasing me until 3 a.m. when I awoke to the sound of sirens.

7: SATURDAY NIGHT AND SUNDAY MORNING

I found that I wasn't in bed. I was sleeping on the landing in front of the paraffin heater. This was becoming my fetal space. I was wearing a Thin Lizzy T-shirt and grey sweat pants. I had no memory of putting them on.

I went downstairs and opened the front door.

The whole street was out.

I walked to the end of the garden path. Number 79 was on fire. The Clawsons' house. I joined the gawkers because who can resist a fire? A wee milly in a dirty frock filled me in on the details. "Chip pan fire. Whole kitchen went up."

With gas cookers and chip pans in every kitchen, the chip-pan fire was by far the most popular method these Proddies had for burning their houses down. The second technique was the ever popular chimney fire and number three had to be the drunken cigarette drop on the carpet. Mind you, why they'd be cooking chips at this hour was anyone's guess.

The crowd grew and I saw people that I vaguely recognized from as far away as the Barn Road. The kitchen burned and despite the best efforts of the brigade it spread to the rest of the house.

Mrs. Clawson screamed about her fish tank and when a second fire tender equipped with foam arrived one of the firemen went in and rescued the fish.

When the blaze was finally contained the crowd erupted into spontaneous applause and tea and biscuits were pressed into the hands of the crew—which had to be nicer than getting bricked in the Catholic estates. They kept pumping in foam and it began to fill the street, taking to the air in huge tufts, blowing this way and that.

We were in the snow again.

Mrs. Clawson was wailing now, standing there, half tore, in her dressing gown with no knickers.

The kids were playing in the artificial snow and the firemen were flirting with the single women and some of the lonely married women whose husbands were over the water.

I yawned and checked my watch.

3:20. Time to head back. I began to walk in that direction.

Someone grabbed my shirt from behind.

I turned. Big guy, 6'9" with a gut, a Zapata moustache, a white wifebeater T-shirt and blue jeans. He was fifty or thereabouts and on his head was what could only be a wig although you'd have had a tough job getting up there to check it out.

"Where's your fancy car now, fenian?" he said.

I ignored him and kept on walking.

He pushed me and I stumbled but recovered my balance in time to see a haymaker coming at me.

Mrs. Bridewell and Mrs. Campbell both screamed.

"Look out, Mr. Duffy!" Mrs. Campbell yelled, her hand at her throat.

Several people turned to look. The haymaker made its painfully slow arc across the air between us. It missed me by nine inches without me having to do anything.

"What's your problem, pal?" I asked.

"What about those people at the Peacock Room, you fucking fenian bastard, what chance did you give them, ya taig piece of shit!" the big ganch said and swung another punch which also missed.

Neither talking nor fighting were his strong points.

"Go home, mate," I told him.

"I'm not your mate. Your fenian pals killed those people for nothing! I hope you all go on hunger strike. I hope you all starve to death! We should have starved you out in the bloody famine!"

Whoever he was, he was cross and the worse for drink and there was no point arguing or getting into a fight with a drunk.

He reached into his pocket and started fumbling with something.

"Oh my God, he's got a knife! Oh, Mr. Duffy, watch him!" Mrs. Campbell called out.

It was a standard flick knife with a button on the handle but he was so pissed he was having difficulty getting the blade to deploy. "If you'll allow me," I said, snatching the knife out of his hands and pushing the button.

"See?" I said as I put the blade in and gave him the knife back. That, I realized later, was my mistake. I had humiliated him.

He was a friend visiting Bobby Cameron and Bobby now felt it was his duty to intervene.

Bobby lived six doors down from me on the same terrace. We'd never spoken, but of course I knew who he was. Medium height, plump, ginger bap, twenty-eight. His wife cut your hair for two pounds in her back kitchen. He was on long-term unemployment benefit but he was also a divisional officer of the Ulster Freedom Fighters, a faction of the UDA, and one of the nastier Protestant terrorist groups; he was a man who, in theory, could have you killed at the drop of a hat, but in practice wouldn't because killing a cop—even a Catholic cop—would mean a feud with every other loyalist faction in Carrick. A feud would be bad news in strategic terms but, of course, few of the loyalists ever thought strategically. (The IRA had a graffito somewhere in Belfast that I always got a kick out of: "The IRA think, while the UDA drink.")

"I'm gonna kill him!" the big guy said to Bobby, still fumbling with the flick knife.

Bobby looked at me. His brow was furrowed and there was that dark light in his eyes that seemed to shine in the eyes of everybody in Belfast who has killed a man or men.

A crowd began to gather.

"You should take your mate home," I said quietly to Bobby.

"Are you telling me to take him home?" Bobby said.

Half the street was watching now, including the bloody firemen who wouldn't do a damn thing to help.

"No, Bobby, I'm asking you to take him home," I said.

Bobby glared at me for a full ten seconds and then seemed to make up his mind. "Show's over, everyone!" he said and the crowd began to disperse.

He took his mate by the arm, pocketed the penknife and led him away. Bobby turned back to look at me, then he grinned and wagged his finger as if to say, you're the Old Bill, but just remember whose street this is.

I went back inside feeling dissatisfied and peeved.

The rain came on. I sat in the cold living room getting steamed until I finally grabbed a coat and went back out. I turned left, away from the remains of the foam and the last few ladies smoking Rothmans and comparing notes on the firemen.

I walked past an end gable where a crude new mural had been painted—a gunman wearing a balaclava standing next to a child with a football. Underneath him was the slogan: "Remember the Loyalist Prisoners, Carrickfergus UDA." No one, of course, could forget the Loyalist prisoners because the UDA "collected for them" in every pub and supermarket across the neighborhood.

Coronation Road. My little universe. The red-brick terraces ran on both sides of the street for half a mile and I knew the houses of quite a few of the residents now: Jack Irwin who worked in the pet shop; Jimmy Dooey who worked in Shorts Aircraft; Bobby Dummigan, unemployed; the Agnews with their nine kids, Da unemployed; widow McSeward whose husband was lost at sea; Alan Grimes, a retired fitter who had been a POW of the Japanese; Alex McFerrin, unemployed; Jackie Walter, unemployed . . .

I walked on.

Coronation Road to Barn Road to Taylor's Avenue.

I went into the field where we'd found the first murder victim. I examined the scene for ten minutes but the Muse of Detection gave me no new insights.

I went back to Taylor's Avenue, past Carrick Hospital and followed a sign to Barn Halt.

Barn Halt, where Lucy Moore went missing. Not that that was supposed to be any concern of mine. Investigating a suicide was a luxury we couldn't afford with an obvious Ripper copycat or nutcase out there.

Still, what else was I going to do?

Barn Halt wasn't an actual train station, merely a red-bricked shelter on each track—one for the Larne line and one for the Belfast line. The shelters were tiny and you couldn't get ten people in on a wet day. The one on this side of the tracks smelled of piss and was covered with the usual sectarian graffiti.

There was an iron footbridge to the other side but at this time of night you could safely cut across the railway lines.

I stepped over the sleepers and climbed up onto the other platform.

Another stinking little shelter. More sectarian graffiti.

Lucy would have been on the Belfast side so I recrossed the tracks and paced along the small platform.

Why did no one see Lucy get on the train? Did she get on the train? If not, what did she do? Walk back to Taylor's Avenue? Cross the iron footbridge?

I walked to the south end of the platform where a six-foot wall prevented you from climbing over into Elizabeth Avenue. She didn't get out that way and the other end of the platform led to a steep, exposed railway embankment where she surely would have been seen.

Her mother's looking for her out the window and she doesn't see her? Where is she? I asked myself. And that guy in the car sees her just a minute or two before the train comes. Where could she have gone in a minute? Not back to Taylor's Avenue. The car driver would have seen her. Not over the footbridge, the passengers getting off at Barn Halt would have noticed her. Not across the railway lines themselves because there was a train in the way. At one end of the platform there's a wall, at the other end there's a railway embankment . . . Is she hiding in the shelter? Why would she be hiding?

The rain was bouncing hard off the concrete.

I turned up the collar on my coat and stepped inside the shelter.

I lit a cigarette and leaned against the wall.

Of course it was busy, it was Christmas Eve. People had other things on their minds. Perhaps you could easily get on and off a train and no one would notice. The great general public were notorious for letting you down when it came to eyewitness testimony.

I finished the ciggie just as the 4:30 Stranraer boat train came rushing by, running express from Belfast to Larne and really clipping it. The train's four carriages were packed and I looked at the brief, flashing, happy faces of people leaving Northern Ireland, perhaps forever.

"Ach, I'm getting nowhere with this," I muttered but I didn't want to think about the other case because that stank too. Stank to high heaven. It was too gothic for Ulster. The Chief was right—we didn't do serial killers in these parts. Even the Shankill Butchers had had the sense to join the Protestant paramilitaries first.

I yawned and ran back across the tracks and walked a minute along the sea front to the police station. I showed my warrant card to the unknown constable at the entrance. "It's the early bird that catches the worm, sir," he said.

"Aye."

I checked to see if that fingerprint evidence had come in yet but of course it hadn't. I reread the killer's postcard and the tip from the Confidential Telephone. Nothing leapt out at me.

I couldn't think what else to do so I took my sleeping bag from out of my locker, lay down on the ancient sofa in the CID room and slept like a log until morning.

8: ORPHEUS IN THE UNDERWORLD

McCrabban and McCallister's faces staring at me. McCrabban holding a mug of coffee.

"Thank you," I said, sitting up in the sleeping bag and taking it. "What time is it?"

"Nine," McCallister said.

"What day is it?" I asked.

"Sunday," Crabbie said.

"You two came in on a Sunday? Why?" I wondered.

"Well, I have a press conference to prepare for tomorrow and Crabbie and you are on an active murder investigation," McCallister said.

Crabbie grinned. "And we're all on time and a half!" he announced with glee.

"I've been here since four."

"Sleeping time doesn't count," McCallister said.

I sipped the machine coffee. "I was just resting my eyes," I muttered.

McCallister rubbed my head. "Back to the coalface for me," he said.

Crabbie was wearing a suit today. As a detective he normally wore his own clothes which consisted of various outlandish jackets, shirts and ties. I hadn't seen him in a proper suit before.

"What gives with the threads?" I asked.

"Had church this morning. And this evening. You wanna come? Leave aside your Romish superstition and follow the one true faith," he said with a glint in his eyes—the only sign of a gag in his Spock-like visage.

I had been to an Ulster Presbyterian church service before. It was a masterclass in boredom. The building itself was deliberately bland with no ornament or accoutrements, merely simple wooden benches and a pulpit upon which a picture of the burning bush had been draped. There was no kneeling, incense, overly stimulating hymns, or raised voices. The sermons were long and focused on obscure passages of the Bible.

"I think I'll give it a miss, mate," I said.

Crabbie's shrug seemed to convey the notion that one hour of tedium was a small price to pay to avoid eternity in the hellfire.

"Where's Matty?" I asked.

"Fishing in Fermanagh," Crabbie said.

"Doesn't he care about this fabled time and a half?"

"Nothing messes with his Sunday fishing."

I yawned and stretched. "Is there anything going on in the world?" I asked.

"The rumor is that the power-station workers are going to go on strike."

"Any more hunger strikers die?"

"Nope."

"Did we ever get that fax from Belfast about John Doe's ID?"

Crabbie shook his head. "We were supposed to get it yesterday morning. You know what I think?" he said.

"What?"

"I think it's being repressed. I think John Doe is somebody important and Belfast is scrambling to lay the groundwork before releasing the information to us."

"You're paranoid," I scoffed and then reconsidered. "Although William Burroughs said that a paranoid is somebody who knows what is actually going on."

"Billy Burroughs said that? The guy that runs the fish shop?"

I drank the rest of the coffee and stood up. "Let's go round the hospital and see if our patho has made any progress," I said.

"All right."

It was only drizzling so we walked to Carrick Hospital along Taylor's Avenue and over the railway bridge at Barn Halt. I stopped when we were halfway over.

"I was here last night," I said. "Checking out Lucy Moore's vanishing act. I don't see how she did it. A guy sees her waiting at the halt two minutes before the train is due to arrive. The train pulls in, her ma's leaning out the window looking for her and she's not there? How?"

"Maybe somebody abducted her."

"Impossible. The platform was full of people."

"Maybe she got on the train but her mum missed her."

"It was only three carriages long and her ma looked in every one."

Crabbie shrugged. "Well, that's all moot now, isn't it?" he said.

"Yeah, I suppose it is."

We went on. The rain and the fact that it was Sunday had deterred all but the hardiest of cases and the waiting room was empty except for one crazy-looking guy with his arm wrapped up in a DIY bandage made of toilet paper.

Hattie Jacques saw us come in. "Good afternoon, gents. You'll have to hurry if you want to see Dr. Cathcart. Her office is along the corridor and the last door on the right."

We walked along the gloomy corridor. I looked at my watch. It was nearly ten and my stomach was rumbling.

"I'm starving," I said.

"You want half a Mars bar?" McCrabban asked.

"Kill for one."

He fished a Mars bar out of his pocket, broke it in two and gave half to me. We ate it outside her door. Inside we could hear her singing along to "Heart of Glass" by Blondie. She was off key by a country mile.

I smiled at McCrabban and he grinned back.

We knocked on the door.

The radio was abruptly switched off.

"Come in!" she said.

Her office was small and dark, packed with books, files and a couple of anatomy charts. There were no feminine or homely touches. The impression she was clearly trying to convey was business, nothing but business.

We said our hellos and sat down. The view behind her head was of the hospital wall and the Knockagh mountain beyond.

She looked stunning today. Her lips were red, her cheeks rosy, her hair cascaded, her face shone. I don't know how I had missed it before. She was gorgeous.

There was a graduation picture of her with her class at the University of Edinburgh and even in her robes and mortarboard she stood out from all the others. The camera loved her. Something about her elfin eyes maybe or those pert, full, downy lips.

"I was going to have these sent over to you," she said, interrupting my reverie and handing across two cardboard files. Her desk was an old cast-iron job with three drawers and a wonky top. You could see through to her legs. She was wearing boots. Riding boots and black jeans and a figure-hugging black sweater. She was trim and athletic in that get-up and I knew that I was going to have difficulty concentrating on the serious business at hand.

"Any surprises?" I asked.

She nodded. "Oh yes. It was all surprises."

"Really?" McCrabban said.

"Listen, we'll have to be quick about this. It's my Sunday morning clinic in ten minutes."

I opened up the topmost file and set it on the desk so McCrabban could see too. We began reading it together. It was her autopsy of Andrew Young.

"And you'll need this," she said, passing across another musical score in a plastic bag.

"This one was rolled up in his hand."

I flattened it out on the desk and peered at the score which had been ripped from a music book with a lot less care than the previous one.

This piece I recognized immediately. It was "the Galop" from Offenbach's Orpheus in the Underworld, Act 2 Scene 2. I had played it on the piano for my Grade 4.

"Shit," I said.

"You know it?" Laura and McCrabban asked simultaneously.

"We all know it. It's 'the Galop' from Orpheus in the Underworld.

A sort of musical joke. A spoof. Offenbach was having a bit of fun at the expense of the more highbrow music lovers."

"I don't know it," Crabbie said.

"Later on in the nineteenth century they called it the Can-can and played it in various musical revues."

"So what does that tell us?" McCrabban asked.

"I don't know. Orpheus in the Underworld is all about being punished and condemned to Hades. Maybe Young is being punished for being gay? You would have thought Benjamin Britten's Billy Budd or Death in Venice would have been more appropriate for that, wouldn't you?"

"I'll take your word for it, mate."

I looked at the score and shook my head. "Or it could just be that he's mocking us again. The Can-can is a famous musical piss-take. Perhaps the most famous musical joke apart from Mozart's K.522."

"Do you want to read the rest of the report?" Dr. Cathcart said.

We read the autopsy.

Young had been shot execution-style in the forehead. The bullet had killed him instantly. His hand had then been cut off and John Doe's thrown on his chest. That was it. He was sixty years old, in good health. His body had not been abused or violated. The score had been shoved into his left fist before rigor had set in.

"How long do you think this whole thing would have taken?" I asked Laura. "You know, shooting him, cutting his hand off?"

Laura shrugged. "If you came equipped with a bone saw—"

"Door opens, silenced 9mm in the brain, killer closes the door, cuts off Young's hand and bags it, leaves the musical score in the other hand and gets out of there in, say, under five minutes?"

"It's possible."

I turned to Crabbie. "And the rest of the house was untouched. No trophies taken, no money, nothing like that."

"What are you thinking?" he asked.

"I think this was all done in a hurry. I think John Doe was killed first in a more premeditated manner and then Andrew Young was murdered because he was a well-known homosexual. The killer shot

Young as he opened the door. There was no conversation, no demands, nothing. He knew he had to kill him fast, cut off the hand and get in and out as speedily as possible."

"Why?" Laura asked.

I shook my head. "I don't know, yet."

We sat there for a minute while thunder rolled across the lough from a storm in County Down.

Laura gave an apologetic look and pointed at her watch. "I have my clinic," she said.

I nodded. "Ok, let's turn to Lucy Moore."

I picked up the second file.

The first shock was the baby.

"Are you sure about this?" I asked.

"Oh yes. She gave birth about a week before she died. It looks like she breastfed the infant for about two days and then stopped."

"It died?" I asked.

"Or she gave it away?" Crabbie said.

Laura shrugged. That was beyond her area of expertise.

"We'll get dogs and go back up to Woodburn Forest. Maybe the baby was buried nearby," I said to Crabbie.

"And I'll check the missions and the hospitals," McCrabban added.

"This might be a better explanation of why she killed herself: you give birth, your baby dies . . ." I said.

"Why did you think she killed herself?" Laura asked.

"Well, her ex-husband just joined the hunger strike last week and we were thinking guilt or something. But this is more concrete," I said.

"And it's probably why she ran away! At Christmas she would have been—what, three months gone?" Crabbie asked.

"She'd know at three months but she might not be showing," Laura said.

"Pregnant! At least this is one case we can start closing the book on, eh Sean?" Crabbie said.

He was dead right. Everybody in Ireland understood this particular trope. Girl gets pregnant out of wedlock, runs away, gives birth, kills herself. Happened all the time. Abortion was illegal on both sides of the Irish border. There were few places a girl could turn. Of course Lucy was a little different in that she was slightly older and she had already been married, but with her ex locked up in the H Blocks and already a Republican hero, there would be just as much pressure, perhaps more ...

She was probably too guilty to even write a note explaining herself. Sad. Sad. Sad.

"Gentlemen, I really should ..." Laura said quietly.

"Yes, yes, of course, Dr. Cathcart. Anything else suspicious here?" I asked.

"I've been told that she's been missing since before Christmas," Laura said.

"That's right," McCrabban agreed.

"There were no bruises on her wrists or ankles, no signs of malnutrition or torture or abuse. Her muscles had not atrophied, her vitamin D levels were high. Which means that she was eating just fine and that she was getting plenty of sunlight," Laura said.

"So she wasn't somebody's prisoner," Crabbie said.

"I think you can infer that," Laura replied.

"Everyone thought she was down South because of the postcards and letters she sent home. Can you tell if she was living down there?" Crabbie asked.

Laura shook her head. "No. She'd eaten fried egg on toast which I imagine you can get on both sides of the border."

"That's a hell of a last meal," I said.

"I like fried egg on toast!" Crabbie said. "I make it for the missus sometimes."

"So, is that everything?" I asked before Crabbie could further depress me with his culinary exploits.

"It's all in the autopsy," Laura explained.

"Good," I said.

"There is one thing," Laura added hesitantly.

"Yes?" I said.

"Well, I don't want either of you to make a big thing about this because it's probably nothing..."

Crabbie and I exchanged a look.

"Go on," I said.

"Well, she died by strangulation, of course: the rope choked off the oxygen supply to her brain and she asphyxiated."

"We saw that," Crabbie said. "She thought it would be quick and it wasn't."

Laura nodded. "And she got a finger between the rope and her neck but it didn't do any good."

"No, it didn't," I agreed.

"Well, it's just that... I'm not entirely happy with the bruises on her neck," Laura said.

Her eyes were narrowed. She was tapping a pencil off the desk. I leaned back in the chair and folded my hands across my lap. "We're all ears."

"The bruising of the rope was the primary cause of contusion on her neck. And there were bruises just in front of the thyroid cartilage from where she'd wedged her forefinger between the rope and her throat, but it seems to me that one of those bruises looked something like a thumb, a thumb that was much bigger than Lucy's. A thumb that pressed directly on her larynx. I should stress that this is only a possibility and it would not stand up in court. I included this observation only in the appendix of the autopsy report and I put no particular stress upon it. The bruising of the rope was considerable and it's possible that this thumb-shaped bruise was either caused by the rope or by Lucy herself. When the coroner asks me the cause of death at the inquest I will say it's almost certainly a suicide."

"Although if this bruise was the result of Lucy being choked, prior to the noose being placed around her neck..." I said.

"It would be murder."

McCrabban and I weren't happy. We had enough on our plate with a lunatic going around shooting homosexuals. We didn't need someone murdering hunger strikers' ex-wives as well.

"You're going to tell the coroner that it was death by suicide?" I said frostily.

"That's what I believe," Laura said.

"That's what we'll put in our report then. That's what we'll tell the family," I replied.

"Fine. Gentlemen, I really must go to my clinic," she said.

We all stood.

Crabbie and I walked back to the station in silence.

We were both thinking about Lucy. "You don't like it, do you, Sean?" Crabbie asked.

"No. I don't."

"It would be the old faithful, wouldn't it? The murder by hanging disguised to look like a suicide . . ."

"Aye."

"Or, as the good lady doctor says, it could just be a common or garden suicide."

I nodded.

"You can't let it sidetrack you though, mate," Crabbie insisted.

"I know."

We went back inside the barracks, sat at our desks and carried on work on the serial killer case. I read up about Orpheus and Offenbach in the station's 1911 Encyclopaedia Britannica. Nothing leapt out at me. I called Special Branch to check that the men on the killer's hit list were getting protection.

They were.

I called the forensic lab in Belfast to see about those fingerprints and was told that it was only a skeleton crew on the weekend and not to expect anything.

I went to see McCallister and he read the patho report on Lucy Moore and told me that it looked like a suicide to him. I told him about Dr. Cathcart's concern.

"What do you think?" he asked me.

"I'd keep an open mind but I'm thinking suicide. A note would have been the clincher."

"Aye. Suicide."

I went out for some air. Carrickfergus on a Sunday was a ghost town. Everything was closed. Even the paper shops and the petrol stations shut at noon.

There was no traffic on the lough and I walked along the shore to Carrickfergus Castle. I was going to actually go in and check it out but it too was closed.

I returned to the police station.

"You want to go back to Woodburn Forest?" I asked McCrabban.

He looked up from his paperwork and nodded.

We rustled up Constable Price who was our canine officer.

The dog was a sensible looking lab/border collie cross called Skolawn.

We drove to the forest in the Land Rover and found the tree where we'd cut down Lucy.

We did a sight line box scan and found nothing suspicious.

We let Skolawn go. After an hour he had failed to find any human remains but he had managed to kill an endangered red squirrel.

"It would be helpful if we could find out where she'd been living for the last five months," I said.

"With all the other stuff we have to do, you want us to look into that?" Crabbie complained.

I nodded.

"All right. I'll ask around," he said.

"Do either of you want to drive up to forensic lab with me and get our fingerprint results on John Doe?" I asked.

"Don't go there, Sean. Not on a Sunday. There's no point making waves," Crabbie said.

He was as impatient as I was but maybe he was right.

We drove back to the station. I poured myself a Johnnie Walker which was the general libation used to liven up the office tea. Johnnie Walker in the tea, Jim Beam in the coffee. Around these parts everyone pitched their tents by the whisky river.

I hummed Offenbach to myself and waited by the fax machine. The John Doe fingerprints came through at just after six.

Of course it was an anticlimax.

The victim was a twenty-eight-year-old guy called Tommy Little, a carpenter originally from Saoirse Street in the Ardoyne. Like everybody else from Saoirse Street he was a player but it looked like a minor one. He was an occasional driver for Gerry Adams and Sinn Fein. He had been interned as an IRA man in 1973 but who hadn't? He had one conviction for possession of a stolen hand gun in 1975 and had spent nine months in the Kesh for that. He had been accused of public indecency in a Belfast lavatory in 1978 but the case had been dismissed. He was not married, had no kids. The next of kin was not listed in the file. He had no crim rec since '78.

I called Brennan at home and filled him in on the John Doe and the fact that Lucy had been pregnant.

"Pregnant?"

"Yes, sir."

"Explains why she ran away, doesn't it?"

"Yes, sir."

"Good, well that's one mystery solved. Who's this Tommy Little's next of kin?" he asked.

"There is no next of kin."

"You say he was a driver for Sinn Fein?"

"It says occasional driver. He's not a major gaffer, sir. Small fry by the looks of it."

"Doesn't matter. Call up Adams and let him know that one of his boys copped it."

"Call up Gerry Adams?"

"Yes. He'll have to do for the next of kin. Is there anything else?"

"We went up to Woodburn Forest. We didn't find the body of Lucy's baby which might mean good news. Maybe she gave it away and then topped herself."

"We can live in hope. Is that everything?"

"Yes, sir."

"Good work, Duffy. Well done."

He hung up. I got myself a coffee and rummaged through the directory until I found Gerry Adams's home number.

Someone that wasn't Adams answered the phone.

"Who is this?"

"My name is Sergeant Sean Duffy from Carrickfergus RUC, I'd like to speak to Mr. Adams about a matter of some urgency."

"Yeah, he's kind of busy. He's doing an interview live on the BBC."

"When will it be over?"

"What the fuck do you want, peeler?"

"A friend of his has been killed and I've been instructed to make the notification only to him."

"Where are you?"

"Carrickfergus RUC."

"He'll call you back."

I turned on the radio and found the interview.

Adams: "The demands of the hunger strikers are very reasonable. They want to wear their own clothes, they went political status, they want the right to do prison work or the right to refuse prison work. They want access to educational materials. We don't understand why the government of Mrs. Thatcher will not give us these reasonable demands. The whole world doesn't understand why she will not give in to these demands."

BBC: "Yes, that's the whole point isn't it, Mr. Adams? She'll be giving in to terrorists."

Adams: "One man's terrorist is another man's freedom fighter. The current Prime Minister of Israel is Menachem Begin and he, if you'll recall, blew up the King David Hotel. Look at Nelson Mandela. The whole world condemns his imprisonment and—"

BBC: "The Secretary of State for Northern Ireland has said that the demands of the Republican prisoners in the Maze can be looked at as soon as the hunger strike is ended."

Adams: "The time to look at these demands is now before more men die needlessly."

I turned off the radio.

I walked around the station looking for food.

The only people in here now were myself, Ray on the gate and a reservist called Preston.

"Have you got any sandwiches, Preston?" I asked him.

He shook his head.

"I'll give you five quid for a bag of crisps."

He had no crisps. I called up half a dozen Chinese restaurants to see if any of them were open on a Sunday. None were.

I waited by the phone.

I got out the whiteboard and wrote a flow chart with labels like "homosexual" and "Daedalus" and "severed hands." I drew a Venn diagram. I drew a labyrinth.

My stomach complained.

The rain outside turned to sleet.

Finally the phone rang. I pressed line one.

"Hello, I'd like to speak to Sergeant Duffy," Adams said. His voice was unmistakable.

"Mr. Adams, I'm sorry to have to inform you about the death of an associate of yours, a Mr. Tommy Little. There was no known next of kin on our files so we thought it best to call you."

"How did he die?"

I filled him in on the details that we were prepared to reveal at this stage: Tommy had been shot and he was possibly the victim of a serial killer targeting homosexuals. I kept back the things I wasn't prepared to reveal yet: the switched hands, the musical scores, the killer's hit list, the postcard to me and the message to the Confidential Telephone.

"You say this was in Carrickfergus?" Adams asked.

"Yes, the Barn Field in Carrickfergus."

"What would Tommy be doing there?"

"That's not where he was murdered. He was murdered somewhere else and dumped there."

"And you think it's a multiple murderer doing this? A serial killer? With all that's going on?"

"This would be an ideal time to do it, Mr. Adams, with police resources stretched so thin."

"Someone's going around killing homosexuals?"

"That's our working hypothesis. Did you know that Mr. Little was a homosexual?"

"Well, we, uh . . . we don't pry into people's private lives."

"Is there anything you can tell me about Mr. Little's movements or acquaintances or . . ."

"No, I can't. Thank you for getting in touch, Sergeant Duffy," Adams said and hung up.

"That was a little abrupt, wasn't it, Gerry?" I said to myself. I got out my notebook and wrote: "Adams . . . what does he know that he's not saying."

Not that I would ever get a chance to interview him.

"All right, I'm out of here!" I informed Preston and told him to man the ship until Sergeant Burke came in at eight o'clock.

I drove home but when I got back to Coronation Road I remembered that there was no food in the fridge and I went to Mrs. Bridewell to beg a can of soup and some bread. Mrs. Bridewell looked like Joan Bakewell from off the telly. The "thinking man's crumpet"—short black bob, cheekbones, blue eyes. Her husband had been laid off by ICI and like half the male population was currently looking for work.

She asked if I wanted to join them for Sunday roast.

"No, I just want some soup if you've got any. All the supermarkets are closed."

"Join us!" she insisted.

I told her I didn't want to impose but she dragged me in.

"Sit down back down, everyone!" Mr. Bridewell said in an old-fashioned country accent that you didn't really hear any more. Everyone sat. There were two kids and a granny. The granny looked at me, pursed her deathly pale lips and shook her head. She was wearing a long black taffeta dress that had gone out of fashion with the passing of the late Queen Mary.

We said Proddy grace.

No wine, of course, but a pot roast, potatoes and mashed carrot and parsnip. I wondered how they could afford such a spread on Mr. B.'s unemployment benefit but he explained that the meat was a free gift from the European Economic Community and there was plenty of it. I'd seen Bobby Cameron distributing this European meat—it was yet another way the paramilitaries got their hooks into people.

Dessert was bread and butter pudding with custard—gooey and crispy and fabulous.

After dinner I played a quick game of chess with their older boy, Martin and tried to lose in a way that didn't look condescending. My condescension quickly turned into a serious ass-kicking from him, as he knocked off my major pieces one by one and forced me to resign.

I went home and flipped through the contemporary section of my record collection. What did I need? Led Zeppelin, The Undertones, The Clash, The Rolling Stones, Deep Purple, AC/DC, Motorhead? Nah, I wasn't in that kind of mood. Carole King, Joan Baez, Joan Armatrading, Bowie? I flipped the sleeves and wondered if Tapestry might be ok to listen to. I stuck it on, made myself a vodka gimlet and lay on the sofa with the window open.

Carole King reinterpreted her own song "Will You Love Me Tomorrow" that she had originally written for the Shirelles. King's was the better version.

Bobby Cameron pulled into the spot in front of his house. He was driving a white transit van. When he got out of it he was wearing a rolled-up balaclava. I could have arrested him on the spot for that. His sixth sense kicked in and he realized that someone was looking at him. He checked both sides of the street. He examined the terrace and spotted the open window.

He saw that the watcher was only me. He gave me a finger wave and I gave him the slightest nod in return.

I made myself another vodka gimlet and switched on the TV. At eleven o'clock the snooker was interrupted by a BBC news bulletin. Time-delayed incendiary devices were exploding all over Belfast and shops were on fire in Great Victoria Street, Cornmarket and the York Road. Key holders were being urged to return to their premises, off-duty firemen were being told to report to their nearest available station.

The snooker came back on but I didn't get to see who won because, at exactly midnight, the street lights went off and the TV died.

The power-station workers had, as anticipated, come out on strike.

9: THE FOURTH ESTATE

Sergeant McCallister was a bluff, old-fashioned copper not *au fait* with the new forensic methods and clinical police work and because of this I tended to underestimate him.

I saw that now as I watched his press briefing. It was masterful stuff. He handled the questions with aplomb and was charming but firm. He played down the sensational aspects of the case and told the media merely that we were dealing with a person who had killed two suspected homosexuals and had threatened to kill more. That was all we knew at this stage.

When asked how we knew that both killings had been done by the same person he said that there were forensic similarities and certain markers that we did not wish to reveal at his stage.

The press turn-out was slightly disappointing.

None of the American hacks had showed up and only three Brits from the *Sun*, the *Guardian* and the *Daily Mail*.

We still had the locals: the *Belfast Telegraph*, the *Irish News*, the *Newsletter* and the *Carrickfergus Advertiser*; and from Dublin: the *Irish Independent* and the *Irish Times*.

We had our own diesel generator in the basement so the power outage didn't bother us. I listened to McCallister talk and gazed out the window at the massive grey Kilroot Power Station, one mile up the coast, which for the first time since I'd come to Carrick was not belching out black smoke from its six hundred foot chimney.

"Why do you think the Yanks didn't show up?" Matty whispered as McCrabban showed the hacks the location of the two killings on a map.

"I suppose that two murders hardly makes a 'serial killer' in US terms," Brennan whispered back.

I had a different view. I reckoned the Yanks hadn't come because this little incident was an unnecessary layer of complication compared to a simple story of peace-loving Irish patriots starving themselves to drive out the evil British imperialists.

That would have been my view too if I'd gone to New York and stayed there.

Felt a bit like that sometimes anyway.

"... will be handled by Sergeant Duffy, who is an experienced detective and is actively pursuing several leads at the moment."

"Can we ask Sergeant Duffy any questions?" the guy from the Belfast Telegraph piped up.

I reddened and looked at my polished DM shoes.

"Sergeant Duffy is busy with the case, but I assure you gentlemen that if there are any major developments you will be kept informed . . ."

There were a few more questions and the guy from the Daily Mail wondered if homosexuality's illegality in Northern Ireland would affect our investigation.

"Keeping pigeons without a license is illegal as well, but we can't have people going round shooting pigeon-keepers, can we? It is the job of the RUC to enforce the law in Northern Ireland, not paramilitary groups, not vigilantes, not 'concerned citizens,' it's our responsibility and ours alone," McCallister said which made me proud of him. Not quite tears-in-eyes but maybe warm-glow-in-tummy.

No one could think of any more questions.

"Ok, gentlemen, I think that's enough for this morning," McCallister said.

I gave Alan the thumbs up and he gave me a broad wink back.

I got my team together in the CID evidence room. Tommy Little's current address had finally come through, not from RUC intelligence, but the friggin tax office. He lived off the Falls Road which would mean another hairy visit to West Belfast.

"Ok, first things first," I began. "Lucy Moore. Patho says suicide and no doubt the coroner will too, but I slept on this last night and I've decided that I want you to keep the file open. We've a lot on our plate, boys, but any spare moment you get, I want you to hunt down leads where she might have been living, who she was seeing and what happened to her bairn."

McCrabban stuck a finger up and flipped open his notebook. "Fourteen babies left at the St. Jude Mission, the Royal Victoria Hospital, Whiteabbey Hospital, the City Hospital and the Mater Hospital in the last week. Apparently that's a pretty standard number. Similar number the week before. All anonymous drop-ins, of course."

"Good. I'm going to go and see her parents and her ex husband tomorrow and see if they offer us any insights. At the very least, I'd just like to close the book on this."

Crabbie's mouth opened and closed in amazement. "Did you say that you're going to go see the husband?" he asked.

"Aye."

"You know he's on hunger strike, right? In the Maze."

"I know."

"You're going to go into all that madness?"

"Yes."

"Count me out of that mess," Crabbie said, shaking his head.

"All right, I'll go by myself."

"I'll go with you," Matty said.

I pointed at Matty and looked at Crabbie. "See? The lad's a thinker. Who's going to have the better story for his memoirs?"

"He'll need to learn to type first," McCrabban said.

"Ok, down to the main business. We'll need to find this Tommy Little character's car. Matty, will you get working on that?"

"Aye."

"And we'll definitely need to visit his house. Today. Did he live alone? With a boyfriend? A cat? What? We'll need to check that out. Crabbie, call up whatever the local barracks is and get a uniform over there to protect the evidence."

"They won't like it."

"But you'll make them do it."

"Aye," he said and made the call.

"Now let's go through what we've got so far . . ."

We reread the patho reports as a team and went through the physical evidence. We discussed motivations and theories. I was the only one who knew anything about serial killers and I gave them some of the standard feeders—childhood trauma, witnessing violence, peer rejection—which unfortunately covered about half the citizenry of Belfast. Another feeder, of course, was juvenile or adult detention—that also covered a healthy percentage of the population.

"Somebody who hates queers probably had a bad experience with one when they were a kid," Crabbie offered, and gave me a quick glance under his eyelids. It was, I knew, the common perception among Protestants that all Catholic altar boys had been raped by priests in their childhood. I saw that there was no point trying to argue so I decided that logic might be a better tack: "I think that kind of anger would be directed at the individual, not at random targets," I said and then a thought occurred to me. "If these are random targets."

McCrabban nodded. "They're linked by the hands and the bullets. Could they be linked some other way?"

"Good point. Matty, will you look into that?"

Matty nodded.

Sergeant McCallister popped his head in through the door. "Mind if I sit in, lads? I won't open my bake."

"Alan, mate, any contributions you could offer would be greatly appreciated."

McCallister sat down next to me. I sipped my coffee and continued: "I don't know what you lads think but I think the key to this investigation so far is victim number one. Tommy Little. Where was he killed, when was he killed, who was he living with?"

Matty picked up a piece of a paper. "According to the notes there was no next of kin in Ireland. Older brother in Australia. He worked for Sinn Fein as a driver and quote security guard unquote. Bit of a loner, I imagine."

"Yes, but we'll need to find out his movements somehow, won't we? A neighbor, a friend. Somebody must know something," I said.

"No one will speak to us. And we'll be lynched if we go up there. He lived on the Falls Road," Matty said.

"He's right. They have a policy with the peelers: whatever you say, say nothing," Crabbie said.

I shook my head. "One of their own was killed by some nut. I think they'll cooperate."

Alan put his hand on my arm. "If I may, Sean... the IRA find out one of their own was killed in some kind of sordid homosexual encounter? I think they're going to brush the whole thing under the rug and pretend he never existed. What if the money men in Massachusetts find out that their hard-earned dollars are going to a bunch of poofs? No, no, no. If you go up there you'll be meeting the stone wall."

He had a point. But if we didn't pursue the Tommy Little angle we didn't have much of anything. Andrew Young was killed in his house with no witnesses and no forensic evidence. Young's record was clean, no abuse allegations, no complaints against him. He may have been a gay man but he was sixty years old and seemed to live a largely celibate life style. Of course we would follow any and all leads on Andrew Young but it would be foolish not to hunt down everything we could on Little, even if it meant another visit to bandit country.

"We've got nothing else. We have to follow up on this," I said.

"Well, I'm not going back into West Belfast after what happened last time. We're sitting ducks. I'll go with you to the Maze but not West Belfast," Matty said.

"Didn't you hear what Sean said about your memoirs? Could be a whole chapter in this," Crabbie said.

"If I'm writing a book it'll be about fly fishing. I am not going to the Falls Road."

Crabbie went to the machine to get us coffees. When he came back he had news. "The uniform we sent to Little's house says he thinks it's empty. Good for us if it is. Don't need a warrant for a vacant property."

"Great for us. I mean, think about it lads, what if there's a note on his fridge: 'Off to see X, hope he doesn't murder me.'"

Alan laughed.

"He was probably going to some well-known poofter place," Crabbie said.

"Aye, but where? Where do you go if you're a poofter in Carrickfergus or Belfast? Is there a hangout? Is there a cottaging area?"

Both Matty and McCrabban looked embarrassed by the very idea. And they were—or claimed to be—utterly clueless.

"Do you know any benders, either of you?"

"No thanks!" Crabbie said.

"It doesn't make you queer if you know a queer," I said.

"It doesn't help, does it?"

"Well, ask around, will ya?" I said.

"Ask who?" Matty wondered.

"I don't know. Use your imagination! Go to the public toilets and ask some of the pervs hanging about."

"They'll think I'm a perv!" Matty said, horrified.

"And let's pull out the stops on finding Tommy's car, there's bound to be forensic in it," I said.

When everyone had finished writing in their notebooks I got to my feet. "Ok lads, so we're agreed, we're going to go up to Tommy Little's house on the Falls Road. Matty, you can either check out the toilets or you can come with us."

"Fine, I'll do the bloody toilets. You boys are old. I've got my whole life ahead of me. I'm not going back to West Belfast after last time."

"What happened last time?" Alan asked.

"Ach, it was nothing, some wee lads threw a couple of bottles at us. No big deal," I said.

Alan looked grave. Of course I hadn't written about this in the logbook which only made it seem worse.

"I'll go with you and I'll drive and we'll bring a couple of cannon fodder just for the laugh of it," Alan said.

I looked at Crabbie. "I'd take his offer, boss. Sergeant McCallister is the best driver in the station," Crabbie said.

"Up the Shankill and down the Falls for the poor wee peeler it's a kick in the balls," Matty sang cheerfully.

"Let's hope not," Crabbie said with a worried look on his beetle brows.

10: SITTING DUCKS

We suited up in riot gear and all the boys checked their Sterling sub-machine guns out of the armory, except for me, naturally, because I still hadn't managed to return mine from Coronation Road.

On the way out the door Chief Inspector Brennan saw us. "Where are you boys headed like it's fucking Christmas?" he asked.

"The Falls, we're going to do a drop on Tommy Little's house."

"Tommy Little is?"

"Victim number one."

"Oh yeah. You wouldn't mind if I tagged along, would you? Bit of a fug now after all the excitement of the press this morning," Brennan said.

"Nah, sir, better not, be a bit of a tight squeeze," I replied, unwilling for this to become even more of a charabanc ride to the circus.

Brennan was not to be deterred. "Won't be a tight squeeze for me. I'll be sitting in the front."

Cut to twenty minutes later: McCallister driving, Brennan next to him in the bird-dog seat, me, Crabbie and two gormless constables in riot gear, sweltering in the back. One of the constables was a woman. First one I'd seen in Carrick. Her name was Heather Fitzgerald and her cheeks were so red it was like they were on fire. Nice looking wee lass with her emerald eyes and curly black hair, timid as a mouse, too; it would be a real shame if we all copped it in some roadside bomb and she got that pretty face blown to smithereens.

"What's the address?" McCallister asked as we hit West Belfast.

"33 Falls Court off the Falls Road," I said.

Falls Road was not as bad as we'd been expecting. Sure there was a mad press scrum outside the Sinn Fein advice center and there were police checkpoints and a couple of army helicopters up, but most people were just getting on with their business, going to the grocers, the butchers, the milk shop and of course the pub and the bookies.

Falls Court was another one of those murderous dead-end streets that peelers hated and number 33, naturally, was right at the end.

"Alan, when you get to the house, turn us round, keep the engine on, me and the constables will deploy and prepare to give covering fire while Crabbie and Sean can go inside and do their fancy-pants detecting," Brennan said.

"Sounds good to me," I concurred.

"And if you hear shooting, come out," Brennan added with a grin.

He was enjoying this, the old goat.

The Land Rover stopped and Brennan and the two reserve constables disembarked, pointing their Sterlings at the cardinal points of the compass.

Crabbie and I walked over to #33. It was the last house in a typical red-brick terrace which had a huge new mural of Bobby Sands and Frankie Hughes on the gable wall and above them in big white letters Patrick Pearse's quote from 1915: "The fools, the fools, they have given us our fenian dead!"

Crabbie and I looked at the mural and each other. We both were thinking the same thing: aye, this is how you grow a movement.

There were two men sitting on plastic chairs outside #33: short hair, spiderweb tats, denim jackets, white T-shirts, drainpipe thin bleached jeans, DM boots. They were IRA enforcers and they were probably packing heat. If we'd wanted to we could have arrested them for that but why give ourselves the aggravation?

I didn't know why they were sitting there or why the front door of the house was open.

The constable I had sent over had put up some yellow "Police Evidence: Do Not Enter" tape on the front door, tape which was now lying in a heap at the men's feet.

"Is this Tommy Little's house?" I asked.

"What the fuck do you want, peeler?" one of the men asked.

"Oh, I don't know, world peace, an explanation for why they stopped making Puffa Puffa Rice, news that Led Zeppelin have finally got a replacement drummer for Bonzo . . . that kind of thing," I said.

The IRA men were unimpressed by the banter. "You're not welcome around here and if I were you I'd tootle on home," the other man said, a greasy character with quite the face full of zits.

I pulled out my service revolver. "Let me be clear about this, sunshine, I don't tootle anywhere!" I said and went inside.

I heard the other IRA man stifle a guffaw.

Crabbie followed me in.

We saw immediately that we were too late.

The house had been completely stripped. No furniture, no carpets, no pictures on the wall, nothing. It was as if Tommy Little had never existed.

We went upstairs but that was stripped too.

They had already sold or burned Tommy's stuff, no doubt distancing themselves from every aspect of his life. Nobody wanted the complication of being mixed up with a gay serial killer just when they were getting their biggest propaganda victory in decades.

"It's like Trotsky. They're erasing him from history," I said.

We went back downstairs to Flunky #1 and Flunky #2.

"What did you do with Tommy's gear? The Salvation Army?" I asked.

Flunky #2 shook his head. "We dumped it all at a Proddy bonfire."

"Does he have any next of kin apart from the brother in Oz? Kids, nephews, nieces?" I asked. Nothing had come up in the files but there was no harm in asking.

"Tommy wasn't the fucking parental type, was he?" Flunky #1 said.

"No friends, family, nothing like that?" I asked.

"Tommy's fucking dead to us! Fucking queer got what was coming," Flunky #1 muttered.

"These lads are no help. Let's get out of here, mate," Crabbie said.

"Tommy was murdered by some nutcase and I want to find out

who killed him, so if either of you can think of something, give me a call, please."

I handed them each one of my cards which had my name and the number of Carrick CID.

Flunky #1 looked at the card and looked at me.

"Are you a Catholic?" he asked.

"Yeah, I am. Well spotted."

He spat on the ground. "You're a fucking traitor, that's what you are. Taking the fucking King's shilling. How do you sleep at night?"

I leaned in close so that my nose was an inch from his pointy neb.

"Usually on my left-hand side, with a big, fluffy pillow and my favorite Six Million Dollar Man pyjamas," I said in a gravelly Clint Eastwood voice.

Flunky #2 and Crabbie both laughed.

We walked back to the Land Rover and everyone got inside.

"Any information?" Brennan asked.

"A total bust," Crabbie said. "They've stripped the house and are moving somebody else in already."

Brennan raised his eyebrows at me. "What did I tell you?" he said.

"You were right, sir," I replied.

"All right, Alan, take us back to Carrick, warp factor 7," Brennan said.

We drove back onto the Falls Road proper. Brennan made us stop at a paper shop to buy the early edition of the Belfast Telegraph. Disappointingly our press conference hadn't made the front page, which was dominated by the headline: "Four More Join Hunger Strike."

We did make page 3 though and there was a nice picture of Sergeant McCallister under the headline "RUC Investigate Homosexual Double Murder."

"They could have given us more coverage," Brennan complained. "I mean it's nice to have a real crime for once. A normal everyday non-sectarian murder. That's man bites dog around these parts. That's news. I have half a mind to call their editor."

We were nearly at the junction of the Falls Road and the new dual carriageway when McCallister slammed on the brakes.

I looked through the windscreen and saw a hijacked Ulsterbus on fire, parked laterally across the lanes and blocking the road. It must have been set alight in the last five minutes because we were the first cops on the scene and it hadn't even been reported yet on the police radio.

Suddenly there were four massive bangs on the steel plate of the Land Rover's right-hand side.

The two reserve constables yelped.

I looked through the peephole. Someone was shooting at us from the two-hundred-foot high Divis Tower, which in a city built on mud flats, was the fifth tallest structure in Belfast.

Two more heavy bangs on the side of the Land Rover and stray bullets dinging into the pavement. Originally Divis Tower and the whole Divis Flats complex around it had been a model slum-clearance project but it quickly degenerated into a high-rise ghetto completely controlled by the IRA.

"What the fuck is that?" Brennan yelled.

"Fifty caliber machine gun, sir," Sergeant McCallister replied placidly. "Seen 'em in the army, unmistakable."

"Jesus! Can it punch a hole in the armor plate?" Brennan asked.

"Maybe. I don't really know," McCallister replied.

Brennan turned round to look at the four of us in the back. His eyes were wild with excitement. I didn't like it.

"All right, lads and lasses, we'll deploy out the back, train your fire on the muzzle bursts, that'll give the bastards something to think about!" Brennan said as more of the fifty-cal tore up the road all around us (difficult to aim those things, I would imagine).

Sergeant McCallister looked at me and shook his head.

He didn't want to say anything but he hoped I would.

"Uh, sir, I don't think that's a good idea. They're probably waiting with an RPG. As soon as we open these back doors they'll fire it and we're all cooked," I said, thinking that one of us had to say something.

"We can't just let him shoot at us!" Heather said, her cheeks redder than ever with her blood up.

"No, by God, we can't! We'll teach them a lesson they'll never forget!" Brennan answered her.

"Sir, we can't fire into Divis Tower. It's full of people," I said.

"Sir, it's actually a standing order for West Belfast, the rules of engagement do not permit return fire into the Divis Flats complex without permission of a Divisional Commander," Sergeant McCallister added firmly.

There was another burst of fifty cal fire that shook us and sent fragments of steel plate sheering from the Land Rover's side. It was like being inside a pin-ball machine.

Inside a pin-ball machine with the added frisson of imminent death.

The reserve constable whose name I didn't get began throwing up between his legs.

"So what do you suggest, ya lily-livered scoundrels?" Brennan yelled.

"Sir, if they hit a tire we'll be stuck here so I suggest we drive around the bus and then maybe call the army, this is more their scene," I said.

"Just fucking leave! What about the big picture? We're here to enforce law and order. We can't run away from every bloody fight."

Yet, much to Brennan's chagrin, run away we did.

We drove round the burning bus, reported the shooting to the army and sat in humiliated silence all the way back to Carrickfergus Police Station.

We parked the Rover and were all very impressed by the big chunks the fifty-cal had carved in the armor plate.

My good kit had a stink of vomit in it now, so I stripped it off, changed into my jeans and desk-drawer emergency Deep Purple concert T-shirt. I got one of the bored looking reserve constables to leave my suit at the dry cleaners and cornered Sergeant McCallister at the coffee machine. "Did you make that thing up about the rules of engagement?"

He nodded. "Of course I did. How would I bloody know the rules of engagement for West Belfast?"

I made a mug of sweet Irish breakfast tea for Constable Fitzgerald and gave it to her when she came out of the ladies toilets, looking pale and trembly.

"That was some fun today, wasn't it?" I said.

She took the tea gratefully. "I've never been in a gun battle before," she said.

"Not really a battle if only one side was shooting," I said.

She was walking to the gloomy area for the reservists but I led her over to my desk by the window. "Sit over here where there's light," I said.

I let her rest her cute bum on my leather swivel chair.

"You have a nice view," she said.

The tide was out and the beach was littered with shopping trolleys, beer cans, plastic bags, decaying seaweed, the remains of a Ford Escort which had been driven off the Fisherman's Quay in 1978, dead fish, dead jellyfish, raw sewage and oil.

"Aye, it's a lovely view," I replied.

She sipped the tea appreciatively. "This is good, what is it?"

I explained the arcane secrets of the Tetley tea bag.

"So where are you from?" I asked.

"Greenisland now, Islandmagee originally," she said.

"Is Islandmagee nice?"

"It's very nice. When you go there it's almost as if there are no Troubles."

"I'd love to visit some time."

She put down the tea and picked up one of my arrow and question mark-filled pieces of A4 paper. I had written in block capitals: "HOW DID HE SELECT HIS VICTIMS?"

"How did he select his victims?" she asked.

"I don't know, but if we can find out then we might—"

There was a tap on my shoulder. It was McCrabban. He was smiling sleekitly at me. "Sorry to interrupt your work, Sean, but there's a call for you on line #4."

"Excuse me," I said to Heather and pushed the button on line #4.

"Is that Sergeant Duffy?" a voice asked.

"Who's this?"

"You don't need to know my name, but we met earlier today," he said.

Flunky #2.

"Go on," I said.

"Tommy Little had a boyfriend. His name is Walter Hays. I don't where he's living now. We kicked him out."

I wrote it down in my notepad. "Walter Hays. Got it. I'll find him. Thank you," I said.

Flunky #2 didn't hang up.

"Is there anything else?" I asked hopefully.

"I read the Belfast Telegraph today."

"Yes . . ."

"Tommy Little was not a man to hide anything. Everybody knew Tommy Little was queer."

I didn't see where he was going with this. "Ok, so what does that mean?"

"So you have to ask yourself, Sergeant Duffy, why were Tommy Little's proclivities tolerated?"

"Why were his proclivities tolerated? What are you trying to say—"

But then it came to me. If Tommy Little was only an occasional driver for Sinn Fein officials he would have been kneecapped and drummed out of the movement long ago.

But he wasn't an occasional driver, was he?

"They were tolerated because Tommy Little was important. Tommy was a player, that's it, isn't it?"

"Have a good evening, Sergeant Duffy."

The line went dead.

I grabbed Crabbie and Matty and took them into one of the interview rooms and told them what had happened.

"What does this mean?" Matty asked.

"It means, Matty, that the RUC files are wrong about Tommy Little. That's what it means. He was big," Crabbie said.

"I want you to find out how important. I want you to bug Special Branch and MI5 and army intelligence if you have to. Somebody knows who this guy was and I want to know too," I said.

Matty nodded.

I turned to McCrabban. "And you and I are going to find out where Walter Hays is living now and we are going to pay Mr. Hays a wee visit."

I walked out of the interview room and smiled at Heather.

"What time does your shift end, love?" I asked her.

"Seven," she said.

"Have you ever eaten Indian food?"

"No."

"Do you fancy a quick bite after work? Unwind a bit after the day's events, you know?"

She looked skeptical. "Its not spicy, is it? I don't do well with spicy."

I shook my head. "Nah, where did you hear that? It's fine. Listen, if I'm not back by seven would you do me a favor and wait for me? Get changed out of your kit and wait for me, ok?"

"Ok," she said and gave me a beautiful smile.

Crabbie came out of the interview room with a piece of paper. "Stone walls on Tommy Little from the Brits of course but Special Branch say they'll look into it. Meanwhile here's Walter Hays's address: 99 New Line Lane, Ballycarry."

"Let's take the Beemer," I said. "I've had my fill of Land Rovers today."

We went downstairs past the noticeboard. Someone had cut out the picture of Sergeant McCallister from the Belfast Telegraph. Unfortunately for Alan his mug was right under the word "homosexual." The station wits had deleted the rest of the headline.

"Is this what passes for comedy around here?" I asked.

"Don't ask me. I'm more of a Laurel and Hardy fan," Crabbie said.

"And of course they slept in the same bed, didn't they?"

Crabbie sighed, "That's what's wrong with the modern world, Sean. Cynical people like you. It was a more innocent time back then. But those days have gone forever."

"They have indeed, mate, they have indeed."

11: THE FRIENDS OF TOMMY LITTLE

The sky was blue and Concorde was doing a big burn above our heads on the outward leg of the TransAt. We watched it for a moment before getting in the BMW and driving through the gate. Outside the police station a bunch of elderly Jesus freaks were singing about homosexuals, the Second Coming, and proclaiming that we coppers were agents of the anti-Christ.

It was a sizeable crowd and a mobile chip van had parked up the road selling chips, fried dough and hot jam doughnuts.

"Doughnut?" I asked Crabbie.

"Wouldn't say no."

We got half a dozen and drove up into the country.

New Line Lane was just off New Line Road about a mile from the village of Ballycarry.

There were a lot of potholes and the bramble bushes closed in tightly on both sides of the track to such an extent that it made me worried about the paintwork.

When we finally came to the cottage it wasn't large: merely one floor, whitewashed stone, cubby windows and a thatched roof. No doubt tourists would have gone apeshit for it and no doubt the occupant complained about the leaks and the damp. Blue turf smoke was curling from the chimney.

I parked the Beemer, got out, and glanced behind me, down the lane, to the grey tongue of Belfast Lough and beyond it to the yellow cranes of the shipyards in Harland and Wolff. The city looked peaceful as it always did from up here. There was no fire but you could tell something serious was going on because of the number of choppers hovering over the Ardoyne: two Gazelles, a Sea King and a Wessex.

The sun had made an appearance so I left my raincoat in the cab. It wasn't that professional to do your police work in a Deep Purple T-shirt, but what could you do?

We knocked on the little wooden door, which had been painted a fetching shade of green.

"Mr. Hays?" Crabbie asked.

The door opened. Hays was tall and thin, about twenty-five. He was wearing blue-tinted John Lennon glasses and his blond hair was gelled. He was wearing white jeans and a white shirt. He had a bruise on his cheek and a split lip, barely healed from when—without a doubt—the IRA had interrogated him about Tommy's death. He was pointing a double-barreled 12-gauge shotgun at us.

"Can I help you?" he asked in a well-to-do South Belfast accent.

"We're the police. We're looking into the death of Tommy Little," I said, showing him my warrant card.

"I've got nothing to say," Hays replied, before reading the card carefully.

"Until recently were you living with Tommy Little on 44 Falls Crescent?"

"Until yesterday," he muttered.

"Until the IRA kicked you out?"

"No comment."

"Maybe you could aim that shotgun away from my bollocks, I'm about to become a father," Crabbie said.

Hays lowered the shotgun.

"Who were you expecting?" I asked pointing at the weapon.

"You never know, do you?" Hays said.

"Is this your house?" I asked.

"It was my da's. We used to come here now and again to get away from Belfast."

"You and Tommy Little?"

"No comment."

"What do you do for a living, Mr. Hays?" I asked.

"I work for the forestry commission."

"Ah, interesting work, I'm sure. I've heard that as late as 1800 a squirrel could go from one side of Ireland to the other jumping from tree branch to tree branch."

"That's about right," he mumbled and narrowed his eyes.

I've seen many a hold-out and this guy was as dour as they came. In normal circumstances he would be a tough interview, but fortunately for us he was frazzled, humiliated and best of all—angry.

"Who told you not to speak to us, Mr. Hays?"

"Who do you think?"

"The IRA?"

"Them and my innate common sense."

"Can we come in, Mr. Hays?"

He shook his head.

"Look, Mr. Hays, I'm a detective sergeant at Carrickfergus RUC. I'm looking into Tommy's death. Unlike your friends in the IRA who want this whole thing just to go away, I want to find the killer. I want to find out who did it."

"Tommy went out that night, that's all I know," Hays said and tried to shut the door.

I got my foot in the jam and held it open.

"Where did he go?"

"I'm not saying anything more."

"Where did he go?" Crabbie asked.

"I don't know anything."

"Come on, we're trying to find out who killed him," I insisted.

His eyes were filling with tears now but he still shook his head. "I can't tell you anything. That much was made clear to me. I was tied to a fucking chair. They placed a gun against my forehead. I was told that I was lucky that I was being let live!"

I took a deep breath and put my hand on his shoulder. "Just tell us where he was going," I whispered.

Hays glared at me but he kept his mouth shut.

I looked at Crabbie. Of course we could take him in, but with a Sinn Fein lawyer in the room with him it would be the stone wall . . . Besides we both could see that he was caving.

He was starting to tremble, not one big tremble but little shunts building towards climax, like people on the bus to the shrine of Our Lady of Knock.

This was the big holy shit. This was grief.

"We need to know where Tommy was going," Crabbie said gently.

"Who was he going to see, Walter?" I asked.

Hays shook his head. "I read the paper. It's nothing to do with Tommy's job, is it? It was some nut randomly going round killing people. Killing queers!"

He said the word "queers" with a sneer—the way he thought we said it.

But it was too late now. He'd given us something important.

Tommy's job.

"What did Tommy do for the IRA, Walter?"

"You don't even know that?" Hays said with contempt. "You boys are fucking clueless."

Crabbie and I shared an excited look.

"What did he do, Walter?"

"I'm telling you nothing!" Hays barked.

Different tack now. Build it like a staircase.

"Did Tommy's car ever show up?" I asked.

Walter shook his head.

"What car did he drive?" Crabbie asked.

"1978 blue Ford Granada, BXI 1263."

I wrote the license plate down in my notebook.

"How long were you and Tommy together?" I asked.

"Four years."

"Four years. He must have meant the world to you. Come on, Walter. Don't you want us to find Tommy's killer?"

"You'll get nothing out of me. Nothing," he said with a sob. "Now you'll really have to leave!"

I reached in my pocket to give him one of my cards but he wouldn't take it.

"If they find it in the house, they'll top me for sure," he said.

There were real tears now.

"It's ok, mate," I said. I gave his shoulder a squeeze. "It's ok," I said. "It's ok."

The tears flowed.

A minute went by.

He sniffed and pulled himself together. I looked him in the eyes.

"Who was he going to see, Walter? Give us a name."

He sniffed again. A hint of flintiness in his expression. A resolution.

"It's two names," he whispered.

"Tell me."

"It won't help you."

"Why not?"

"Neither one of them is the killer. The IRA already did an internal investigation and both of them are still alive."

"Tell me anyway. Tell me the whole thing."

He wiped his nose. "All right. If it'll get rid of you."

"We'll leave, I promise."

He sighed and took a deep breath. "Ok. Ok, so it's half seven at night and the snooker's on BBC2 and it's Alex Higgins and Tommy loves seeing Alex play, but he puts on his jacket and so I ask him where he's going and he says something about having to see Billy White about the rackets. I don't think anything of it as he goes to see Billy once a fortnight, more or less. And I'm not really listening to him. And he's literally going out the door and the phone rings and he picks it up and he's talking for about a minute and I'm not paying a lot of attention cos I'm watching the snooker too and then he hangs up and I say who was that? And he doesn't answer. And so I turn to look at him and I ask him what's up. And he mutters something about business to take care of and after that he's going to have to go down to Freddie Scavanni's house. And then he goes out. And that . . . that's the last I ever saw of him."

"What was at Scavanni's house?" I asked scribbling in my notebook.

He opened his mouth, closed it, looked away.

"There's more, come on, Walter, out with it."

"No. There's not much more. That same night, one of the higher-

ups phoned looking for Tommy—about an hour after he left home—
and I told him what Tommy had said."

"What do you mean 'higher-up'?"

"One of the big bosses. But you won't be getting his name from
me, ever."

"Do you mean one of the big bosses in the IRA?"

"Yes."

"How big?"

"The top. The very top. That's all I'm going to say."

I looked at Crabbie. He couldn't believe what he was hearing either.

"Ok, Walter, so you told this big boss what exactly?"

"That Tommy had gone out already. That he was going to see Billy
White and Freddie Scavanni."

I wrote it down. "And then what happened?"

"Well, Tommy didn't come back and the bosses called again at midnight looking for him and I said I hadn't seen him yet. A lot of times
Tommy will do an all-nighter for the boys so I wasn't that worried. But
then the bosses starting calling again in the morning and all that afternoon. And I began to get really concerned, and then that evening a
couple of thugs wearing balaclavas knocked at my door and they took
me away for the third degree . . ."

He hesitated and then stopped speaking as if he had just caught
himself doing something terribly wrong. "Informer" has always been a
poisonous word in Ireland and these days "informer" was anyone who
so much as opened their mouth in the presence of a policeman.

"Ok, Sergeant Duffy, that's it. You know what I know. Please leave
and please don't ever come back," Walter said wearily.

He pushed me out onto the porch.

"Wait, a minute, Walter, I—"

Before I could get another word out he shut the door.

I stood there for a moment and then turned to Crabbie. "Either of
those names ring a bell?"

"Don't know who Freddie Scavanni is but Billy White is a Prod paramilitary in Newtownabbey. UVF divisional commander for East Antrim."

"Why would an IRA man be going to see a UVF divisional commander?"

"Lots of reasons."

"Drugs?"

"Aye, dividing up territory for drugs, arranging truces, sorting out territory for protection rackets, that kind of thing. But the thing is, Sean, the question we have to ask ourselves, is why Billy White is seeing some low-ranking IRA guy?"

"And we know the answer, don't we? Because Tommy Little isn't some low-ranking IRA guy at all, is he?"

"Nope. I reckon he isn't," Crabbie agreed.

We drove back to Carrick station and while Crabbie filled in Matty I looked up the file on Billy White:

Born 1947, Belfast. Smart kid. Methodist College. 10 O-Levels. 2 A-levels. 1966–71 moves to Rhodesia where he joins the police. 1971 expelled from Rhodesia for unspecified reasons. 1972 arrested for receiving stolen goods in London. '72–'74 Her Majesty's Pleasure in various English Stretches. '74 returns to Belfast. Joins UVF, arrested for attempted murder. Witness disappears. Never arrested again. Suspected hitman, suspected bagman, suspected narco distributer. Current UVF rank: senior commander and quartermaster.

The file didn't say what Billy did now for the UVF but if he was a liaison officer with other paramilitary groups it would make him almost untouchable.

I looked up the file on Freddie Scavanni:

Born 1948, Ravenna, Italy. Relocated to Cork 1950 and to Belfast 1951. Father one of the many Italian immigrants who came to Ireland just after the war. Educated on a scholarship at the Portora Royal School, Enniskillen. 12 O-Levels. 3 A-Levels. Another smart kid. Interned for IRA membership 1972 and released in 1973. BA in journalism from Queen's University Belfast 1976. Currently Sinn Fein press officer. Current IRA rank: unknown.

I closed both files and put them on my desk.

I called up Sinn Fein HQ and asked to speak to Scavanni but they told me to take a long, spiritually fulfilling walk into the nearest peat bog.

"Oi, Crabbie, remember when the chief said that it was great that we had a nice wee normal murder case for once that didn't involve the paramilitaries or have a sectarian angle?"

"Yeah," he said sourly, looking at his watch.

"I'm not sure we have that anymore."

I rubber-banded the files on Scavanni and White and chucked them over to him. He read them and whistled.

It was five o'clock. "Tomorrow's going to be a busy day, mate," I said. "You better go home."

"Busier than today?" he asked.

"Oh aye. We're going to interview Lucy Moore's ma and da and her husband in the Maze to close that investigation and then we're going to have to interview our two new best friends: Freddie and Billy."

"I'll be late in, Sean. I have to go to Derry tomorrow for me Uncle Tom's funeral," Crabbie said.

"All right then, it'll be a busy day for Matty."

"I'll write those names up on the scoresheet."

Crabbie wrote FREDDIE SCAVANNI and BILLY WHITE on the whiteboard.

He put on his coat. "Is it really ok if I go on home?"

"Aye."

"What about me?" Matty asked.

"Jesus, you're here? Where are you?"

"Lying on the floor by the radiator."

"Why?"

"My back's killing me. I must have done something to it. I could barely reel in that ten-pounder yesterday. I should be off on sick leave."

"No sick leave! Did you find out where the homosexuals go to do their business?"

"No."

"Did you find where Lucy Moore's been hiding since Christmas?"

"No."

"Did you find out if there was a link between Tommy Little and Andrew Young?"

"No."

"Did you find out what Tommy Little really did for a living?"

"No."

"Brilliant. All right, you can go home too."

Matty grinned and thanked me. When they were both gone, I turned on the portable TV to catch the Six O'Clock Northern Ireland News. Our story was only the fifth lead, behind a bus bombing, the Royal Wedding, the hunger strikes and an attack on an army helicopter: Two homosexual men had been shot in possibly related incidents. The BBC, in their wisdom, interviewed Belfast City Councilor George Seawright of the DUP, who, as a responsible elected representative called homosexuals an "abomination under God deserving of the very worst torments of hell."

I turned down the sound and called Special Branch and asked them to send me their latest intel files on the IRA High Command and Army Council. Then I called the Northern Ireland Prison Service to ask how you went about interviewing a prisoner on hunger strike.

Until Heather Fitzgerald's shift ended I killed some time working up my psych profile of the killer, but there wasn't a whole lot to go on. Male 25–50. Intelligent. Into classical music. Into mythology. Knowledge of Greek? That didn't really narrow it down as I'd learned Latin and Greek as did most kids who went to Catholic school or a Proddy Grammar.

At seven o'clock Heather and I walked to the Taj Mahal Indian Restaurant on North Street. We were the only customers.

She had changed into her civvies: a black sweater, long brown skirt and short-heeled boots. She'd kept her end up and she looked lovely.

I ordered half a dozen things off the menu and instead of any of that they just brought us what they'd already made. The waiter grew strangely evasive when I asked for details so I didn't press him. She pecked at her food like a bird, eating practically nothing. I hadn't had a proper meal in days and I scarfed what she left.

We were both on three Kingfishers when we walked hand in hand down to the Dobbins on West Street. She wanted a gin and tonic and I got a pint of bass.

Two more drinks and we were getting on famously.

She went off to the toilet and I stood by the fireplace watching the peat bricks crack.

"I thought you might be here," a voice said.

I turned round. It was Laura.

"I came looking for you," she said. "I wanted to ask you if you wanted to go to the cinema this week."

"I thought the IRA had blown up all the cinemas."

"Not all of them," she laughed.

"What's playing?"

"*Chariots of Fire*? Have you heard of it?"

"Some kind of Ben Hur remake?"

"It's about the Olympics."

Just then Heather came back from the toilet. She saw me talking to Laura and immediately put her arm through mine and kissed me on the cheek.

Laura blinked a couple of times.

"Laura, this is my friend, Heather. Heather, this is Laura," I said.

The two women looked at one another and said nothing.

Heather put her hand on my cheek, turned my face to hers and kissed me on the lips.

When the kiss was done, Laura, naturally, was gone.

"Let's finish our drinks and get out of here," Heather said.

We went outside and called a black taxi.

It took us to her house in the wilds of Greenisland.

It was a surprisingly big house for a young reserve constable.

If I hadn't seen her in the RUC van with us today, I would have been thinking: oh shit, IRA honey trap.

She stripped off her clothes revealing fishnet stockings and a black basque.

What the fuck is this? I was thinking when she grabbed my cock through my trousers.

"We were nearly killed today," she said.

"Not really."

"Doesn't it turn you on?" she said.

"You turn me on," I replied and kissed her again.

She tasted of gin and better times.

I kissed her breasts and her belly and laid her down on the bed.

"Fuck me, you bitch!" she moaned.

I didn't need any more encouragement.

We had hard, rampant animal sex and then she climbed on top of me and we fucked again.

I fell asleep until 1:30 when she shook me hard.

"My husband gets back from the night shift at two," she said. "Get your clothes on and get the fuck out of here."

"Are you serious?"

"He's a sheet welder, he'll fucking break you in half, wee man, now get out."

I had to walk five miles home in the rain.

When I got back to #113 Coronation Road I was shattered. I ripped off my wet clothes, lit the upstairs paraffin heater and put on the Velvet Underground and Nico. I slid the stylus across to "Venus in Furs" and clicked the repeat switch. When John Cale's crazy viola and Lou Reed's ostrich guitar kicked in, I went to the bookcase found the Britannica Encyclopaedia of Art and skipped through the centuries until I came to the painting of Orpheus in the Underworld by Jan Velvet Brueghel. I lay in front of the heater as the rain came on and the wind rattled the bathroom windows. I looked at Brueghel's hell: flying demons, fires, tormented souls and in the foreground two ladies in rather nice frocks.

I lay there and let the minutes wash over me. The minutes. The hours. All eternity. I thought of Orpheus searching for his beloved in the realms of Hades. I thought of Laura and Heather. I thought of Tommy and Walter. I looked for meaning. But there was no meaning. It was nonsense. All of it. There was method but no key. They're all just playing with us, I thought. And then at three o'clock exactly the lights went out again.

12: BITING AT THE GRAVE

If the papers were to be believed there were two things going on in the world: the Royal Wedding and the IRA hunger strikes; one focal point was the baroque dome of St. Paul's Cathedral, London, the other was the middle of a sour, boggy portion of the Lagan Valley just west of Lisburn—the Maze Prison.

The Maze was built in the aftermath of the disastrous Operation Demetrius in 1971 when hundreds of IRA "suspects" had been arrested in a desperate attempt to stop The Troubles from escalating. Initially they were kept in huts at the former RAF base of Long Kesh, but eventually the Maze prison was built around them with its massive perimeter fence and eight concrete "H Blocks."

Many of the internees had had no links whatsoever to the IRA but that had certainly changed after six months or a year's detention by the British. The Brits have always been experts at pouring gasoline on every situation in Ireland: The Easter Rising, Bloody Sunday, Internment— all of them excellent recruiting tools for the radicals.

After Internment ended and the prisoners were released it was decided that IRA volunteers would only get jail time if they were actually convicted of a crime: murder, conspiracy to cause explosions, possession of illegal weapons, etc. Initially, however, IRA prisoners had been granted a Special Category Status because their offenses were considered to be political in nature. But then in 1976, on a whim, this status had been revoked by the Secretary of State for Northern Ireland. The prisoners had protested in various ways, most famously by refusing to wear prison clothes and smearing excrement on their cell walls.

In 1979 the Tories were returned to power but of course Mrs. Thatcher had refused to "give in to terrorists" and would not backtrack on the Special Category Status. The hunger strikes had begun. I'd been sympathetic. Bobby Sands, Frankie Hughes and the others were merely attempting to return things to the status quo ante of 1976.

Bobby Sands's election to parliament and death after sixty-six days on hunger strike had been the media event of the decade in Ireland and IRA recruiters were now having to turn away hundreds of young men and women. It did my heart no good at all to know that I was working for the same people who had been responsible for such utter incompetence.

Matty drove up to the Maze Prison walls, which were grey and thick and topped with coils of razor wire.

I turned off the tape of Led Zeppelin's *Presence* album that despite a dozen listens, still sounded crap. Matty breathed a sigh of relief.

It was raining hard and the prison officer did not come out of the guard hut to check the warrant card I was holding up.

That too inspired zero confidence.

"All you need is a hijacked police Land Rover and anybody could get into this joint," I muttered to Matty who was sitting beside me in the front seat. Neither of us were even in uniform. I was wearing a black polo-neck sweater under my leather jacket and he was wearing some kind of white pirate blouse thing that he must have seen Adam Ant sporting on *Top of the Pops*.

The thick steel gate slid across on rollers and I drove to a small car park in the lee of a brown concrete watch tower.

"It's going to be terrible in here, isn't it?" Matty said.

I nodded grimly. I could only imagine what the hospital wing of the prison looked like with a dozen emaciated men hooked up to drips—dying by heartbreaking degrees while family members wept and priests gave extreme unction.

"Aye, Matty, I think so."

Fortunately we'd come early. It wasn't nine so the hacks wouldn't be out of bed yet and the rain had kept away the demonstrators we'd been told to expect outside the prison gates.

Scowling, a chubby, blue-faced man regarded me through bullet-proof glass.

"Sergeant Duffy of Carrick RUC. I'm here to see Seamus Moore," I said.

"Sign here," he replied, passing me a clipboard through a horizontal slit.

I signed and passed the clipboard back.

He did not inspect my ID. I gave Matty a wry look and shook my head. A buzzer sounded and a metal gate opened.

With that we were into the main prison compound.

There were eight H Blocks in separate wings for Republican and Loyalist prisoners—in fact separate wings for the various Republican and Loyalist groups. There was a Provisional IRA wing, an INLA section, a UVF section, a UFF/UDA wing and areas for various other smaller factions.

We parked the Rover and got out.

"Sergeant Duffy?" an aged, grey mustachioed, sad-faced man in a prison officer's uniform asked me from under a giant black umbrella.

"That's me."

"I'm Davey Childers, RUC liaison."

We shook hands.

"We've arranged to have you meet Moore in the visitor's area."

"He's not in the hospital?"

"Oh no, he's only been on hunger strike for a week. That's not necessary yet."

I looked at Matty and we were both relieved.

We went through a series of narrow-fenced easements topped with razor wire until we came to a bunker-like one story building that was also surrounded by a razor-wire fence.

This place was not like the Victorian prisons of England with their imposing red-brick and neo-gothic architecture that was supposed to impress inmates with the power of the state; no, this place looked cobbled together, shoddy and temporary and the only thing it impressed upon you was how current British policy on Ireland was dominated by short-term thinking.

We walked through a set of double doors, checked in our weapons, patted an amiable sniffer dog and immediately saw a fairly healthy looking Seamus Moore sitting waiting for us at a long Formica table. He was bearded, long-haired and wearing pyjamas. He was smoking a cigarette and drinking what looked like a mug of tea.

"I didn't know they were allowed tea," Matty muttered.

"Don't comment on it, we don't want him to take the huff and storm off," I hissed.

We sat down opposite and I did the introductions. Seamus was a good-looking wee skitter with green cat's eyes, arched eyebrows and a bit of a sleekit grin; he had a violet-colored scar running from his chin to his lower lip but that didn't detract from his easy-going, handsome face. He was thin, of course, but he didn't look emaciated. He was in for possession of a stolen shotgun, which had only garnered him a two and a half year sentence. Why he had taken it upon himself to go on hunger strike was a bit of a mystery to me. You could understand why a lifer or a ten-year man would do it, but not someone who'd be paroled in twelve months. Maybe it was just to establish his credentials and he'd be one of the ones who pulled out of it in a fortnight "after listening to the pleas of his family."

"You've got five minutes, peeler," he said. "I've got a phone interview with the Boston Herald at half nine."

"All right. First, let me say that I'm very sorry about your wife, Seamus. I was the one who found her," I said.

"Ex-wife."

"Regardless. Ex-wife."

"Suicide, right?" he asked.

"That's what it looks like."

"Silly bint. And she'd got herself knocked up, hadn't she?"

"Where did you hear that?" I asked.

He laughed and blew smoke. "You hear things, you don't know where," he said.

His attitude needed serious work, but that was not a job for me—I had to be relatively gentle with him. At any moment he could turn round and waltz back to his cell and there wouldn't be a damn thing I could do about it.

"When did you last hear from Lucy?"

He shook his head. "Jesus. Last November? After the divorce came through. She said I owed her two thousand pound for her car which was total bollocks. We agreed to give that wee Mini to my ma. I didn't owe her bloody anything."

He stubbed his cigarette out in the ashtray, lit another and looked at his watch.

"I heard that she ran away to Cork," he added.

"How do you know that?" I asked.

"Cos she sent postcards to her ma and her sister Claire. I mean, who fucking runs away to Cork? Stupid wee milly. If you're knocked up ya go to fucking London and get it fucking seen to."

"I would have thought you'd be upset that she'd gotten pregnant while you were stuck in here?"

"What the fuck do I care? We were divorced. She could marry fucking Prince Charles as far as I'm concerned."

"So you haven't heard from her at all since Christmas?"

"Nope," he said with thin-lipped finality.

"Did you ever threaten her at all, Seamus?"

"Did I fuck. I haven't wasted two seconds thinking about her since last year."

"So you wouldn't have objected if she'd taken up with someone else?"

"Are you deaf, peeler? I've fucking told ya, I didn't give a shite."

I rubbed my chin, looked at Matty, but he said nothing.

"Borrow a smoke?" I asked.

"Help yourself," he said.

I lit a Benson and Hedges and gave Matty one.

"What makes a man want to starve himself to death?" I asked.

"For Ireland!" Seamus said vociferously.

"You know what my barber said?"

"What did your bloody barber say?" he asked.

"He said that nationalism was an outmoded concept. That it was a tool capitalists used to divide the workers and keep them down."

He shook his head. "In a free Ireland, rich and poor, Catholic and Protestant will be united!" he said.

"Do you really believe that? Is that what's happened in the Republic?"

He stood up. "I've had enough of you, peeler. I have important people to talk to."

"Seamus, sit down. You told me you'd give me five minutes. Come on, mate. Is neamhbhuan cogadh na gcarad; má bhíonn sé crua, ní bhíonn sé fada," I said in the glens dialect of Irish that I had grown up with.

He was taken aback by the Gaelic and blinked a couple of times before sitting down again.

"Can you think of any reason why anyone would want her dead?" I asked.

"Somebody topped her?" he asked with what looked like genuine surprise.

"We're awaiting the coroner's verdict on that. It seems like a suicide but you never know. I was just wondering if anybody would have wanted her dead."

Seamus shook his head, but I could tell he was thinking it over.

"I don't think so," he said at last.

There was a but in there.

"But . . ." I began.

"Well," he looked behind him and lowered his voice. "The old-timers might not have taken too kindly to her getting knocked up while I'm up for me stretch."

"Even after you got divorced?" I said.

Seamus laughed. "In the eyes of the church there is no divorce, is there?"

I was about to follow up on this but before I could a voice yelled to us from the other side of the visitor's room.

"What is going on in here?"

I turned and saw Sinn Fein President, Gerry Adams, and another tall man that I didn't know, marching towards us. Matty and I stood up.

Adams was furious. "Are you a peeler? Are you a cop? Who gave you permission to talk to one of the martyrs?" Adams demanded.

"Shouldn't you wait to call them martyrs until after they're dead?" I said.

This was the wrong thing to say.

Adams's beard bristled.

"Who gave you permission to talk to our comrade?"

"I'm investigating the death of his ex-wife."

The other man got in my face. "You are not permitted to talk to any of the prisoners in our wing of Long Kesh without a solicitor being present," he said in a soft southern-boarding-school/almost-English accent.

"Seamus doesn't mind," I insisted.

The other man ignored this. "Seamus, get back to your section. Remember you've got a phone call with America this morning!"

"Ok, Freddie," Seamus said and, with a little nod to me, walked quickly towards the exit.

"And now, you might want to be running along, peeler," Freddie said. He was a big lad, six three and built, but he was relaxed and he wore his size well. He had a dark complexion and he was wearing a tailored blue suit and a green silk tie. His black hair was tied back in a ponytail. A little badge on his lapel said PRESS OFFICER. Adams was in his bog-standard white Aran sweater and he looked scruffy in comparison with his companion. The contrasts didn't end there. Freddie had dark brown, almost black, eyes and a long, continental nose and he was a good-looking cove and he knew it. Adams's vibe was all puffy left-wing history teacher, with his full beard, thick glasses and unkempt brown hair flecked with the occasional strand of grey.

"You're not Freddie Scavanni, are you, by any chance?" I said to the second man.

He was taken aback. "What of it?" he asked, visibly nonplussed.

"I've been trying to have a wee talk with you too," I said. "I called up Sinn Fein twice yesterday, I got nowhere."

"We don't have wee talks with the peelers," Freddie said.

Adams and Freddie turned to go.

"Hold the phone, lads, this'll only take two seconds," I begged them.

"We have a busy morning, we have to get back to headquarters," Adams said.

"I just need one second of your time, boys," I said, getting in front of them.

It was alleged that Gerry Adams was on the IRA Army Council and thus could pretty much have anyone in Ireland killed at any time if he wanted. His "Get out of our way, constable, or you'll regret it" stare was therefore a solid down payment on a year's worth of nightmares.

"Aye, let's get some fresh air, Gerry," Freddie said.

"Wait! You're going to want to listen to this: I think we can help each other," I said.

"How so?" Adams asked.

"I spoke to you, yesterday, Mr. Adams, I'm the lead investigator into the death of Tommy Little and I need to speak to Mr. Scavanni about Tommy. Tommy was on his way to see Mr. Scavanni when he disappeared."

I had hoped to maybe surprise Adams with this information but he obviously knew it already. It made sense. Scavanni wouldn't still be working for the movement if he hadn't been investigated and cleared by the IRA.

"Now what we probably have on our hands here, Mr. Adams, is a serial killer preying on homosexuals. That's a pretty sensational story and as soon the Ripper Trial concludes in England, the British tabs are going to be desperate for something like that until the actual Royal Wedding. This is where our interests coincide. You'd like the press to keep its focus turned on the hunger strikes but if this serial-killer story gets momentum, it's going to be bad news for you and your lads. Imagine dying for Ireland and nobody cares because the new Irish Ripper has taken all the headlines. They're not going to like that, are they?"

Adams shook his head dismissively "I don't like your flippant tone, young man. It's trivializing an important matter. Now, if you don't mind—"

"An IRA man is mixed up with a gay serial killer? Is that really a distraction you can afford to have this summer? Wouldn't you rather have your boy Scavanni cooperate with us, tell me what he knows, help me catch this nutcase and hey presto: distraction over, hunger strike number one story again and the brave struggle by your volunteers can resume its rightful place on all the front pages."

Adams looked at Scavanni who merely shrugged.

I could see that it made sense to both of them.

"Again, I don't like your tone, but in this case I suppose our interests do converge. We, uh, we have not made much progress finding out who killed Tommy Little," Adams said.

"Mr. Scavanni?" I said.

"I'm not sure how I can help. Tommy never made it to see me that night but if you want to chat about it come to my office at noon today. Bradbury House #11," Scavanni said. "I'll give you fifteen minutes."

"See, I knew we'd all become fast friends," I said with a wink at Matty.

"Maybe we could all go to the pictures some time," Matty said dead pan.

"Aye, if those cheeky boys would only stop blowing up all the cinemas."

They walked away from me in disgust.

When they were gone Matty and me allowed ourselves a little laugh.

I was quite pleased with our work and after we got back in the Land Rover I put in a tape of Stiff Little Fingers. It was bucketing now and the rain was coming in sideways from Lough Neagh. Matty was no Stiff Little Fingers fan and was less impressed with what we had achieved. "That was a waste of time," he muttered.

"We got an interview with Scavanni."

"What's that, another bloody trip to Belfast? Another pointless interview. He's IRA, he's not going to tell us anything. And if he did, what difference would it make? He says Tommy Little never made it to his house and if that's a lie the IRA would have found out about that and he wouldn't be standing next to Gerry bloody Adams, would he?"

It was a valid point but I didn't like Matty's negativity.

If McCrabban disagreed with you he just sat there and said nothing. And if he agreed with you, he also just sat there and said nothing.

"I just don't see where this gets us in either investigation," Matty went on.

"We've made progress! I don't think the husband had Lucy killed," I replied as I flipped the volume and the window wipers to maximum.

"We didn't think he'd had her killed before. We didn't think anybody had her killed," Matty protested.

We drove through the gates past a long line of protesters, journos and other rabble gathering outside the fence.

"Bloody hunger strikers, they're never going to win," Matty said sourly.

"What's the matter? Don't you ever root for the underdog? You'd be on the side of the Sheriff of Nottingham."

"We are the Sheriff of Nottingham, Sean."

I pulled over the Land Rover at a spot where cameramen were jostling for position on a little hill that gave you a shot down onto the H Blocks themselves.

"Hey friend, I'll give you twenty pounds if you'll let me take some snaps from the roof of your vehicle," a Yank photographer said to me as I walked round to the passenger's side.

"The cheek of ya. This isn't Bongo Bongo Land mate. We are the incorruptible representatives of Her Majesty's Government. I will, however, accept a hundred-quid donation to the police widows benevolent fund and you're to be quick about it."

He climbed onto the bonnet, took some nice shots and gave me two crisp fifty-pound notes.

I gave one to Matty and kept the other.

Matty put the Land Rover in gear and headed for the M2 motorway.

"Where to?" he asked.

"Betty Dennis Florist on the Scotch Quarter in Carrick," I told him.

We avoided the rush hour and were back in Carrickergus in fifteen minutes.

A dock strike had been called so there were panicked queues of people outside the supermarket and the grocers but no one wanted to waste their few coppers on flowers so I had no problem at Betty Dennis's. I bought carnations, which are a nice neutral sort of flower. Boring yes, but neutral.

"Carrick Hospital," I told Matty.

We parked the Rover and walked to reception with the flowers.

Hattie Jacques. Unsmiling.

I gave her the flowers.

"These are for Dr. Cathcart," I said.

"I'll make sure she gets them," Hattie said.

"Is she in at all?" I asked.

Hattie gave me a severe look. "Dr. Cathcart has given me explicit instructions not to let you or any policeman into the surgery area. Now if you'll excuse me I have to work to do."

Matty grinned, slapped me on the back and steered me back outside into the rain.

"That's harsh, brother, the good doctor is not a fan. You were shot down, mate! Shot down like the Red Baron," Matty said.

"The Red Baron shot the other people down."

"Not in the end, Sean. Not in the end!"

"Shut up! Shut up and drive us to Lucy Moore's house. I wrote the address out on the map."

"Will do boss, will do," he said and laughed again.

Lucy's parents lived on a large farm not far from Carrickfergus. Her father Edward O'Neill had been an old-school Nationalist, one of the few Catholic MPs in the Stormont Assembly and he was still well respected in Republican circles. There had been two girls, Lucy and Claire, and a son, Thomas. Claire was a contracts lawyer based in Dublin and New York. Thomas was a barrister in London. Lucy must have been the black sheep marrying a ne'er do well like Seamus Moore.

We parked the Land Rover and were shown in to the conservatory by Daphne O'Neill, a prematurely aged, grey-haired lady.

Edward was sitting by the window with a blanket over his knees. He was a big man brought low, like an exiled king or politician.

We drank tea.

Talked.

Neither Lucy's mother nor father had anything to add. They were in mourning for a lost girl.

The worst thing in the world that could happen had happened.

Chief Inspector Brennan had already informed them about the baby.

They were bereft. Adrift in a sea of grief. They showed us the post-cards and letters Lucy had sent from the Irish Republic. We, of course, had the photostats in our file and the originals gave us nothing new.

"Did Lucy drop any hint at all that she might have been pregnant to either of you or possibly to Claire?"

Lucy's mother shook her head. She had high, arched cheekbones and a dignified white bun. Tears had been pouring down her face and she was somehow extremely beautiful in all that pain.

"Not a peep and she wasn't showing or I would have noticed at Christmas."

"Was she seeing anyone? A boyfriend or anyone new?"

"No! Not that we knew of. After finally divorcing Seamus? No. She had a lot of friends in the Sinn Fein crowd, but we all thought she'd lay low for a while. Oh Lucy, my darling, darling girl. I don't under-stand it, I don't understand it at all!"

"Is the baby still alive?" Mr. O'Neill asked.

I was choking and I looked at Matty for help.

"We have every reason to think that it might be," he said hesitantly. "Certainly we found no traces of a body in Woodburn Forest. Nearly two dozen infants have been left at hospitals and missions in the last week."

The room grew quiet. Mr. O'Neill cleared his throat and stared out the window. The long seconds became a minute.

"I know what some people say. They say it's an Irish tradition. That it's an ironic commentary on the famine. I don't find anything ironic about it. Do you, sergeant?"

I was genuinely baffled. "Sir?"

"In India the Jains starve themselves to death to obtain purity in the next life. The philosopher Atticus starved himself in Rome because he had become sick and wanted to hasten the end. In Ireland there has never been honor in such a course. I don't know how this so-called tradition got imported into our country!"

I had no answers for him. Clearly he blamed the hunger strikers for guilting Lucy into killing herself.

"Mr. O'Neill, if we could find out where she'd been staying for the last six months it would help us a lot to piece together—"

"We don't know!" Mr. O'Neill snapped. "I wish we had known."

"Perhaps one of Lucy's friends would know?" I asked.

"We've asked everybody again and again!" Mr. O'Neill said, banging his fist into the flat of his hand to emphasise his words.

"We'd like to talk to them anyway," I said.

Mrs. O'Neill calmed her husband down and they gave us half a dozen names, all of whom Carrick CID—that is, Matty and Crabbie—had interviewed after the initial disappearance.

Still we went back to the station and made the calls. Nobody had heard from Lucy since her disappearance, nobody had any insights into boyfriends or a pregnancy. The friends were Catholics, we were the police . . . it was a brick wall.

"Where to now?" Matty asked.

I looked at my watch. "I suppose we'll go see our new friend Freddie Scavanni."

We drove into Belfast along the M5. Burnt-out buses. A wrecked Saracen. A post-office van on fire. Soldiers walking in single file.

We parked the Land Rover at Queen's Street RUC station.

Because of endemic fire bombs, blast bombs and bomb scares the roads into the city center had been blocked. No cars were allowed into the heart of Belfast and all shoppers and civilians were searched at one of a dozen hastily built "search huts."

A long line of uniformed civilian searchers patted you down, looked into your bag and waved you on past the canine officers. Once through the search huts you were free to walk the area around the City Hall.

This inner area was still heavily patrolled by the police and the army and with all these precautions it meant that the square mile of Belfast City Center was one of the safest shopping precincts in the world. Bombers couldn't get in and muggers, rapists and shoplifters couldn't get out. Still, the search huts were a major fucking hassle and sometimes it took fifteen minutes to get through.

Of course plain-clothes detectives could just show their warrant cards and skip to the head of the line.

We heard "fucking pigs" and "SS RUC" behind us as we pushed through.

The civilian searchers were usually women and usually attractive young women at that, so it was a mixed blessing avoiding their attentions. The reason they were universally called civilian searchers was so that they could be distinguished from the agents of British Imperialism: the police, the army and prison officers. It was hoped that the IRA would never issue a communiqué designating them as "legitimate targets" and so far they had not. Unlike Matty and me, of course, who could be killed with impunity.

We walked to Bradbury Place and found Bradbury House in a cobbled street near Pottinger's Entry. It was an older building that had recently been renovated and divided into various subunits: an optician, a travel agency, a hairdresser.

Suite #11 was on the second floor.

It was packed with chippies and painters and men in white boiler suits laying down phone lines.

Scavanni was standing there with one of the sparks examining a complicated fuse box that must have been put in shortly after World War Two.

He saw us and came over with a hand out although he looked annoyed as if he hadn't really expected us to actually show up. I shook the hand.

"Mr. Scavanni, if we could just steal you away for a few moments," I said.

He sighed. "All right, Sergeant Dougherty, this way."

"Fucker forgot your name," Matty muttered as we followed him along a pastel-shaded corridor.

I shook my head. "No. He didn't," I replied.

Scavanni's office was new and had nothing in it apart from a phone, a desk and a few plastic chairs.

He sat behind the desk, took his watch off and set it on the table.

"You have fifteen minutes," he said.

Behind him there was a view of the Cornmarket where they had executed Henry Joy McCracken and the other leaders of the northern branch of the United Irishmen during the 1798 rebellion. That rising had been the last time when Protestants and Catholics had been on the same side; since then it had been divide and conquer in spades.

"The clock's ticking," Scavanni said.

"What is all this?" I asked pointing at the offices.

"It is an adjunct press office for Sinn Fein. We're getting a thousand calls a day for interviews and quotes. We just couldn't cope on the Falls Road."

"And what do you do for Sinn Fein, Mr. Scavanni?"

"I'm just a lowly paid staffer."

"And what do you do for the IRA?"

He rolled his eyes at me. "Sergeant, I have absolutely nothing to do with the IRA."

"Why was Tommy Little coming to see you the night he disappeared?"

"Admin stuff. Nothing that interesting."

"It might have been a wee bit interesting. It was a sudden change of plans, wasn't it? We've been told that Tommy was on his way to see a certain Billy White and then he got a phone call and then he said he had to come see you too."

Freddie didn't flinch. "Talking to Walter, were you? Yes. I called him. I just wanted to have a chat about getting more cars. Tommy was one of our drivers and we've been having to double and triple up on cars for American journalists."

"You called him? To talk about cars?"

"Yes. Check the phone records."

"We will," Matty said.

"So was this a long conversation?"

"As far as I recall we settled the whole thing in about a minute. I asked him if he could make more cars available for the US media and he said he'd take care of it."

"So if it was all settled why was he coming to your house?"

"I have no idea why Walter told you that he was coming over to see me, but I do know that he never made it."

"Did you see him at all on Tuesday night?"

"No."

"Do you not find that a bit strange, that he said he was coming to see you but then he didn't?"

"Yeah, it would be strange if he hadn't been shot in the head somewhere between Belfast and my house."

"Where do you live, Mr. Scavanni?"

"Straid."

"Where's that?"

"Near Ballynure," Matty said.

"And you've no idea why Tommy felt the urge to come and see you in person?"

"None at all. I asked him if he could sort out more cars for the American hacks and he said that he'd take care of it. I thought the matter was settled."

"What did Tommy do for the IRA?" I asked.

"I have no idea. I know very little about the IRA. I'm a press officer for Sinn Fein," Scavanni said.

"Will you be going to Tommy's funeral?"

Scavanni shrugged. "I'm very busy. And I didn't know him that well."

"We've been told that Tommy's death is something of an embarrassment. No military honors, no firing squad, nothing like that," I said.

"There's no point asking me. I have no clue."

I was getting nowhere with this character. I looked at Matty and gave him a kick under the desk.

"You father came over from Italy?" Matty asked.

"He did."

That was it.

There was no follow up.

Jesus, Matty.

"How do you feel about homosexuals, Mr. Scavanni?" I asked.

"I think they're great. More women for the rest of us," he said sarcastically.

"How does Sinn Fein feel about homosexuals?"

He laughed. "We don't have a policy."

"Where were you on the evening of May twelfth?"

"I was at home watching TV."

"Alone?"

"Alone."

"What time did you go to bed?"

"I don't know. Eleven?"

"What were you doing the whole night?"

"Watching TV."

"And you went straight to bed?"

"Yup."

"And you fell asleep?"

"Almost immediately."

I frowned and bit my lip.

"Frankie Hughes was dying on May twelfth. Hunger striker number two. All of Sinn Fein must have been abuzz with excitement and you just went to bed?"

"There was nothing I could do for Frankie. And I knew that the Wednesday was going to be an emotional and busy day. And busy it was, I can tell you that."

Freddie pointed at his watch.

"Look, I'm sorry but . . . time, gentlemen, please."

We got to our feet and on the way out I did one more question Columbo style: "You didn't know Lucy Moore, did you?"

"Lucy who?" he asked with a blank face.

"Seamus's wife."

"The wee doll who topped herself?"

"Aye."

"'Fraid not. What's she got to do with anything?"

"Sweet Fanny Adams, by the looks of it," Matty grumbled.

"You speak Italian, Mr. Scavanni?"

"Of course."

"Che gelida manina . . . you know what that means?"

"Well, obviously the dialect is important . . . something to do with hands?"

"Yeah."

He pointed at his watch again. "Officers, please, it's been fifteen minutes."

He gestured to the door with a look that told us that if we had any more questions we shouldn't hesitate to "fucking get lost."

I took Matty to the Crown Bar and we got a fantastic pork rib stew and Guinness for lunch. A couple of lasses were sawing away on fiddle and acoustic guitar giving us Irish standards about the famine, horses, the evil Brits . . .

"What do you think, chief?" Matty asked.

"About Scavanni?"

"Aye."

I took a sip of the Guinness. "I think he's hiding something," I said.

"My vibe too."

"Did you notice the typewriters? All electric."

"Aye. Did you hear what he said about Tommy? 'I have no idea why Tommy told Walter that he was coming over to see me.' What's the implication behind that?"

"That Walter is lying?"

"Or maybe that Tommy was lying to Walter? And what was with his wee bit of cluelessness about Lucy when he knew that that was the reason for our visit to the Maze this morning? Was he so concerned with concealing something important that he decided to conceal everything?"

"You've lost me," Matty said.

We finished our excellent lunch, chewed the fat with the peelers at Queen Street cop shop, spent twenty minutes checking the phone records at British Telecom (Scavanni had indeed called Tommy Little on the night of May 12) and arranged an appointment with Billy White.

We retrieved the Land Rover and drove to Rathcoole Estate in North Belfast.

This was a Protestant ghetto made up of bland, grim, tower blocks and rows of dismal terraces. There were few services, much concrete, much sectarian graffiti, no jobs, nothing for the kids to do but join a gang.

They didn't throw petrol bombs at us as we drove into the estate but from the four iconic tower blocks we got a good helping of eggs and milk cartons.

We pulled into the strip mall and easily found Billy White's joint wedged between a Bookies and an Off License. It was grandly named the "Rathcoole Loyalists Pool, Snooker and Billiards Hall."

The graffiti on the walls all around announced that this was the territory of the UVF, the RHC (the Red Hand Commando, yet another illegal Protestant militia) and the Rathcoole KAI, a group I hadn't heard of before.

The hall had a bullet-proof grille, speed bumps in front of it and half a dozen guys in jeans and denim jackets hanging around outside.

Matty and I parked the Rover, walked through the riff-raff and went inside the place.

There were a few pool tables and more men in denim playing darts and snooker.

"Are you the peelers come to see Billy?" one of them asked, a giant of a man whose skinhead was brushing against the nicotine-stained ceiling.

"Aye," I said.

"Let's see some ID," he demanded.

We displayed our warrant cards and were shown into a back room.

An old geezer was sitting behind an unvarnished pine desk in a scary, claustrophobic little room that would have given the Führerbunker a run for its money. There were UVF posters on the wall and a large what you might call naive art portrait of Queen Elizabeth II sitting on a horse.

Behind the old man were cases of cigarettes of every conceivable brand.

The old man was watching a gardening program on a big TV.

"Are you Billy?" I asked.

The old man did not reply.

I looked at Matty. He shrugged. We sat down in a couple of plastic chairs.

The old man looked at me suspiciously. "Are you from the taxes?" he asked.

"No."

"From the excise?"

"We're from the police, we've come to see Billy."

"And you're no here from the missionaries of the apostates?"

"I don't even know what that is. Is Billy around?"

"He'll be back in five minutes. He's just getting more petrol for the generator. We had no electricity last night."

"Neither had anybody," Matty said.

"Would you like some tea?" the old man asked.

"I wouldn't mind," Matty said.

The old man went out the door and came back a couple of minutes later with three mugs, a bottle of milk, sugar cubes and a packet of McVitie's Chocolate Digestive biscuits. He added milk and sugar to both mugs and stirred them with his nicotine-stained forefinger.

"Ta," I said when he handed me a cup.

The old man started nattering away, first about the buses and the football but eventually somehow the trenches and the Great War where, he said, he was the only survivor from a platoon of men in the Ulster Volunteers on day one of the Battle of the Somme. I looked at my watch. This was some five minutes.

"I'm just going to step outside," I said.

I went through the games room, opened the front door and took a breath of God's free fresh air. It was raining now and all the men in denim were inside waiting their turn at the snooker tables.

A black Mercedes Benz 450 SL pulled up. It was your classic hood auto beloved of terrorists, pimps and African dictators.

Two men got out.

One of them got a drum of petrol from the boot and began rolling it round the back of the club. He was a young guy, blond hair, about twenty-two. Good-looking imp wearing brown slacks and a plain black T-shirt.

The other guy lit a cigarette and nodded at me. I knew that this was Billy. His hair was mostly black but with a Sontagian grey mohawk up front. His bluey-green eyes were sunk deep in his head and the lines around his mouth were deeper still. He had a square Celtic face, which reminded me a bit of Fred Flintstone or Ian McKellen.

"Are you the peeler who's been ringing up looking for me?" he asked.

"Detective Sergeant Sean Duffy from Carrick RUC," I replied.

"Is that a Catholic name?"

"Yes."

He laughed a nasty wee laugh. "Ok, so what's this all about?"

"Tommy Little."

"Let me guess, you interviewed Walter Hays and he said that Tommy was coming over to see me? Is that right?" he said with animal cunning.

"That's right."

"You want to know how I know that?"

"You have telepathic abilities?"

"Because the IRA has already been on the phone to me, asking me when I saw Tommy last. Very polite they were too."

Of course the IRA and the UVF were sworn enemies who in theory tried to kill each other at every opportunity. In practice, however, there were many contacts between the two organizations. They cooperated to reduce friction between the two communities and to facilitate the distribution and the collection of protection money.

"When did you see Tommy last?"

"Tommy came over here about eight o'clock the night he was topped. The Tuesday."

"Why?"

"We had business to iron out."

"What business?"

"It's not relevant, copper," Billy said with menace.

Like with Gerry Adams and Freddie Scavanni I knew where the power lay here. It was all with him. I had to go softly softly: he could terminate this interview any time he wanted and I'd never get another chance to talk to him again.

"Was it about drugs?" I asked.

He shrugged.

"I'm homicide, not a narc," I said.

"Off the record then?"

"Off the record."

"Swear it on the fucking Pope's life."

"I swear on the Pope's life."

"All right. Well, I can tell you're dying to know so I'll put you out of your misery. Some very bad lads had killed an enterprising young man up in Andy town who we had given a safe conduct to; and I was a bit concerned about this and I was also wondering what had happened to the three bags of brown tar heroin that this young man had been carrying."

My mind was racing. Brown tar heroin? A safe conduct? What had Tommy Little to do with all of this?

"And what did Tommy say to that?" I said placidly.

"He didn't say much of anything. We went into my office and he gave me two of the three bags and asked me if I was happy with that and I said that I was."

"What time was this at exactly?"

"Like, I say, about eight."

"How long did your meeting last?"

"Two minutes."

"And then he was gone?"

"And then he was gone."

"And you never saw him again?"

Billy shook his head but didn't speak.

"You never saw Tommy again?"

"No."

Billy was dressed in a red tracksuit, with Adidas sneakers and a golden chain around his neck. He had a spiderweb tattoo on one side of his neck and a red hand of Ulster on the other. It was very much the look of your middle echelon Protestant paramilitary, and yet there was something about it that didn't quite fit.

This was the external. This was the image he was projecting. But there was more going on underneath. Billy was clever and his accent wasn't Rathcoole at all. There was more than a hint of Southern Africa still.

"You were a copper too for a bit, weren't you, Billy? In Rhodesia?"

"Copper? Is that what your file says? Give us some credit. We were practically running that country. Only thing holding it together. Those were days. High times! That place could have been paradise. Look at it now! We should have killed Mugabe when we had the chance and we did have the chance, believe me."

I could imagine some of those high times: prison beatings, raids into Mozambique, torching villages, burning crops . . .

"How many people did you kill in Rhodesia, Billy?"

"More than enough, copper. More than enough," he said chillingly.

I rubbed my chin. Was any of this relevant? He was a stone-cold killer but I knew that already. "You ever hear of a wee girl called Lucy Moore?"

"Who?"

"Do you know who Orpheus is?"

"What?"

"Are you a music lover, Billy?"

"Of course."

"Do you like the opera?"

"The what?"

"Opera. Wagner. Puccini."

"No fear."

"Not your line?"

"Not my line."

We looked at one another while Billy lit himself a cigarette. He offered me one and I took it. A plane was landing at the Belfast Harbour Airport and I watched it stick rigidly to its landing vector along the shore of Belfast Lough.

"Let me get this straight. Tommy Little came over to see you on Tuesday night at about eight o'clock. He was defusing a potentially serious dispute about who owned the heroin of a dead drug dealer. He stayed here for five minutes and then he left and you never saw him again."

"That's about right," Billy said and again there was that look in his eyes that I didn't quite like. If this was the truth it was not the whole truth.

"What did you do after Tommy left?"

"I played snooker until about twelve and then I went on home."

"Witnesses?"

"Everybody in the club."

"They'd swear on oath that you were the Shah of Iran."

"That they would," Billy laughed.

"How do you feel about queers, Billy?"

"Me personally?"

"Yeah."

"I don't give a fuck. Who cares what people get up to in their own bloody home."

"Very enlightened. What would you do if you found out one of your boys was a queer?"

"You know what we'd do."

"You'd kill him?"

"We'd have to. The higher-ups would demand it."

The drizzle turned to rain.

"Are there any more questions?" Billy asked.

"One or two," I said.

"Then we better go inside."

We went to the stuffy back room. Billy turned off the TV and kicked out his grandfather. He sat behind the desk.

"Shane, get in here!" he called and his young, blond-haired assistant came in. Shane sat down next to Billy, facing us. He was winsome and pretty and annoying and perhaps there was even a shade of Jupiter and Gannymede. Perhaps.

"You are?" I asked Shane.

"Shane Davidson. Davidson with a D."

"Sergeant Duffy wants to know if Tuesday night was the last we ever saw of Tommy Little?" Billy said.

Shane's eyes narrowed. "Of course it is," Shane said, looking at Billy with a glance I could not interpret. Matty saw it too and gave me the minutest nod.

"Holy shit, lads! You didn't have a falling out with Tommy and fucking shoot him, did you?"

"Don't you read the papers, mate? Tommy was killed by some nutcase doing in queers. Although I say nutcase, but the truth is, I'll bet you most people think he's doing everybody a favor," Billy said.

"And besides, we know better than to fuck with Tommy Little!" Shane said.

"Aye, we do. The Great White Chiefs would kill us before the IRA ever did," Billy added.

"What exactly did Tommy do for the IRA? What was his position?" I asked

Billy laughed and slapped his hand on the table. "Yon boy's been dead four days and you don't even know who he was? Christ, are you the Keystone Cops or what?"

"What was Tommy Little's job for the IRA?" I insisted.

"You really don't know?" Shane said again, sending his boss into hysterics.

"No."

"Tommy Little was the head of the FRU," Billy said.

"Tommy Little was the head of the IRA's Force Research Unit?" I said incredulously.

"That he was."

"That's an Army Council position," Matty gasped.

"So, you can see why anybody who killed Tommy would have to be a nutcase, wouldn't you?" Billy said.

Yeah I could.

All the other angles had collapsed.

Tommy Little was the head of the FRU—the IRA's internal security unit. The FRU was responsible for uncovering police informers and MI5 moles within the organization. They were the most feared group of men on the island of Ireland. Scarier than any of the paramilitaries, Special Branch or the SAS.

When the IRA got you, they'd kneecap you or shoot you in the head. When the FRU got you and they suspected that you were a police informer or a double agent the fun could last for a week. Torture with arc-welding gear, with hammers, drills, acid, electric shocks. Castration. Blinding. Dismemberment. These were the methods the FRU used to get at the truth.

No one but a lunatic would ever fuck with the FRU's big cheese.

The blow back would be swift and terrible.

You'd have to be crazy.

I got to my feet. Matty stood next to me.

"Here, gents, take your poison," Billy said offering us half a dozen cartons of cigarettes each.

I shook my head.

"Go on, lads, they've called a dock strike. Ciggies are all gonna be out of the shops by morning," Billy said.

"Fuck it," I said in a daze and took a carton of Marlboro. Matty took one of Benson and Hedges and we got a case of Virginia pipe tobacco for McCrabban. We walked out of the office into the wet battleship-grey Rathcoole afternoon. "Back in the Rover?" Matty asked.

"Let's walk for a bit, clear our heads."

We walked among the drab tenements and crumbling 1960s tower blocks. Everything was achromatic and in ruins less than twenty years after it had gone up. A massive social engineering experiment gone horibly wrong. "Where do you think the women are, Matty?" I asked. "It's all men, here. No women, no kids."

"Inside washing the clothes, hitting the weans, cooking the chips."

I stopped at a twenty-foot-tall graffito: Look Out, Look Out, The Rathcoole KAI's About. "What does KAI stand for?"

"Kill All Irish."

"Kill All Irish. Nice. Rathcoole is from the Irish Rath Cuile meaning 'in the center of the ring fort.' Once this was a royal palace for the kings of the Ulaidh. Now look at it. Concrete towers and row upon row of soulless terraces."

"If it was a palace these scumbags would still have messed it up, believe me," Matty said.

I looked at my watch. It was four o'clock. Where had the day gone? "We should go home," Matty said. "If Tommy Little was Force Research Unit, The Angel of Death wouldn't go near him with a ten-foot pole. This is obviously the wrong angle. These boys are not that stupid."

"Aye, I know. All right. All right, we'll get back in the Rover. We'll head off, but I want you to drop me round the corner away from the prying eyes in the tower blocks."

"What are you going to do?"

"I am going to go round the back of those derelict tenements and I'm going to sneak into one of them and wait for our boy to come out."

"Billy?"

"I'm going to wait for Billy's wee friend, Shane. I think he knows something he's not saying."

"Everybody in Belfast knows something they're not saying."

We got in the Land Rover. Matty drove me to a doomed basketball court that was now a rubbish dump filled with skips, shopping trolleys, prams and the odd burnt-out, hijacked car. I got out of the passenger side and put my gun in my raincoat pocket. "You be careful, Sean, ok?" Matty said.

"Careful is my middle name. That and Aloysius but you don't need to tell anybody that."

He smiled and I walked through the swirling circles of garbage to the abandoned terrace.

13: HE KISSED ME AND IT FELT LIKE A HIT

I waited in a gutted living room among the rats and human excrement, drug paraphernalia and dead pigeons. Outside the rain was pouring so hard it was as if hate rather than gravity was sucking it down to Rathcoole.

I had a perfect view of the snooker hall and the sad little strip mall. Only the bookie was doing any business but that wasn't surprising with the Derby coming up and the beautiful bay stallion Shergar, even at 1-6, a horse to bet your pension on.

Evening.

The scene at the snooker hall began to wind down and Billy drove off in his Merc at seven on the zero zero. Shane came out at 7:01 with a leather jacket over his head in lieu of a raincoat. I turned up the collar on my mac and followed him at a discreet distance, into the estate, along the Doagh Road, through Abbots Cross (the very place where Bobby Sands had been born) past Whiteabbey Hospital and down the Station Road.

He stopped at the station bar for a drink. I followed him inside and got a whiskey against the cold. The local news was on. The murder of Tommy Little and Andrew Young was now the sixth lead. No one was interested. I wondered if that would piss off our killer. Perhaps he'd go bigger or perhaps he'd take his game over the water where it would play better. The story ran for less than a minute and that included another incendiary remark from Councilor George Seawright who said that homosexuals should be shipped to an island in the Atlantic and left to starve to death.

Shane finished his drink, bought a book of matches and left by the side door.

I waited ten beats and went out after him.

Several times Shane looked back to see if he was being tailed, but he never checked the far side of the street, two hundred yards behind. There were many ways to shake a tail and he knew none of them. "Who do you think's after you, Shane, my lad? Or is just the dark you're afeared of?"

He turned left on the Shore Road and walked a good quarter of a mile to Loughshore Park, a pleasant little bit of greenery right on the water. We were nearly at the University of Ulster now but instead of doing the obvious and turning up the Jordanstown Road or going straight on, he cut across the busy Shore Road and went to the public toilets at the park.

I waited for him to come back out.

He didn't come back out.

The wind was whipping up the boats in the lough and forcing spray onto the highway. It was freezing and the rain was running down the back of my neck.

I saw that there was an exit to the toilets on the park side so I crossed over the Shore Road and waited under the branches of a small confederacy of white oak trees.

At least with the rain there will be no rioting tonight, I said to myself. And I'll bet that the power workers' wives forced their hubbies to keep the light and heat on too. The minutes ticked past. This is why peelers need a book. A wee paperback to stick in your pocket.

I stood there for a good fifteen minutes. "Has he fallen down the bloody hole?" I muttered. And then I began to have a darker suspicion.

We were on the trail of a killer after all . . .

I took the service revolver out of my raincoat pocket and checked there were six .38 rounds in the cylinder. I stepped out from under the branches and began walking towards the bogs.

I got half way there and saw someone leave the toilets from the Shore Road side and walk briskly to a parked car I hadn't noticed before. A Volkswagen Beetle. I began to run, but he began running too to get out of the rain.

He got in the Beetle and it drove off in the direction of the M5 motorway and the sliproads for Belfast.

"Jesus! You bloody blew it, Duffy!" I cursed myself. You wanted to be dry so you stood under the trees rather than a place where you would be equidistant between both exits. "You bloody idiot!" I said to the rain and the crashing surf.

Didn't even get a license plate, although if it was Shane and Shane's car it would be easy enough to check.

"All right, all right, let's see what you were doing in the bog for the last twenty five minutes," I said, keeping my gun ahead of me as I went inside.

For some reason I'd been expecting a junkie but of course it was a fruit instead.

He was about nineteen or twenty, blue eyes, pale skin, black hair in a sort of Elvis quiff. High cheekbones and his fingernails were lacquered red. He was far too attractive not to be a poofter and he was wearing a leather jacket, jeans and converse high tops—standard rentboy garb.

He looked at the .38 and I put it away.

"Ahh, you're a policeman," he said nonchalantly.

"Well, I ain't your fairy godmother."

He took a step towards me. "Look at you, coming on so tough," he said.

"Aren't you the brave lad? What's your name, son?"

"John Smith. You can call me Johnnie."

He didn't seem at all concerned that I could possibly shoot him or kneecap him. This toilet must be a well-known queer hang-out. I checked the graffiti on the wall: the usual Fuck The Pope, Remember 1690, UVF, UDA, UFF, but not as much of it as you would expect so close to Rathcoole.

"Who was that that was just in here?" I asked.

"His name?"

"Aye, his name."

"I've seen him around, peeler, but I don't know his name. Not really my type."

"What was he doing in here?"

The kid smiled. "You know what he was doing."

"Don't play games with me, pal, I'll fucking slap you round the head."

"Is that how you get your kicks?"

"All right, sunshine, enough of the smart remarks. Spread 'em up against the wall," I said.

"That's not the first time I've heard that tonight."

I pushed his face against the tiles, patted him down and searched him. He had about 100 quid in one of his jacket pockets, a tiny bag of cannabis resin wrapped in cling film in the other. Not enough to get him on a distribution wrap and certainly not worth the hassle of the paperwork.

"Where did you get this?" I asked him.

He didn't reply. I pulled out the .38 again and shoved the barrel against his cheek. "Where did you get it?"

"From him," he said. "The one you were talking about."

I nodded and put the cannabis in my raincoat pocket.

"What did he want from you?" I asked.

The kid turned round and stared at me.

A long searching look. Even in the darkness his eyes were very blue. He took a step closer and moved the revolver with a finger so that it was no longer pointing at him.

"The same thing you want," he said.

He slipped a hand behind my neck, pushed me forward and kissed me on the lips. I pulled back, startled, horrified. He kept the pressure on the back of my head and kissed me again, gently at first and then deep, letting his fingers caress my scalp.

"What the hell are you doing?" I hissed.

"If you want to go, you should go now, copper," he said.

Of course I wanted to go. But I stayed where I was.

He ran his hands under my shirt and over my back.

He looks like a girl was what I told myself. Except that he didn't, not at all.

He explored my mouth with his tongue.

I was confused, guilty, hungry for more.

"I'm not a fairy," I said.

"Shut up and enjoy yourself," he said.

I ran my hand down his spine. I cupped his tight, girlish arse.

I closed my eyes.

Let him kiss me.

Relaxed.

We caught our breaths for a moment.

"Well?" he said and leaned his head against my forehead and grinned.

"This will be something new for my next confessional," I said.

He laughed. "A Catholic boy! How charming."

"I . . . I better go," I muttered.

"Are you sure?"

"Yes."

"Maybe next time then."

"Maybe."

I walked the seven miles back to Carrick along the Shore Road.

It was lashing. I tried to hail a taxi but none of them stopped and every single phone along the route had been vandalized.

I went into the Dobbins and got a pint of Guinness and sat steaming by the fire. I was the only customer. I stared at the flames and the black hearth and the peat logs turning grey and then white.

All the newsagents were closed so I asked Derek behind the bar to sell me some cigarette paper, matches and loose leaf tobacco. I walked to Carrickfergus Castle and found the smugglers steps down to the black lough water. Sheltered by the big eight-hundred-year-old outer castle wall, I took the cigarette paper and crumbled in the tobacco. I removed the cannabis resin from the cellophane, cooked it in the flame of a match and crumbled half of the wad between my thumb and forefinger on top of the tobacco. I stirred it together with my finger and rolled it up.

I lit the end of the spliff and sat there watching the lough traffic and the occasional army helicopter zipping from crisis to crisis. The cannabis was hardcore skunk and I was toasted when I walked across the harbor car park and over the Marine Highway to Laura's apartment.

I knocked on the door. And knocked and knocked.

It had started to storm now and lightning was hitting the conductors on the County Down side of the lough. The rain was cold and horizontal.

She opened the door.

She was wearing an Oriental bathrobe and had a towel wrapped around her wet hair in that mysterious way only women can do.

"What do you want?" she asked.

"I don't know . . . What does anybody want? Heidegger said death is the central fact of life after being. We can't experience our own death but we can fear it."

She was shook her head. "No, Sean, what do you want with me? What are you doing here?"

A loose strand of wet hair unhooked itself from the towel. She looked beautiful like this. "The movies," I said. "The one about the chariot race. Let's go before they firebomb the cinema."

She folded her arms across her chest and sniffed.

"I got your flowers," she said.

"Can I come in?" I asked.

She shook her head but smiled. "Call me. In a day or two," she said and closed the door.

I walked to the police station. The top floor was dark. I checked my desk. A fax from Special Branch answering Matty's intel request: they knew nothing about Freddie Scavanni and they had heard no rumors that Tommy Little was involved with the IRA's Force Research Unit. Geniuses.

I walked back to Coronation Road across the railway lines.

I stopped at Barn Halt. I crossed the tracks to the Belfast side.

Lightning struck the conductor on Kilroot power station's six-hundred-foot chimney.

"Her mother's on the train, looking out the window for Lucy but she doesn't see her. How the fuck does she not see her? A guy in a car saw her just seconds before."

I walked to the little shelter. It was basically just three walls and a roof. You couldn't hide in there.

"Did the fucking aliens take her?" I yelled at the storm.

I stood there getting wet, disgusted at my own denseness.

I went into the shelter and relit the joint. I sat down on the concrete.

The boat train came flying through express from Belfast to Larne.

The boat train. Again. The boat train.

Of course!

The reason her mother didn't see her was because she wasn't going to Belfast. She'd been on the platform all right—the other platform. The guy in the car had seen her waiting, but she'd been waiting on the other side of the tracks. She had lied to her ma. She wasn't going to Belfast, she was going to Larne.

She'd been going to Larne to catch the ferry to Scotland.

The abortion special.

What was it she had said? "I might stay over with some friends, but I'll be back on Christmas morning."

Train to Larne. Ferry to Stranraer. Train to Glasgow. Abortion. Overnight in the hospital. Train to Stranraer. Ferry to Larne. Train to Carrickfergus. Home for Christmas. She'd been planning to get an abortion. But something had happened. She had vanished instead. Hmmmm. I threw the stub of the joint onto the railway tracks and walked home along Taylor's Avenue and the Barn Road.

Despite the downpour the DUP were electioneering in Victoria Estate. Dr. Ian Paisley himself riding atop a coal lorry. "Do not allow the British Government to bow their knee to terrorists! Vote DUP!" Paisley was bellowing in an Old Testament prophet voice. Behind Paisley was Councilor George Seawright, originally from Glasgow and now the most militant and crazy of the DUP's rising stars. There were dozens of DUP security men walking alongside of the coal lorry. And behind them there was another coal lorry piled high with boxes of foodstuffs and milk that were being given out to anyone who wanted one. The boxes were stamped with the words "EEC Surplus Not For Resale."

Bobby Cameron beckoned me over to the lorry. "You like bacon?" he asked.

"Who doesn't?"

"Fucking Muslims and Jews. Here," he said. He offered me a box of German bacon. I shook my head. "Take it," he insisted.

"Ta," I said and grabbed the box. "And Bobby, listen, times are tough so you might want to rethink the rates you've been charging for protection around here."

"Have people been squealing to you?"

"Nobody's been squealing but times are tough."

I left him to it and headed for my house. I put the bacon in the fridge, grabbed a book at random, stuck *Liege and Lief* on the hi-fi, went upstairs, lit the paraffin heater and ran the bath.

I thought about him. About what had just happened. There was no getting away from it. "What the hell have I done?" I said to myself. Was I a fairy? A homo? A queer? Well . . . ?

Unlike those crazy Prods, I needed someone to talk to but there was no one. I lit and crumbled the rest of the cannabis into a tobacco-filled cigarette paper and got in the bath. I smoked the spliff, coasted on the paraffin fumes, and opened the book. It was a volume of German poetry. A birthday gift from an uncle that I'd never opened.

I read Goethe, Schiller, Novalis.

Nach innen geht der geheimnisvolle Weg, the poet said.

Inward goes the way full of mystery.

Indeed.

14: THE APARTMENT

And then … nothing. Twenty-four hours of nothing. Not so unusual in the life of a copper. Action stations, red zone, 100 mph and then zilch. Another reason why you need a good book.

Zilch in our case meant no leads, no further developments, no witnesses, no tips to the CID or the Confidential Telephone. The gay angle was probably hurting us. No one wanted to leave a tip about a homosexual murder. Not everybody in Ulster was George Seawright crazy but this was Northern Ireland in 1981 which was slightly less conservative than, say, Salem in 1692. If they knew anything about such things it probably meant that they were queer too.

Procedure keeps you going. I checked for bombs under my car and drove to work. We tabbed the files, filed the reps. I called up the DMV and found out that Shane drove a VW Beetle. I pestered Special Branch about Tommy Little until a chief super came on the blower to tell me that I was barking up the wrong tree, that the police's intelligence was very good and that if Tommy Little was a player he was a minor actor in the play.

We interviewed Lucy Moore's pals in person and got nothing from them. We examined the Boneybefore postcard and the only prints were mine and the letter carrier. We looked and looked again for any links between the victims but there were none that we could find. We checked for Tommy Little's missing Ford Granada but came up empty. I examined the music scores and played the records. I looked at the "hit list" and asked Crabbie to see if there were any links between the people there. Again none beyond the obvious. The inferences we drew from our inquiries took us down several blind alleys just like in a real labyrinth.

On Tuesday afternoon we got a fax from the coroner's office. Sir David Fitzhughes, the Coroner for East Antrim, had read Dr. Cathcart's pathology report and our notes and had issued a preliminary finding of death by suicide on Lucy Moore. The full inquest would be in November but this preliminary finding was enough to have Brennan breathing down my neck to bin the case.

On the one hand we didn't know where Lucy had been staying since Christmas. On the other hand hiding a pregnant woman wasn't a crime. Not even in Belfast. Brennan wanted my full attention on the murders. The patho said Lucy killed herself, the coroner said Lucy killed herself, the papers said Lucy killed herself.

I wasn't that happy about it. I agreed to suspend the investigation but not close the case. I wrote "Possible suicide" on the file.

I completed my psych profile of the killer. It was standard stuff from the Wrigley-Carmichael index: A white male, 25–45, moderately high IQ, almost certainly an ex-prisoner, and almost certainly a sex offender of some type. We ran the names through the database. We got twenty-three matches but no one who was still around. Every single one of them was living in England, Scotland or further afield. As soon as they got out of prison sex offenders fled Northern Ireland because they knew that sooner or later they would be kneecapped or murdered by a paramilitary chieftain looking to make a name for himself.

In a normal society that's where you'd look for your leads.

But this was not a normal society.

No leads. Brick walls. And then there was Shane. Shane boy was as bent as a five-bob note. Billy and Shane jungled up together? Or was Shane a heroic loner in a murderously intolerant world? If Shane and Tommy Little were having an affair, Shane might have killed him to cover it up. Anything could have happened: lovers' quarrel, fear of exposure, you name it. Sure he talked the talk about incurring the wrath of God from the IRA but in the heat of a fight you don't think of such things.

The problem with Shane was his alibi. After Tommy Little left he said that he played snooker with Billy and the other lads until midnight. They would cover for him as a matter of course.

I thought about the angles. Shane didn't seem like the type who embraced opera and Greek culture, but you never knew, did ya? It would be nice to have a nosey around his place . . .

On Tuesday night Laura and I went to see Chariots of Fire. It was about running. The two British guys won. I had a feeling they might. No one, however, blew up the cinema and there were no bomb scares.

Laura asked me about Heather. I told her part of the truth. A reserve constable who was a little drunk and freaked out after a riot in Belfast had briefly come on to me. She was, I added, married.

"You've every right to see whoever you want, we're not really going out," she said.

"I'm not going to see anybody else," I told her.

I walked her to her apartment door but she wouldn't let me in for a coffee. I didn't mind. She kissed me on the cheek and said something about the weekend.

I said something in reply.

I was distracted.

I was thinking about that other kiss.

Trying to get it the fuck out of my mind.

On the way home from the station I met Sammy, my Marxist barber, walking his bulldog. He told me that I looked depressed. I said that I was. He said that it wasn't surprising because the collapse of capitalism was imminent. He said that this was a reason for celebration, not anxiety, and that I should start listening to Radio Albania on the shortwave.

I went home, made myself a vodka gimlet and found Radio Free Albania. Sammy was right—it did cheer me up. The Americans were denounced, the Russians were denounced, Mao was praised, Comrade Enver Hoxha's achievements at chess, athletics, in research physics, agricultural innovation were all saluted . . .

Wednesday morning: I checked under the car for bombs, drove to the cop shop and sat staring at McCrabban's ugly mug from 9 until 10.

"Crabbie, you want to go up to Belfast with me?"

"What for?"

"Let's go see Scavanni."

"Why?"

"I'd like to get your take on him, Crabbie. I didn't like him and I think he's hiding something."

Crabbie yawned. "Aye, why not? I've just been pretending to work."

We signed out a Land Rover and drove up the Shore Road. We passed the Loughshore Park in Newtownabbey. There was no point telling either McCrabban or Matty about Shane. Not yet. Not until I knew something.

The rain was heavy, the traffic light.

We drove past a fresh bombsite that was, with ruthless efficiency, being bulldozed into a car park. Soon Belfast would be the only city in the world with more parking spaces than cars.

We left Queen's Street RUC and walked through the search gates into the center of town.

"Oi, chief, I'm starving, I had no breakfast this morning, can we get something to eat?" Crabbie said.

"No breakfast?" I said, staring at the ghost of his black eye. "Are you sure everything's sweetness and light at chez McCrabban?"

"The, uh . . . she's been a bit . . . pregnant, you know."

This, I felt, was a major breakthrough in my attempt to get him to open up.

"My treat. Breakfast. Question is where?"

Because of the sky-high insurance rates there were no major chains in Belfast: no McDonald's, no Burger King, no Kentucky Fried Chicken, nothing.

"Anywhere."

We found a greasy spoon off Anne Street and I got the cornflakes. Crabbie got the Ulster fry and I waited while he scarfed: pancakes, potato bread, soda bread, sausages, bacon, egg, black pudding, white pudding—all of it fried in lard. A heart-attack special.

We walked over to the Cornmarket and found Bradbury House.

The painters were in doing the lobby in Mental Hospital Beige.

"Scavanni's in a new Sinn Fein press office up on the second floor," I was explaining when I noticed on the directory that the offices of Councilor George Seawright were on the ground floor.

That was interesting. It was like finding Rommel and Montgomery sharing the same tent.

I pointed it out to Crabbie.

"I've heard rumors about him," McCrabban said.

"About who? Seawright?"

"They say he's tight with the paramilitaries."

"Let's go pay him a visit."

"What for?" Crabbie asked.

"He hates homos, doesn't he? Let's see what he was doing on the night Tommy got himself topped."

"You're reaching, mate," Crabbie said.

"Exactly the sort of thing you do when you have no leads."

I was wearing my black polo neck and leather jacket and Crabbie was in his orange shirt and tie so Seawright's secretary had to be convinced that we were peelers by our warrant cards. She showed us into his office which, like Scavanni's, also overlooked Cornmarket Street where they had hanged the United Irishmen, the last time Protestants and Catholics had ever come together to fight the blah, blah, blah . . .

Unlike Scavanni's digs, however, Seawright's office was adorned by several Union Flags and boxes and boxes of a little DUP pamphlet entitled Proof The Bible Is True. Seawright was a big guy with a mop of greasy hair and thick 1970s glasses. He was wearing a grey checked suit that was a size too small. The Napoleon haircut and the suit gave him a comedic air and in truth he wasn't that funny.

"What can I do for you gentlemen?" he asked after his secretary showed us in.

I told him that we were from Carrick RUC and were investigating the murders of Tommy Little and Andrew Young.

"The two fruits? That guy should get a medal, so he should," he said with a hideous grin.

"Where were you on the night of Tuesday the twelfth?"

"I was in bed with my wife, so I was."

"She'll vouch for that?"

"She better."

"Did you know either Tommy Little or Andrew Young?"

Seawright leaned back in his chair. "Your investigation must be in a sorry way if you've come to question me just because I've said a few things about the queers. I mean, excuse me, officer Duffy, but isn't being queer still illegal in Northern Ireland?"

"Being homosexual isn't, homosexual acts are, but there is an interesting case up before the European Court of Human Rights that—"

"Fucking Europe. The fucking whore of Babylon will bring about the apocalypse. Sixteen years, Sergeant Duffy, 1997. Not 2000, no. The fenians got the calendar wrong. 1997, that's the Millennium. That's when our Lord Jesus Christ will return and cleanse this world of the idolaters and fenians and queers and all the mockers of the holy Bible."

"Any particular day I should keep clear?" I asked him.

"August twenty-ninth," he said immediately. I was a little thrown by that and I glanced at Crabbie and he asked Seawright if any of his followers had been bragging about the murders. Seawright denied that they had.

Seawright's secretary spoke through the intercom: "Councilor, I'm afraid you have another appointment."

Crabbie gave me a "Why are we wasting our time here?" look.

I nodded and got to my feet.

"If any of your followers do feel the urge to hasten the work of the Millennium I hope you'll dissuade them, Councilor Seawright. Murder is a crime too," I said and left my card on his desk.

I picked up one of the Proof The Bible Is True pamphlets and walked out into the reception area. It would be an understatement to say that I was surprised to see Freddie Scavanni talking good-naturedly to Councilor Seawright's secretary. He was wearing a tailored black silk suit with a black shirt and a black tie. Anywhere else you wouldn't have given Freddie a second look but in Northern Ireland terms Scavanni was a bit of a dandy.

"Hello, Freddie," I said cheerfully, "We were just coming to see you. Fancy you hanging out here. With Councilor Seawright of all people. That's interesting isn't it, Detective McCrabban?"

"Very interesting," McCrabban agreed.

"What do you want to see me about?" Scavanni asked, clearly irritated.

"We'll wait for you upstairs and then we'll talk," I said, winked at him and we went up.

Freddie's office was buzzing with earnest young men with beards and bell-bottomed corduroys. The women were in mini-skirts and tight Aran sweaters and looked as if they'd bang you at the drop of a hat if you said you were on the run from the Johnnie Law.

I nodded at Scavanni's secretary and waltzed into his office.

"Don't worry, Freddie's expecting us," I said.

McCrabban lit his pipe and I read Proof The Bible Is True until Freddie came in fifteen minutes later.

"What can I do for you?" he asked, apparently in a better mood.

I passed him across the DUP pamphlet. "Fascinating stuff, Freddie. Your buddy Seawright down there thinks the fossils were placed under the ground by God to test our faith. Is that what you think?"

Freddie took the pamphlet and dropped it in the trash can.

"I don't have time for games. As you can see, we are very busy at the moment."

"What were you doing hanging with George Seawright? Aren't you supposedly mortal enemies or something?"

"Don't be naive, peeler."

I nodded. Yeah. I had been naive. Freddie had something that Seawright didn't. An aura, a charisma, an arrogance. He was relaxed. Too relaxed. Two detectives had come to see him about a murdered man and he didn't even break a sweat. He was cool as a goddamned Irish summer.

When people like Freddie came into a room the gravity changed. You could feel it. Freddie had presence, like Billy Wright and Gerry Adams. Perhaps all players had it. Was that what Freddie was . . . a player?

I thought about it for a heartbeat or two.

"This job is largely a front isn't it?" I suggested.

"What?"

"A front, a cover, a beard."

"What are you talking about?"

"You work for the Force Research Unit too don't you, Freddie?"

McCrabban looked at me in amazement.

"Never heard of them," Freddie said.

"The FRU, the 'nutting squad,' the IRA internal security unit."

"I have no idea what you're going on about," he said with a shake of the head.

"Something's been troubling me, Freddie. Tommy Little was the head of the Force Research Unit. He was coming over to see you the night he was murdered. If I'm an ordinary foot soldier and the head of the FRU is coming to see me I'd be shitting my pants. I'd be on a plane to fucking Indochina. But not you. Why is that, Freddie?"

"I called him. About cars. Remember?"

"The story about the homosexual serial killer didn't break for two full days after Tommy went missing. That's two days in which the IRA knows one fact and one fact only: Tommy Little, the head of their internal security branch, is on his way to see you. Why aren't you dead, Freddie? Why didn't they torture you and kill you?"

He sighed. "I'm assuming these are not rhetorical questions."

They had been twenty minutes ago but they weren't now. If you were setting up a press office why have Councilor Seawright from the DUP in the same building? Surely office space in Belfast wasn't that precious, was it? Why share a building with Seawright? I suppose the real question was why not? What have you got to fear if you're FRU? If you're FRU everybody else better watch out, not you. You certainly don't fear a punk like Seawright.

I smiled, leaned back in the chair and tried another bluff: "I know who you are, Freddie. You're FRU too, aren't you? More than that. You were Tommy Little's deputy, you were the second in command of the FRU."

"Brilliant!" he said and laughed.

"Why was Tommy coming to see you? It crossed my mind that you and Tommy were having an affair. You're a good looking guy, but that can't be it, can it? If you're homosexual you wouldn't still be in this job, would you? There's a purge going on right now to distance the IRA from this nasty business."

"You have quite the imagination, officer. You're clearly wasted in the RUC."

"And Tommy wasn't coming over to brace you, was he? If he was coming over on orders from the IRA Army Council he would have brought an entire team, wouldn't he? Nah, he was coming over to consult you about something. The reason you're not dead, Freddie, is because you're still a valued member of the team, aren't you?"

"Maybe he's the one who's leading the investigation into Tommy Little's death? Maybe he's the one bracing other people?" Crabbie said, jumping on the bandwagon. I liked that and I grinned at him.

"All this, the new job, the new office with the DUP just one floor below. Seawright's UVF isn't he? Seawright's UVF, Billy White is UDA and you're the brand new head of FRU and the new liaison between the loyalist paramilitaries and the IRA," I said.

Freddie folded his hands across his lap and chuckled. "That's a very good story. You boys should turn pro."

"You want to hear a story? How about this? You wanted Tommy's job so you fucking topped him and then you went and shot some random gay guy that you knew about. And you did this because the IRA army are a conservative bunch and they'd buy any old shite about poofters killing each other or a lunatic running around killing homosexuals," I said.

Freddie grinned at me. He looked at McCrabban. "You must have a great time keeping up with him, I'll bet you lads don't even need TV down the station."

"Do you like opera, Freddie?"

"Some."

"Do you play an instrument?" I asked.

"A piano," Scavanni said with an open easy grin. "Where the hell are you going with any of this?"

"What about Greek? Do you know Greek, Freddie?" I asked quietly.

"Ancient Greek?"

"Yes."

"I studied it in school."

"You know the story of Ariadne?"

"The Minotaur, of course."

He didn't deny it. He didn't hum and ha. He just sat there, amused by me. Fifteen seconds went past. His grin widened a little.

I began to think that I was the one lost in the labyrinth.

I closed my eyes and tried to think.

The secretary said: "Mr. Scavanni, the calls are stacked up, if you're through here . . ."

"Gentlemen please, I'm really jam-packed today," Freddie said.

I opened my eyes, got to my feet. "Let's go, Crabbie," I said and, turning to Scavanni, I added, "You and I will be talking again."

"The next time you try and barge in here you better have a warrant, Sergeant Duffy. Some of us have work to do."

I nodded, but did not reply.

We went outside and walked back to Queen's Street police station.

In the cop shop we ate sandwiches and I found their local Special Branch rep and asked him if there was any intel at all on Freddie Scavanni. He pulled the folders. Freddie had a file, of course, but he'd been out of the game for at least six or seven years and had restricted his activity purely to the political side.

"Not a player?"

"Not a player."

In the Land Rover back to Carrick Crabbie put on Downtown Radio and we listened to Kenny Rogers and Dolly Parton. When we got through the roadblocks and army checkpoints McCrabban turned to me in the passenger's seat.

"I'm surprised you're not seasick, Sean," he said.

"Oh, aye? Why's that?"

"After that fishing expedition."

"You're funny."

"No, that was really something."

"You don't think Scavanni's holding out on us?"

"He's definitely holding out on us. But even if he is FRU it means what exactly? We're looking for Tommy Little's killer and if Freddie Scavanni was that man, he'd be dead by now, wouldn't he?"

"You may have a point."

"You want me to drive us home?"

I shook my head. "Let's take this old trawler to Rathcoole and see if we can piss off Billy White and his dashing young assistant Shane the same way we pissed off Freddie."

North Belfast. The Shore Road. The M5 motorway. Rathcoole Estate. All the previous beats: Drizzle, tower blocks, terraces, murals of masked gunmen proudly displaying that icon of the second half of the twentieth century: the AK-47.

Stray dogs. Stray cats. No women. No cars. Rain and oil separating into strange colors and patterns by a process of organic chromatography.

The snooker hall. The back room.

The boxes of ciggies and UDA posters. Billy pouring over a ledger filled with accounts. Shane reading a comic book.

"You again?" Billy said, looking vaguely disappointed.

"What? You thought you'd bought me off with two cartons of cigarettes?"

"I thought you weren't going to bother me since I was so nice as to answer all your questions."

Shane was looking at me over the top of the comic.

Batman.

Do you have a secret identity, Shane my lad? What do you get up to after dark?

"Are you a married man, Billy?" I asked conversationally.

"Aye, two kids."

"Boys? Girls?"

"One of each, Caitlin, two, Ian, four. You want to see pictures?"

"Love to," I said.

We saw the pictures. They'd been taken on a pilgrimage to the site of the Battle of the Boyne in County Meath.

"Charming," I said.

"Lovely," Crabbie added.

"So," I said. "Tommy Little."

"Jesus! Not this again, peeler."

"Aye, this again. And again and again until we are satisfied," Crabbie said, not liking Billy's tone one little bit.

I looked at McCrabban. You run it, mate.

"What time did Tommy come by here last Tuesday?" he asked.

"About eight," Billy said with a sigh.

"Why did he come here?"

Billy looked at Crabbie and then he raised his eyebrows at me. "You can mention the heroin to my colleague," I said. "We're not interested in that."

Billy sighed. "Tommy gave us a couple bags of dope, we chatted about one or two things and then he left. That's it," Billy said.

"What things did you chat about?" McCrabban asked.

Billy shrugged. "He was reassuring us that despite the craziness around the hunger strikes all of our bilateral deals would be intact. He said that there would be a lot of rhetoric from Gerry Adams and Martin McGuinness but underneath it all we would keep to our arrangements regarding territory, rackets and narcotics. It was standard stuff but it was still good to hear."

"The conversation would have taken how long? Ten minutes? In which case he left at ten past eight? Eight fifteen?"

"I don't know, but no later than eight twenty."

"He got in his car and drove straight away?"

Neither man spoke.

McCrabban and I exchanged a look.

"Well?" McCrabban insisted.

"He didn't exactly do that," Billy said.

I felt a little burst of electricity along my spine.

"Go on," I said.

"It wasn't a big deal," Shane said.

The Sphinx speaks. Excellent.

"What wasn't a big deal?" I asked.

"He said he was going to Straid to see someone."

Freddie Scavanni.

"And?"

"Well, it was lashing and I asked him if he could give me a lift," Shane said. "I live in a flat out on the Straid Road."

"You've a car though, don't you, Shane?"

"It was banjaxed."

Convenient.

"So what happened next, Shane?" I asked.

Shane bit his lower lip and shook his head. "Fuck. This is why I didn't even want to mention it. Nothing happened. He gave me a lift. He was in a big hurry. I was at the house five minutes later and then he went on his way."

"This would have been eight thirty?"

"Yeah."

"He gave you a lift and then he drove off?"

"That's it. Like I say, he was really pressed for time."

I let silence sink into the room for thirty seconds or so.

Silence is also a form of conversation.

Billy spoke through his hard man look, Shane through his gaze which never left the floor.

"Why didn't you lads tell me all this the other day?" I asked.

"There was no point complicating things. If we'd told you, you'd have thought we had something to do with it. And we had nothing to do with it. We wouldn't be that buck daft," Billy said.

"And why are you telling us now?" Crabbie asked.

"Shane and I were talking and we wondered what would happen if you found Tommy's car with Shane's fingerprints in it," Billy said. "You might get the wrong idea."

"Or the right idea," I said.

Crabbie didn't know what I knew about Shane. And I wondered for a moment how exactly I could tell him.

"Are you sure Tommy didn't meet with some kind of unfortunate accident when he was here?" Crabbie asked.

Bobby shook his head. "Come on, peeler. Why would we do that? There's no angle in it for us."

"Maybe Detective Constable McCrabban's on the right lines. Maybe it was an accident. Maybe you were showing Tommy your brand new Glock 9mm when . . . boom!"

"Wise the bap!" Billy muttered.

I looked at McCrabban. He shrugged. I stood up. "Are the pair of you going to be here for a while? We might have more questions," I said.

"We'll be here," Billy said.

We went back outside to the Land Rover. While we'd been talking some wee shite had graffitied "SS RUC" on the rear door.

"Oh my God," I said. "If Brennan sees this!"

Crabbie put his hand on my shoulder. "Don't have an eggy fit, Sean. We'll drive past a garage, get some white spirit and clean it off before we get back to Carrick."

"Wee fucking shites!" I yelled at the estate and my voice echoed off all the concrete at right angles.

I checked underneath for a mercury tilt bomb and we climbed in and I called up Matty on the radio. They took forever to get him because he was on the bog.

"Yes?" he said.

"Give me the addresses of Billy White and Shane McAtamney and make it sharpish," I said.

He took his sweet time about it. "18 Queens Parade, Rathcoole and, uhm, number 4, 134 Straid Road, Whiteabbey. Oh, and I've got a bit of news," he said at last.

"What news?"

"Your man, Seawright. Back in his Glasgow days, him and a bunch of welders allegedly beat up a couple of transvestite hookers. Beat them near to death," Matty said.

"Cheers, Matt," I said.

I looked at Crabbie. "What was that you were saying about fishing expeditions?" I added.

"Back to Belfast, talk it over with Seawright?" McCrabban wondered.

I shook my head. "Nah, I don't really see it, mate. He's hardly going to go on the BBC calling for death to the queers if he's actually out killing queers."

"What was it your man on the telly says: the only two things that are infinite are the universe and human stupidity."

"It's a fair point."

"Oi, lads, I'm not done yet!" Matty said over the radio.

"There's more?" I asked.

"There's more."

"Go on then."

"I cross-tabbed all the pervs and kiddie fiddlers that have been released from prison in the last year. The probation office tells me that every one of them has left Northern Ireland except for three. Lad called Jeremy McNight who is in Musgrave Park Hospital with terminal lung cancer, a guy called Andy Templeton who was killed in a house fire. Suspicious house fire, I might add. And finally after a lot of grueling leg work and—"

"Just get on with it."

"One name. Could be our boy. Got four years for homosexual rape. Released two months ago."

"Better not give his name out over the airwaves," I said.

"Of course not! I'm not a total eejit. Give you it back at the station."

"Ok. Good work, mate."

We turned off the radio.

"Where to then, kemosabe?" Crabbie asked.

"Billy's first. 18 Queens Parade. We've got a wee window here."

We drove about half a mile to an end terrace with a big mural of King William crossing the Boyne on the gable wall. It was a modest home. A council house, which made me think that Billy had all his money in a secret bank account—either that or he had lost it all down the bookies like every other medium-level crook. Which reminded me: 100 quid on Shergar for the win even if it meant an overdraft.

We walked along the path and rang the bell. While we were waiting we heard an explosion in Belfast. "Two hundred pounder by the sound of it," Crabbie said.

A woman opened the door. She was an attractive, skinny blonde in a denim skirt and a union jack T-shirt. She had a cigarette dangling out the corner of her mouth, a glass of gin in one hand and a crying baby in the other. I assumed this must be Caitlin.

"Who the fuck are you?" she asked.

"We're the Old Bill," I said.

"He's not in."

"That's why we're here," I said.

We brazened our way inside. I sent Crabbie upstairs to get the gun Billy no doubt kept under his pillow, while I hunted downstairs. The place was filled with boxes of cigarettes, crates of Jameson whiskey and two or three dozen Atari Video Game consoles. I ignored all of this and went to the record collection.

Sinatra, Dean Martin, Buddy Holly, Hank Williams, more Sinatra.

The baby screamed.

The TV blared.

I looked in the laundry basket for bloody clothes and I looked for traces of blood in the washer/dryer. Nothing.

Caitlin followed me with the screaming baby, saying nothing, looking anxious.

I went into the back garden and examined the clothes on the line. No blood-stained items there either.

Back inside. Crabbie came downstairs and showed me the piece, a Saturday Night Special, snub-nosed .38. He was holding it on the end of a pencil. I slipped it into an evidence bag.

"Well take this," I said. "And you might want to give your wee girl there something to eat."

We drove to 134 Straid Road, #4.

It was a small square apartment complex. A dozen flats, each with a little balcony. It could have been nice but for the fact that they'd painted the exterior a kind of sheep-shit brown.

The front door was open and we walked up one flight of steps to #4.

"Now what?" McCrabban said.

"Now this, me old mucker," I said and took out my lock-pick kit.

Crabbie put his hand on my arm.

"Sean, get a grip! We can't break in!"

"I shall note your protest in the log," I said doing an English naval officer's accent.

McCrabban shook his head. In Protestant Ballymena such things were not tolerated. It was one thing to take the occasional carton of ciggies from a paramilitary, but a man's house was sacred.

It was a Yale standard and I had keyed the mechanism in under a minute.

"Don't touch anything," I said.

"I'm not going in," Crabbie said petulantly.

"Yeah, you are."

"No, I'm bloody not."

I flipped on the light switch with a knuckle. A small two-bedroom apartment with a neat two-person leather sofa, bean bags, red-painted walls and several framed posters of boxers: there was Ali versus Frazier back in the glory days; there was Joe Louis versus Max Schmeling at Yankee Stadium.

The apartment had a 22-inch TV, a Betamax video recorder and a dozen tapes: The Godfather, The Sting, Close Encounters of The Third Kind, etc.

Shane had a sensitive side: in perhaps an echo of Katsushika Hokusai's Thirty-six Views of Mount Fuji he had done half a dozen watercolors of Kilroot Power Station. The last two weren't bad although a magenta sunset was somewhat fanciful.

It was the laundry bin and the record collection that I was after.

Laundry first: briefs, T-shirts, a pair of jeans. No blood.

Records next. I put on a pair of latex gloves and looked through them. Shane's tastes were similar to mine: David Bowie, Led Zep, Queen, The Police, Blondie, The Ramones, Floyd, The Stones. What did they say about the pair of us?

"What did you find?" Crabbie asked from outside.

"No classical. No opera," I said.

"I can see his bookcase from here. They're all comics and Enid Blyton. The guy's sub-literate."

"Let's do a thorough shakedown before we jump to any conclusions."

"You do it. I'll keep watch."

I worked the bedroom and the bathroom. I found some grass, a sheet of acid tabs and a couple of body-building magazines.

"Let's get out of here," I said.

We left the .38 at the ballistics lab in Cultra and told them to match it against the slugs on Tommy Little and Andrew Young and then headed for home.

We drove back to Carrick and picked up Matty.

The released perv was one Victor Combs of 41A Milebush Tower, Monkstown. Ex-schoolteacher, currently unemployed. He'd been caught having sex in a park with another man. The other man—a seventeen-year-old—had accused him of rape and the judge had bought it.

It sounded like he'd gotten the shaft but we drove over to see him anyway.

Milebush Tower was another of those shit-colored four-storey concrete blocks of flats that had grown up in the sink estates of Ulster in the '60s and '70s. They were damp, cold and seemingly deliberately unlovely. The day the Northern Ireland Housing Executive gave you your key they probably gave you a suicide information leaflet.

We parked the Land Rover and hoofed it up to 41A.

Mr. Combs was in.

He was wearing a bathrobe and listening to classical music which got our attention.

He was heavy, balding, forty-five, but he looked twenty years older and he walked from the door back to the sofa with a cane.

The flat was as nice as he could make it.

There were books, records and he kept it clean. He had a cat.

I let McCrabban run it while I looked through the books and records.

"Where were you on the night of May twelfth?"

"I was here."

"All night?"

"Yes."

"Can anyone vouch for that?"

"What's this about?"

"Can anyone vouch for the fact that you say you were here all night?"

"Not really, no."

"Do you own a car, Mr. Combs?"

"No."

"Do you know a man called Tommy Little?"

"No."

"Do you know someone called Andrew Young?"

"No. What is this about?"

The records weren't that impressive. Boring collections of classical music done in the early '70s by cheapo German firms. No sheet music.

I looked at Crabbie and he shook his head. Combs certainly didn't look as if he could get too physical with anyone.

"Under the terms of your probation I have the right to search these premises for a firearm. I am exercising that right," I said.

No gun. No contraband. Nothing suspicious.

But there was the fact that he had no alibi.

"Why are you still in Northern Ireland, Mr. Combs? Aren't you afraid that you'll be kneecapped because you're a sex offender?" I asked.

Combs's grey face became greyer. "Let them kneecap me. Let them do anything they want. I don't care. Let them kill me. I didn't do anything wrong and they know it. My life's ruined. Everything's ruined. My family won't speak to me. My friends. Fuck it. Let them come. Let them do their fucking worst."

"I like the defiance. Do you have anything to back it up? A wee pistol maybe?" I asked.

"What did you find?" he asked.

"Nothing."

He nodded. "Who'd sell me a piece anyway?"

"Just about anybody," Matty said.

I sat on the sofa and looked at him. "What happened to you, mate?"

He didn't reply for a long time.

"Love happened," he said at last.

I looked into his strangely pale eyes.

"Go on."

He shook his head. "It was my mistake. I flew too close to the sun."

We took our leave and drove back to Carrick Police Station.

"Big tubby," Matty scoffed. "He flew too close to the bun more like."

Crabbie laughed and then pointed at me.

"Remind Matty about Icarus, why don't you, Sean."

"Icarus was the son of Daedalus who was famous for building the labyrinth before he got famous for building wings that didn't work."

"Coincidence," Matty said.

"Probably," I agreed.

We got to the station. I sent the lads home and I went in and briefed the Chief. Brennan poured me some Jura while he listened to my report.

"Not much progress, eh, Sean?"

"No, sir."

"Well, at the least the nutter hasn't struck again, has he?"

"Not that we know of."

"What else is new?" he asked.

I drank the whiskey. "In my life, sir?"

"In your life, Sean."

"I went to the flicks, saw *Chariots of Fire*."

"Any good?"

"They go for a run along the beach at the Old Course in St. Andrews. I think you'd like that bit, sir."

He yawned. "All right. Sally forth! And take my advice and go to bed early. We'll be needing you before dawn."

"What for?"

He tapped his nose. "Top Secret VIP on her way."

Her could only mean Mrs. Thatcher or the Queen. Either would be bad news.

I went home but I couldn't go to sleep early. Never could. I took some of the EEC bacon, fried it with eggs and potato bread. I ate it in front of the TV. There was a brand new cop show on called *Magnum P.I.* He was a PI. He was called Magnum. Like Serpico he had an impressive moustache. This, I realized, was my problem.

I phoned Laura but she told me that she was just on her way out.

"Who with?"

"A friend."

"What friend?"

"A friend from college."

"Man or woman?"

"Oh, you're impossible!" she said and hung up.

I called an old mate of mine, Jack Pougher, from Special Branch intel. I span him my "Freddie Scavanni is a major player" theory. He'd heard nothing about it. He told me I should stick to detecting. I told him I was shite at that. We discussed cop moustaches and agreed that they were on the way out.

I took a pint glass out of the freezer and made myself a vodka gimlet.

The phone rang. It was ballistics. "This gun did not fire the bullets that killed your homicide victims," some fucking Nigel said in a home-counties accent.

"Are you sure?"

"We can say it with 99 per cent confidence."

I thanked him and hung up the phone. Billy White did not shoot Tommy Little. At least not with that gun. I drank the vodka and thought about the killer. He'd been so quick to get our attention before with postcards and sawn-off limbs and now nothing: no new victims, no new communications. Surely that meant something. But what?

I thought about Dermot McCann, a boy I'd known at St. Malachy's. Dermot had been very sexually adventurous even for 1968 . . . Dermot was now inside doing ten years for bomb making.

I thought about *him* from Loughshore Park. Stopped thinking about him. Got annoyed. I opened the front door and left out the milk bottles. I went back in, stripped down to my jeans and T-shirt, got an oil can from the garden shed and pretended to oil the squeaky front gate. If Mrs. Campbell came out now and did her "Oh, Mr. Duffy, it's such a shame about the Pope" thing I'd lift her over the fence, carry her into the living room and fuck her goddamn brains out.

I oiled the gate. The rain came on. Mrs. Campbell did not come out.

15: THURSDAY, MAY 21, 1981

Tuesday had been a bust. Wednesday had been a bust. Two days of nothing. And then on Thursday all hell broke loose.

4 A.M. CARRICKFERGUS

They didn't phone. Crabbie rang my front-door bell at four in the morning. I was convinced it was an inept terrorist attack and opened the door with my service revolver cocked.

"Don't shoot, it's me," he said.

"Oh."

"Get a move on, Sean. We're meeting the Chief in half an hour."

"Let me make a cup of tea," I murmured.

"No time for tea, the others are waiting in the Land Rover, come on, I'll help you. Lemme get your kit off."

"Don't touch me! Wait in the living room."

I quickly threw on my dress uniform and body armor. "Last night I told a mate in Special Branch my theory about Freddie Scavanni," I yelled from the bathroom.

"What did he say to that?" McCrabban asked.

"He said I was a genius and he sent over the file on Jack the Ripper."

"Have you solved that one too?"

"It was Queen Victoria."

"I knew it all along. Easy to conceal a machete under all that crinoline."

I grabbed my electric razor and the pair of us went outside.

"I cleaned that graffiti off the back of the Rover," Crabbie said.

I had completely forgotten about that. "Thanks, mate," I told him.

"You can go in the front, Sean," Crabbie said. "I can see you're fragile today."

I got in the passenger's seat. Sergeant McCallister was driving, McCrabban, Matty and three reservists were in the back. No one had mentioned the name "Thatcher" yet but this had to be about her.

"We're to rendezvous at Ballyclare at 04:30 hours," McCallister said.

"'04:30 hours?' Is that what he told you? Does he think we're the bloody army?"

4:30 A.M. BALLYCLARE

Brennan was sitting there like Lord Muck in his famous Finn Juhl armchair that he must have transported in the back of the Land Rover. He tapped his watch and grinned at us as we pulled up in front of the Five Corners Public House, which was open and serving Irish coffee to the lads.

The sun was just coming up over the Slieve Gullion and Lough Neagh and if the big line of black clouds to the north would keep away it might be a fine morning. The landlord of the Five Corners passed an Irish coffee into my hands and I took it gratefully. Brennan was enjoying himself, surrounded by his men, in the wee hours, in his full dress uniform and leather gloves.

"Men, we are to proceed to Aldergrove Airport in convoy where we are to meet with the brave boys of Ballyclare RUC and establish a roadblock, in co-operation with units of the British Army, on the Ballyrobin Road in Templepatrick so that an unnamed very important person can drive to Belfast," he said.

"Why doesn't she take a helicopter like everybody else?" McCallister wondered.

"Wrecks her hair, doesn't it," Matty offered.

5 A.M. TEMPLEPATRICK

The army had the whole village sewn up and a brigadier general told Brennan that we were surplus to requirements.

"We were ordered up at four in the morning for this!" Brennan said furiously and after some negotiation we were allowed to set up our three Land Rovers further along the road.

"They're on the way! Attention!" one of the squaddies yelled and the soldiers stiffened. We did not. Instead we fidgeted in our body armor and Crabbie explained to the reserve constables that because this was both out of regular hours and perilous we could claim hardship allowance and danger money at the same time.

At 5:30 a.m. two police motorcycles were the heralds for two fast-moving army Land Rovers, two equally speedy police Land Rovers and two bullet-proofed Jaguars that presumably contained the Prime Minister and her staff.

I didn't see her. All I saw was a blur.

"Was that it?" Matty asked me. Nobody knew the answer and we got back in the Rovers feeling deflated.

Fifteen minutes later on the way back to Carrickfergus we were diverted to young Shane Davidson's muse, the Kilroot Power Station, where there was trouble.

6:10 A.M. KILROOT

Two dozen workers backed by another hundred and fifty men from God knows where had formed an illegal picket line in front of the power plant. The shift change was trying to get in and if they couldn't all the lights in north Belfast and East Antrim would be out, which wouldn't impress Mrs. Thatcher during her news conference about how everything in Ulster was just tickety boo.

We parked the Land Rovers a hundred meters away.

"Machine guns away, lads," Brennan ordered and we advanced with side arms only. In my case this was an easy instruction to obey since my SMG was still back on my hall table in Coronation Road.

"You lads wait here, I'll go talk to the fucking scum," Brennan said with the diplomatic *savoir faire* we had all grown to know and love.

"I'll go with you," Sergeant Burke said and McCallister gave me the nod. I sighed and joined them. We walked to the picketers who were holding up signs that said "Thatcher = Traitor" and "No Deals With Terrorsits [*sic*]."

The headman was frickin Councilor George frickin Seawright who was rapidly becoming the Rosencrantz and Guildenstern of my little drama.

"You have to let the day shift in. This is an illegal picket!" Brennan said in a voice that you could have heard at the top of the power station's six-hundred-foot chimney.

"We will not countenance deals with the blackguards in the H Blocks! Mrs. Thatcher and the British government will know our wrath as the Amalekites knew the wrath of the Lord! Just as the Sodomites have tasted the fruits of their evil ways. Just as the Antichrist in Rome felt the wrath of the Lord's divine justice!" Seawright yelled in his apocalyptic Glaswegian accent.

Chief Inspector Brennan hooked his thumbs under the Velcro straps of his flak jacket. "I just saw Mrs. Thatcher. We were part of the honor guard at the airport and after telling us what a lovely day it was she assured us all to a man that no deal would ever be done with IRA terrorists!"

There was a cheer from some of the picketers. Seawright seemed to waver and Brennan grabbed the initiative. "Ok, lads, you've had your fun, now let these hard-working lads through to do their job!"

"Aye, let them though," someone yelled from the crowd.

I walked over to the first car waiting beyond the picket line.

The driver was a thin, jumpy young man with tissue paper plastered over his shaving cuts.

"Drive in, mate, don't stop and you'll be fine," I told him.

"It's me mother-in-law's car. She'll go ape if they break me windows."

"Didn't I just say you'd be fine? Drive, or I'll bust your bloody windows."

He set off and the others followed behind. And with that the night shift went in and day shift came out and heat and light and power flowed to the citizens of Ulster and for once the Amalekites were triumphant.

7 A.M. CARRICKFERGUS

Back in the RUC station we began hearing rumors that not one but two hunger strikers had been given extreme unction (or as the Proddies insisted upon calling it—the last rites).

Two hunger strikers on the same day. Jesus. Already shops and businesses in Belfast were telling their staff to stay away in anticipation of a massive riot.

Mrs. Thatcher had planned a full day of events but at 8:15 she flew out on an RAF aircraft to London, which could only mean one thing: the rumors were bloody true.

I somehow kept my eyes open until 9:15 and then I walked home, checked under the Beemer for bombs and drove to Ballycarry.

10:30 A.M. BALLYCARRY

A country chapel overlooking Larne Lough and Islandmagee and beyond that the North Channel and the blue, hazy outline of Scotland.

Lucy's Moore's coffin just in front of the font where, presumably, she had been baptized and confirmed.

"Lucy Mary Patricia O'Neill," the Priest said.

They had given her double protection. The mother of God. The patron saint of Ireland. It hadn't helped. About fifty people were crammed into the chapel.

I watched and listened. Prayed.

The service ended in tears.

She was waked at The Harp and Thistle four doors down the street. I went there and took a cup of tea and a sandwich and sat by myself.

I wasn't going to impose. This wasn't the appropriate venue. Claire, the sister, came to me. I didn't go to Claire.

"You're the peeler?" she asked.

I nodded.

"Let's talk outside."

We walked round the back of the pub. Sheep fields and Larne Lough and the North Channel and Scotland again.

"Kill for a ciggie," she said.

I gave her one of mine and lit it for her.

She was a chubby, attractive lass, about thirty, with dirty-blonde hair in a Lady Di haircut.

She pointed back at the chapel. "We had to get special dispensation because of the suicide thing."

I knew what she meant.

We smoked and didn't say anything.

"Go on, ask the questions you've been asking everyone else," she said.

"Did she ever confide in you about the baby? Make you promise not to tell your parents?"

"Nope. We weren't that close. Big age gap. But still, a thing like that . . ."

"After she went away did she ever call you?"

"No."

"When was the last time you got any communication from her?"

"About a month ago. A wee letter. More of a note really. Posted in the north. I looked at it yesterday. There were a few others before that. They don't really tell you anything except that she was alive."

"She never mentioned that she was pregnant in any of them?" I asked.

"Not once. I still can't really believe that."

"She was pregnant. And she did give birth."

"Then why? Why would she kill herself?" Claire said.

"I don't know. I'd like to see those letters, especially the later ones. When you get back to Dublin, you couldn't send them on to me at Carrickfergus RUC?"

"Of course . . . I don't think they'll help you though. There was nothing odd in any of them. Except of course that the whole thing was odd. Running off. Running off to the Republic. And why wouldn't she mention that she was up the spout? To me? Her sister?"

"Because she knew she was going to have to give the baby away. She wasn't going to have the abortion, but for some reason she couldn't keep the baby."

"What reason?"

"I don't know."

We finished our cigarettes.

Below us, on the Irish Sea, a tanker was chugging out of Larne Harbour heading for Glasgow, leaving a scarlet line of filth in its wake.

"She ever talk to you about labyrinths?"

"Labyrinths? No."

"Opera? Rossini, Offenbach?"

"No."

She looked at me and gave a half sort of smile. "You don't believe she killed herself, do you?"

I thought about my answer for a long time.

"No," I said. "I don't."

12 NOON. THE CITY OF BELFAST CREMATORIUM, ROSEWOOD CEMETERY, EAST BELFAST

Rows of neat, well-tended graves, gravel paths, trees. Signs of trouble already over the Lagan in the west and north of the city. Smoke curling from a dozen hijacked cars. Army helicopters hovering over potential foci and already that *atmosphere* that you only ever find in cities on the brink . . .

I had never been to the crematorium before. Didn't even know it existed. A worker told me that in England the majority of people now got cremated whereas here they barely got one "customer" per day.

Despite his years of long service Tommy Little had exactly three people at his funeral: me, Walter and a venerable priest that Walter had dug up from somewhere. Not a single gentleman or lady of the press, which was surprising given the sensational nature of Tommy's death.

The service was brief. The priest mumbled the words.

I watched as the simple pine coffin made its way through a hole in the wall into the fire.

The priest shook Walter's hand.

And that was that.

The priest nodded as he walked past me and then shuffled out quickly, rushing to get home before the riot started.

Walter stared after the coffin for a moment or two and then turned. He smiled when he saw me. I stood up and offered him my hand.

"I'm sorry for your loss," I said.

"Thank you," he said, shaking my hand.

We walked outside.

"You couldn't give me a lift to a train station, could you?" he asked.

"I can take you to Carrick station if you want."

"Ta."

I drove the long way back, avoiding the city center completely, taking Balmoral Avenue and Stockman's Lane which were in the leafy, comparatively well-off southern suburbs. At Uni I had not only learned that Belfast rioters hated rain but also any neighborhood that was close to a golf course.

Still we had to drive around hijacked cars and a jack-knifed bus.

I stuck on the radio. The BBC were confirming the bad news. Raymond McCreesh and Patsy O'Hara were either both dead or dying. I didn't know McCreesh but O'Hara was the INLA commander in The Maze so those boys would definitely put on a big show of force in Belfast and even more so in Derry where O'Hara was from.

I turned off the set. Aye. It was going to be bad.

"Why did you come today?" Walter asked. "Hardly to pay your respects."

"Hardly. How many men do you think Tommy killed? I mean, personally."

Walter nodded and we drove in silence while I rummaged in the cassette box.

"What's your feeling about The Kinks?"

"The usual love-hate."

"Look for something else then. I need to keep my eyes on the road."

Eventually he stuck in Bessie Smith which was a nice soundtrack to the unfolding Belfast tragedy.

We avoided the worst of the trouble and I pulled in at Carrick railway station.

"Thank you," Walter said.

He opened the car door but didn't get out.

"So," he said. "Do you have any leads?"

I shook my head. "Not really, but I did learn something today. If somebody wanted to kill Tommy, mixing him up with a homosexual serial killer was a smart move. Tommy's the head of the IRA's internal security wing and not a single comrade shows up? He's being wiped from history commie style."

Walter nodded.

We stared at one another. I was waiting for it.

Waiting...

"Do you know Cicero?" I asked.

"They beat him into us in school," he said.

"Us too. Father Faul made us read his murder trials. His defenses of accused killers. Cicero would always start his orations by asking cui bono? Who benefits? So I've been wondering who benefits from Tommy's death?"

"You tell me," he said.

"Let me run a few ideas past you. Tommy's the head of the Force Research Unit and if he dies there are many current FRU investigations that would get suspended. That might buy someone some time."

Walter shrugged. "What else are you thinking?"

"A rival? Tommy had to have made many enemies and rivals at the top."

"They wouldn't dare."

"The people he interrogated, over the years. Important people. They could hold a grudge."

"Perhaps."

Now the time for my ace . . . "And then there's Freddie Scavanni, isn't there? Tommy dies and Freddie Scavanni moves into Tommy's place."

He nodded and crucially did not deny that Freddie was next in line.

"But if Tommy Little died when he was on his way over to see Freddie, wouldn't that set off all the alarm bells in the world? Wouldn't Freddie get the full Spanish Inquisition from the FRU and the IRA?" I said, airing my doubts as much as asking him.

He sighed. "That's why it can't have been Freddie."

"Do me a favor, Walter, tell me again about that phone call Tommy got the night he was killed."

"He got the phone call. He talked. He hung up. He was on his way out anyway, but . . . I don't know . . . maybe the phone call gave him an added urgency."

"What precisely did he say to you?"

"He said that he had to, let me think . . . he had to 'see Billy White and then he had to take care of some business with Freddie.' Yeah, that's it."

I flipped open my notebook and skipped back through the pages. "Previously you said Tommy told you he was going to 'take care of some business with Billy and then go see Freddie.' Which was it? It's important, Walter."

He thought for a moment.

"I don't remember. It wasn't important at the time. I didn't know then that it was the last thing I would ever hear him say."

"You'll let me know if anything else occurs to you?"

He nodded, got out of the car and went to catch the train.

2 P.M. CARRICKFERGUS

I was reading the killer's postcard to me and making no headway with it when the CID phone rang. Daedalus—inventor—Athenian—labyrinth—mirrors—bull worship—Crete—Poseidon. Ring. Ring. Ring. Ring. Ring. Ring. Ring.

"Will somebody please get that?"

Matty was in the bog again, Crabbie was still out at lunch.

I picked up the phone. "Hello, I'd like to speak to Sergeant Duffy, please," a Dublin-accented voice said.

"This is Sergeant Duffy."

"Sergeant Duffy, this is Tony O'Rourke from the Sunday World. We've just received a letter on a sheet of A4 here in our Dundalk offices. It's a hit list. It says above it, 'Queers who will die soon.' There's half a dozen names. The first two, Tommy Little and Andrew Young, have been crossed out. The others are all prominent people in Northern Ireland. We've photocopied the note and sent the original to the Dundalk peelers."

"Ok," I said.

"Listen, we're going to run the list and the story about the killer in this Sunday's paper and we were wondering if you had any comment."

"Wait a minute! You can't run that. You'll be putting those people's lives in danger."

"You've seen it then?"

"Yes. He sent it to us too," I admitted.

"We're publishing the list, Sergeant, it's newsworthy. We just wanted to know if you had any comment."

"You will be putting those people's lives in jeopardy! Let me speak to your editor."

"I am the editor, Sergeant. Look, we already know from our sources that the people on the list are getting Special Branch protection. We're endangering no one."

"You can't publish it! It's dangerous and it's libelous."

"It's not libelous to publish a list of alleged homosexuals."

"You can't do this, Mr. O'Rourke, it's completely irresponsible. I don't want to have to threaten you—"

"I'd love to hear you threaten me, Sergeant."

"Come on, Tony, please. Surely you can see that this is completely the wrong thing to do."

"Ask me that on Monday when our circulation has doubled."

"Don't you see that he's using you?"

"So you've no official comment then?"

"No. Of course not."

"All right then," he said and hung up.

I ran into Brennan's office and told him. He hit the roof.

"How could you let this happen?" he yelled.

"The killer must have sent them his list. We've got to stop them publishing it. We've got to take out an injunction."

"They're based in the Republic, right?"

"Yes."

"How in the hell could we can get an Irish court to issue an injunction restricting prior publication?"

"I don't know but we have to. You have to make some phone calls, sir!"

Brennan nodded and dismissed me with a wave of his hand.

He summoned me back into his office an hour later.

"There's nothing we can do, Duffy. They're publishing," he said.

"How can they—"

He held up a hand. "Don't speak. Don't say a fucking word. There's nothing we can do. Sit down, Duffy."

I sat. "Sir?"

"What progress are you making finding this guy?"

I cleared my throat. "Well, like I say in my report, I've interviewed Freddie Scavanni and Billy White and I've talked to Walter Hays and uhm . . ."

"Were you in Ballycarry this morning?"

"Yes, sir."

"What were you doing there?"

"I was at Lucy Moore's funeral."

"Why?"

"I don't know. I thought maybe I would talk to her parents or her sister or—"

"Why are you going to the funeral of a suicide in the middle of a double homicide investigation?"

"Sir, I—"

"You complain about a lack of resources and having to do riot duty and how precious your time is and you're off at a wake for some dead wee lassie who got herself knocked up and whose husband is an IRA hunger striker?"

I had no answer to that.

"You're in over your head, aren't you, Duffy?"

"No sir, I don't think so, sir."

"You know the Chief Constable's office is involved now, don't you? The Chief Constable's breathing down my neck!"

"I'm sorry, sir, I've been doing my best."

"Your best clearly isn't bloody good enough, is it? The Chief Constable!"

His eyes were blazing and his face heart-attack pink.

"Sir, I—"

"Get out of my office!"

I slunk out with my arse kicked, almost literally.

At four the entire station was called out to go up to Belfast on riot duty. It was going to be a big one. "But you and your team can stay here, Sergeant Duffy, you're busy! You've got work to do!" Brennan said with childish sarcasm.

The station emptied out.

At five we began hearing the rumble of controlled explosions and the kick of plastic bullet guns.

Dusk.

Incendiary-device fires. Searchlights from army helicopters. Confused reports of trouble on the BBC.

I sent the lads home.

I put on the news. Yup, it was a bad one.

I stared at the killer's note and our accumulated evidence.

We had nothing.

I reread the case notes three times until I was sick looking at them and then I went out to my Beemer and drove to Rathcoole.

9 P.M. RATHCOOLE

Billy pacing the snooker room, barking orders. The riots had spread to north Belfast and chez Billy it was crisis mode: gunfire, bombs, riot control; the concrete bunker back room very April '45.

"This is a bad time. What do you want, peeler?" Billy asked.

"Aye, what do you want?" Shane echoed.

"What happened after Tommy Little left here?" I asked Billy.

"He dropped Shane off and went about his business. He went wherever he was going next," Billy said.

"He never made it there."

"Says who?" Shane said.

"Says Freddie Scavanni, the new head of the IRA's Force Research Unit."

Billy shook his head. "We didn't kill him. We were all hanging out here until midnight. Ask any of the lads. The snooker was on the box and we were hanging out."

Shane was looking at me. There was something other than contempt in his eyes.

He knew that I knew. That he and Tommy had been having an affair.

If I mentioned this in front of Billy, Billy would have him summarily executed. Was it worth the threat? I wondered if Shane had the wherewithal to be my prime suspect? To turn Queen's evidence?

"Let me show you something," I said.

I took out my notebook, drew a labyrinth on a piece of paper and passed the notebook across.

Shane took a gander at it. Not a flicker. Billy took a look. Similar reaction.

Still, they were lying about something. I could feel it in my cop bones.

Was Tommy being followed by a suspicious and jealous Walter? Was Freddie lying? Jesus, there were a million possibilities. I needed to talk to Shane on his lonesome. I needed to arrest and get him away from Billy, bring him down to the station under the bright lights.

My beeper started ringing. "Can I use your phone?" I asked.

"Be my guest," Billy muttered.

I called Carrick station. "You better get back here, Sergeant Duffy. There's been another incident," Sergeant Burke said.

"Where?" I asked.

"The Mount Prospect Pub, Larne. It's a poofter bar."

"When?"

"Ten minutes ago. The details are still coming in."

"I'll be right there."

I put the phone down. Looked at them. "Another attack on homosexuals. In Larne," I said almost to myself.

Billy grinned. "And this time *you're* our alibi."

10 P.M. THE MOUNT PROSPECT PUB, ESSEX STREET, LARNE

Apparently a gay-friendly establishment in a gay-unfriendly town. If port cities are always more cosmopolitan than the hinterland then Larne was either the exception that proved the rule or else the hinterland had quantum tunneled itself all the way to Iran.

Larne announced its credentials on every route in to town with massive murals of an equine King Billy crossing the River Boyne on an almost equine horse. The Mount Prospect Pub was a sad little breeze-block building that said nothing about itself or its clientele on any sign, but which must have been a bit of an open secret.

When I arrived the street was cordoned off and filled with uniformed officers, plain-clothes officers and an army team examining the explosive.

A young copper filled me in on the details. The bomb had been attached to a grille covering the window, IRA fashion. Two pounds of high explosive packed around nails and screws. One man was dead, sixteen seriously injured.

Soldiers were picking up the nails where they had found them and peelers were trampling over the bits of brick and broken glass.

"All right, people! Everybody stop moving! This is a crime scene and you're all marching around like a herd of bloody elephants!"

Everyone stopped and turned to look at me.

"Excuse me, who are you?" a gangly man asked. He was wearing a green gabardine knee-length raincoat, and a brown toupee. He had a moustache, round glasses and a North Down accent but all I could see was that big plank of green.

"I'm Detective Sergeant Duffy. Carrick RUC. This is my investigation," I said.

He pushed his glasses up his nose and shook his head.

"Go back to your work, gentlemen!" he ordered.

"Don't listen to this big lump of snot, I'm the gaffer here," I said and tried to push past him. He put his hand on my shoulder. I grabbed his hand and twisted it back against his wrist.

"Touch me again and I'll shoot that thing off your fucking head," I snarled at him.

"You're not in charge any more, Duffy," the man said in a nasally, civil servanty tone. "You've been superseded."

The beat coppers and the squaddies turned to look at me.

"Who the fuck are you?" I asked.

"I'm Detective Chief Inspector Todd of Special Branch," he said in a loud voice meant to carry to the end of the street and back.

"On who's authority have you—"

"The Chief Constable's authority, Sergeant Duffy, the Chief Constable of the RUC. I'll send an officer over in the morning for your evidence and your report. I expect the full cooperation of you and your team."

I stared at him open mouthed.

"Do you understand, Duffy?"

"Yes," I muttered and—after an insolent pause—added "sir."

There was nothing more for me to do here.

I got in the BMW and drove back to Carrick at 100 mph on the line.

I kept going until I hit Greenisland and then Monkstown.

I went to see Victor Combs.

Up four flights. Screaming wives, screaming children, yelling men.

I knocked on Combs's door.

"Who is it?" he asked.

"Peelers," I said.

He opened the door. He was still in his dressing gown. I walked into the kitchen, opened his fridge, got myself a can of Harp and sat on his sofa.

"Account for your movements from seven o'clock onwards," I said.

He told me the story of the TV shows he'd watched and of a brief phone call to his sick mother.

"What's this about?" he asked.

I finished the beer, crumpled the can, chucked it at the TV set and drove back to Carrick.

I sped up the Tongue Loanen to Walter Hays's. He was half drunk and watching the riots on TV. But again he had no alibi.

I searched the house for musical scores or manual typewriters. Nada on both.

He offered me a martini. I took it. He offered me another. I went out to the Beemer and drove home.

11 P.M. CARRICKFERGUS

I knocked on Laura's door but she didn't answer. I drove back to Coronation Road. Kids had spent the day painting the curbstones red, white and blue.

"You look as if you've had a day of it," Mrs. Campbell said, putting out the milk bottles.

"Who are you talking to?" a man asked from inside the house.

"Our neighbor," she told him and then in a whisper to me, "he's back."

"Haven't met him. Invite him in," the voice said.

"Would you like to come in?" Mrs. Campbell asked.

"No thank you, I better go," I replied.

"What's he say?" Mr. Campbell asked.

"He wants to go home. He hasn't had his tea," Mrs. Campbell said and smiled.

"Nonsense! He'll have tea with us. Sure I'm just sitting down now," Mr. Campbell bellowed.

Mrs. C shook her head at me. "He won't take no for an answer," she whispered.

A very late tea with the Campbells: sausages, fried eggs, chips, beans, fried soda bread.

Mr. Campbell looked like somebody's dangerous uncle who only came down from the hills to whore and drink and take revenge for petty slights. He had a hedge of black hair, a black beard and a crushing handshake. Easily six six, 250.

I ate the food and the kids looked at their father for the first time in a couple of months with a mixture of awe, excitement and terror. For this household, tea, especially tea at eleven o'clock, was a time for eating not talking. When we were nearly done Mr. Campbell asked me my team. I told him Liverpool. He seemed satisfied with that. One of the kids asked me my favorite color. I told him it was a tie between red and blue. That also elicited murmurs of approval.

I finished up, thanked the Campbells, went next door, turned on the midnight news. The riot was still going on. The cops had lost control of the situation and the army had been called in. Eighteen police officers had been injured by petrol bombs. Fifty cars had been hijacked and set alight. Eighty-eight plastic bullets had been fired. A helicopter had been forced down by gunshots. A paint factory had been set on fire.

In other news: Mrs. Thatcher had paid a brief visit to the City Hospital in Belfast this morning; Courtaulds were closing down their remaining factories in Northern Ireland putting five hundred people out of work; Harland and Wolff were laying off twelve hundred welders for an indefinite period; a "gay bar" had been attacked in Larne ...

16: PATTERNS

Victoria Estate opened her eyes in the morning light. Birdsong. A whistling milkman. The sound of kids throwing milk bottles at brick walls. I went downstairs. Through the living-room window I could see children kicking around a football. Others were playing hopscotch and hide and seek while women with curlers in their hair chatted across the fences.

Lou Reed was on the radio, singing "Sweet Jane."

Coffee. Toast. Jeans. Sweater. Trainers.

Car. I checked underneath for bombs.

Not today. I drove along Coronation Road. Kids waved, adults nodded. In a council estate or housing project there is a feeling of intimacy, a feeling of togetherness that perhaps can only be replicated among a ship's crew.

I liked it.

I stopped short.

There was a big plate of wobbly yellow iron placed over a large pothole at the top of Coronation Road. In any other country in the world you just would have driven over it, but here, time and again, coppers had been blown up by explosive devices such as these. You dug a hole in the road, you filled it with C4 and nails, you covered it with a plate of iron to make it look like it had been done by a road crew as a temporary fix. You blew it up by remote. This was Protestant Coronation Road in Protestant Victoria in Protestant Carrickfergus and there was a 99 per cent chance that this really was a temporary fix by a road crew but I wasn't going to drive over it.

I reversed the car and went south along Coronation Road instead.

Chicken? Sure. Alive? Aye.

I went to the newsagents, collected my free papers from Oscar, told him I'd had a word with Bobby Cameron, which, technically, was true. Oscar was selling paint and hardware now to make ends meet. I took the sample sheets of every shade of blue and drove to the barracks.

Normally I was the first one in but this morning Brennan was waiting for me.

He pointed to his office and when I had sat down, he got up from behind the desk and closed the door. He offered me a whiskey.

"Too early for me, sir," I said.

He poured himself one.

"So," he said.

"So," I agreed.

"I sent off the files, case notes and the physical evidence this morning, but Chief Inspector Todd would appreciate a full report from you," Brennan said.

"I'll get working on it straight away," I said with a neutral tone.

Brennan sipped his whiskey. "Apparently there was some kind of incident last night in Larne?" Brennan asked.

"Sir?"

"Todd says that you yelled at him."

"That's not my recollection, sir," I said.

"You had a week, son. A week is a fucking geologic era in a murder investigation. You had a week and you turned up nothing. You haven't had one person in here for questioning. Face it, Sean. You were in over your head."

"I'm not sure I would categorize it quite that way, sir."

"The killer made a monkey out of you. Sending you postcards, sending you on wild-goose chases up to Belfast to get anonymous notes, writing you codes! That sort of thing doesn't happen in Northern Ireland."

"Neither does a gay serial killer, sir."

"You were being played, son."

"You may be right, sir, in fact I think that the notes, the list of names, the music score, the murders subsequent to Tommy Little's may have been a smokescreen to cover an assassination of a high-ranking IRA operative who—"

Brennan held up his hand. "Save it for your report. It's not your worry any more. Nor mine. It's that most glorious of things now: someone else's problem."

"Yes, sir."

"It's my fault, Sean, I should have reined you in. You're very young. It was my job to supervise you, to mentor you, to get you to take all this in a more deliberate manner. I thought Sergeant McCallister would help, I thought an experienced man like McCrabban would help. It should have been me."

"No, sir, if there's any blame to be apportioned for my handling of this investigation, it's mine alone."

"Detective Chief Inspector Todd is a good man. He worked the Shankill Butchers case. He'll have a couple of inspectors under him and three or four sergeants. An entire forensic team. They'll find this freak and get it sorted in no time at all."

I tried a last desperate throw of the dice. "I thought the point of this, sir, was that in these troubled times resources were at a premium. Surely someone of Detective Chief Inspector Todd's caliber would be best served looking into terrorist-related offenses?"

"Not now that the Chief Constable's taken an interest. Not now that the Secretary of State has been on the blower. Not now that the Sunday World has got involved. This has become big. This has become an embarrassment. It needs to be nipped in the bud."

"In that case, sir, my team could help with—"

"No!" Brennan exclaimed. "No, Sergeant Duffy. DCI Todd has his own team and resources and he doesn't want you cluttering up his investigation. You are not to interview any of the witnesses or interfere with this investigation in any way. Is that understood?"

"Yes, sir."

Clearly Todd not only didn't like me but had utter contempt for the work that I had done so far on this case.

And who knew? Maybe he was right. Maybe I had cocked this whole thing up through lack of experience.

Brennan and I stared at one another.

"You're not being reprimanded or anything. Don't get that idea. This is just a simple reassignment. And in case you're wondering, I did fight for you, Sean. But this thing has just become...The names in the Sunday World...It's just another distraction. You're right. We're stretched very thin here. Very thin indeed. We need to close the book on this nut. And then focus on, you know, preventing a bloody civil war."

"Yes, sir. But I can still help, sir, I've got a lot of ideas."

He coughed and looked uneasy. "I'll be blunt, Sean. Todd was furious at you last night. He wanted me to put you on report. I put him straight on that but he doesn't want you poking your nose in. He wants you to forward all tips and evidence straight to his team at Special Branch."

I nodded. I had heard enough. I had heard enough and I was desperate to get out of here. "Of course...So what do you want me to do now, sir?"

"You're to type up your report on Tommy Little and Andrew Young, fax it off to Todd's team at Special Branch and when that's done... Well, when that's done, you can go back to your work on the Ulster bank fraud. They're all important. Every case."

"Yes, sir."

"And you can stick Matty and Crabbie on those bike thefts from Paddington's Warehouse."

"Yes, sir."

"All right, go. Type that report. Don't mope! And get your bloody hair cut!"

"Yes, sir."

I left the office and took a deep a breath. I sat down at my desk.

Crabbie and Matty were looking at me through the door.

"Do you already know?" I asked them.

Crabbie nodded.

"It's probably for the best," Matty said. "I mean, who wants to be known as the detective who solved the Belfast Queer Murders? It's not like catching the Yorkshire Ripper, is it?"

"No, I suppose it isn't...Listen, lads, I have this report to type up and you two are to get onto that bicycle theft case . . . ach, fuck it, who fancies a pint?"

We retired next door to the Royal Oak, waited until the bar opened, got three pints of Guinness and sat near the fire.

"Seawright was in Larne yesterday," Matty said as he lit up a smoke.

"Tell Todd. You're to forward all tips or information to his team at Special Branch," I said.

"What about the evidence we gained illegally?" Crabbie asked.

"What evidence?"

"Breaking into Shane Davidson's apartment."

"We didn't gain any evidence, except about his really quite good musical tastes."

He had a point though. When I typed my report should I mention the fact that a man I'd had a homosexual dalliance with had implied that Shane also had the occasional homosexual dalliance? Did that mean that Shane was a homosexual? Were Sean and Bobby more than just good friends? Did any of this have a bearing on the case?

On reflection it probably did, but how to broach it?

"I'll tell them. I'll say that I had 'an opportunity to examine Shane Davidson's flat and found nothing of interest.' If he asks me how I'll tell him the stupid wee shite left his door open. Don't worry, I'll leave you out of it, Crabbie."

Crabbie looked hurt. "You don't have to take the fall for me. I'm old enough and ugly enough to look after myself."

"Nobody's taking the fall for anybody. Come, let's drink up."

We swallowed our Guinnesses and went back to the station. I closed my office door and laid out the blue paint strips on my desk. My favorite color is blue.

Klein blue. Sapphire. Persian blue. Midnight blue. Columbia blue. Indigo. I lit a cig. I swam in blue. I tripped on blue.

I sat there for a while and then I swiped the strips off my desk into the wastepaper basket.

I typed up my report mentioning that I had "followed Shane to a public lavatory where suspected homosexual cottaging took place."

My report was nine pages long. I showed it to McCrabban and he thought it was fine. I showed it to Sergeant McCallister and he thought there was a distinct sarcastic tone that I should probably remove.

I faxed it anyway. At lunchtime I saw Todd on BBC Northern Ireland news which was more than I had ever managed to achieve—so perhaps the powers that be were right in firing me.

"His dad's a viscount," Sergeant Burke told me over bangers and mash in the Oak. "He has three older brothers and if they all die and he outlives them he'll become Lord Todd of Ballynure."

"Seems like the sort of cunt who would do precisely that," I muttered.

After lunch I went to get a haircut. Anything but work on that bloody Ulster Bank fraud case. After a murder investigation all other cases were anticlimactic.

Carrick was a goddamn mess.

There were two more TO LET signs in empty shop windows, three stores had been boarded up completely and the library had a notice in the window that said "Book Sale! New, Old, Fiction and Non Fiction! Thousands of Books!" which could not be a good thing.

West Street had two competing street preachers, one of whom was saying "Repent for the millennium is at hand and ye are doomed" but the other felt it was the time to "Rejoice now, for Jesus died that we might live!"

Sammy, as usual, was doing a roaring trade. Of course Friday evening was his busy time. Men getting "a little something for the weekend."

He had three guys lined up in the chairs and another two waiting.

I picked up a paper. The English press was dominated by the Yorkshire Ripper trial. A verdict was expected today.

Sammy looked at me, nodded. "Guilty on all counts," he said. "It just came through on the wireless."

Good. That was one less bastard for us coppers to worry about. When it was my turn in the chair, I ordered a short back and sides. Sammy went to work with the scissors. "You like your music, don't you, Sean? Thought I'd let you know. Town hall. Auction tomorrow morning at nine. The entire stock of CarrickTrax."

"Paul's going out of business?"

"Moving to Australia. Selling everything. Three thousand LPs. It's breaking his heart. Classical. Non-classical. You name it. Rarities. Everything."

"I'll be there," I said.

"Aye, me too. You're not a Beatles fan, are you?"

"No. Not really."

"Are you more of a Stones fan?"

"Aye."

"Well, look, if you don't bid on the Beatles, I won't bid on the Stones. Ok?"

"Ok."

"What about Mozart?"

Like ghouls we split up his collection between us and I wondered exactly how much money I had in the bank. A hundred quid? One fifty? I'd saved up six years pay to buy the house for cash. Still, this was a once-in-a-lifetime opportunity. CarrickTrax was the deepest and best record shop in East Antrim and had been in business forever. The stuff they might have . . .

We moved on to other topics. He told me about the record renting shops in Moscow and then he got to talking about the Red Army choir and finally about his father who had been interned by the Japanese. "Fascinating people, the Japs. They say that death is lighter than a feather but duty is heavier than a mountain . . ."

I had heard the story of his father's experiences in Burma twice already so I changed the subject. "What do you think of yon girl marrying Prince Charles?"

"When I think of that wee lassie in the clutches of that corrupt family of decadent imperialists . . ."

When I left the rain was heavier. I crossed the railway lines at Barn Halt and channeled Lucy Moore again.

"Your mother didn't see you, Lucy, because you were on the Larne side of the tracks waiting for the Larne train to get you to the ferry. Isn't that right? You and your boyfriend were going to Glasgow to get an abortion. But you got cold feet. You decided to have the baby and live with your boyfriend until it was born. Decent enough plan. What went wrong, Lucy?"

What went wrong? I stood there getting soaked. Walked home. Heated soup. Drank vodka and lime. I put on La Bohème again. This time the classic 1956 Sir Thomas Beeching version.

Read the lyrics as I listened. Mimi's solo aria.

"My name is Lucia. But everyone calls me Mimi. I don't know why. Ma quando vien lo sgelo. Il primo sole è mio. When the thaw comes, the sun's first kiss is mine."

I lifted the needle and put it down on the record and played it again. And again. I'd heard it before but this time it struck a nerve. Lucia = Lucy? Was that a stretch? Could Lucy Moore's death have something to do with the murders of Tommy Little, Andrew Young and the others? A deliberate or even a subconscious link?

I listened to the record over and over, getting drunker and drunker. At midnight I played Orpheus in the Underworld. I began to see patterns there too. Eurydice is a daughter of Apollo, the lord of light. Lucia means light. The more I listened I began to see links everywhere, in everything. In Mozart, in Schubert, in Bowie.

Human beings are pattern-seeking animals. It's part of our DNA. That's why conspiracy theories and gods are so popular: we always look for the wider, bigger explanations for things.

The more I delved the clearer it all became. DC Todd was in on it. Brennan was in on it. It was the masons. It was the Hermetic Order of the Golden Dawn. Yeats was in on it. All the crazy Prods were in on it. I drank so much vodka that I made myself sick. I kept on drinking. The one smart thing I did was unplug the phone lest I call Laura or my ma. I climbed upstairs and hugged the toilet. Alcohol poisoning. Pathetic. What was I? Sixteen? I began to cry. Eventually the power went off and I closed my eyes and fell asleep dry heaving.

17: ARIADNE'S THREAD

I woke on the bathroom floor sometime after first light. I was a sorry spectacle in the mirror, and the house was worse.

I put on the Ramones, cleaned up the vomit, had a cold shower, brushed my teeth, made a Nescafé, drank the coffee, replugged the phone and called Laura.

"You wanna get breakfast and go to an auction?" I asked her.

"I have my clinic in the afternoon."

"This is at nine. Come on. We'll get breakfast at the Old Tech and bid on some records."

The Old Tech. I couldn't face the Ulster fry so I just got a cup of tea instead.

Laura got pancakes.

We talked and read the papers.

The headlines on all the tabs were the same: GUILTY over a picture of Peter Sutcliffe, the Yorkshire Ripper. The broadsheets too were obsessed by the Ripper with his trial and the verdict occupying most of their front pages with a little bit about the hunger strikes. According to The Times, senior figures in the Tory party were speaking about "compromise" and "new ideas" but Thatcher was having none of it; she had come to Ulster to stiffen the resolve of the troops: the lady would not negotiate with terrorists, the lady was not for turning.

Only the local papers, the Irish News and the Newsletter had the attack on the gay pub in Larne.

One dead. Twenty hospitalized.

The report was done in a restrained, let's not talk too much about this, style.

The killer had used a tried and true terrorist grille-bomb method. Had Todd seen that? Maybe I should call him?

No.

I shouldn't.

I went to the cashier and asked if she had any aspirin.

She said that she did and I popped a couple and splashed my face in the bathroom and went back to Laura who was reading a fold-out special on Lady Di's wedding plans from the Daily Mail.

I didn't tease her.

We finished our breakfast and went round to the auction in the town hall.

The place was packed.

Word had got out and the vultures had come in from high and low. Only Paul himself had not come by to watch his valuable records gets sold to the hoi polloi.

I nodded to Sammy.

He nodded back.

I ignored the first few lots which were '30s–'40s Americana.

I bought some '60s Motown and a mint condition, first pressing of Dusty in Memphis for a pound, which was an absolute sin.

It was when we were into the classical section that I noticed our old friend Freddie Scavanni in the audience.

He was buying early Italian stuff with not much competition.

I watched him bid and buy.

He was initially cautious but eventually he lost his patience and jumped on the things he wanted like everybody else. I let Sammy take most of the Mozart. I bought the Schubert.

I bought some knick-knacks too: some anti-static cloths, an oil lamp from Chess Records in the shape of a guitar, Beatles pencil sharpeners.

None of it was terribly interesting and I could see that Laura was bored out her mind. I had spent about ten quid but had gotten enough records that I was going to have trouble getting them home.

"Do you want to head?" I asked her.

She nodded.

I went to the auctioneer's assistant, gave him my lots, paid my money and got my discs. The Dusty in Memphis album turned out to be number eleven of a limited edition signed by Dusty Springfield and Jerry Wexler. Karmically there was no way I could keep it. "Laura, here, this is for you," I said, giving her the album.

We were leaving when I saw that a low-key bidding war was going on between Freddie Scavanni and Sammy.

They were both after a pressing of Richard Strauss's Ariadne auf Naxos by Karl Bohm and the Vienna State Orchestra that had been recorded live for Strauss's eightieth birthday on June 11, 1944, in the presence of many top Nazis. It was a very rare record indeed but the bidding was only going up in twenty-pence increments and now stood at two pounds sixty.

I was disgusted and sad for Paul. I went outside with Laura.

"Do you want to go back to my place for a cup of tea?" she asked.

It was a good idea. I could leave the records at her house and come back for them when I had the car.

We went to her flat and she put the kettle on. I hadn't been there since we'd made love. Nothing had changed. Except spiritually. Emotionally.

I sat in the easy chair and looked at the harbor.

"Thank you so much for this album," she said.

"You're welcome."

"I've never heard her before."

"You're going to love it."

"Why don't you put it on?"

I went to the turntable, cleaned the record with my anti-static cloth and put on the B-side, which begins with the Randy Newman song "Just One Smile."

"You probably shouldn't play this too much, it's very valuable," I told her as Dusty's breathy vocals competed with the heavy strings on what was really a subpar song.

"How do you take your tea again?" she asked.

I didn't answer. It suddenly hit me. Richard Strauss. Ariadne auf Naxos. After they kill the Minotaur in the labyrinth, Ariadne is abandoned by Theseus on the island of Naxos; bewailing her fate, she mourns her lost love and longs for death. Three nymphs, Naiad, Dryad and Echo then announce the arrival of a stranger on the island. Ariadne thinks it's death's ambassador but it is in fact the god Bacchus. He falls in love with Ariadne and promises to set her in the heavens as a constellation.

I remembered the killer and his talk of labyrinths. And here we had Freddie Scavanni bidding on Richard Strauss. Was this a coincidence? He wasn't a stupid man but, my God, there were getting to be a lot of coincidences in this case.

I stood up. "I've got to go to the auction. I won't be long," I yelled. I jogged across the harbor car park to the town hall.

The auction was over now and I found Freddie Scavanni getting help with his purchases. Loading milk crates full of records into the back of a Ford Transit van. Even on a Saturday he was wearing a suit and tie. A rather nice cashmere blue suit. A rather nice silk tie.

"Hello, Freddie," I said.

He squinted his eyes as if trying to recall who I was.

"Sergeant Duffy, Carrick CID," I said.

"Oh yes, of course. I meet so many people, as you can imagine."

"Did you get the Richard Strauss?" I asked.

"No, I was outbid," he said cheerfully. "But I got plenty of other stuff."

"Interesting record that. Ariadne conquers the labyrinth with Theseus but then Theseus shows his gratitude by abandoning her on an island where he leaves her to die."

Scavanni shrugged. "Well ... yes. If that's your thing, sure, great. But with that record it's more the rarity of the recording, isn't it?"

"Why are you in Carrick, Freddie? Do you live around here?"

"You know where I live, Sergeant Duffy. Near Straid."

"Oh, that's right."

I stared at him. His smile began to falter a little.

"Is there something I can help you with, Sergeant?"

"I didn't see you at Tommy Little's funeral."

He shook his head. "No. Too busy."

"I suppose it would have been seen as a distraction. A dilution of the message in this time of great sacrifice, is that it?"

"Perhaps. I don't really go into the politics. I just do as I'm told."

"You didn't go to Lucy Moore's funeral either."

He shook his head. "No. I read about that. We did send along a representative from Sinn Fein."

He looked impatiently at the sky. "Well I suppose I should—" he began.

"Maybe we can help one another," I said.

"How so?"

"As one professional to another, Freddie, you wouldn't mind telling me how the FRU investigation in Tommy's death went? Any suspects? Any leads? We're both after the same thing, aren't we? The killer."

"The FRU?"

"The FRU. The Force Research Unit, the IRA's internal security outfit."

He sighed. "How many times do I have to tell you? I know nothing about the IRA. Nothing at all."

So that's the way he wanted to play it. "Labyrinths, Freddie? *La Bohème*? Who knows about that stuff? Nobody. It's classic misdirection, isn't it? Somebody wanted us to get caught up in the minutiae, to get distracted. So we've all run off like a crazy fox hound on a scent trail."

"I'm afraid I'm not following you at all," he said cheerfully.

"I think you are, Freddie," I said grimly.

"I think you're barmy!" he laughed.

"Do you own an Imperial 55?"

"A what?"

"Can you account for your movements on Thursday night?"

"I can actually, I was at work in Belfast sending out press releases."

"You didn't get a moment to pop down to Larne by any chance, did you?"

"Larne? Why would I go to Larne?"

"To lead the trail away from you. To close the book forever on Tommy Little. He was a queer mixed up in some filthy queer business. Let's forget him and move on."

Freddie shook his head. "I've had enough of this. I'm—"

I took a step a closer to him. "It's a good move, but he's layered the cake too thick, our murderer. He was too clever by half. He's too smart for his own good. Like you, Freddie."

Freddie shook his head. "Excuse me, Sergeant, I have to go," he said and brushed past me.

"Don't think this is over, mate. You know something and by God I'll find out what it is!"

A crowd of bidders, assistants and ringmen were looking at us now.

Freddie gave his shaggy head an embarrassed little shake. "I have no idea what you're talking about, Detective, but you're not going to intimidate me. We've put up with eight hundred years of intimidation by the English and we're not to stand for it any more. That, I promise."

"What are you going to do? Shoot me?" I said.

"If you don't stop bullying me, you'll certainly be hearing from my lawyer," he said, closed the van door and drove off with his purchases.

"Bloody peelers," somebody muttered but when I looked to see who it was everyone hid their faces.

The crowd dispersed and I stood there watching Freddie's car drive along the Marine Highway. I walked back to Laura's. My tea was still warm. She asked me what I'd been doing but I was too embarrassed to tell her. If Crabbie had heard me spout all that he wouldn't have been able to look me in the eye. That wasn't police work. That was frustration. That was a man clutching at straws.

Dusty Springfield was singing an early version of that weird Legrand-Bergman song "Windmills of Your Mind":

The circle it is closing, like a compass on the page,
A curve that's always ending, a silvered metal cage,
No ending or beginning, like an ever turning wheel,
No escape or exit from the way that you must feel . . .

I sipped the tea and nodded in agreement.

18: LIFTED

Days. As Philip Larkin says: days, they come, they wake us, where can we live but days? Friday. Saturday. Sunday. Monday. This particular day was a Tuesday. The mood was black. A policeman in Lurgan had been killed by a mercury tilt bomb under his Mini Cooper. That's what happens when you skip the routine.

"The Chief wants to see you," Carol said as I came in.

I wonder what I've fucked up now, I thought.

I sat down opposite him. "What have I fucked up now?" I said.

He handed me a letter. Scavanni had followed through on his threat. The eejit. It was a boilerplate lawyer's letter. Words like "intimidation" and "harassment."

I read it and handed it back.

"You know that you're off this case, don't you, son?"

"Yes, sir."

"Are you sure you realize that? Am I going to have to explain how the fucking chain of command works around here?"

"No, sir."

"Tell me you're not a maverick, Duffy."

"I'm not, sir."

"Then why were you hassling a senior Sinn Fein press officer, on a Saturday, outside an auction?"

"I ran into him by accident. It was a coincidence. It won't happen again, sir."

"You know what you have, Duffy?"

"What sir?"

"A lean and hungry look, that's what."

He glared at me, shook his head, opened a drawer, took out a packet of cigarettes.

"Only child, aren't you, Duffy?"

"Yes, sir."

"It's been my experience that only children never learn when to keep their fucking traps shut. An older brother would have beat that out of you."

"Yes, sir."

"How are you getting on with the Ulster Bank Fraud?"

"Oh, we solved that easily enough. It was a guy over the water. He didn't think we Micks would have had the wherewithal to check into the offshore deposits."

Brennan sniffed and took a draw on his ciggie. He did not seem particularly jubilant about our success. "What are you working on now?"

"The bicycle thefts."

"Any leads?"

"A couple, sir."

He nodded. "Do me a favor, Duffy?"

"Yes?"

"Stay the hell away from Freddie Scavanni and anybody else who has access to a scary team of barristers, or hit men, ok?"

I nodded. He waved his hand at me. "Be fruitful and multiply."

"Yes, sir."

I was being dismissed but I didn't move.

"I was telling you to fuck off in a jocular manner, Duffy," Brennan said.

"I know that, sir. But I have a question."

"Quickly."

"Have DCI Todd's team made any progress on the homosexual murders? I'm only asking because I've heard nothing. I was taken off the case after a week because I had made no progress and they've had it since Thursday and ..."

"You take things personally, Duffy, that's your trouble. I suppose it's some kind of Catholic thing. Now, please, get out of my office before I bloody kick you out."

"With respect, sir, they've made no progress because they may be looking in the wrong place. The list of names, the attacks. Why hasn't there been an attack since last Thursday? Because he doesn't need to do any more attacks. The scent trail has been sufficiently laid now. We're off and running. I think there won't be any more attacks because—"

"Did you not hear me? Get out of my fucking office!"

I skulked back to my desk. Again my cheeks were burning. I'd always been an A student. A good pupil. House Captain. Deputy Head Boy. I had never so much as been sent to the Principal. This was humiliating. Humiliating and I knew that every mother-fucker in here was looking at me. Constable bloody Price was positively beaming: that's taken the uppity fenian down a peg or two.

At lunchtime I went to see Laura at the hospital but she was busy at her surgery.

From the phone box on Barn Road I called my mum. I told her I was well.

"When are you coming to see us? It's been a month."

"Next weekend, I promise."

"Are you sure you're well? You sound like you've got a bit of cold."

"Nah, nah, I'm fine. Tell Dad I was asking for him."

I turned up the collar on my coat and walked back out into the rain. A car pulled up next to me with a screech of brakes. Mark 2 Jag. Tinted windows. I looked in my raincoat pocket for my service revolver but of course I'd left it at the station.

Billy White opened the rear door and pointed a 9mm at me.

"Let's go for a ride, Duffy," he said.

"You're not going to shoot me in broad daylight," I said.

"Won't I?" he replied, grinning.

I shook my head and took a step backwards. "You don't kidnap peelers from the middle of the street."

"Don't fucking test me. Get in the fucking car," he said.

His eyes were wide and they had a dangerous whiteness to them. I got in the back of the Jaguar. Billy leaned across me and closed the door.

I noticed that Shane was the only person in the car. In the driver's seat. Where was Billy's crew? What was this?

Shane's face was badly bruised. His lip was split. That was the face. The pretty part. What did the rest look like?

I began to panic now. No witnesses. No problems. He wasn't crazy enough to top a copper in the middle of Carrick, was he? The Jaguar centrally locked.

"Drive!" Billy said and Shane took us out onto the Marine Highway.

"What is this?" I said trying to keep my voice level.

"This is just a couple of friends having a chat," Billy said. "A little bird tells me that you've been kicked off the Tommy Little investigation."

I said nothing.

"You've been kicked off the investigation yet you've been slandering young Shane here. You've been telling your bosses that he's been hanging around the toilets in Loughshore Park near Jordanstown. That he's a fucking poofter! Isn't that right?"

So he had seen my report. It had been leaked to him. He had connections with the RUC. But then why wouldn't he? He'd been a copper in Rhodesia, and perhaps dozens of ex-Rhodesian police had joined the RUC.

"You've got no proof and if you fucking repeat that lie you'll be hearing from our solicitors, or worse."

He waggled the gun. Shane stopped the car at the red light at Carrickfergus Castle and my heart beat quickly until he released the central locking.

I got out of the car.

"And then, of course, there's the good lady doctor to consider," Billy said.

"What did you say?"

Billy closed the door, the light went green and the Jaguar drove off. My hands were shaking. I ran to the hospital and sprinted down to Laura's office. She was eating a sandwich.

"Are you ok?"

"Yes. Why?"

"Has anyone been bothering you?"

"No. What's going on?"

I breathed a sigh of relief. Billy was bluffing. For now. "It's probably nothing. Nothing. Everything's fine."

"Are you sure?"

"Can I see you later?"

"Ok," she said, giving me a funny look.

I went back to the station. The duty officer was Sergeant Burke. I typed up an incident report about my ride with Billy and left it in Sergeant Burke's in-tray.

Typing.

I had a bit of a brainwave. I got out my notebook and wrote: "The killer sends us a hit list and a letter and types it flawlessly. Freddie Scavanni would have learned to type in journalism school. Where else did you learn to type? The police! And our friend Billy was in the Rhodesian police for four years..."

Food for thought...

I worked the bike theft case and at five I went to the hospital to meet Laura. "Have dinner with me," I said. "My house, I'm making spaghetti."

"You can make spaghetti?"

"Lived on it for three years at Uni."

"That doesn't sound encouraging, but all right."

I walked her up Coronation Road where she noted the red, white and blue curbs with disapproval. I put on Ray Charles and opened a bottle of Italian red that had been out in the garden shed for a month. I cooked the spaghetti with some Parmesan from the cheesemonger. "Delicious," she said as if she meant it.

I had no appetite. I told her about my ride with Billy.

She was horrified. "How can they just lift you off the street like that? The nerve of them!"

I told her about my pet theory. "Billy and Shane are an item. Shane was seeing Tommy Little on the side. Instead of killing him, Billy has forgiven him. But the rot has to stop here. I had to be threatened with the law and the gun. If the big bugs ever found out that Billy is a queer, minimum he gets kneecapped and exiled and divorced, but more likely they'd just kill him."

"Do you have any proof of this?" she asked.

"None at all," I said with a grin.

We drank the wine. Sufficient time had obviously passed: I didn't need to ask if she wanted to go upstairs. We made love in the double bed.

I lit the paraffin heater and, when the lights went out, the Chess Records guitar shaped oil lamp. We lay in bed. "I can't believe a man pointed a gun right at you in broad daylight," she said.

She clearly had no idea the shit I had to deal with on a daily basis.

"How can you live here, among them?" she asked.

"Among who?"

"The Protestants! We're like Anne Frank and her family up here," she said.

"It's not as bad as all that. They're ok to me."

"For now. And it's a question of class too, isn't it? What's going to happen when you hear one of them get drunk and start knocking his wife about? What are you going to do then?"

"I'll stop it," I said.

"And how do you think they'll treat you after something like that?"

"I don't know."

She shook her head, smiled and kissed my furrowed brow. Her lips were soft and she smelled good.

I kissed between her breasts and I kissed her belly and I kissed her labia and clitoris. She was a woman. I wanted that. I needed that.

We made love until the rain began and the light in the guitar lamp turned yellow, and the bishop on the Chess logo faded and finally guttered out.

19: THE SCARLET LETTER

Letters. Words. Aren't you bored looking at them? Line after line. Page after page. Dream me away from the letters and the words. Dream me away even from logic. Take me to a land of alien typography. Away from Ireland, where there's always a fight, always a duality, never a synthesis. Protestant:Catholic; Green:Orange; Beatles:Stones; Presta valve:Shrader valve. How tedious it all is. How wearying.

One would have to be mad to stay here.

Or indolent. Or masochistic.

What does it matter? What does any of it matter? The girl was dead. Tommy was dead. Andrew was dead. None of it was my business. Truth was something to be debated in philosophy 101.

"Morning," Laura said.

"Morning," I replied and kissed her.

"I'll fix breakfast," she said.

"You don't have to."

"I want to."

None of my clothes were clean so I pulled on my jeans and a battered red New York Dolls sweatshirt that I had picked up in America.

We ate and I looked under the BMW for bombs and I drove Laura to the hospital.

I went to the paper shop, listened to Oscar complain about the paramilitaries, scanned the headlines in the newspapers: The Pope was out of hospital, a dress designer had been picked for Lady Di's wedding, no hunger strikers had died overnight. I rummaged in the glove compartment and found the mix tape I'd made of Ray Charles, Aretha Franklin, Etta James, John Lee Hooker and Howlin Wolf.

I put the windows down and drove up into the country to clear the cobwebs. When I finally got back to Carrick police station Matty and Crabbie were expectantly waiting for me in the CID incident room.

Matty was holding something in his hand.

"News," he said.

"Have we got a break in the bicycle theft case?"

"Better. The letters and postcards Lucy Moore sent to her sister in Dublin."

"What about them?"

"You asked her sister Claire to send you the letters, right?"

I put on latex gloves and took them to the desk by the windows in the CID incident room. Two letters, two generic white postcards and one picture postcard of the Guinness brewery.

"We read through them a couple of times. She only says the blandest things. 'I'm doing well, it rained today, I had toast for breakfast,' that kind of thing," Crabbie said.

"It's as if she had someone looking over her shoulder censoring ever single word," Matty said.

"Here's a typical one," McCrabban said. I picked it up and read it:

Dear Claire,

I hope you are good. I am well. Things are nice here. Don't worry about me. I'm looking after myself. I saw The Horse of The Year Show on TV last night. Your favorite, Eddy Macken was the quare fellow.

That's all for now.

Lucy

"Ok, so why are you so excited?" I asked. "Fingerprints?"

Matty shook his head. "No. Nothing like that. No prints and I checked the stationery, same as the others, nothing special. I ran the letters under the UV light. Nothing. But then I did the same with the envelopes . . . I don't know if you're still interested, Sean, but have a wee gander at this . . ."

He handed me one of the envelopes and a copy of the UV photo.

"In visible light there's nothing on the envelope, but under the UV light you can just see an 'S' in the upper left-hand corner of the envelope."

I was electrified. "How did that get there?"

"In your bog-standard Irish way some diligent person had been writing the return addresses on all the envelopes in a stack. Top left-hand corner, name and address," Matty said.

"Of course they kept the envelopes that Lucy used free of a return address," McCrabban added.

"But whoever was writing the return addresses on the regular envelopes leaned all the way through to the envelope that Lucy used for this letter to her sister. Cheapo paper and a heavy hand. Only the 'S' though. You can just see traces of the rest of the address, but nothing else is legible."

I nodded. "So what do you think we have here, lads?" I asked.

"I think we have the first letter of the name of the person Lucy was staying with. You always do the name first. Name and address in the top left-hand corner, that's what I was taught," Crabbie said.

I rubbed my chin. I wasn't entirely convinced and Crabbie could see that.

"I mean, Sean, it's only the first letter of a first name, but it's still a lead, isn't it?" Crabbie insisted.

"It could be that," I said skeptically.

"Come on, Sean!" Matty said.

"I don't want to piss on your cornflakes, boys, but the imprint of an 'S' in the left-hand corner of an envelope isn't exactly Nathan Leopold's glasses prescription, is it? And I know what the Chief's going to say. He's going to say that this case is closed, isn't he?"

"Do you still think Lucy's death is connected to Tommy Little's?" Crabbie asked.

Of course I had told them my bullshit theory about the line from La Bohème: "My name is Lucia but everyone calls me Mimi" . . . Lucia = Lucy?

I shook my head. "Nah. Lucia, Lucy? I was just spouting off, Crabbie. It's a coincidence," I insisted, but Crabbie looked me in the eyes and he saw that I wanted to be convinced.

"Let's just say for the sake of argument that there's a link between these two cases. These two murders that occurred at approximately the same time, not a million miles away, where does that get us?" Crabbie asked.

"There are two 'S's in the Tommy Little case, aren't there?" Matty said.

"Aye. There are. Freddie Scavanni and Shane Davidson."

The three of us stared at the envelope. Outside rain was lashing the windows. A coal boat was struggling out of Carrick harbor. An ambulance roared by on the Marine Highway.

Crabbie filled his pipe and lit it. "So," he said.

"So," I seconded and lit another ciggie.

"What do we do with this?" Matty asked.

"What can we do?" Crabbie asked.

"I don't know. If I or either of you go near Scavanni or Shane Davidson we'll get a bollocking."

Matty jabbed his finger into the envelope. "But we have something here!"

Suddenly the incident-room door was kicked open. Chief Inspector Brennan was standing there larger than life. Eyes wide, fag end drooping from his mouth. I immediately hid the envelope under a sheet of A4.

"Oi, Sergeant Duffy!" Brennan bellowed.

"Yes, sir?"

"Remember in the dim distant past of yesterday you gave me this big fucking speech about how there wouldn't be any more queer murders? About how the queer angle was only misdirection? A false trail?"

"Yes."

"Well, wise guy, they just found another dead poofter. You're fucking brilliant, aren't ya?"

"Where?"

"Loughshore Park, near Jordanstown. In the bogs. Somebody just called it in."

Loughshore Park.

The toilets.

"Is there a description of the victim?" I asked.

"Young white male, twenty, Elvis quiff, black hair, what's it to you?"

I grabbed my leather jacket and my revolver. I pushed past Brennan. He grabbed at me.

"Where the fuck are you going, mate?"

"Loughshore Park."

"This isn't your case anymore, arsehole!"

I ran down into the car park and reversed the Beemer out of its spot.

I hit 80 on the Shore Road.

I made it to Jordanstown.

Todd was there with his team. Ten officers in all. White boiler suits, photographers, the whole thing. I was impressed.

I showed my warrant card, kept out of Todd's sightline and went down into the bog.

Of course it was him.

He was lying there in the fetal position with his hands duct-taped behind his back.

Billy and Shane had silenced him.

They'd tortured him first to get any information out of him. He'd been stripped and beaten black and blue. This also was a lesson for Shane. A lesson in the way the world worked.

I walked closer to the body.

His face was bloody but there was no blood pool around the corpse. He hadn't been shot.

"How did he die?" I asked one of the forensic officers.

"Very unusual," the nearest FO guy said.

"Oh?"

"Yeah. They taped over his mouth and taped his hands behind his back. They killed him by putting a Speedo nose clip over his nostrils. Swimmers use it to stop water going up their nose."

"So, he suffocated?"

"Yeah, but that's not the unusual bit."

"What's the unusual bit?"

"They cut off his eyelids with a pair of scissors. Don't know why they did that."

"So they could watch him die," I said.

Part of the moral lesson.

Shane was forced to watch the light go out of his eyes.

"What in the name of fuck are you doing here?" DCI Todd said.

"Fuck off," I snapped and pushed him away from me.

"Did youse see that? He fucking pushed me," Todd said.

I made a fist. "I'll fucking do worse if you don't get out of my fucking way!" I said.

I shouldered him aside and went out.

"I'll tell your gaffer about this!" Todd screamed after me. "You'll be giving out parking tickets in Free Derry when I'm done with you!"

I walked to the BMW.

I drove across the four lanes of the Shore Road and up into Rathcoole.

I screamed the Beemer through the estate and hand-braked it to a halt in front of the Rathcoole Loyalists Pool, Snooker and Billiards Hall. I took the police revolver out of my jacket pocket, checked the cylinder, cocked it and stormed inside.

A cocked .38 doesn't feel the same as an unprimed revolver. The frame tightens differently, the trigger is on a hair and this tension is communicated to you and the people around you.

There were a dozen men playing snooker and pool. They looked at me and looked at the gun. Said nothing. Didn't move.

I marched to the cigarette room, kicked in the door.

Shane and Billy were having Chinese for lunch. I swiped the food onto the floor and put the barrel of the .38 in Billy's right eye.

"I'm lifting you. I'm taking you in, fucker!"

"I was expecting you," Billy said, wincing away from the revolver in his face.

"Like fuck you were. Get on your feet!"

"I'm not going anywhere," Billy said.

I shoved the revolver deeper against his eye.

"You're going down, Billy. You killed that boy to cover your tracks. Shane and Tommy were having an affair, weren't they? Shane here can't keep his dick in his fucking pants, can he?"

"You have some imagination, copper," Shane said.

"I'm taking you down too. Separate cells, let's see who cracks first."

"On what charge?" a voice purred behind me in an Anglo-Irish accent.

I kept the gun in Billy's eye but turned to see who was talking. A tall, thin, grey-haired man in a black suit.

"Who the fuck are you?"

"Anthony Blane, QC, Mr. White's barrister. On what charge are you arresting my client, Sergeant Duffy?"

"Murder with malice aforethought."

"What evidence do you have linking my client with such a crime?"

I wracked my brain for a second. "I have motive."

Blane crossed the little room. "Put the gun away, Sergeant, before someone gets hurt," he said.

I wanted to squeeze the trigger. I wanted to wipe the smile off Billy's fat fucking face.

I closed my eyes.

I could see blood.

Words.

Letters.

Typography.

I lifted the revolver from Billy's eye, disarmed it and put it in my pocket.

"Please show me your warrant for entry into this private room and please tell me your grounds for suspecting my client of murder. When I talk to the Chief Constable this evening, I'll want to have all the facts before me."

Shane was laughing now. Billy too. Pistol-whip the pair of them. Kill all three of them. Shane. Billy. Mr. Tony Blane, QC, mob lawyer to the scum of the earth.

I bit my lip. Shook my head.

"Aye, I thought so," Shane said.

I slapped his face. Billy was on my back in a second. He rugby-tackled me to the ground and we tumbled out into the snooker hall.

One of the goons raised a pool cue and smacked it down towards my head.

I got my wrist up just in time and the cue smashed into two pieces.

I scrambled to my feet. There were half a dozen guns pointing at my chest.

Billy got up. Still grinning. Still laughing. It drove me mental.

"Yak it up, Billy boy. I'll find the proof. I'll muddy the fucking waters. You and Tommy Little. You and Shane! A pair of benders? How will the higher-ups like that? I'll fucking dig until I find something! And then you'll be toast!"

Billy looked around the room at his men. Some of them wanted to know what I was talking about.

"Empty threats!" he said. "He's spouting off. It's all bollocks, so it is."

"We'll see! We'll fucking see!" I screamed and stormed out to the Beemer.

I put it into gear. I drove. Someone threw a milk carton onto me from one of the tower blocks. It smashed over the windscreen scaring me shitless.

"Shite!" I yelled. "Shite! Shite! Shite!"

The Shore Road. Traffic. My wrist was banjaxed. Hurt like a bastard. And my beeper ringing so insistently that I finally had to turn it off. Whoever it was, I didn't want to know.

By the time I got to Carrick my wrist was agony. "Might as well go to the hospital," I said.

I got the end of Laura's afternoon clinic. "Police business?" Hattie Jacques asked.

"This time I'm a customer."

Laura saw me in her surgery. "What happened to you?"

I told her the truth. She was appalled. She gave me an x-ray and it turned out that there was a micro-fracture in the ulna.

"I'm afraid there's very little we can do about that," she said.

"It hurts like hell," I said.

"I'll prescribe anti-inflammatories and codeine."

We got the medicine and went back to Coronation Road. She drove the Beemer through the biblical rain. I self-medicated with vodka until the codeine finally kicked in. We ate the rest of the spaghetti and lit the fire and listened to Etta James.

She had news. Good news, she said, but I saw it differently. She told me that her parents were buying her a house. She was leaving Carrick but she wouldn't be too far away.

"Leaving? Where will you be?" I asked groggily.

"Five minutes up the road in Straid. It's my great-aunt's house. We're buying it from her. It's lovely. It backs onto Woodburn Forest. She wants to move to Tenerife. Have you ever been to Tenerife? Black sand. And the mountain with snow on it even in summer. You go up to the top—they give you hot chocolate with brandy in it."

"Don't go. Move in with me."

"Here? In this house?"

"Yes. It's bought and paid for. Move in with me."

"I can't. I can't live here with all these . . . I can't live here."

"They don't bite."

"Not so far."

We went upstairs to bed. I lay on the mattress and I was so beat she made love to me in the cowgirl and swan positions with my cock deep inside her and she grinding with her hips and knees. We came together and she lay beside me laughing.

"All that riding was good for something," she said. I lit the paraffin heater and took a couple more codeine to help me sleep. And the rain came and the wind blew.

"It's all going to be all right, isn't it?" she asked.

"Aye," I said. "Don't worry. It's going to be fine."

20: WHO KILLED LUCY MOORE?

Dreams. Dreams of labyrinths. A labyrinth is not a maze. There are no dead ends. All paths lead inexorably to the center. All paths lead from the outside in. From the inside out. Daedalus was no genius. Only a joiner. Only a chippie in the yard.

Labyrinths are shaped like nooses.

Lucy Moore's finger was in the noose. She wished to see the baby again. She wished to live. The man wished death upon her. Motherless child, you have no protector. I am your voice. I am your avenger.

The darkness.

Falling, tumbling, into that black pit.

The falling will never stop. The numbers will go on counting until the end of time. The integers are infinite. The spaces between the integers are infinite. Let me tell you about the trees, Lucy. We climbed out of the trees. We walked away from the trees. Trees are a step backwards.

Everyone calls me Mimi, I don't know why because my name is Lucia. Straid.

The woods. Woodburn Forest.

The letter S.

The labyrinth.

He killed her.

He was the man.

I opened my eyes wide. Rain had flooded the gutters. Liquid skitter clinging to the windows like a beaten wife clinging to a bad marriage.

I bolted out of bed.

Laura looked frightened.

"What's wrong?" she said.

"Where did you say you were moving to?"

"Straid."

"What did you say about the forest?"

"What are you talking about?"

"You said something about your grandmother's house backing onto the forest!" I said, grabbing her by the shoulders.

"You're scaring me, Sean."

I let her go. "You said something about the house backing onto the forest."

"Oh . . . yes. I said that her house was nice because it backs onto Woodburn Forest."

I grabbed my jeans and fell over trying to put them on. My wrist had swollen to the size of a marrow.

"Help me get dressed!"

"What's going on?"

"Please!" I yelled at her.

"All right, all right, keep your hair on."

She pulled up my jeans and buttoned them and I grabbed a black sweater.

I went out onto the landing and down the stairs.

I looked at the kitchen clock. 8:45. I waited until 9 and called up the Sinn Fein press annex in Bradbury House.

"Hi, this is Mike Smith from the New York Times, I'd like to speak to Freddie Scavanni, please," I said.

"Just one moment," his secretary replied.

"Hello?" Freddie said.

Freddie was at work. Good for him. I hung up. I called Jack Pougher in Special Branch. "Hi, this is Duffy from Carrickfergus RUC. You couldn't do me a favor and find out Freddie Scavanni's home address, could you? It's never been in our files but I assume you boys must know, cos you boys know everything."

Jack didn't see through the compliment and after a minute he came back on: "This is a weird file, Sean. Lots of blank pages and I'm not supposed to give out Scavanni's home address to anyone beneath the rank of Superintendent."

"That's all right, Jack, I'll get it from a mate of mine in army intelligence. Those boys are always a wee bit better at giving you stuff."

Of course I had no mate in army intelligence and even if I had they'd give me shit. Jack didn't know that though. "Hold your horses, Sean. You'll owe me a favor, all right?"

"I'll owe you a favor."

"All right then. 19 Siskin Road, Straid and you didn't hear it from me."

I hung up, opened the drawer under the phone, grabbed the ordnance survey map of East Antrim and looked for the village of Straid. I found it and then I looked for Siskin Road. It ran parallel to Woodburn Forest

I got my raincoat and checked that the .38 was in the pocket.

I pulled on my Converse Hi-Tops and looked for my car keys.

"Oh, no, you're not driving anywhere with that wrist," Laura said, snatching the keys out of my hand.

"Gimme the keys!"

"No way. You're not driving. Doctor's orders," she said. Her eyes were firm.

"I need the car," I said in a quieter tone.

"Get one of your constables to drive you."

"Impossible. I can't involve them in this. I'm not supposed to be looking at these cases any more. They'd be up the shite sheugh with me."

"Where are you going?"

"Siskin Road, Straid, near Woodburn Forest."

"What's there?"

"Answers, goddamit!"

"Calm down, Sean."

Calm? We should be out in the street screaming: Death is coming. For ever and ever. And there's nothing we can do.

Nothing we can do, but bring down his disciples.

"Sean, what—"

"He killed Lucy Moore, I don't know why, but he did and I'm going to take him in for it."

"Who?"

"Freddie Scavanni."

"What?"

I grabbed my car keys from her.

"Where are you going?"

"His house near Woodburn Forest."

She had performed the autopsy. She had never been completely happy with her report.

"I'll drive you," she said.

"No way!"

"I'll drive you or you don't go. Let me tie up your laces while you think about it."

She tied my laces while I thought about it.

"You'll do as I say, if it looks dodgy, you'll wait in the friggin car."

"You're so butch! I like it," she said, mocking me.

We got in the Beemer and we drove down Coronation Road as far as Taylor's Avenue when I screamed, "Hit the brakes!"

The BMW screeched to a halt.

I got out and looked underneath for a mercury tilt bomb but didn't find one.

"Ok, let's head on."

We drove up the Prospect Road to the New Line and along Councilors' Road to the Siskin Road. For the last half mile of our journey the forest ran alongside the road. That familiar dense, exterior pine forest and the older deciduous wood behind.

"Where's Straid from here?" I asked.

"Oh, it's another few miles on up the road."

"I'd heard of the village of Straid but I had no idea at all that it was so close to Carrickfergus, so close to Woodburn Forest."

We passed a sign on a gate that said #19 Siskin Road.

"Here!" I said.

She pulled the BMW over and I got out and examined the gate. It had an electronic-locking mechanism that opened by remote control. Freddie could open it without leaving his car, which was the sort of thing you wanted if you were a high-ranking IRA man. A subject getting out of his car, fumbling with his keys in the early morning or the late evening was the ambushers' dream.

The gate was made of thick, shipyard steel and ran on a roller across the entranceway. A stout high stone wall went all the way around the property and the wall was topped by rotating iron spikes.

Nasty.

"You're breaking into this guy's house? Don't you need a warrant or something?" Laura said.

"Nah, we'll be fine."

"We'll be fine he says. And how are you going to get in there?"

"Easy enough for a resourceful chap like me," I said.

I took out my lock-picking kit and unscrewed the cover from the remote control box. I fused the exposed wires in the control box and the gate slid open.

"Quick, back in the car before the thing closes again," I said.

Laura had a disapproving frown. "I'm not sure about this. If he comes back and finds us . . ."

"When he comes back we'll be waiting here with half the RUC to arrest him."

We drove along a short tree-lined gravel drive until we came to Freddie's house.

It was a large four- or five-bedroom tower house—one of those fortified farmhouses that had been built in the seventeenth century during the Irish and English civil wars. It had thick, white-washed stone walls and one of the sides rose up into a three-storey round tower.

I saw now that the thick exterior wall was a bawn, a badhun—this whole place had been a cattle stronghold in the time of the Plantation. A good place for a player to have as his sanctuary.

The roof was thick slate and there were cast-iron grilles on the windows. The front door was a massive oak affair with an iron lock. I knew from my history that badhuns had large basements for storing food and grain and many of them were built over their own well or spring. You could easily survive a machine-gun or RPG attack and you'd do pretty well in the face of a zombie invasion, comet strike or the apocalypse.

It was the kind of place that cost money. Of course he had his press officer's salary but what other readies could he be pulling in? Kickbacks from the rackets? Drugs?

"How are you going to get inside? That's six inches of Irish oak," she said, examining the front door.

"I'll just have to pick the lock."

Laura smiled at me. Her nostrils were flaring and her cheeks were flushed. She was enjoying this. Getting off on it.

I better get us inside then. Old locks were tricky, old seventeenth-century locks might be impossible, but we'd see.

I probed the mechanism with a pick. It was ok. A tension wrench was unnecessary, all I had to do was insert the pick into the bottom part of the keyhole and make sure it slid under the lock bar to act as the bottom of a key. I inserted my next hook pick above the first pick and slid it under the lock bar. I tapped around until I felt resistance, which came in the shape of a series of hanging pins at the back of the pick. I pushed up on the hanging pins to reproduce the top of the key turning.

The door unlocked.

I put on latex gloves and lifted the latch.

"What exactly are we looking for?"

"I'm looking for. From now on you're waiting in the car."

"No fear, not after all this fun and games."

I knew she wouldn't listen to reason and she might even be able to help. I gave her another pair of latex gloves. "All right. We're looking for evidence that Lucy Moore was staying here. Anything. Women's clothes, baby clothes, any kind of ID. Anything like that! And a manual typewriter. Imperial 55. If you move anything put it back exactly the way it was. He'll never know anyone was here," I said.

"Hey, if there are three bowls of porridge can I have the one for baby bear?" she said.

We went inside.

Timber frame. Interior white-washed stone walls. Small windows. Not much light but an undeniable rustic charm. There were watercolors on the wall and when I examined one of them it was a tiny but valuable Jack B. Yeats.

A huge living room that contained a piano, two sofas, a big TV.

I went to the piano. There were no books of sheet music, which was a little strange. If you played you always had one or two sheet books lying around, didn't you? I checked the bookshelf but there were no sheet books there either, and nothing interesting. A lot of Leon Uris.

I went upstairs and searched the bedrooms. They weren't fancy. Simple, Irish, even minimalist. Wood furniture, whitewashed walls.

Clean. No women's clothes, no baby's clothes.

There was a study with a locked roller desk. I picked it open and rummaged through a dull assortment of bills and financial statements. Nothing out of the ordinary.

I went down into the basement but all I found were a few bottles of wine. Probably expensive, but who knew? No old typewriters.

My last port of call was the record collection in the living room.

He was a connoisseur.

After me own heart.

A thousand albums. Easy. Maybe three hundred classical records arranged alphabetically.

"Look at this! Puccini!" I said taking out the 1956 Sir Thomas Beecham recording of La Bohème.

"What does that prove?" Laura asked.

"I don't know," I said putting the record back on its bulging shelf. "What have you found?"

"Nothing."

I was depressed. "It's a fucking boy scout's house."

"Maybe's he's innocent."

"He can't be. It's too big a coincidence. Lucy Moore's body was found in Woodburn Forest. She died the same night as Tommy Little. That piece of music. Your tiny hand is frozen. My name is Lucia but everybody calls me Mimi! It's a tell. He was rushed. He didn't know he was doing it. And Eurydice, remember? Eurydice doesn't make it back! Lucy didn't make it back! Apollo taught Orpheus to play the lyre.

Apollo is the lord of light. Lucia means light. Don't you see? Ariadne's thread. The labyrinth leads us right back here!"

Laura folded her arms and sighed, "Jesus, is this how you do your police work? You wouldn't get away with this in pathology."

I was babbling and I fucking knew it. And she was right: this wasn't police work, this was intuition, guesswork. It was feeble.

I went back upstairs, hunted under beds, in the back of cupboards, in the bathroom . . .

When I came back down, Laura was sitting on the sofa.

"Shall we go?"

She was disappointed. She wasn't impressed with my detecting skills. Join the club, sister.

"He killed her. He's the 'S' that was seeing Lucy," I insisted.

I sat next to her on the leather sofa.

"Where's the evidence that Lucy was here?"

"He got rid of it all."

"Why would he kill her? What possible motive could there be?"

"She was a hunger striker's wife. He knocked up a hunger striker's wife."

"Ex-wife. And so what?"

"It would look bad. It would hurt his career."

"Come on. Murder hurts it even more."

"Maybe they had a fight."

She squeezed my hand. "There's nothing here, Sean. He lives near Woodburn Forest? His name begins with 'S'?"

"And Tommy Little was coming to see him. And he listens to Puccini."

"Let's go before he comes back. You'll lose your job, Sean."

"No. It's all about Tommy! It has to be. Tommy Little did come to see him. Tommy Little was here in this room."

"He killed Lucy and he killed Tommy?"

"Yes! They're linked. They've always been linked!"

"Maybe you can pin all the unsolved murders in Northern Ireland on Freddie Scavanni," she said sensibly enough, but I barely heard her.

"It's him. It has to be," I said, with a touch of panic now.

"Why does it have to be? So you can solve the case and be the hero? Come on, Sean, let's go."

"Five more minutes. We'll find something."

"Yesterday you were saying that it was Shane Davidson. That he had an affair with Tommy Little and killed him to cover it up. That he was the one who made the false trail . . ."

"I was wrong about that! They had nothing to do with killing him. Shane is Billy White's boy and Shane was having an affair with Tommy Little but he didn't kill him."

"I'm sure Shane will be relieved to hear that."

The grandfather clock ticked.

Crows cawed from the woods.

Laura got to her feet and pulled me up with two hands.

"Let's get out of here," she whispered.

I stood there for another minute, thinking, desperately . . . but finally I had to admit defeat.

"I was so sure," I said.

"I know," she replied and kissed me on the cheek. "Everyone wants a chance at redemption."

We went back outside and I closed the door behind me.

"Come on. Let's go get lunch somewhere," Laura said.

I hesitated. "Let me look in the woods for two minutes and then we'll head."

She was much happier now that we were out of the house. She took my hand.

"Let's say he topped both of them. He's got to get rid of Tommy's body well away from here. And her. He can carry her over his shoulders and hang her in the woods," I said.

"Why doesn't he just bury both of them?"

"I've been thinking about that. Time is a factor. He's got a couple of hours at the most before Tommy going missing rings all the alarm bells. A couple of hours to concoct a plan . . ."

"But why is he doing all this, Sean? Don't you need a motive?"

We went to the badhun's cast-iron back gate, lifted an interior latch and walked in the wood. It was damp and dark. Strange white mushrooms were pushing their way through the sodden earth. Giant ferns were growing from the shells of fallen trees. There was a dungy smell, the smell of rotting leaves, autumn, graveyards.

"Just a couple of steps and we're in Woodburn Forest," I said.

"But remember Lucy wasn't found anywhere near here. It was all the way over that hill, wasn't it?" Laura asked.

"Obviously he can't hang her right next to his house."

"How does he carry her?"

"Over his shoulder. Fireman's lift. You could carry someone for a mile like that."

She was skeptical.

"Let me show you."

"Ok."

Favoring my good wrist, I lifted her up onto my right shoulder and slapped her bum.

"Hey!" she yelped.

I walked for about fifty feet and stopped.

"See? You're out of breath and—"

I put her down.

"Jesus! Look! There!" I said, pointing through the trees. About thirty yards from the road in a broad valley between two enormous chestnut trees there was a burnt-out Ford Granada.

I ran to it.

The glass had melted and buckled, the interior was a mess of black debris and blackened foam but there was no rust or erosion. This had been done recently. Within the last month. I opened a door and looked inside.

It had been doused with gasoline and burned but then someone had killed the fire with a foam extinguisher. The number plates had been stripped off and when I lifted the bonnet I saw that the serial numbers on the chassis had been blow-torched away by arc-welding gear.

"Mother of God!"

"What is it, Sean?"

"It's Tommy's car. Has to be."

"He drove a Ford Granada?" she asked, but I wasn't even listening.

"For some reason Tommy comes over and Freddie kills him. The girl's a witness so he has to hang her. He cuts Tommy Little's hand off and shoves a musical score in his rectum. He drives to the home of the only other poofter he knows. He shoots him. He cuts off his hand. He leaves Tommy's hand there."

"Are you sure this is Tommy Little's car?"

"It's Tommy's car. Freddie can't be caught driving it and he can't have the IRA finding it at his house, so he gets it off the road and burns it out."

"I don't get it. He killed Tommy Little and drove him to Carrick?"

"He kills him. He puts Tommy in the boot of his car. He drives carefully through the police and army roadblocks. He gets far away to the Barn Field in Carrickfergus, he dumps Tommy's body where he hopes it will be quickly found along with Andrew Young's hand. He hurries back here. He drives Tommy's car off into the woods and torches it. But he doesn't leave the car burning all night in case it attracts attention. He waits until Tommy's body is found and then he calls the police and finds out my name and writes a bunch of gibberish on a postcard and sends it off to me. He calls the Confidential Telephone and starts in with the threats and false clues. He calls the Sunday World. He leads every one of us on a merry dance through the labyrinth. His bosses in the IRA know that Tommy is coming to see him but he tells them Tommy never made it over. The IRA are suspicious, skeptical, but when they find out that Tommy is mixed up with a sordid homosexual serial killer the whole thing is brushed under the rug. The misdirection works."

"But why, Sean? Why kill Lucy? Why kill Tommy?"

"I don't know. But I'll find out. I'll arrest him and charge him with terrorist offenses and question him and crack him. Come on! Let's go back to his house and call Carrick RUC. I don't care if I do get bloody suspended, I'm taking him down."

"I still don't see—" she began but was interrupted by a loud crack and bark flying from the chestnut tree behind her.

"What was tha—"

"Hit the deck!" I yelled at her. "And stay down!"

She dived into the thick layer of leaves on the forest floor. I took out my service revolver and turned to look behind me.

No one.

Another crack and this time the bullet missed my head by inches.

Where had it come from?

Somewhere up ahead in the direction of the house.

I ditched my raincoat, slithered through the undergrowth, got back into a crouch and ran through the trees in a big semi-circle to my right.

I kept Laura and the car in view and looked for him.

He had anticipated my move and was waiting for me near a lightning-struck oak. I saw him out of the corner of my eye a split second before he fired. I dived to the ground and heard the crack of the 9mm three more times, I rolled behind the nearest tree, a slender Scots pine and then kept on rolling down a little embankment.

Back on my belly again, moving sideways, silently, deliberately, holding my breath.

"Where are you?" he yelled and I could see his profile ten yards to my right. He was still wearing his office suit, holding the gun in two hands and looking into the space where I had been.

This time I had successfully outflanked him.

I got to my feet.

One step in front of another, carefully, toe then heel in my Converse gutties. Gently down onto the leaves, onto the twigs, gently right up behind the fucker.

I placed the barrel of the .38 on his neck.

"Drop the gun and slowly put your hands on your head."

He did as he was told.

I took a step backwards. "Laura! It's all right now! I've got him."

"Are you sure?" she called back.

"See if you can find my raincoat, it's got my handcuffs in it."

Scavanni turned and looked at me. He was grinning. I felt like pistol-whipping that smile off his fucking face.

Laura gave me the raincoat. Her face was flushed. Her chest heaving. For an insane second I wanted to blow his brains out and lay her down and fuck her into next week.

"Hold your hands out!" I said to Scavanni. "Laura, reach into the pocket, take out my handcuffs and cuff him."

She seemed reluctant.

"Don't worry, if he so much as twitches, I'll put one in his left ear."

"It's not that. How do these things work?" she asked.

"Put his hands in and close them tight," I explained.

"Oh, I see."

She cuffed him.

"What now, Sergeant Duffy?" Scavanni said.

"Now, Mr. Scavanni, we go back to the house, I call Detective Chief Inspector Todd and he shows up with a bunch of men anxious to have a wee chat with you. You get lifted, I get a fucking medal and maybe a promotion and you get life in prison. Probably in solitary cos I think they'll be out to make an example of you, won't they?"

Scavanni did not seem ruffled or concerned in any way.

"There's a phone in my living room," he said.

"All right, let's go."

We went back inside the garden walls. His car was in the driveway and the front door was open. The phone call to his office had obviously spooked him and he had driven home to see what, if anything, was up. Better for me.

"Why did you kill her?" Laura asked him.

"My dear, I don't believe we've been introduced," Scavanni said.

"Dr. Laura Cathcart. Pathologist."

"Charmed. Freddie Scavanni, Sinn Fein Press Officer," Freddie said.

"Why did you kill her?" she asked again.

"I don't know what you're talking about. I didn't kill anyone. I've never killed anyone in my life."

"Who were you shooting at in the woods?"

"I thought it was that dreadful fox again. He causes havoc in my bird feeder. I suppose I should have gotten the shotgun."

"Fox my arse. You saw us near the car. You knew the game was up. There's no point running your bullshit any more, Freddie."

We reached the living room and I put Freddie in the beanbag chair. Laura sat in the sofa and I sat in the chair next to the phone.

"Before you call Carrick RUC, would you indulge me in my one phone call?" Freddie asked.

"No fucking way."

"I think you'll find that it explains everything."

"Yeah, it goes right to an IRA hit squad who'll speed down here and try and save you before the coppers come."

"Oh no," Freddie said. "Nothing like that. It's a London number. 01 793 9000. When you get through and they ask who's calling, tell them it's Stakeknife. And when they ask for the reference number, tell them 1146."

"Pardon?"

"01 793 9000. When you get through and they ask who's calling, you tell them Stakeknife. And when they ask for the reference number, tell them 1146."

"What are you playing at, Scavanni?"

"Dial the number. You'll see. If you don't, your entire career will go down the shitter."

"Don't threaten me, my lad!"

"That's not a threat, believe me. Call the number. And if at any stage you are not completely happy, immediately hang up and call Carrick RUC. What have you got to lose?"

"Well, I'm slightly curious," Laura said, still flushed and excited by it all.

"All right, I'll indulge you. Consider this your phone call. And if I don't like it I'm hanging up."

"It's a deal."

I dialed 01 793 9000.

"Hello? Who's calling, please?" a young female, English voice said.
"Stakeknife."

"What is your four-digit reference number, Stakeknife?"

"1146."

"Thank you, Stakeknife, I'm putting you through to Mr. Allen."

There was a pause and then a man came on. An older Englishman.

"What is it, Stakeknife?"

"Who is this?"

"Who's this? How did you get this number?" Allen demanded.

"My name is Detective Sergeant Duffy of Carrickfergus RUC," I said.

"Where's Stakeknife?"

"He's nice and safe. He's under arrest."

"Where? At the police station?" Allen barked.

"Who the fuck are you?" I asked.

"Let me speak to Stakeknife. How do we know he's still alive? Who are you?"

"I've told you, I'm a policeman and—"

"What's your warrant card number?"

"Let me speak to him," Freddie said. "I think I can cut through this dismal swamp of mistrust."

"Is that Stakeknife?" Allen asked.

I looked at Scavanni. "I'm getting fed up with this. I'm going to hang up."

Freddie shook his head. "No, no, let me speak to them for a second or two."

I glanced at Laura. She shrugged.

"All right. You got two seconds. Anything I don't like and you're toast."

I carried the phone over and held it in such a way that we could both listen.

"Oh hello, Mr. Allen, this is Stakeknife. I'm afraid I've been arrested by a member of the Carrickfergus police. He wants to bring me to his local station. We're still at my house."

"Has he told anyone else?"

"He's brought a lady friend with him. A pathologist."

"Shit."

"Mr. Allen, he's very skeptical. I'm concerned that he's not going to take your word for it. You'll have to get the Minister."

"Tell him to hold on," Allen said. "And give him the phone back."

"He wants you to hold on," Freddie said.

"I heard him."

"Can you hold the line please, Sergeant Duffy?" Allen asked.

"Yes."

I sat back down on the sofa. I found that I was trembling.

A minute went by. A minute and a half.

A voice on the phone said: "Hello."

"Yes?" I replied.

"Hello, Sergeant Duffy, do you recognize my voice?"

It was William Whitelaw, the Home Secretary, Margaret Thatcher's Deputy Prime Minister.

"Yes, sir, I recognize your voice."

"Sergeant Duffy, would you mind awfully waiting at your present location for a few minutes? We're sending out a couple of chaps who will explain things to you much better than I can."

"Yes, sir."

"Thank you, Sergeant Duffy. There's a good chap."

I hung up the phone. I looked at Laura.

"What is it?" she asked.

"He's MI5. He's an MI5 undercover agent in the IRA. He's a fucking spook."

Half an hour later, two men pulled up in a silver Jaguar.

I sent Laura upstairs and kept Freddie handcuffed and the gun pointed at his head until I saw their IDs.

They were both in their forties. Ex-military. Old-school agent handlers. After they uncuffed Freddie, I had a stab of panic.

The easiest way out of this would be to immediately kill me.

Kill me.

Kill Laura.

Make us go away.

But they didn't kill us. They put us in the back of the Jag and drove us to Thiepval Army Barracks in Lisburn. HQ of the British Army in Northern Ireland. They took us to a fenced-off, high-security area and then to an even tighter security installation within that.

They took us to separate rooms and debriefed us.

I told them about the evidence I had against Scavanni.

They told me that it sounded pretty flimsy to them. They told me that Stakeknife was a valuable asset. A very valuable asset. He was now the head of the IRA's internal security branch, the Force Research Unit, and thus a very important person indeed.

"He might be the key figure in ending the hunger strikes. He might be the key figure to ending the Troubles."

I listened. I understood. I was made to sign a document that I was not allowed to read. I was made to sign The Official Secrets Act. A new team came in and it was all explained to me again.

I signed more documents. A third team came in. It went on until ten o'clock at night. Finally they were satisfied. I would not talk. I would not prosecute Freddie. I would return to my bicycle theft case and never speak of this again.

They asked me if I understood the big picture. I told them I understood the big picture. A middle-aged woman in a grey skirt and white blouse appeared.

"In that case," she said as if resuming a conversation, "we can let you go, Sergeant Duffy."

I stood up and looked into her brown eyes. "There's a condition," I said.

Her mouth opened and closed like a Lough Neagh roach wondering if you're going to throw him back or not. "You're not in a position to—"

"You tell Freddie that the killing has to stop. He's done enough to leave his trail. The killing has to stop!"

"I'll tell him."

They dropped Laura and me in the harbor car park in Carrick-fergus next to my BMW which was already there.

She was shivering. "Cold?" I asked.

She shook her head. "Did they make you sign all those forms?" she asked.

I nodded. "What will happen to us if we talk?"

"I don't know."

"What will we do now?" she asked.

"I don't know."

"Let's get a drink," she suggested.

We made it to the Dobbins for last orders. I got two triple whis-keys and two double gin and tonics. We sat by the fire. The rain came on outside. "What's going to happen to Scavanni?" she asked.

"Nothing."

She gulped her gin and tonic.

"Drink up, folks!" Derek boomed.

"I'll walk you home," I said.

She shook her head. "Let's go to your house. I want to be with you tonight."

I didn't feel sober enough to drive the car so I left it in the car park.

"So that's that, he'll never be punished for any of that?" she wondered.

"It's best not to think about it anymore," I said and my voice sounded like it was coming from the bottom of a well.

We walked up Taylor's Avenue, Barn Road, Coronation Road. We went inside #113. I lit the paraffin heater. We went upstairs and hugged under the blankets and closed our eyes and maybe even slept until the men in balaclavas came down the path and sledgehammered the front door and stormed violently into the house.

21: CORONATION ROAD

I reached under the pillow but the revolver was still downstairs in my raincoat pocket. I put my hand over Laura's mouth before she could scream.

"Get under the bed. Don't make a sound. You'll be safe."

I heard the men thumping up the stairs.

I had three or perhaps four seconds.

If I hesitated I/we were dead.

I grabbed a fire iron from the malfunctioning fireplace and ran naked onto the landing. I reached the top of the stairs at the same moment as the first gunman. His balaclava was impeding his field of vision but that didn't really matter as he was a micro-second too slow onto the final step.

I smashed the fire iron into his head, screaming as I did so.

Metal into bone.

He crumpled instantly and fell backwards down the stairs into gunman #2.

Gunman #2, however, put his hand out and stopped his mate from knocking him down. He shot at me twice with a big .45 that banged horribly in the enclosed space of the staircase. The two .45 rounds missed me by inches.

I ducked my head back round the staircase wall and desperately tried to think of a plan. They'd kill me if I went out either of the front bedroom windows and there might be a man waiting out the back too.

Another .45 round smashed into the yucca plant at the top of the staircase. Gunman #2 had recovered and was walking slowly up the stairs.

"C'mon, Gusty!" a voice said, a voice I recognized as Shane

Davidson. So it was Billy White and his crew come to kill me before I told the world what I knew about them.

Behind me Laura came to the bedroom door.

"What can I do?" she asked.

I ran to the end of the landing and picked up the five-foot-tall paraffin heater by one of the handles at the top.

"Take the other handle!" I said.

The heater was never supposed to be moved when fuelled up and it was never supposed to be moved when burning.

We carried it along the landing to the very edge of the stairs. It was at full capacity and it blistered and burned our hands.

"Now, get back!" I said lifting it from the rear by both handles.

It was searingly hot and the enameled stainless steel scalded my chest.

I screamed as I heaved it to the very top of the stairs.

The scream stopped Shane in his tracks, half way up.

He saw me and the heater, didn't compute it for a moment. He fired his gun but the .45 slug only smashed into the heater's plate steel spraying paraffin over him and the unconscious man beside him. I tumbled the heater at him and dived back behind the stair wall but I wasn't quite fast enough to avoid the blast as the heater crashed into Shane and the glass flue shattered and all the fuel ignited at once. There was an explosion and the shock wave flung me against the landing wall.

I tried to stay upright but I couldn't manage it and I fell down the stairs into the horror of burning men and white-hot metal.

I went head over heels into the glass phone table by the front door.

An eviscerated, burning Shane slid down the stairs on top of me. I yelled in horror and kicked him off.

I managed to stand and through the open front door a machine gun opened up on me from the street.

I dived to the carpet and crawled into the hall as AK-47 rounds tore up the vacuum above my head and broke and span and yawed off the walls and the ceiling.

Splinters, sparks, Libyan 7.62x39mm tracer rounds racing right through the house and across Carrickfergus towards their destiny in Belfast Lough.

I did a quick triage to see if I was in one piece.

Pain everywhere but there was nothing broken and I wasn't on fire.

"Sean!" Laura screamed from upstairs.

"I'm all right!" I yelled.

I could see the rest of the hit crew now in a black Transit parked in front of my house. A guy with a Kalashnikov in the passenger's seat and that wasn't the worst of it—the van's side door was open and there were two more men inside priming a rocket-propelled grenade launcher.

An RPG.

A Land Rover killer.

But then I saw my SMG. The Sterling M4 9mm sub-machine gun that had been sitting on the hall table for two goddamn weeks.

I grabbed it and snapped in the curved clip.

Thirty-four rounds between me and death.

Thirty-four rounds and skill. I had one crucial advantage. I had put the hours in on the range and they, obviously, were firing their weapons for the first or perhaps second time in their lives.

I got to my feet, unfolded the stock and braced the weapon against my shoulder.

I put my left hand on the ventilated barrel casing and walked into the valley of the RPG.

I squeezed the trigger and fire spat from the barrel and the weapon hummed and the open bolt sang like Ella Fitzgerald.

I walked down the garden path looking through the iron sight. Bullets whizzed all around but I was aiming, they were shooting. I aimed first at the men with the grenade launcher.

I hit my target and Death opened their eyes and they fell into his radiance, blood pouring from head wounds, chest wounds, ripped arteries and veins. Eternity revealed to them its mysteries and they tumbled backwards into the van and dropped the RPG launcher at their feet.

I turned the Sterling on the man with the AK-47. In his excitement the muzzle on his weapon had already ridden so high that he might have been trying to bring down the Space Shuttle. I gave him a burst that ripped through the transit van's aluminum door and ricocheted inside his body, slicing up his internal organs so badly that while the AK was still firing, blood was filling the balaclava and pouring out of his mouth.

That was enough for the driver who hit the accelerator pedal. The van leapt forward, the clutch slipped and it stalled. The driver didn't panic.

He leaned across his dead partner, reached for something on the floor, and before I had time to react, gave me both barrels from a sawed-off shotgun.

Shotgun pellets travelled towards me at 1200 feet per second.

That's 120 feet in a tenth of a second.

White-hot lead in my chest, neck and shoulders.

My beloved Sterling tumbling from my arms.

White-hot lead and a feeling of weightlessness.

Weightlessness and then hard cement.

Stars.

Footsteps.

The driver got out of the van. He rolled up his balaclava and walked towards me. From his jacket pocket he removed a Browning pistol fitted with a suppressor.

I almost laughed.

Why a silencer after all this?

He stood above me and looked down.

"You had to stick your fucking neb in, didn't ya? You had to open your big yapper. Can't you fucking take a hint? After all them ciggies we give you too," he said.

He raised the gun.

I closed my eyes.

Held my breath.

A bang.

Silence.

When I opened my eyes again Bobby Cameron was staring at me and shaking his head. Billy White was dead to my left with the back of his head blown off.

Bobby was grinning.

"Why?" I managed.

He shrugged. "They didn't ask me first. They didn't ask me for permission and this is my street!"

His grin faded.

The stars faded.

I saw Laura run out of the burning hall with a blanket over her head. Smart, that lass.

I was losing a lot of blood. My head was light.

I heard sirens.

Bobby safetied the 9mm, wiped it clean and left it next to me.

I nodded.

If I lived, I'd tell them it was me.

"This is my fucking street," Bobby said again.

22: THE CONVERSATION

In and out of the whiteness. In and out of the silence.
  Faces:
  Mum and Dad. Laura. Matty. McCrabban. Brennan. McCallister. Doctors. Nurses. My mum again, holding my hand. Tears on her cheeks. Tears on her good blue dress. Fear in her blue-grey eyes.
  Night.
  An alarm.
  A crisis.
  Doctors younger than me. An old man I did not know. An old man startled from sleep, muttering words over me and holding a crucifix above my forehead. "Dómine sancte, Pater omnípotens, aetérne Deus, qui, benedictiónis tuae grátiam aegris infundéndo corpóribus, factúram tuam multíplici pietáte custódis: ad invocatiónem tui nóminis benígnus assíste; ut fámulum tuum ab aegritúdine liberátum, et sanitáte donátum, déxtera tua érigas, virtúte confírmes, potestáte tueáris, atque Ecclésiae tuae sanctae, cum omni desideráta prosperitáte, restítuas."
  A night boat. A night boat crossing the Irish Sea. A journey through darkness. The moon smothered by fragments of the dark. The stars mouthing hermetic songs.
  A curlew on the lava beach. Auguries in the movement of the birds . . .
  Time passed.
  I could tell the different nurses by their perfumes.
  I could sense the difference between the shifts.
  I could tell when I was awake and dreaming.
  "Ach, you're doing much better now," the one with the lovely Scottish accent said, touching my bruises with her fingers.

I had had surgeries to remove shotgun pellets from my stomach, right lung, ribcage and one that was nestled against my aorta.

The surgeries had been long though not difficult.

Then there had been complications.

Hemorrhaging.

An immune system attacking itself.

I had been put in an induced coma for four weeks after they had trepanned my skull to relieve the pressure on my brain.

For another fortnight they had kept me medicated and semi-conscious.

When I became fully aware of where I was, it was the middle of July.

Six weeks of intensive care followed.

My condition moved from "critical" to "serious" to "improving."

I wasn't starved for visitors.

My mum and dad. Aunts and uncles dredged up from all over Ireland. Most of Carrickfergus RUC.

Laura.

Eventually I was moved to an open ward.

I got to know the heart patients and the car-crash victims.

The world outside the hospital continued without us.

Prince Charles married Lady Di in St. Paul's Cathedral.

Shergar won the Derby by ten lengths.

The Deputy Chief Constable came by to tell me that I had been recommended for the Queen's Police Medal. He also told me that he personally had seen to it that I would get my full pay, minus my uniform allowance, until I could return to duty, but that to do this I would have to wave my claims under the Victims of Terrorism Compensation Act.

I signed his forms and he went away happy.

My dad went round my house, ripped out the stair and rebuilt and repainted it.

He told me that everyone on Coronation Road had been "asking for me."

The riots continued.

The hunger strikes continued, but it was clear that they were winding down. The families of the hunger strikers appealed to the Primate of All Ireland, Cardinal Daly; he pleaded with the men in the H Blocks and many of them began ending their fast.

Seamus Moore came off along with several others.

Michael "Mickey" Devine was the last man to die on August 21, 1981. I'd known Red Mickey in Derry. Not a bad lad. He'd been arrested and sent to prison for possession of a stolen shotgun.

In the English papers the suspending of the hunger strikes was portrayed as a massive victory for Mrs. Thatcher. She had not given in to the terrorists. She had won.

Nevertheless, she quietly sacked her Secretary of State for Northern Ireland—the incompetent Sir Humphrey Atkins—and brought in James Prior. Prior immediately flew to the Maze Prison and promised that if the hunger strike was formally brought to a close then the British government would "strongly consider all of the prisoners' demands." Journalists began leaving Belfast for new trouble spots around the globe.

In my world it was much the same.

The "gay serial killer" case was closed. Billy White was tagged as the chief suspect. Shane Davidson had been his accomplice. Two repressed self-hating secret homosexuals. They had killed Tommy Little and Andrew Young and all the others . . .

They were disowned by the UVF and their families. Who knew why they had done it? As a pathology or because of some dispute with Tommy Little and then the others to cover up their crime? Who can see into the hearts of men?

But I knew. There had never been a gay serial killer. Northern Ireland was not the soil in which serial killers grew. If you wanted to murder a lot of people you joined the paramilitaries and used that as cover for your sociopathic tendencies . . .

Anywhere else this case would have been big news, but Ulster in 1981 had other things on its mind.

I tried to forget it. I had physiotherapy to do and water therapy and exercises.

I began exercising in the hospital. My mum bought me a Sony Walkman. Crabbie brought me a mix tape of country standards. Matty brought me a mix tape of Adam and the Ants and The Human League.

I learned to walk again and I listened to music and an audiobook novel Laura brought me called Midnight's Children.

One morning in the papers I read that at the European Court of Human Rights in Strasbourg the case of the Dudgeon v UK had been decided against the British government. A panel of judges had ruled 15:4 that Northern Ireland's laws against homosexuality violated the European Convention on Human Rights. Mrs. Thatcher's Attorney General said that the law in Northern Ireland would have to be changed. That homosexual acts between consenting adults would have to be made legal.

The Catholic Church objected. The Free Presbyterian Church objected. The political parties objected. The paramilitaries objected. Something had brought the Protestants and Catholics together at last. But there was little they could do. Britain couldn't leave Europe, or renounce the Treaty, the law was going to change . . .

I got a new doctor. An intern from Nigeria. He told me that as soon I could walk fifty feet without a stick he would let me go. In a week I proved it to him by walking from one side of the ward to another.

I was released from hospital on September 23.

Laura drove me back to Coronation Road. My grass had been mown and roses planted in my garden. The hall was filled with cards and letters. I could barely get through the front door.

Chief Inspector Brennan came to see me and told me to take my time before coming back to work.

I told him I would.

The next day Bobby Cameron came to see me. He brought bacon, milk and sausages. He told me that I had taken out a six man UFF assassination team and that under normal circumstances, me being a fenian and all, I'd be well advised to leave Northern Ireland, or at the very least Coronation Road.

"But these aren't normal circumstances, are they?" Bobby said with a sleekit grin.

"Aren't they?"

He pointed heavenwards. "They see it as a rogue cell that they would have had to take out anyway. And Bobby and Shane being queers and all? You fucking did them a favor. What an embarrassment."

"So they're not going to kill me?" I asked.

"Only if, in the course of a future investigation, you step on anyone's toes."

I grimaced. "It's my job to step on people's toes."

"And you're still a peeler and a fenian peeler and a bit of a famous fenian peeler at that, so the other side will still be trying to kill you, won't they?"

"I suppose they will."

Bobby walked to the front door. "Congratulations on your police medal. Say hello to her majesty for me. I'll see myself out."

Out he went.

Days, nights. Autumn turning into early winter. I went walking around Carrickfergus. Along Coronation Road and the sea front and sometimes all the way to Whitehead and back.

I grew stronger. I began lifting weights. Eating steak.

I went to the range at the UDR base and practiced my shooting.

I had been home ten days when the great Maze hunger strike was formally ended at last. Two days later Secretary of State James Prior announced that IRA prisoners would be allowed to wear their own clothes, have separate cells and free association: "political status" would be returned in all but name.

For the first night since April Belfast had no rioting.

It was over.

The very next day the man came to see me.

He rang the bell just after I had gotten back from a run.

I was in sweat pants and my Ramones T-shirt.

He was dressed in a tweed suit and handmade shoes. It was a relatively dry day but he was wearing a raincoat, a trilby and carrying an umbrella. He was about sixty years old with a handsome face, sunken blue eyes and a grey pallor. He reminded me a little of Sir John Gielgud and his voice had the same commanding authority although tinged with a West Country accent.

"Detective Sergeant Duffy?" he said when I answered the door.

"Yes?"

"My name is Peter Evans. May I speak with you for a moment?"

I was breathing hard.

"Are you quite well?" he asked.

"I've just got back from a run. Let me get myself a drink of water, go on into the living room."

I got my water and followed Mr. Evans into the living room.

He had sat himself down on the leather sofa and was examining the copy of *The Thin Red Line* that I had left there.

"A good book?" he asked.

"Yes," I said.

"I was in Burma under Orde Wingate, quite an extraordinary fellow. Unorthodox."

I sat opposite him in the recliner. "You're MI5, aren't you?"

"We don't like to use that name."

"You've come here to put the fear of God into me, haven't you? Have you seen Laura? You better not hurt her."

"Oh, there's no question of that. Oh, my goodness, no. We're quite sure about you both. We've had many conversations about you and Dr. Cathcart."

"We won't talk. We get it," I agreed.

He smiled. "Yes, we know. I told them that all the way back in June. I said, gentlemen, these two young people are good eggs."

The proverbial cold chill. Of course if we hadn't been good eggs we wouldn't be having this conversation. We'd be dead.

Evans sighed and tapped *The Thin Red Line*. "War is so much easier than this business that we're in. You know who your friends are and, most of the time, who your enemies are. Usually they're the ones shooting at you."

"But you work in the grey area," I said.

"Not quite. In my world everything is binary. Black and white. Friend and enemy. Traitor and hero. The problem is that today's friend is tomorrow's enemy and vice versa. It can be confusing. It can destroy the finest minds. I had a colleague, an American colleague, who rose to the top of a well-known agency but became convinced that everyone working in that agency was a traitor. Everyone was in a conspiracy except for him. The President, the Vice-President, they were all working for the Russians. Poor chap. He couldn't trust anyone in the end. He used to speak about the 'wilderness of mirrors,' a line from Eliot I think (not my bag, the modern stuff). Anyway, a wilderness of mirrors where faces were reflections of reflections and nothing was as it seemed."

"Would you care for some tea?" I asked.

"That would be lovely."

I made it and brought chocolate biscuits, which Mr. Evans seemed inordinately excited about.

"You're getting the Queen's Police Medal," Evans said.

"So they tell me."

We sipped our tea and I looked through the window at the rag and bone man's balloon-filled cart making its melancholy way down Coronation Road.

"What have you come here to talk about, Mr. Evans?"

He laughed. "*Brevis esse laboro, obscurus fio*, and I wasn't even very *brevis*!"

"Why don't you just tell me what you want to tell me?"

He nibbled at his biscuit and smiled. "Three quick things and then we're done, Sergeant Duffy. Firstly, I want to tell you that we've thoroughly examined your psychology assessments and I believe we can trust you and Dr. Cathcart completely. So please put any residual uneasiness out of your mind."

"I will."

"Secondly, the so-called 'gay serial killer' case is now closed both officially *and unofficially*. You do see that, don't you, Sergeant Duffy?"

"Yes."

"Thirdly, we do not want you going near Stakeknife. We don't want you going to his office in Belfast, or his house in Straid . . . or to his home in Italy where he will be until the end of the month."

"Italy?"

"A little town called Campo on the northern shores of Lake Como. Charming place by all accounts. Tells everyone he got it from his grandfather. There's a little article about it in August's . . . in fact, hold on a minute . . . I just happen to have . . ."

He reached into the pocket of his raincoat and placed August's *Architectural Digest* on my coffee table.

I looked at the magazine, looked at him.

He smiled and got to his feet.

He pointed at the room.

"Love the color scheme. Striking. Such a breath of fresh air after all the usual dreary Sybil Colefax stuff."

"Yes."

"Well, I suppose I should be jollying along. Just wanted to check in. For a long time everything was so delicate, so finely balanced, but now, well, the hunger strikes are over and we have a new broom as Secretary of State and . . ."

"Everything's changed?"

"Yes . . . well . . . look, it was awfully nice meeting you."

He reached out his hand.

I shook it.

"I'll see you out," I said.

I opened the front door and he walked onto the porch.

"When do you return to duty, Sergeant Duffy?" he asked.

"I was thinking about next week but the Chief says I can take until the end of October if I want to."

Evans put on his hat and waved to a man in a black Daimler who turned the engine on and threw his cigarette out the window.

"It's been my experience, Sergeant Duffy, that after a traumatic event the best thing to do is to leap back into the saddle as soon as you can. Although you have been through so much that perhaps it would be best if you take a little holiday abroad first."

"You think so?"

"Oh yes. Yes indeed."

"Then perhaps I'll go."

23: THE ITALIAN JOB

I landed at Linate Airport just before dusk. I changed two hundred quid into lira and at the airport gift shop I bought a hunting knife and a map of the Como area. I had an espresso and some kind of meat filled pastry which made me feel that this was the first time I had tasted food in my life.

A taxi took me to the Central Bus Station in Milan without too much trouble. It was off season, too late for summer travel, too early for the skiers.

The bus to Como left at 6. A Red Brigade bomb scare delayed it until 7:30 and made me feel at home.

At Como I caught a local bus up the Via Regina.

We arrived at Mezzagra in the middle of a street party. It was a harvest festival and kids were dressed as grapes and ears of wheat.

It was cold and braziers had been set up to warm the crowd. More good food. Beautiful women. People enjoying themselves.

Italy with its chaotic politics and twenty-plus prime ministers since World War Two was still the inverse of Ireland—bomb threats notwithstanding. This, I thought, is what normality looked like.

I found a stand selling home-made toys and, changing my mind about the knife, I bought a realistic-looking cap gun in the shape of an ACP. In Ireland all toy guns had to be orange so weans didn't get shot by cops or soldiers on foot patrol. But this one, from a distance, looked like the real thing.

I laughed.

It would be funny if this worked and funny if it didn't.

I watched a puppet show about the capture of Mussolini by the Resistance which, if I understood it correctly, happened on this very spot.

At 9 o'clock I caught the last local bus to Campo.

Lake Como was the black empty mass to my right as we hugged the shore and drove past the homes of the very rich. Beautiful villas from the baroque and rococo right up to the present day. Father Faul told us that the Younger Pliny had owned two villas on Lake Como. One on a hill and one on the lake. The upper home he called Tragedy, the lower Comedy.

The bus stopped at every village and went slowly along the shore road. It finally left me off at the hamlet of Campo at around 11:30.

A quiet, attractive, unearthly little place in the foothills of the Alps.

There were no people.

No cars.

Occasionally a truck roared by under the vast yellow arc lights of the SS36. The rest was silence.

Snow had been falling since the day before and the bus station car park was a frozen world.

An ice mirror reflecting the winter constellations. A landing strip for migrating birds.

I unfolded my map, strapped the rucksack across my shoulders and headed east.

The house was at the end of a long track off Vicolo Spluga.

The incline was steep and I had to catch my breath a couple of times.

Wind was whistling down from the Swiss border, eight miles to the north.

These were not the high Alps but it was still freezing. According to the map we were up at 1400 meters which I reckoned was over 5500 feet. I was wearing a leather jacket, jeans and Adidas trainers. I was underdressed. I hadn't expected it to be this frigid in early October.

I took another breather to steady my nerves.

From up here I could see the lights of planes landing at Milan and boats putting across the black waters of the Lago di Mezzola.

I walked on. I passed a ruined mill, a couple of small cottages and a barn that had been destroyed by fire.

Freddie's house was built in a typical Tyrol style: wood beams, a deck facing south, a steep timbered roof. It wasn't particularly large but I knew that he owned much of the surrounding forest too. He told everyone that he had inherited the place from his grandfather but that wasn't true. The whole shebang was bought and paid for by MI5.

Since June and Freddie's ascension to the Army Council things had really begun to happen for him.

Gerry Adams had been out here. All the top guys in Sinn Fein and the IRA.

Even a couple of US Congressmen.

I imagine that it was bugged. And since people were chattier out of their natural environment the intel must be pouring in.

There was a brand new silver Mercedes SL parked under the deck.

The moon was out and I could read my watch without hitting the backlight. 12:20 now. Getting late. I walked around the ground floor looking for a way in but there was none.

You had to go up the steps and enter from the first level.

The stairs were sparkled with frost so I gripped the hand rail and took them cautiously.

The deck had sliding French doors, large plate-glass wraparound windows and a view to the south-west of Lake Como and to the north, between two mountains, the 4000 meter-tall Piz Bernina.

The view, the mountains, the chalet, Freddie and his scary pals— the whole thing had a Berchtesgaden vibe circa 1939.

At the top of the steps I took out the knife and the cap gun. I weighed the two options. "Aye, let's try the bluff, Freddie will appreciate that," I said to myself.

I pulled on a pair of leather gloves and re-shouldered the backpack.

I walked round the deck, looked in through the glass windows and saw Freddie standing there in front of a large TV set. He had videoed an Inter Milan match on his Betamax and he was fast forwarding through the game in search of goals.

I took a step backwards and retraced my steps around the deck until I came to a door.

I had brought my lock-pick kit but when I turned the handle and pushed, the door opened.

I stepped cautiously inside.

I took off the rucksack and set it down on a tiled floor. I removed the note I had written on the plane and looked again at the cap gun. Was it convincing? We'd soon see.

I walked through a large, modern kitchen illuminated by night lights.

I pushed the kitchen door and tiptoed my way along a hardwood corridor until I made it to the enormous living room.

Freddie was sitting now, watching and re-watching a beautiful goal by a blond-haired Inter player.

"Lovely stuff," Freddie kept repeating to himself.

I slipped behind Freddie's reclining leather chair.

The knife would have done just as well.

I shoved the cap gun against Freddie's ear.

"What the—" he began.

I put my finger to my lips and still keeping the cap gun in his ear, handed him the note.

He looked at me and read the note. It said: "Turn off all the recording equipment and make no sound until you do so."

Freddie was reassured by this. It told him that I was a reasonable, forward-thinking young man, not a nutcase bent on some vendetta.

He nodded. I took one step backwards keeping the cap gun pointing at him and letting the sleeve of my jacket droop over it so that he wouldn't get a good look at it.

He got to his feet and pointed to a door at the end of the living room. I gave him the OK sign.

We walked into his study and he turned on the light.

There was no tremble in his gait and he didn't look frightened in the least. I didn't like that and it put me on my guard.

The study was small, with a desk and a few metal filing cabinets.

There were signed pictures on the wall.

Freddie with Vanessa Redgrave. Freddie with Senator Ted Kennedy.

He pointed at the desk and began walking towards it. I shoved the gun in his back and he froze. I pushed him to the ground, stepped over him and opened the desk drawer.

The gun in the drawer was a Beretta 9mm.

I checked that it was loaded and put the cap pistol back in my pocket.

Freddie sighed.

"Can we speak now? There's no tape going. It's not turned on, is it? I mean, what's the point? It's just me here," Freddie said.

"Show me," I said.

He got to his feet and looked ruefully at the gun barrel of his own pistol aimed at his chest. He pulled open the top drawer of one of the filing cabinets.

"Look in there," he said. "If it was recording, the spools would be going round, wouldn't they?"

I looked in the filing cabinet.

Two enormous spools of tape on an expensive looking recording device.

The thing was evidently turned off and the spools were not going round.

Of course there could have been a back-up somewhere in the house.

"Is there a back-up? The truth now, Freddie," I whispered to him.

"Back-up? That one cost two grand. Those cheap bastards are not going to install a bloody back-up, are they?" he said with an attempt at levity.

I tried to impart the seriousness of my question with a waggle of the Beretta.

"No! There's no back-up. This is it."

I believed him.

We returned to the living room.

I switched off the TV.

I motioned him to sit down in the leather recliner and I sat on the glass coffee table opposite him.

"Talk," I said.

"About what?"

"Tell me everything."

24: THE WILDERNESS OF MIRRORS

That sleekit handsome hatchet-face broke into a grin. "What do you wanna know?"

"What happened on Christmas Eve, 1980?" I asked.

"With Lucy, you mean?" he asked.

"Aye. With Lucy. The train. The aborted abortion."

"You know about that?" he asked, surprised.

"You got her pregnant and there was only one way out of it. The abortion special. Ferry to Larne, train to Glasgow. One night in the hospital. Back for Christmas Day."

His left cheek twitched, the first minute chink in that force field of confidence. We're all projecting multiple images of ourselves all the time but for Freddie it must be so much harder to maintain the likeness . . .

"Her mum decided to get the Belfast train and she was looking for Lucy at the Barn Halt but she didn't see her because Lucy was on the other platform, wasn't she? The Larne side. She was going to Larne," I said.

"She was. Lucy saw her mother stick her big bonce out the train window and the poor girl almost had a heart attack."

"What did she do? Hide in the shelter?"

"She hid in the shelter until the train left. But that was where it all fell apart. Seeing her mother really spooked her. We'd arranged to go to Scotland together on the boat train. I got off the train at Barn Halt but of course she wasn't bloody there. She was supposed to meet me on the platform but she'd got cold feet. I knew she'd bottled it. She finally came to see me and I suppose I should have ended it there and then but she was bawling her eyes out and I felt sorry for her."

"How long had you been seeing her?"

"A few months. It wasn't that serious. She was very beautiful but there was no way I could ever get heavy with a comrade's wife. Even an ex-wife. The powers that be wouldn't allow it. They're very conservative. And of course then she got pregnant . . ."

"And refused to get the abortion."

"Quite the dilemma, eh?"

"So what did that big brain of yours cook up, Freddie?"

"You know what we did, Sergeant Duffy."

"Aye, I do. She moved in with you and you got her to write a bunch of postcards and letters to her family and you went down to the Republic and posted them. Everyone thought she was living in Dublin or Cork or wherever but in fact she was only a hop skip and a jump away living with you—until she had the baby, right?"

"It wasn't so onerous. The thing was due in five months. What was five months? She could stay with me. Cook and clean the place. Nice wee feminine touch. The baby's born, we give it away and then she goes back to her parents like the prodigal daughter. And who knows, maybe after a decent interval and with Seamus's OK, we could begin a formal courtship."

"But then Seamus went on hunger strike. Didn't that complicate things?"

Freddie shook his head. "Not really. I knew he wouldn't go through with it. Not him. He didn't have the stones for it. He was only in for gun possession. That's a hell of a thing to die for. Lucy was a little upset though. He joined the hunger strike just a couple of days before she was due. I told her not to worry about it, that I'd have a word and we'd get him off. And we did too. He was no martyr."

I understood. It had to be exhausting to be in cover this long, to play that game.

"So the plan is: Lucy gives birth, gives the baby away, returns to her parents and no one knows that she was ever pregnant or that you're the father of her baby."

"That's the plan. Of course people would gossip and her mother's an intelligent woman but with no actual proof . . . I mean, technically Lucy and Seamus are divorced. But not in the eyes of the church."

"Seamus told me as much."

"The first sin was divorcing him. That was bad enough. But then to get herself pregnant with some other bloke while her husband was martyring himself for Ireland? Not good my friend, not good. I was protecting her as well as me. Maybe 'after her return' she even goes to see Seamus in the H Blocks. Or you know what? Maybe we'll get lucky and Seamus will go through with the bloody hunger strike or have a heart attack or something and she'll be the grieving widow. Ha! And after a decent interval I could see her on the QT."

"But you weren't worried about her living with you during the pregnancy?"

Freddie tapped the side of his head and grinned. "Who do you think you're dealing with? My house is out of the way and I don't encourage visitors."

"What if they did find out?"

"Trouble!" he laughed. "Best-case scenario they kneecap me, court martial me, kick me out of the IRA and exile me permanently from Ireland."

"So Lucy lived with you and she gave birth and you gave the baby away."

"Yes. Mind if I smoke?"

"Go ahead."

He lit up. He licked his dry lower lip and took a long drag on the cig. He was a young man still, but his eyes were hollow. He looked a little like one of those old priests you found in the West of Ireland who was weary after decades of the same dreary confessions.

"You knew how to deliver a baby and everything?"

"God no. I got a midwife. You never did find her, did ya?"

"What do you mean?"

"You see what I'm talking about? I outsmarted all of you. She lived in East Belfast. Wee flat by herself. I told her there was an emergency job. I drove her and she delivered the baby and I paid her well. And of course after it all went wrong I had to call on her again and disappeared her."

"You killed the woman who acted as Lucy's midwife?" I asked.

"Yes. You don't need to know about it. It's all taken care of. I did it the night I got back from my IRA interrogation in Dundalk. Before she would have heard the news about Lucy. It was a busy couple of days for me."

"I can imagine."

"But unlike the queers, I didn't want the police to find her body. I buried her in the Mourne Mountains. She's gone forever. Don't worry about it."

Don't worry about it? Don't worry about it? Why did he think I had come here? Just for a chat? To clear the air?

He was talking again: "So everything went according to plan. Plan B anyway. Lucy lived with me from Christmas onwards. We wrote letters to her family. Boiler-plate stuff. She said she was doing ok, she wanted a second chance in Dublin. And then when I was down South, I posted them. Easy. Piece of cake."

"And you liked having her around? She wasn't moody?"

"I loved having her around. Very good-natured girl. Lovely wee lass so she was. Have you seen any pictures of her? She was gorgeous."

"So what went wrong? Why'd you kill her?"

"Well, the baby's born. I give the midwife a thousand quid, tell her to keep her mouth shut, everything's fine. Wee baby girl. We keep it for a couple of days, but then it's time to give the little bairn away, isn't it? That's part two of the plan. Lucy comes back from Dublin, moves in with her parents for a bit, all is forgiven . . . But nobody can know she was ever pregnant. Too many questions. So I take the bairn and leave it in a stolen car in the Royal Victoria Hospital car park. I call them up and I watch them come out, look in the window and take the poor wee thing away. I suppose we were lucky they didn't think it was a bomb and blow the car up!"

He started laughing at that.

"So they took your daughter away," I said loudly to stop his cackling.

"Aye, ok, my daughter, big deal. Maybe if it had been a wee boy ... but that's another story, isn't it?"

"Did you tell MI5 about Lucy?"

"Why would I do a thing like that? They'd go crazy."

"It's quite the game you're playing, isn't it, Freddie? Deceiving your handlers, deceiving Sinn Fein ... I'm amazed that you could keep it all together."

"A lesser man would have cracked."

"So what happened next, Freddie? After you gave the baby away?"

"So then I get back from the RVH and she's acting very strange. This is the climax of the hunger strikes, you understand. Bobby Sands is in the ground just a couple of days before and it's my busy time. We're all running round like mad things, driving people places, doing interviews with American TV. I'm protecting the top guys, doing this, doing that, getting orders from Tommy Little as well as my regular press job. Running myself ragged from morning till night and every time I get home it's yap yap yap, where's my girl? Boo fucking hoo. And then she starts with the yelling and the screaming, 'You're this and you're that' and I give her a wee slap or two just to get that noise out of my head. And then she's really bawling. It does your head in that stuff. I'm going for a drive, says I, you better get your fucking act together."

"Something happened then, didn't it? After you hit her and left the house."

"Something happened all right."

"You go for a drive and she ... what? She starts rummaging in your stuff looking for a gun to shoot you with when you come back. But instead of finding a gun she finds ... something more interesting."

"Oh, you're good, Duffy."

"She finds checks from MI5? A book of contacts?"

"Very good. It was receipts. Those incompetent fools make me get receipts for everything. I had an envelope full of receipts and I had them all itemized for my handlers. And she finds them and she doesn't really know what it all means. But she knows it's not good."

"She finds the receipts and she knows you're an informer."

"She's gotta turn me in, but I suppose she's worried that we'll both go down for it. Both of us dead in some border sheugh with a bullet in the brain. So she calls up Tommy Little. She tells him to meet her at my house and she gets Tommy to promise not to tell a soul about it until he talks to her."

"And Tommy is surprised to hear from her cos he thinks she's in Dublin or dead or whatever, so of course he comes," I said. "So what happened when you got back from your drive?"

"Tommy parked his car in a layby a little further down from the house, so I waltzed into the kitchen expecting Lucy to have made me a cake as a way of apologizing and there's Tommy Little, my bloody boss at the FRU, standing there with her. He must have just got there a couple of minutes before me. 'How do you explain all this?' he asks holding up the receipts. 'Like this,' says I and I pull out my Glock and shoot him in the chest. Jesus! What an eejit. I mean, what is he doing standing there in my kitchen like that? He must have heard the car. If it was me I'd have been out the back door and into the woods. Instead he had to be a hero, had to confront me!"

"What about Lucy?"

"Lucy. Jesus. She's another eejit. She's screaming her head off and I put my hand over her mouth to shut her the fuck up and she's fighting me and I'm covering her mouth and she's still screaming. Christ! The lungs on her. 'Who else did you tell?' I ask her and she says only Tommy and I give her the old one two in the gut and she's screaming again. So I can't take it no more. 'Give my head peace!' says I and I locked her in my elbow and choked her to death."

He was exhausted by this little speech and he reached over for his bottle of Peroni. I shook my head. No beer bottles. Nothing he could throw.

"What did you do next?"

"You're me, what would you do?" Freddie asked.

"You tell me."

"Well, you have two options. The first is that you pull the plug. You call the boys in County Down and they come and—"

"The boys in County Down?"

"MI5!"

"Oh, I see."

"They come and you tell them what's happened and they parachute you out. And I'm fucking living in some god-awful Sydney suburb for the next forty years getting skin cancer and trying to acquire an interest in rugby league. I'm a low priority agent so there's no secret knighthood or a million a year retirement salary for me."

"Couldn't they just clean it up for you? Fix everything."

He shook his head and smiled condescendingly. "You're a bit simple, aren't you, Duffy? At that stage I was only a cog in the machine. A cog that's just killed Tommy Little and a hunger striker's wife! Tommy they might give me at a squeeze but not Lucy and certainly not both of them. Saluta Jesus da parte mia! as they say in these parts. Thank you for your services, Freddie, now here's your ticket for Australia, don't call us, we'll call you. And, hell, maybe they'll even chuck me in prison. Who knows? Perfidious Albion and all that!"

"So what was the second option?"

"Get rid of the bodies. Make like I never saw them. Rub out all connection with them. Just go on with my life, oblivious. Pity about Lucy but them's the bloody breaks."

"Sounds like a plan."

"Yeah. And I've done it before. You saw off the hands, saw off the head, bury the torso in a bog, dissolve the head and hands in HCL. Piss easy."

"What went wrong?"

"Well, I'm literally just done killing Lucy. Like, not even time to make a cup of tea and I get a call from Ruari McFanagh. He's the chief of northern command. Number Two in the Army Council. (That's just between us, by the way.) So he asks me if Tommy came by. Tommy was a cautious cove, he stopped at a call box and told Ruari he had business at Billy White's and then he was on his way over to see me. And I said, 'Tommy didn't come over here, did he say what it was about, Ruari?' And Ruari says no and nobody can reach him. 'Well,' says I, 'I have no

idea where he is, I'm just in myself.' So he says ok and he hangs up the
phone and literally a minute later it rings again and it's Lee Caldwell.
Lee is the IRA Quartermaster for Down and Armagh and he asks me if
I could come to see him tomorrow morning about shipping a new lot
of AK-47s up from Newry. So I say ok, no problem. But I know, I know.
Tomorrow morning while I'm down at Lee's place Ruari is going to
have a couple of boys over, going through my house from top to bloody
bottom."

I understood. I understood it all now. The necessity of doing everything quickly. Why he had to get rid of Tommy immediately. Why he
had to get rid of Lucy as fast as he could. "Go on," I said.

"So now what do I do? I'm fucked. They're sending a couple of
boys over to my place to suss me out. I've got seven or eight hours at the
most. And the streets are full of rioters and army and peelers are everywhere and there's checkpoints and roadblocks. So again I'm thinking:
parachute your way out. Escape. Run."

"But you didn't."

"No. Because I am the alpha wolf. I am fucking Finn McCool."

"You knew you could outwit them?"

He was grinning at the memory of it. He was impressed by himself.
"I had to think quickly. Nobody would buy an argument between
me and Tommy or something crazy like an accidental discharge of
my weapon. No way. They wouldn't buy Tommy getting killed by the
army, the cops, or the loyalists. Tommy's a protected man and nobody's
killing him without starting World War Three."

"So you thought outside the box."

"The IRA high command is ultra-conservative. Tommy was a
queer, everybody knew it and they didn't like it. Tommy was only tolerated because he was very good at his job. Tommy was the best of us. But
he was vulnerable because he was a poofter. I mean, who knows what
they get up to?"

"So you killed him to make it look like that?"

"The queer angle was my lifeline. He had to be meeting someone
before he met me and that someone was a queer pal and that queer pal

killed him. That was the story I was going to go with. No, sorry lads, never heard from Tommy, don't know where he is. And then Tommy's body shows up. Some sicko's killed him. Shock, horror!"

"You had to make it weird."

"Something to get the lace curtains twitching. Something to get you coppers all in a tizzy. And then I thought why not a serial killer? Tommy is just the first in a series of victims. The IRA Army Council is not even going to want to think about that. A serial killer going around shooting queers? How dare he take publicity away from the hunger strikers? How dare Tommy get himself mixed up in this disgusting business?"

"So you realized you were going to have to kill Andrew Young too?"

He sighed. "Andrew Young was the only other queer I knew. I'd seen him at the record shop and at the Carrick festival. Nice enough fella but a bender and so he had to die, poor sod. I had eight hours. The clock was ticking. I mean, first things first. I carried Lucy deep into Woodburn Forest. I hung her from a tree and I left her ID at her feet so everybody would know who she was. I wasn't worried about her at all. Her husband's on hunger strike, she's run away from home, she's feeling guilty, your pathologist is going to find out that she gave birth, more guilt, guilt, guilt. That's the Irish condition. So that's an easy one."

"And you're not worried because there's no link to you."

"Right. Nobody knew about us! Nobody. We were so careful. Only the midwife and I already told you about her. Anyway I hung Lucy, went back to the house, removed all traces of her from the place and burned all her clothes in the incinerator out the back. Even hosed down the ashes and scooped them out."

"And then you cut off Tommy's hand and put the note up in his rectum?"

"Did you like that? I had to link him to Young. Make you peelers think this was a sex crime. More importantly, make the IRA and FRU think it was a sex crime."

"Why not cut his dick off?"

"I considered cutting his dick off and swapping his dick with Andrew's dick, but then I wondered if your patho would spot that, you know? One dick looks pretty much like another. And hands have fingerprints, so I settled for his hand. I cut his hand off and shot him in the head. I took the hand, got in the car and drove to Young's house in Boneybefore."

"How did you know his address?"

"He was in the phone book like you. Anyway, I park the car. Knock on his door, check there's no one around. Knock, knock, knock. Finally he opens the door. I ask him if he's alone. He says yes, I shoot him in the forehead with my silenced Glock and push him into the hall. Then it's out with the old hacksaw. I leave Tommy's hand with him and I take his. I knew you boys would eat up the stuff about the music so I left another wee note. I'm in and out of Young's house in two minutes flat. He could have had the Vienna Boys Choir upstairs and I wouldn't have known about it."

I nodded. "It was easy after that. You drove Tommy's body to Barn Field where it would be discovered fairly soon. Then you went down to your meeting with the quartermaster in Newry while the FRU boys searched your house and found nothing."

"That's right. Easy. I burned and buried everything: receipts, women's clothes, the whole shebang. Drove Tommy's car deep into the woods, torched that. They searched the house and they found nothing. I was as clean as a whistle. So they told me afterwards when I became their boss."

"What about me? Carrick CID?"

"I needed to get that serial-killer angle running as quickly as possible so I found out your name from your switchboard and the address was easy."

"The stuff you wrote on the postcard was just meaningless? Right? Like the list?"

"Of course. Just random shit off the top of my head."

"I spent days looking at that bloody thing."

"Sorry about that."

"Then what?"

"And then I went and took care of Martha."

"Martha?"

"The midwife!"

"You killed her?"

"Of course. I had to. She knew everything."

"And then I just waited for twenty-four hours cos I knew that when it all came out I would be in the clear. Tommy got mixed up with some queer nutcase, poor old Tommy."

"What about the others? The bar in Larne?"

"Hell, yeah. I knew I had to do maybe one or two more attacks just to establish the pattern. You boys love your patterns."

"After you typed that hit list you got rid of the Imperial 55?"

"Nice work tracing the typewriter. I knew you would, though, so, aye, of course I got rid of it. Thought about planting it in your man Sea-wright's office, but that was only a passing fancy."

I sighed. "You got us excited, Freddie. We finally thought we had an ordinary, decent killer on our hands."

Freddie laughed. "Yeah. I got you jumping. Patterns. Codes. Once I had the time I read up on the Yorkshire Ripper and the Zodiac killer and I . . ."

I stopped listening.

Of course there were more questions: the phone calls, the hoaxes, was it all part of the smoke trail or did he just enjoy messing with us? But none of that mattered.

It all seemed so distant now.

It was like events that had happened long ago in another age.

He talked and I pretended to listen and finally his mouth stopped moving.

He was looking at me. He had asked me a question.

"Sorry?" I said.

"Did MI5 contact you after the hospital?" he wondered.

"Yes, just a few days ago," I replied.

"Aye, that's when they pulled me in for questioning. I told them everything of course. By then I knew it was ok. It didn't matter how close you got. I had been appointed head of FRU. I knew I was safe. They needed me. I am the head of IRA's internal security. Can you imagine it? The head of IRA internal security is a British agent! The guy who's in charge of investigating every informer, double agent, and piece of intel. What a joke!"

He leaned back in the chair and put his hands behind his head. He was smiling again. It was a confident, infectious smile that I could not bring myself to hate. Even after all he had done.

"Why did you pick those particular pieces of music? Puccini and Orpheus?"

He shrugged. "I liked them. I played them on the piano."

"And of course che gelida manina. Another joke, right?"

"I thought that was hilarious! Even with all the shit going down, that cracked me up. Of course I had the score for the piano and I hoped that you'd find out the words . . . I considered writing them in but I just didn't have the bloody time. I knew a detective with time on his hands would really burrow into that. Go off on some fucking tangent, really think it was a devious psycho nutcase."

"That I did."

Freddie laughed. "That's brilliant, isn't it?"

"They weren't clues? To Lucy? In La Bohème Mimi's real name is Lucia."

He seemed shocked. "God no! Lucy? The last thing I wanted was anybody thinking about Lucy."

I nodded. They were tells. Maybe I'd exaggerated them but they'd been tells none the less. If he hadn't been rushed maybe he would have seen that.

"You were lucky, Freddie," I said.

That ticked him off a little and his expression clouded. "No, you were lucky! Your government was lucky to get someone as sharp as me. Look at me! The head of FRU! Everything the IRA does for the next twenty years will be known about by me. And hence by your government. In advance. You were lucky!"

I reached in my pocket and took out the box of Italian cigarettes.
I lit one and blew smoke towards the ceiling,
I let the ash fall on the carpet.
Yes, we were lucky to have Freddie Scavanni on our side.
He had killed five people to protect his sorry ass.
He had killed dozens in a sordid career.
As head of FRU he would undoubtedly kill and torture dozens more.

He was a monster. He was a serial killer by any definition of the word. It didn't matter if it was for politics or to protect his own skin. He was a sociopath.

He looked at me, and seemed a little worried. "What are you doing here, Duffy? They told me that they put the fear of God into you. They told me that the Sean Duffy problem was finished."

"It's not finished."

"Yeah. I didn't think so. I knew different. I knew that your sort can never see the big picture."

"What's the big picture, Tommy? The hunger strikes?"

"Of course. It's a big victory. For both sides. Mrs. Thatcher hasn't publicly conceded anything to the IRA prisoners and her reputation as the Iron Lady has only become enhanced among the electorate. The martyrdom of ten IRA and INLA prisoners who starved themselves to death has been a recruiting poster for both organizations. They were desperate to find volunteers in the late '70s and now they're turning away men by the score. And there's the political angle: Sinn Fein has shifted from being a minor political party of extremists into a major electoral force in Northern Ireland politics. The whole match has changed."

"And you're at the center of it."

"Damn right!"

"You can't blame people like me for feeling like pawns."

He shook his head. "I don't blame you, Duffy, but you're tang-ling with the big boys now and, as Clint Eastwood so rightly says, a man's got to know his limitations."

I took another draw on the ciggie, coughed and looked out the window. Snow was falling in big flakes.

"I've investigated six murders since becoming a detective and not had a conviction on any of them."

"That's a shame," he replied with a sneer.

"What am I going to do with you, Freddie?"

He laughed. "You're not going to do anything. We're on the same side. Like I say, it's a win/win for everyone, isn't it?"

You could look at it that way. Freddie had only been protecting himself. The war was long but one day peace was going to come to Northern Ireland and it was going to come because of people like him.

"Don't you feel bad for the innocent civilians, Freddie?"

"Who? The fucking queers? We probably should ship them all off to some island like Seawright says. And Lucy? Fucksake, look at the state of her. Her husband's up for a stretch and she's banging me? Come on, you don't do that."

"No, I suppose not."

He yawned. "Look, Duffy, it's getting late and I've told you all you need to know. So grow up, put the gun away, get out of my sight and we'll say no more about this. I won't report you to your betters."

I didn't know what I was going to do.

I still wasn't sure.

After all this time and travelling.

"I don't think I can go just yet, Freddie," I said.

"Well, I've had enough of this. You're boring me. You've bored me from the start. I don't need to explain myself to the likes of you. What's going on in that head of yours, Duffy? Forget your wee stupid case and appreciate the big picture. Appreciate it on the plane back to Belfast."

I nodded and stamped the cigarette out on his living room floor.

"I see the big picture, Freddie, but I wonder . . . I wonder if you're missing the big gallery the picture's hanging in?"

"What do you mean by that?" he said with a snarl.

"If you're so valuable why have I been allowed to live? Why have I been allowed to know. Why am I here? Who's pulling my strings?"

"Sorry?"

"Let me give you one possibility that's occurred to me and that might intrigue you. What if there's an even bigger rat than you, Freddie? What if it's one of the very top guys. I mean the very top guys. Gerry Adams, Martin McGuinness, Marty Ferris, Ruari, one of them boys. What if MI5 turned one of them and has been running them for the last decade?"

His brown eyes darkened and he shook his head. Ah, so this thought had occurred to him too.

"I'm their agent, I'm the best they've bloody got! I'm the best there's ever been. I'm Garbo. I'm Kim Philby!"

"I'm sure you are, Freddie. I'm sure you are. But it makes me wonder a wee bit why I was told that you were in Italy. It couldn't possibly be that MI5 didn't want to rub you out, but some crazy, pissed-off copper . . . well, that would be quite another thing, wouldn't it? I mean, look at the mess you've made. Look at the big bog trail of shite you've made covering your tracks. Maybe, just maybe, Freddie, you've become, oh, I don't know . . . dispensable. Did you ever think about that?"

He leapt at me, one hand going for the gun, another punching me in the kidney. He took me completely by surprise, knocking the gun out of my hand and winding me. The gun flew across the room and clanged off the plate-glass window.

He hit me with his left, a hard metallic blow in my ribcage, and he followed quickly with a gut punch. He shoved my shoulders, forcing me down into the glass coffee table which smashed underneath me. He dived for the gun and grabbed it.

"Nessuno me lo ficca in culo!" he yelled delightedly.

I ducked as Freddie's first shot missed me by a cigarette length.

I scrambled out from under the smashed coffee table, rolled to one side, grabbed a broken table leg and threw the bloody thing at Freddie. He dodged it and shot again. I picked up a shard of glass with my gloved hands and threw it at him and this time he couldn't get out of the way. I hit him on the forearm and before he could shoot again I jumped him. He smacked me with the butt of the Beretta, but it was a glancing blow off my scalp and with both my hands I squeezed the wrist of his gun arm until he winced in pain. His fingers slackened and I wrestled the gun out of his grip and pistol-whipped him across the face.

He collapsed to his knees, got to his feet and then staggered backwards into the TV set, knocking it off its stand and exploding its cathode ray tube.

The lights flickered, went out for two seconds and then came back on again.

"Now you've wrecked my telly! This has gone beyond a joke, Duffy! Get the fuck out of here!" Freddie yelled.

I shook my head. I wasn't going anywhere. Not now that I had seen the real Freddie Scavanni. It was a question of trust, wasn't it? I knew Freddie's identity. Freddie knew that I knew. Laura knew. He knew about her too. Could we really leave our lives in the hands of a man like him?

I raised the Beretta.

"You know why they sent me to Carrick RUC? They sent me to learn, Freddie. And you know what? I have learned. I've grown up."

"Is this about the queers, Duffy? Fuck the queers! And Lucy? I gave her every chance. At least it was over quick!"

"Quick? Is that what you think? I cut her down, Freddie. She was still alive when you strung her up. You hadn't quite killed her. She got one finger between the rope and her neck. She wanted to live. She fought to live."

"This isn't justice, Duffy, this is revenge!"

"What's the difference?"

The nearest house was 400 meters away.

Perhaps they heard a crack and then one more crack almost immediately after the first. Perhaps if they'd been looking in the right direction at the right time they would have seen a sudden flash of light through the plate-glass windows.

I had thought about making it look like a suicide but there wasn't much point after all this.

I left the gun on the floor and went into Freddie's study.

I checked myself in the mirror. There were a couple of holes in my leather jacket from the glass table, a few cuts and bruises but hopefully nothing that would attract too much attention.

I opened the filing cabinet and took the big spool of tape from the MI5 machine and put it in my rucksack. This would be my insurance from the blowback.

I closed the front door and walked down the valley, back into Campo to the bus station. At 6 a.m. a van dropped off the morning papers outside the cafeteria. I looked at the headlines. The big news was from Egypt: President Sadat had been assassinated in Cairo. The story came with pictures. Men with machine guns firing into a crowd.

Finally the bus pulled in on ice tires. It had set out early from St. Moritz and was nearly full.

The driver was cautious and I arrived at Milan Airport with only minutes to make my plane.

The flight was uneventful. I bought Laura a bottle of Chanel in the duty free. We touched down at Prestwick Airport outside Glasgow just after 11.

I knew that if I really hoofed it I could catch the noon ferry from Stranraer to Larne . . .

The crossing was rough, the North Channel a mess of chuddering green sea and white-storm surf. I had a smoke, buttoned my duffle-coat hood and went to stare at the cauldron-like wake over the rear deck rail.

I watched Scotland slowly fade behind me.

I watched Ireland loom ahead.

This was the only acceptable place to be in these barren lands. On that grey stretch of sea between the two of them.

It was raining in Larne.

It was always raining in Larne.

I caught the train, got off at Barn Halt, said a brief Ave for Lucy, grabbed a six-pack of Harp from the off license and a fish supper from the chippie. I strolled up Victoria Road eating the chips in the rain. On Coronation Road there were few cars and only a couple of kids kicking a ball around. A man was walking the streets with a handheld megaphone proclaiming the imminent return of the Messiah.

"Are you ready for Christ's return, son?" he asked me.

"In about twenty minutes I will be," I replied.

#113.

I opened the gate, walked up the path, put the key in the lock, went upstairs, lit the new paraffin heater, stripped out of my wet clothes.

I poured myself a pint-glass vodka gimlet and listened to Ghost in the Machine, the brand new album by The Police. Classic case of three good tracks and eight fillers.

I called Laura in Straid and she asked how I was doing and I said I was doing just fine. I drank the six-pack and the vodka and by 8 o'clock I was a long way gone. I went to bed singing rebel songs.

The next morning, early, there was a knock at the door.

Big guys. Plain Clothes. Special Branch/MI5/Army Intelligence. Something like that. One with a ginger moustache, the other with a black moustache.

"Are you Sean Duffy?" Ginger asked.

"Could be," I said cagily.

Ginger pulled out a silenced 9mm and shoved it in my face. I took a step backwards. His mate followed him into the hall and closed the door behind him.

"First things first. Where's the tape?" Ginger said.

"What tape?"

Ginger pointed the revolver at my right kneecap.

"We'll shoot you in both knees, both ankles and both elbows. Then we'll go to work with the blowtorch. Why don't you save us all some trouble?"

"In my rucksack. It's still in my rucksack in the kitchen."

Ginger's mate went and got it.

"Ok. Now we'd like you to come with us," Ginger said.

"Let me get my kit on," I said.

They watched while I got changed and they led me outside not to a Land Rover but to an unmarked Ford Capri—which was a bit of a bad sign.

A tight squeeze too. A driver. Them two boys. Me.

We drove through Carrick, Greenisland, Newtownabbey, Belfast.

After Italy I saw the city anew.

A fallen world. A lost place.

Ruined factories. Burnt-out pubs. Abandoned social clubs. Shops with bomb-proof grilles. Check points. Search gates. Armored police stations.

Smashed cars. Cars on bricks.

Stray dogs. Sectarian graffiti. Murals of men in masks.

Bricked-up houses. Fire-bombed houses. Houses without eyes.

Broken windows, broken mirrors.

Children playing on the rubbish heaps and bombsites, dreaming themselves away from here to anywhere else.

The smell of peat and diesel and fifty thousand umbilical cords of black smoke uniting grey city and grey sky.

We drove to the top of Knockagh Mountain.

There was no one else around.

No one for miles.

"Get out," Ginger said.

"What is this?" I asked, scared now.

They pushed me out.

"What is this?" I asked again, panic clawing at my throat.

They shoved me to the ground, took out their revolvers.

"For some reason. For some unearthly reason, they like you, Duffy," Ginger said.

"Who likes me?"

"*They* like you and that's why they're letting you live," Ginger said. He pulled the trigger, the cylinder turned, the hammer came down. It was only a mock execution. They should have told me about the reprieve afterwards. I wanted to laugh. They'd botched it.

"The Moore case is over. Is that understood, Inspector Duffy?" black moustache said with an English accent.

"Aye, I understand," I replied.

"You watch your step, now, ok?" Ginger added.

They got back in the Capri and drove away.

The rain pattered my face.

The tarmac under my back felt reassuringly solid.

I lay there and watched the clouds drift past a mere hundred yards above my head.

I got to my feet. Belfast was spread out before me like a great slab of meat in a butcher's yard.

Who liked me?

Why had they let me live?

Why had they called me Inspector?

These were things to think about.

It would keep my mind busy on the long walk home.

GLOSSARY

bairn	baby
bap	head
banjaxed	broken/messed up
bog	toilet/shitter
charabanc	bus/motor coach
eejit	idiot
fenian	Catholic (derogatory)
ganch	guy/bloke
Jaffa	Protestant (derogatory)
Kesh/Long Kesh	Maze Prison
kit	clothes
muckers	boys
neb	nose
Old Bill	Police
peeler	policeman
pochle	a mess
Proddy	Protestant
sheugh	ditch
sleekit	sly/crafty
taibhse	spirit (Gaelic)
taig	Catholic (derogatory)
Twelfth of July bonfire	a bonfire celebrating the 1690 Battle of the Boyne
wean	kid

ABOUT . . . *THE COLD COLD GROUND*

I was born at home on Coronation Road, Carrickfergus, Northern Ireland in 1968. Coronation Road was one of the many red-bricked terraces in a Protestant housing estate in a town five miles north of Belfast. The street where I grew up and Victoria Estate itself was controlled by two rival Protestant paramilitary factions: the UDA and the UVF. The paramilitaries ran protection rackets, administered "street justice," dealt drugs, etc.

In 1980 Carrickfergus's major employer, ICI, shut down and almost the entire town was, overnight, thrown out of work. Carrickfergus was relatively untouched by the Troubles, but things changed in 1981 when the IRA hunger strikes began and the whole of Northern Ireland was engulfed by rioting, bombings, assassinations and, for a time during the summer of '81, after the death of Bobby Sands, it seemed that Ulster was on the verge of civil war.

The central idea of The Cold Cold Ground was to follow a young police detective trying to do his job in the midst of all this chaos. He's a bright Catholic cop in a primarily Protestant police force, who has recently moved to Carrickfergus. The homicide he's asked to solve is what looks like an ordinary execution of a police informer, but it quickly becomes clear that the case is far from ordinary. The victim is homosexual and when more gays are killed it looks like the Ulster police are dealing with their first ever serial killer. The police resources are stretched thin by endemic rioting and the case is further complicated by the fact that in 1981 homosexuality was illegal in Northern Ireland and punishable by up to five years in prison.

I remember 1981 extremely well. I remember the bomb attacks in Belfast and trouble in the Estate. I remember getting a lift to school from a neighbor who was a captain in the British Army: he had to check under his car every morning for mercury tilt switch bombs and sometimes when it was raining or cold he would skip the check and my little brother and I would be in the back seat waiting for the first hill when the bomb might go off...

I wanted to set a book in this claustrophobic atmosphere, attempting to recapture the sense that civilization was breaking down to its basest levels. I also wanted to remember the craic, the music, the bombastic politicians, the apocalyptic street preachers, the sinister gunmen and a lost generation of kids for whom all of this was normal.

The Cold Cold Ground is a police procedural, but a procedural set in extremely unusual circumstances in a controversial police force cracking under extraordinary external and internal pressures...

ABOUT ... *ADRIAN McKINTY*

I was born and grew up in Carrickfergus, Northern Ireland. After studying philosophy at Oxford University, I emigrated to New York City where I lived in Harlem for seven years, working in bars, bookstores, building sites and finally the basement stacks of the Columbia University Medical School Library in Washington Heights.

In 2000 I moved to Denver, Colorado where I taught high-school English and started writing fiction in earnest. My first full-length novel *Dead I Well May Be* was shortlisted for the 2004 Ian Fleming Steel Dagger Award and was picked by *Booklist* as one of the ten best crime novels of the year. The sequel to that book *The Dead Yard* was selected by *Publishers Weekly* as one of the twelve best novels of 2006 and won the Audie Award for best mystery or thriller. These two novels, along with *The Bloomsday Dead*, form my trilogy of novels starring hitman Michael Forsythe, the DEAD trilogy.

In mid-2008 I moved to St. Kilda, Melbourne, Australia with my wife and kids. My book *Fifty Grand* won the 2010 Spinetingler Award and my last novel, *Falling Glass*, was longlisted for Theakston's Crime Novel of the Year.

Visit Adrian's blog at http://adrianmckinty.blogspot.com/